AUTUMN
SAGE

LAS MORENAS, BOOK TWO

Genevieve Turner

Book Layout ©2013 BookDesignTemplates.com

Autumn Sage/ Genevieve Turner. -- 1st ed.
ISBN 978-0-9906298-3-2

For K—my middle child, who feels deeply and is often misunderstood, just like Isabel

CHAPTER ONE

San Jacinto Mountains, Southern California
Autumn, 1898

US Marshal Sebastian Spencer watched the man across from him fidget—and waited. Waited for that flutter of hands like the last flicker of a butterfly's wings before it succumbed—that sign that his subject was fully focused on Sebastian, rather than his own anxiety.

There it was. A tight clasp of the arms of the chair, one last shift in his seat, then a release of his hands and a relaxing of his shoulders.

Mr. Jace Merrill was ready.

Sebastian waited one moment more, raising a finger to the marshal's badge pinned to his breast. Ostensibly the motion was to adjust it, but in reality it was a reminder of the difference in position between himself and his subject. This wasn't an official interrogation, but Sebastian always preferred to keep the upper hand.

"The sheriff ought to be here soon," Merrill offered.

Perfect. Merrill was volunteering words without prompting. Silences unsettled most people—they needed to fill that void with something, anything. The voids

1

that Sebastian created, either due to his heft or impassivity—or his innate nature—were especially unsettling to others.

Keep quiet long enough and they'd sing like birds in the end.

After catching the three a.m. mail train from Los Angeles, followed by a jarring ride up the mountain, Sebastian's temper should have been thin. A lesser man's would have been. But Sebastian's temper was commanded by himself, not circumstance.

He flicked a glance around the back room of the blacksmith's shop. "How often is the sheriff here in Cabrillo?" he asked.

Likely not often, if the sheriff had to use this as an office when he was in town.

"We've seen him twice since he was appointed," Merrill answered. "With Sheriff Obregon wounded and the outlaw on the loose, the new sheriff could show more interest in catching the man." The words curdled as they came off Merrill's tongue.

"And your sister-in-law wounded as well," Sebastian offered neutrally. "How is she?"

Tension stitched through the set of Merrill's shoulders. "Isabel? She's..."

Sebastian let the silence continue, at ease in it.

"She can speak again," Merrill finished.

Odd choice there. A more direct probe was needed. "She must be overset after such an attack."

"Overset?" Merrrill's laugh was leaden. "No, not Isabel. Angry might best describe her. You'll see when you meet her." A pause. "I have to tell you, the entire town is angry. We can't find this bastard and the new sheriff has no interest in doing it himself. If anyone besides a lawman captures him…"

Sebastian sighed inwardly. Vigilantism would not be tolerated. This outlaw was going back to Los Angeles intact. Judge Bannister would accept nothing less. *Justice* would accept nothing less.

Therefore neither would Sebastian.

"If anyone besides a lawman captures him, he will be immediately brought to me," Sebastian warned. "Please ensure that anyone… *angry* about the situation understands that." He paused, then said pointedly, "Your father will make certain any vigilantism is punished."

Merrill leaned away, eyes narrowing, jaw tightening. "Is he coming here?"

Interesting. Although Merrill had reached out to Judge Bannister, it seemed that the thirteen-year estrangement between the two wasn't to be repaired.

"No." Sebastian studied Merrill closely. Merrill was very much a younger version of his father—dark hair, blue eyes, rather stern set to his mouth. But a looser, freer version of Judge Bannister. As if Merrill had found contentment in his long years outside of his father's shadow.

Merrill didn't remember Sebastian, but Sebastian remembered Merrill. Merrill had been William Bannister, Jr. then, fifteen years ago in Los Angeles. Judge Bannister had dragged young Willliam to Sebastian's father's funeral, where Bannister had wept at the loss of his fellow defender of justice.

Sebastian hadn't wept. Not then, not ever for the late Judge Spencer.

His impression of Merrill had been one of youthful sullenness, so it was no surprise the boy had run away from home two years later.

It *was* a surprise that he'd surfaced in this little mountain town. His first contact with his father had been to request aid in apprehending the man who'd attacked his sister-in-law and her fiancé—the Deputy Sheriff for the area.

Judge Bannister had ranted over the reappearance of his son, raged over Merrill's choice of wife—such things that Sebastian wouldn't repeat to the lady's husband, things about her heritage and her people unflattering in the extreme—but once he'd seen the outlaw named in his son's letter, his response to the request could be nothing but affirmative.

Cole McCade. Yes, a marshal would certainly have to be sent for him. One Judge Bannister could trust completely, both to get the job done and to be discreet about the entanglement of son and judge and outlaw.

And so Sebastian was sent to Cabrillo.

"Good," Merrill said, the strength of it emphasizing how far away he wished his father.

Sebastian returned to the situation at hand, tugging his cuff a hair back into place.

"You were one of the first ones to find them after the attack, weren't you?" he asked briskly, the better to pull Merrill's attention away from Judge Bannister.

"Yes." Merrill's focus sharpened on him once more. "It was three weeks ago. Catarina—my wife—we were... talking, when we heard the shots."

Talking. They'd been arguing, more like. Newly married and arguing—that was a new wrinkle. Estrangements between father and son, husband and wife—such things marred a person's inclination toward truthfulness.

Sebastian disliked wrinkles.

"Señor Moreno—my father-in-law—and Felipe, the foreman, and I went to investigate." A shaky breath left him. Clearly, the man was unused to the aftereffects of violence. "We found them maybe a half mile out of town. Sheriff Obregon was bleeding from a belly wound—we didn't expect him to live. There were two dead outlaws and signs of a third. A trail of blood led to the high country." He shook his head. "We searched and searched, all of us, and never could find him."

Not surprising. These men weren't trained to bring in a fugitive. They knew the country they were searching, but hunting a man was very different from hunting stray steers. Especially a man the likes of Cole McCade, who had years of experience evading the law. At least, if the rumors whispered about him were true.

"And your sister-in-law? Miss Moreno?" Sebastian reminded him.

Merrill colored and dropped his head a fraction. "She was in the brush, insensible. The one who got away, he'd dragged her there. Her clothes were... mussed." He pointed to his neck. "Her throat had livid prints."

The embarrassment at having to confess this crawled across the man's skin.

"You were the one who found her?"

The other man nodded, without elaborating on what else he might have noticed about the wounded woman.

Merrill had said she wasn't overset—she was *angry*. Given the discomfort itching through Merrill's frame, Sebastian wondered if he ought to ask the next, obvious question.

No, he'd save it for the sheriff. Asking a man if he thought his sister-in-law had been raped would be taking this interview too far.

"How long did you pursue McCade?" Surely they hadn't been searching all this time.

Merrill's unease slid into frustration. "A week. It was all we could afford—we all have stock to send to the stockyards in the valley. My father-in-law and I are already behind."

Of course. In a rural area, fall was the time to prepare for winter. If one didn't, one died. Sebastian hardly took note of the seasons himself, there being no need in Los Angeles.

"Well, I'm here now," he assured the other man.

Assurance was not what crossed Merrill's face—it was suspicion. "My father sent you solely because I asked, did he?"

So Merrill didn't recognize the McCade name. He'd no idea why Sebastian had really been sent.

The judge had never admitted the reasons directly—he'd given Sebastian a speech about justice being served, with no mention of the political rivalry that had stewed for years between him and Cole McCade's father. Even Judge Bannister didn't dare speak of such things within the hallowed walls of a courthouse.

Sebastian didn't give a fig for the unspoken political aspects—a man had gunned down a sheriff and attacked a woman. He had to be brought in. Powerful father or no.

"Your father wouldn't want a dangerous man running free," he answered, "escaping the judgment of the law."

And if bringing in Cole McCade and having him stand trial for attempted murder ruined the political hopes of his father, Edwin McCade, so much the better.

Merrill didn't need to know any of that. The judge had chosen Sebastian for his silences as much as his tracking skills.

Before Merrill could press the issue further, the door opened to reveal a man with pale, thinning hair, wearing a careless aspect as he entered the room, a badge pinned to his wrinkled shirtfront.

Sebastian rose to shake his hand, the man's grip as lazy as his demeanor.

"Sheriff Williams," the man said in introduction. "You must be the marshal." Insolent and overfamiliar.

If Sebastian allowed himself to dislike anyone, he'd dislike this man, with his sloppy manners and clothes. Thank goodness he'd eradicated such weaknesses from his nature.

"Merrill, you can go now," Williams tossed over his shoulder. "I'll take it from here."

Merrill sent the sheriff a sour look, which the other man missed, nodded to Sebastian, and was gone. No doubt off to spread the word of Sebastian's arrival.

Hopefully he would include Sebastian's warning about forming a lynch mob.

Williams sat at the desk and began pushing around some papers. He might have been looking for something, but his movements were too purposeless.

"While I am glad to have you here," Williams began, "you likely wasted a trip up the mountain." He continued to shuffle the papers.

The silence stretched, but Williams wasn't a master of it like Sebastian was. The sheriff wouldn't stop moving, wouldn't allow the stillness to grow.

Amateur.

"Did I?" Sebastian asked, right before he sensed Williams preparing to speak again. He'd show Williams that he would set the pace.

"You'll have a hell of time catching him," Williams said. "It's been three weeks since the attack. Who knows where he is now?" He shrugged.

You *ought to know.*

Sebastian had once successfully tracked a man using a six-month-old lead. But he wasn't one to boast. "I'll do my best."

Of course, he'd tracked that man to Sacramento—tracking a man through a city was easier. Each brush with a fellow human left a lingering imprint that could be sought out with proper questioning.

In this wild terrain, whatever memories the mountains might hold would be unknown to anything human.

"They ought to have sent the man who brought in Lashlan." The sheriff chuckled, which he wouldn't have done had he actually met Lashlan. "I bet that son of bitch could capture anyone."

"That was me," Sebastian said levelly.

"Oh." The sheriff's eyes went wide, the indolence leaving his frame. "I heard that was a six-hour gun battle."

"Five," Sebastian corrected.

"You waited him out for five hours?"

"I recited poetry to pass the time." And some spiritual exercises and choice bits of Seneca—he hadn't spent the hours in idleness. "May I see your report?"

Williams located the report beneath a stack of papers—the third such stack he'd searched.

What was Williams doing? That report—this entire case—ought to have been foremost in the man's mind and papers. And why wasn't any of this filed properly? No wonder the townspeople were annoyed with him.

Sebastian read through it quickly, never letting his frustration at the contents burn higher than a flicker.

Nothing that he hadn't learned from two minutes' conversation with Jace Merrill.

Useless. He set it aside.

"Do you want me to write out a copy of that?" Williams offered.

"No. When was the last time you interviewed Sheriff Obregon?"

"Oh, right after I was appointed, about a week and half ago. He can't hardly talk—gut shot, you know—so it was pointless."

"You haven't been back?"

"There's no need." Williams looked surprised at such a suggestion.

There was every need. Which the sheriff ought to know.

"Miss Moreno?" Sebastian let his finger tap the arm of his chair once, hard. "I assume you've interviewed her as well?"

"Oh, I talked to her." Williams rubbed at his forehead as if a headache had come on. "*Frigid* isn't near cold enough to describe her. She behaved like we were in a boxing match. She can talk better than Obregon—but she certainly didn't want to."

Interesting. He wondered if that was because Williams bungled the interview—or if she were naturally difficult.

"*Angry might best describe her.*"

A sheriff so wounded he couldn't speak and a witness so angry she wouldn't—that promised difficulties.

Sebastian couldn't heal the sheriff's wounds, but he knew exactly what to do with irrational, unrelenting anger: smother it with frigid calm.

A possible excuse for the lady's anger remained, one the sheriff hadn't mentioned. The one Sebastian hadn't wanted to ask Merrill about.

"This wasn't in your report," Sebastian said, "but I must ask: Was she raped?"

He didn't quail at the word—he didn't quail at anything anymore.

"She said no," Williams replied, "but that's likely just missishness. I asked her several times, trying to get her to be honest, but she always said no."

"Several times?" Sebastian might not quail at the word, but he wouldn't have used it *several times* when questioning a victim.

"Yes," Williams answered. "She had to have been. Although why she won't admit it, I don't know." The man appeared completely insensible of his own boorishness. Or of how admitting such a thing might affect a lady. "Perhaps she's worried the news will get out. But the whole town knows."

Or perhaps you got her back up with your clumsy questioning.

That would be a mystery to solve once he met the frigid Miss Moreno.

"I see," he replied, hoping to put an end to the subject.

Williams leaned in, imparting a confidence between them. "This town—there's a serious vigilante element. The sheriff before Obregon was murdered. Now that Obregon's been hurt, they're tetchy. Ready to be set off by the slightest spark." He shook his head. "Although, what were they expecting? They put a Negro behind a sheriff's star and he gets killed, so they put a greaser behind the next one—and he gets shot. Ought to have had a white man from the very beginning."

Like yourself? Sebastian refrained from pointing out that the marshal here was half-greaser, as Williams so charmingly put it.

"I'd like to stamp out any troublemaking," Williams went on. But it wasn't righteousness holding the muscles of his face taut—it was fear.

The sheriff had no control over matters and he was frightened.

"I'll deal with any mobs that form," he assured Williams. *Better than you ever could.* "First, I have to find this outlaw."

"Of course," the sheriff said. He tilted his head consideringly, a kind of dumb cunning coming to his eyes. "You know, you don't move."

As if Sebastian were a statue Williams was studying.

"What?" Sebastian heard his voice drop in register, only just kept his internal flinch from transfiguring into true emotion.

"You don't fidget," Williams explained. "You hardly seem to breathe."

The silence that followed wasn't intentional on Sebastian's part—it was required, a stretch of time needed to keep hold of his self-control. Perhaps Williams saw more than he gave him credit for.

"Economy of motion," Sebastian finally said. "Fidgeting accomplishes nothing."

"Suppose you're right." The contemplation left Williams's expression and he was the careless rube once more. He half rose from the chair. "I'll get you a map then, and you can start your hunt," he said brightly.

"Not quite yet." Sebastian let the silence pull on purpose this time, long enough for uncertainty to flash across the sheriff's face, long enough for the advantage to swing back to himself. "I'd like to speak with Obregon and Miss Moreno first."

And properly do this investigation that you've botched.

"Are you certain? Obregon's all the way in the sanatorium in Pine Ridge—that's a three-hour ride, and I've already—"

Sebastian rose suddenly from the chair, stopping Williams's babbling more effectively than a fist to his throat.

"Take me to Obregon." More silence, darker this time, as he loomed over Williams. "Now."

~~~

A gunshot to the gut was a terrible thing to endure. Given the state of Sheriff Joaquin Obregon, perhaps even more terrible to survive.

Sebastian noted the waxy cast to the other man's skin, the tortured pull of his breathing, the limpness of his limbs in the bedclothes. A man this broken might not remember what had brought him to this state.

There was only one way to find out.

"His pulse is dangerously elevated and erratic," the nurse fussed at Sebastian. "Perhaps you can question him later?"

If he dies, there will be no later. "The doctor assured me it would be fine," Sebastian said.

The thunk of the nurse's bottom hitting her chair spoke to her displeasure, though her expression remained serene. Dealing with the rich consumptives who came to these mountains for a rest cure must have given her a great deal of experience in hiding her irritation.

He studied Obregon for several moments. If not for the agony weighing down every inch of him, the man would have been handsome.

Miss Moreno was likely handsome as well. In Sebastian's experience, those blessed with fair features tended to couple with each other.

He was not so blessed—not that he intended to couple with any lady.

"Sheriff Obregon," he said firmly.

Obregon turned his face toward Sebastian, his eyes open but glassy, unfocused. This was a man in the grip of a pain so deep, he could perceive little else.

Sebastian's task was to pull the information he needed from this man, pain or no. If Obregon were more alert, he would understand. He was a lawman.

Or had been.

"Sheriff Obregon." Closer to a command now.

A long blink. A clearing of his gaze, slightly.

"I am Marshal Spencer. I've been sent to track down the man who attacked you. I need you to tell me about the events of that day."

Silence. Obregon's gaze remained steady, but nothing came from his lips.

Sebastian waited. And waited.

"I don't think he remembers."

Sebastian trained his gaze on the nurse, watching her flutter under it, flutter and flicker and...

She dropped her gaze, her cheeks going red.

Good. There'd be no more interruptions from her.

He turned back to Obregon, whose breathing had grown more labored.

"They came from the trees," he finally forced out.

Sebastian leaned forward so that his ears could catch each dropped word.

"I shot them," Obregon said.

"Them?"

"Three. Careys and the other."

The Careys were the Carey brothers, both found dead at the scene of the attack. And the other—well, he was the one Sebastian must find.

"Who fired first?" A crucial question, one Sebastian couldn't find the answer to in Williams's report. If Obregon had fired first, and the three men were defending themselves... that put an entirely different cast on the affair.

"They did."

Hard to discern if Obregon was truthful. There was no inflection in his voice—only effort.

"So they fired first," Sebastian allowed. "All three of them?"

Obregon shook his head. Sebastian waited for him to elaborate, but nothing more came.

"Did they hit you, when they first fired?" Sebastian asked. "Or Miss Moreno?"

Obregon shook his head again, his eyes shut in agony.

All right. Shots fired—not by Obregon—no one wounded. "What happened next?"

For several long moments, Obregon did nothing but fight to breathe. At one point the nurse rose, then fell back into her chair after catching Sebastian's expression.

"Killed the Careys." The rasp under the words made them difficult to decipher.

Now that didn't make sense. Was Obregon saying that he'd killed both the Carey brothers with no one else getting a shot off?

Of course he wasn't. Such a happening was impossible. Obregon was confused.

"After the Careys were killed, what next?" Whatever Obregon remembered was suspect, but Sebastian wanted it anyway. He'd only know if Obregon's memories were worthless if he had them to examine.

The other man's brows drew together, his gaze clearing. "She screamed. She never screams."

That wasn't true. Anyone could be made to scream, if one only applied enough pressure. Sebastian's father had proved that particular point multiple times during his childhood.

Sebastian tightened his grip on his control. His father was dead. Those screams were in the past.

He had to focus on *her* screams now.

"Miss Moreno? She was the one screaming?"

Obregon was lost to pain once more, his jaw clenching tight. Clamminess broke out across his skin while he struggled with his agony.

Silence wasn't working, and neither was waiting. "Miss Moreno?" Sharper, louder, a call to Obregon to come back to this world. "Was she the one who was screaming?"

A minor point, really—of course she'd screamed. Any woman would have, even one as frigid as Miss Moreno supposedly was.

But for some strange reason it mattered, to have Obregon say, yes, she had screamed.

"She *never* screams," was all Obregon got out.

Sebastian pushed down his rising frustration. He wouldn't allow himself the luxury, to feel that sharp bite of irritation, not so far from his notebooks and the absolution they provided.

Time to start from the beginning, see if he could lead Obregon to the finish from that direction. "You and your fiancée, Miss Moreno, were out for a drive that Sunday."

The sheriff's report had included at least that much.

Obregon managed a nod.

"Three men ambushed you," Sebastian went on. "One of them fired first. Which one?"

Nothing from Obregon. If the man's eyes weren't half open, Sebastian would have thought him unconscious.

"Who fired first?" he demanded.

Still nothing.

"He can't remember." A dart of exasperation from the nurse. "Return later—today is a bad one for him."

Sebastian didn't look at her. "He has to remember. Otherwise this case is already lost. If he were awake and aware, he'd realize that."

"Then question him when he's awake and aware." The nurse sounded as though she were holding Sebastian's irritation as well as her own.

She was welcome to his—he didn't want it.

"I'm here now," he said. "I need to know what happened."

"She screamed." Finally, Obregon was speaking again. "I don't remember after."

It was more exhalation than statement, the effort of which had Obregon closing his eyes completely.

The nurse was up and at his bedside before Sebastian could blink. "His pulse is weaker." Closer to accusatory than she probably should have dared. "You'll have to leave."

"I'll wait until he's recovered." He settled himself more securely in his chair.

"I don't believe the doctor would approve, not with the condition Mr. Obregon is in." She crossed her arms, sending Sebastian a look of implacability that even he, the master of such looks, had to admire. "Shall I fetch him?"

He *could* battle with this nurse, and likely the doctor as well, and wait who knew how long for Obregon to be fit to speak. Assuming Obregon's memories of the attack were more intact than the interview suggested.

Or he could seek out the other victim and interrogate her. She wasn't curled in agony in a sanatorium bed. She'd answer whatever questions he put to her. He'd make certain of that.

"Very well," he said, rising and settling his hat on his head. "As soon as he's recovered, send word to me in Cabrillo."

Time to find this Miss Moreno and see if the stories were true. And to wrest every last bit of the story from her—willing or no.

CHAPTER TWO

Isabel Moreno set aside *Tess of the d'Ubervilles* and took up her pen.

She'd picked up the novel—about the violation of an innocent young girl at the hands of a villain and her tragic end—the way one would poke at a sore tooth, tongue probing until it triggered that sweetly stabbing pain. But the exercise lost its appeal after a few chapters.

Lesson plans. There were always lesson plans to prepare. Pen poised, she looked toward the sheet of paper at her right hand—only to have her bedroom window pull her gaze toward it.

Low sagebrush, taller, brighter pines, gently rolling hills. And boulders poking up like cracked teeth. Nothing novel in that landscape.

But he was out there somewhere. The man who'd attacked her.

Breath-stealing, heart-rattling, mind-blotting panic came upon her each time she looked out at where he might be. Panic that she hid as well as she could, panic that was stealing upon her even now.

He could be watching her. Might be imagining his hands around her throat once more, dreaming of all the disgusting, depraved acts he'd promised to visit upon her...

She reached for her collar—the collar that was strangling her—but forced her hand to stop at her breastbone. She must not pull at it. She'd torn off a button the other day, struggling in one of her attacks. She'd had to hurriedly sew it back on before anyone could notice. Because the only thing worse than these attacks of paralytic fear were the looks of pity she received when one was upon her.

She lingered on the scene for a moment, using the time to master herself.

Only greenery, mountains, and the creek appeared.

He wasn't lurking outside. She was two stories above ground. This fear would not control her.

A terrible thing to no longer be able to trust one's own sense of fear. To be at such pitched trembling that one couldn't discern true dangers from the ones manufactured by one's own mind.

Tightening her grip on her pen, she turned back to her paper and began to write. Not on *Tess of the d'Urbervilles*—that was much too racy to teach to impressionable young minds. No, only a lesson on sentence diagramming. Always difficult, to find a way to present that subject in the detail required without losing the students' attention. Perhaps if she tried—

A knock at the door had her tossing her pen across the room, the fear so thick and hot upon her she could hardly breathe. She slowly rose, the better to give her shaky limbs time to settle, crossed the room to retrieve her pen, wiped it clean, and set it carefully on the desk. By that time she'd managed to erase the worst of her shock, although her heart was still racing. But no one could see that.

"Come in!"

Her elder sister, Catarina, bustled in, moving at a slightly faster pace than usual. "That marshal went to the sanatorium to speak with Joaquin. He'll likely head here after; I wanted to come warn you."

The marshal. Sent here by a man who hated her mother, a man who must never learn Señora Moreno's true identity. While Isabel understood Mr. Merrill's impulsive request for help had been noble, part of her wished he hadn't done it.

This marshal could expose her mother's true identity to their family's greatest enemy—or he could capture the man who'd tried to murder her and her fiancé. Isabel prayed that the latter could be achieved without triggering the former.

To have played such a part in endangering her mother... Well, once this marshal was gone, their mother's secret still safe, Isabel's guilt would dissipate.

"We'll need to prepare refreshments if he is coming." Always best to focus on mundanities—it helped keep the fear away.

Catarina walked toward her, her eyes focused near Isabel's neck.

What is she looking at?

"I've already prepared tea and food," her sister said. She raised her hand toward Isabel, coming straight for her throat—

Isabel slapped her hand away before the command to do so had taken shape in her mind.

Catarina pulled her hand into her chest, rubbing it as she took two quick steps back. "I'm sorry, I forgot—"

"No, I'm sorry," Isabel rattled out before Catarina could go on. Thank the Lord Catarina hadn't managed to touch her neck—Isabel might have slapped her cheek.

Someday Isabel would have control over these reactions again, wouldn't give herself away. But until then...

She moved further out of Catarina's reach.

"You have a speck. Near your collar," Catarina explained.

Rather than simply tell Isabel so she could deal with it herself, Catarina had done as she always had and taken the task upon herself. An accident of birth made Catarina five years older than Isabel's twenty-one, but that accident meant Isabel would forever be treated as a child by her sister.

"Thank you. I can remove it myself." She brushed her bodice clean with a flick of her wrist.

"There—it's gone." Catarina's expression remained downcast—and green. But still eye-achingly beautiful.

An angel with morning sickness. A nasty thought, to be sure, but if Isabel couldn't be honest in her own mind, she'd go mad. Catarina was married, mistress of her own house, the green cast to her skin a testament to the coming baby she hadn't yet announced to the world. Her sister wanted nothing more than what she already had.

Isabel sometimes thought she might never assuage her wants, that she might hunger and hunger and never fill herself—she certainly felt empty now. Joaquin, the man she was to marry, might never rise from his bed again. This town, the one she'd hated for as long as she could remember, might never release her to find the life she'd always dreamed of.

"What were you doing?" A strained attempt at conversation from Catarina.

"Writing a lesson plan." She didn't much feel like talking, but it was better than staring out the window.

"A lesson plan?" Catarina asked. "But you've no teaching position this term."

Thank you for the reminder. She hadn't even the escape of practicing the profession she loved. She'd *had* a teaching position, one in the valley at the base of the mountains—not quite as far as she'd like, but certainly forward movement.

Then she'd been attacked, and there was no question—she was staying in Cabrillo, in her parents' house, until the man was found.

The worst part was, she wanted to remain in the house, behind the illusion of security these walls and her gathered family provided.

There was always next term.

If the man had been caught by then.

If she had the courage to leave the house by then.

Of course she would.

"I'll return for the spring term." Firm, confident, as if she could will such a thing with only the force of her voice.

"Certainly." Catarina put a pinch of pity there.

Pity. She was choking on everyone's surfeit of pity.

"What were your impressions of this marshal?" Isabel asked. Catarina and her husband had met the marshal at the train depot. Any impressions Catarina had formed would aid in the coming interrogation.

"He was very still. Almost menacingly so."

Menacing. Isabel doubted this marshal was half as menacing as McCade had been. No doubt the marshal thought to make himself mysterious and intimidating with his silence. No doubt he'd ask the same questions the sheriff had, grow as frustrated with her answers—

and then hopefully leave her alone while he hunted the outlaw.

He'd gone to see Joaquin, then. Three hours to Pine Ridge, an hour at the sanatorium, three hours back— he'd be here soon.

Isabel had made that same trip a few days ago to visit Joaquin. Sheer torment, to drive in that same buggy, passing places identical to the site of her attack. She'd reminded herself that her brother Juan was sitting right next to her and had a pistol strapped to his thigh, that there was a rifle just under the buggy seat...

But Joaquin had been carrying a pistol that day, and there'd been a rifle at her feet as well. Such things hadn't saved them the last time.

No matter. She was safe at the moment.

There was no one at the window.

"Well, I suppose I'll find out about this marshal for myself," Isabel said evenly.

Uncertainty pulled at Catarina's features. "Do you think... do you think he knows exactly who our mother is? And how she's related to Judge Bannister?"

Panic spiked high in Isabel's breast. "How could he? Unless your husband told him?"

Catarina stiffened. "Of course not! He might be the judge's son, but Jace would never betray our mother."

So certain her sister was, after only a few weeks in an initially unwanted marriage. Isabel wasn't yet ready to put her certainty in a man so closely related to Judge Bannister. Estrangement or no.

"As long as we *all* remain silent, she's in no danger," Isabel reminded her pointedly.

Not that Isabel had the choice to be silent. About her mother, yes, but about this attack... Over and over again she'd had to recite the story, first to her parents, then to the sheriff, then to the parade of townspeople coming to offer their sympathy—and to obtain the salacious details from the source herself.

Immediately after, her throat had been too bruised to allow her to speak. When her throat had healed, she'd gone downstairs to meet everyone, to prove that nothing had changed. To prove that she was still Isabel Moreno—intelligent, composed, accomplished—that the assault had left her unmarked.

Her resolve had not been enough to stem the whispers. Eyes wide with pity and prurience, their neighbors had pressed her for details she'd refused to give. She'd seen the sidelong glances, the whispers behind cupped hands.

She could well imagine what they whispered. *That Isabel Moreno. Thought she was higher in the instep than all of us. Not so high now, is she?*

The sheriff's questioning had been worst of all. Over and over he'd asked if she'd suffered the ultimate violation at the outlaw's hands. And over and over she'd said no, each and every repetition unheard. It was as if he wanted her to have been raped.

Remembering his eager harassment made her stomach roll. Hadn't she suffered enough? How much more blood should she have shed?

"Of course we'll all remain silent about Mama," Catarina answered rather waspishly. She went to peer out the window.

Flickers of panic flashed through Isabel as an ache echoed through her skull.

He's not out there. She's looking at something else.

"The marshal is coming," Catarina announced, the afternoon sunlight falling across her face as she leaned in for a closer inspection.

Isabel remained where she was. She'd face him soon enough.

Her stomach continued to roll in time with the sharply rising throb between her temples.

Dear Lord. Of all the times for a headache to come upon her... Since McCade had attempted to knock her wits out with a pistol butt to her temple, she suffered from the most vicious headaches. Nasty, nauseating things that incapacitated her for hours at a time.

Paralytic fear, debilitating headaches—sometimes it felt as if her very body was betraying her.

"Well, then," she answered resolvedly, "he'll want to speak with me, won't he?"

She shoved away the fear, the pain, and straightened her shoulders. The mirror showed her spectacles firmly in place, her hair tucked into the twist at her nape. She looked as she always had—rather stern, perhaps too severe for her age.

But she *was* stern and severe. That hadn't changed in all this. She would meet this still, menacing marshal measure for measure—and he would not best her.

~~~

They'd all been correct, Sebastian reflected—Miss Isabel Moreno was difficult. And frigid. And *angry.*

With her sensible gray dress wrapped around her thin form, polished spectacles shielding her black eyes, and pins trapping her dark hair, she was a painting come to life—*Portrait of a Schoolmistress.*

The Moreno family parlor was quite ordinary, with portraits of venerated ancestors staring from the papered walls, along with overstuffed chairs, a table, and a mirrored side table, all likely ordered from the more expensive pages of a catalogue. Fine indeed for the small mountain town of Cabrillo—which wasn't very fine at all.

Sebastian preferred the stark severity of his own furnishings in Los Angeles. Miss Moreno wouldn't be out of place in his parlor, not as she was in this one.

Thin and sharp, she should have brought to mind something pinched and mean, but instead he was reminded of a saber: slim, shining, keen-edged. If he set his will against hers, as he wanted to, she might leave him torn and bloodied.

This interrogation was to be a battle of wills—and he had the unsettling thought that his will might not prevail.

"Miss Moreno," he began after the introductions, greetings that each member of the family—mother, sister, and Miss Moreno herself—had returned with distinct chill. "You understand why I am here."

He let the silence stretch after that, wanting her to reassure him that yes, she understood. Wanting her to flutter or fidget and then yield. As a normal lady would.

Instead, she sent him a look of icy rage. And waited.

So the battle began. Well, he knew how to wait.

He sipped from his cup, the tea leaving an ashy residue on his tongue.

The silence went on, her fierce expression never easing. Her sister, Mrs. Merrill, began to fidget, her gaze bounding between Miss Moreno and their mother—who was as still as her younger daughter. For every glance Mrs. Merrill flicked toward her sister, she sent two toward her mother, the dots and dashes of her gaze coding a deep unease.

Interesting. Perhaps there was more at play here than simply one loose outlaw.

The clock on the mantel ticked off fifteen more seconds, and still this witness would not open her mouth.

Very well. He would concede this round. But only the one—he hadn't the time to humor her endlessly.

"Of course you know why I'm here," he said. "To find this fugitive, I need to hear your story. From your own lips."

Those same lips compressed further. If not for the anger coming off her like heat from a stove, she might have been striking. Certainly the fierceness of her intrigued him.

"I understand that it's distressing to speak of," he offered.

"Do you?" Miss Moreno gave him an assessing look, one that crept along his skin, before turning her face back to the weak sunlight filtering in through the lace curtains.

If this was how she was going to behave on the witness stand, the trial would not go well. This lady would evoke no sympathy in a jury.

His own sense of justice demanded he do his utmost to capture McCade—but if the man went free because this woman wouldn't open her mouth...

Sebastian wouldn't feel a thing. Not a single blessed thing.

"What do you wish to know?"

A grudging concession, but one he'd take.

"All of it," he ordered. "From the very beginning."

Her pulse ticked hard where her jaw met her throat, the only indication she wasn't as stone-like as she pretended.

Excellent. There might yet be a way to pry her open, if he could exploit that unease.

"Sheriff Obregon and I were going for a Sunday drive." Some of the anger left her voice, but it remained blade thin.

"Sheriff Obregon is your fiancé?" he asked, wanting to probe her feelings for the man.

"He *was*."

The back of his neck tingled. "I see."

A broken engagement was not a wrinkle Sebastian wanted to deal with. It spoke of deep emotions that had turned on themselves. He loathed such things.

"Did you often go that way?" he prodded.

"Yes."

Good God, the woman could best a Spartan at being laconic.

"But you didn't make it to town that day."

Her dark eyes and thin face were unreadable. "No."

He'd meant the statement to lead her to elaborate on the story—he didn't need a stark confirmation of what he already knew.

She'd only answer direct inquiries? Very well, he'd be as blunt as a rusty blade. "Where did the attack happen?"

"On the road to town. Two to three miles from the rancho."

"Would you recognize the place?"

"Of course." A cold sneer, that. "Perhaps you should be writing down some of this?" As if he were a schoolboy who'd forgotten his slate.

"No need to." He placed one finger to his temple. "I couldn't forget if I tried."

"How... *interesting*." The way an insect might be interesting.

"We'll visit the site tomorrow," he bit off. If visiting the place where she'd been assaulted didn't knock her out of her stony facade, nothing would.

"I don't think—" her mother cut in.

Miss Moreno raised a slim, imperial hand. "It's quite all right. If Mr. Spencer wants to see the scene of the crime, I can certainly show him."

The pulse beat hard in her throat.

"It's Marshal Spencer." He showed his teeth, releasing a fraction of the frustration building within him.

"Of course." She showed hers. "After all, Judge Bannister sent you all this way to hear and see exactly what happened."

His frustration turned cold. That was much too sharp for a woman who ought to know nothing of why Judge Bannister had really sent Sebastian.

"Thirteen years with no word from his son," Miss Moreno mused, "a son who changed his name to hide from him, and he immediately sends a marshal at his request?"

Another lady would have made the question sticky with sarcasm, but not her. The words were bone dry.

Her mother flinched before smoothing herself back to impassivity. Mrs. Merrill went a deep shade of red.

Interesting.

The judge might have had hidden motives for sending Sebastian, but there was something hidden between these three. Had it only been Miss Moreno and her mother, he'd have missed it. Mrs. Merrill was a poor prevaricator, thank the Lord.

With every turn in this, he came upon a new wrinkle, a perhaps deeper game here than he'd anticipated.

Just so long as none of it interfered with apprehending McCade.

"Judge Bannister cares about justice," he told Miss Moreno. "Especially when a lawman has been injured." Even if it was a Mexican lawman. And the judge *did* care about justice—but he cared about embarrassing Cole McCade's father more. "Please finish your account."

Miss Moreno studied him for a long moment and he prepared himself to deflect more questions he shouldn't answer.

But luck—and the lady's difficult nature—were with Sebastian this time, and she continued her story.

"As we drew up," she went on, "they came out from behind the trees." She spoke as if reciting a poem she'd been forced to memorize.

"Who was there?"

"The two Carey boys—Billy and Thomas—and another man." Her expression slipped into bleakness for half a moment. "McCade. Sheriff Obregon had been keeping a close eye on him. There were rumors in the valley that he'd killed a man. They started a fight at a dance, and Señor Obregon broke it up."

Finally, several complete sentences of exposition. The bit about the dance hadn't been in the sheriff's report. That gave McCade and the Careys a motive for attacking Obregon.

Although Cole McCade wouldn't need an excuse for harming someone he'd consider a lesser member of society.

He tapped a forefinger once, hard, against the arm of his chair. Enough to allow himself to focus back on the matter at hand.

Miss Moreno caught that movement, her face hardening as she did. "You know this man, the one who attacked us?"

"I know of him." He glanced away from her accusing gaze, saw his cuff was a hair out of place, and tugged at it, the fabric scraping the skin of his wrist.

So she hadn't connected Cole with his father, Edwin. "Perhaps you might have heard of his father?" he asked her.

Realization chased the accusation from her expression. From all three of their expressions.

"His father is Edwin McCade?" That bit of incredulousness came from Mrs. Merrill.

"He is," Sebastian admitted.

"So that's why you were sent after him." Miss Moreno's contained rage had returned.

She was hitting too close to the truth. "I told you why I came." He put ice on that. "Your story?" he prompted. "What happened after they came out of hiding?"

She turned her gaze back to the window, as if she expected someone to come down the drive.

"They raised their pistols at Señor Obregon." Her hands began to twist in the gray fabric of her skirt while she looked out at nothing. "Then he—McCade—said, 'We're going to teach you a lesson, Sheriff.'"

The silence stretched between them.

"What happened next?" He gave the command force, urging her onward, not wanting to lose this forward motion.

She blinked, staring at something only she could see. Finally, she took a shaky breath. "Then the shooting began."

She looked at him then, her eyes saying, *What more is there to know?*

But there was more, a thousand painful details that she leapt over, to keep from falling into the crevasse.

He needed to have those details.

"Who shot first?" The key point, and they were finally getting to it. His fingers wanted to tap on the chair arms, but he commanded them to stillness, smothering his eagerness.

"McCade." Her hands began to twist in her skirt again. "Señor Obregon then drew his pistol and shot both the Carey brothers."

The flatness of her recitation made it sound as if he'd been shooting bottles, not men.

"Just like that?" he asked. "No one else got another shot off?"

Her eyebrows lifted. "Señor Obregon was quite good."

Sebastian swallowed the whistle that wanted to sneak past his lips. Obregon *hadn't* been confused, then.

"She screamed. She never screams."

He could well believe that, now that he'd tangled with her.

He retraced the story in his mind—the fight at the dance, the Sunday drive, the ambush on the road. The killings.

"The sheriff shoots both the Carey brothers," he mused half to himself. "McCade shoots the sheriff." He let the moment draw out as he stared at her. "When did you shoot McCade?"

Her hand rose, hovered near her throat, then settled below her collarbone. She was agitated, that succession of tiny movements betraying her internal state.

She was cracking. He had her. But there was no glory in the victory.

"At the very end," she answered. "There's... there's more before that."

He took a moment to study her mother and her sister. They were watching Miss Moreno intently, waiting for the rest of her tale. They didn't appear as though they'd object to the question he had to ask. Not that their objections would stop him, but he wanted to be prepared for an outburst of indignation.

"Tell me the rest." Gentler, in light of her agitation.

"After Sheriff Obregon fell, I fired at McCade from the buggy seat. The shot went wide." Her lips put on a mocking twist. "My hands, you see, were shaking quite badly."

"Anyone's would have shaken," he said. "Even mine."

Her look was pure contempt. "I very much doubt that."

Of course she would spurn his attempt at comfort. Very well, they'd go on as they had before.

"What did he do after you fired at him?"

"He threw me into the brush. I couldn't hold onto the rifle." Self-blame dripped through the words. "Must I expose every detail?"

He almost regretted what he was about to do, but he squelched the urge before it bloomed into a full-fledged emotion. "If he violated you, Miss Moreno—"

Her face twisted in disgust. "Of course he didn't violate me."

If he were a man who cursed, he might have done so, silently. She likely understood what he'd meant by *violated*... but he had to be certain. "Miss Moreno, I'm speaking of rape. Did he rape you?"

"No." She drew the word out to three times its length. "I understand what you meant. I understood it all six times the sheriff asked that same question."

Her mother and sister had dropped their gazes to their laps, Mrs. Merrill red as a ripe tomato and her mother's cheeks heading for that same shade.

Miss Moreno showed no embarrassment—just that icy rage of hers.

"I found a rifle lying next me," she went on. "This time I hit him. Only in the shoulder, but he was bleeding."

Merrill had mentioned a trail of blood, as had the sheriff's report. She'd marked him, and McCade had trailed the evidence of it behind him as he'd escaped. Was likely wearing that badge of hers even now.

"I can't imagine he was too pleased." An admiring understatement, but he was impressed.

"No, he was not." A gleam entered her eyes, lightened her voice. Oh, she liked telling this part. She'd drawn blood and she'd enjoyed it.

He'd understood that sensation. Once. But never again.

There were consequences for drawing blood, terrible ones. Now he must force her to describe the consequences she'd suffered.

"The marks on your throat. Did that happen after you shot him?"

She turned away, stone once more. "Before. He did that before."

He'd lost her again. "And the wound on your head?"

The final piece of her story—or at least this half-story he was getting from her.

"He struck me with his pistol. After that, I only recall waking in my own bedroom."

The set of her jaw indicated that as far as she was concerned, her tale was finished.

Sebastian allowed his forefinger one more tap to focus himself as he reviewed what she'd told him. It sounded plausible—yet it was so free of particulars, it likely bore no more resemblance to the memories trapped in her mind than a child's scribbles did to a Rembrandt.

There was nothing about McCade's demeanor, Obregon's reaction to the first shot, her own response to any of it.

The most powerfully altering experience of her life, and she'd told it with an almost complete lack of passion.

He sensed more hiding behind her reserve, perhaps that same something that had sparked Mrs. Merrill's uneasy glances.

He wanted to know what it was. But she'd give him nothing more here.

No matter. Tomorrow he'd have her out at the site itself. Alone with him, the physical presence of her memories impossible to ignore—she was certain to crack.

"Thank you, Miss Moreno," he said. "I appreciate your honesty." Thin though it was. He remained in his chair, waiting for the inevitable offer. As an old Spanish family, they were certain to hold to the old ways of hospitality. In fact, he was surprised they hadn't offered him a place to stay earlier. It would have been the very first thing his mother would have done.

Mrs. Moreno and Mrs. Merrill exchanged a quick glance. Miss Moreno continued to ignore him.

"You'll want to return with Mrs. Merrill," Mrs. Moreno said firmly. "My daughter is happy to share her hospitality with you."

She didn't look like it. And it wasn't *her* hospitality he needed to share. It appeared Mrs. Moreno didn't hold with the old traditions.

He'd have to force his way instead.

"Mrs. Moreno, I am very sorry to impose upon you, but I must remain here. With Miss Moreno under my guard. A man has already been sent to guard Sheriff Obregon."

Miss Moreno turned to face him, pale tension gripping her expression.

Oh yes, she was hiding something from him. His resolve to remain doubled.

"I'm certain you'll be more comfortable at my daughter's," Mrs. Moreno said, without a hint of give.

He pondered his next course of action. The best thing would be to expose who he truly was. Having people assume he was a full-blooded Anglo usually made things easier—but the Morenos wouldn't be impressed by his father's name.

They would be by his mother's.

Smoothly, in his best Spanish, he said, "Señoras, Señorita, I know how distressing this has been to your entire family." He placed a hand on his heart. "I promise you, I will apprehend this cholo, and he will face justice. I wish to keep the Señorita safe in the meantime."

Oh, that set them on their heels, their mouths dropping to shape identically incredulous expressions. He let a bit of pleasure rise within him at this small victory. He'd repent for it tonight.

"You're not American. You're Spanish." Señorita Moreno's expression might be surprised, but her words were accusing—and also in Spanish.

Let her be suspicious—he didn't owe her any explanations.

"My mother is a Vasquez." He tapped the badge on his chest. "I am, of course, also an American."

"A Vasquez?" The Señora raised an elegant eyebrow. "I am an Alvarado, myself. Perhaps I know your mother?"

The Alvarado connection certainly explained the haughtiness. The family may have lost the Rancho Alvarado decades ago—to Judge Bannister's father, no less—but they had held on to their oversized arrogance.

"My mother is Señora Maria Carmen Vasquez Calderon de Espencer." As it normally did whenever he spoke his mother's language, *Spencer* came out in the Spanish fashion. He didn't bother to keep the reverence he felt for his mother from his voice; it was the truest emotion he could summon these days. It had been the hard-fought achievement of years to eradicate every other one—including the hatred of his father.

"She's a cousin to Raul Calderon, is she not?" the Señora inquired. "Don Raul is married to one of my cousins on my mother's side."

Of course they would be related. As decimated as the old Spanish families were, the pool of marriageable people shrank each year.

Which was why his Spanish mother had found herself married to an American.

"I believe my cousin, Don Enrique Jaramillo, knows your mother," the Señora went on. "He's mentioned her in his letters." She paused. "But he's never mentioned her son."

Don Enrique wouldn't. His mother was an occasional visitor to the Jaramillo house—Sebastian had visited only once. He'd felt like a bear on a chain, Don Enrique's daughters watching him in appalled fascination. Silly girls often did that, when faced with a man of his size and wearing the scars that he did.

Sebastian disliked such social occasions.

"I've only had the pleasure of meeting Don Enrique once," he replied. "My duties keep me busy."

"Of course," the Señora allowed. "Well, then, you must stay here with us. You'll want to rest before dinner. Isabel can show you your room. We dine at six."

A firm dismissal.

He rose. "Yes, I am tired after all my traveling. I thank you for your hospitality, Señora."

He nodded to each lady in turn, leaving Señorita Moreno for last.

Her mother's nod was short, correct—polite, but nothing more. Mrs. Merrill's nod was more uncertain—and a touch relieved. He unnerved that lady. Too bad her sister wasn't similarly affected by him.

For her part, Señorita Moreno gave him nothing but chilled arrogance. Yet, even in the midst of such pinched pride, he saw a glimmer of *something*. Not prettiness, for a lady as sharp as she could never be *pretty*. Pretty was for the flowers that didn't survive the storm.

Certainly not beauty. Beauty never had such a keen edge.

He kept looking, trying to put a name to what he'd seen. Slowly, he realized she was gazing at him as hard as he was at her, the fierceness of her gaze quite beyond intriguing. It was almost... captivating.

Without warning, she turned away, leaving only the shell of her ear for him to peruse.

She could try to hide from him—but tomorrow he'd study her all he liked.

~~~

Isabel's head throbbed in time with her heartbeat, each pulse sending an agonizing echo through her skull.

A dull hum before the interview, the headache was a piercing screech by the time the marshal asked the only question anyone wanted to know.

Were you violated?

She knew what questions lurked behind that one.

Did he force open your legs, hammer between them, spill your virgin blood?

He *had* violated her—he'd taken her fiancé, her teaching position, the privacy she'd so carefully cultivated behind her imposing reserve. He'd taken it all and left her with nothing but the paralytic fear and the headaches.

With each hammer blow to her head, she wanted to fall to the floor. But she kept dragging herself up the stairs—if only to get away from the man at her back.

His footsteps fell as steady as a metronome. If she glanced behind her, he'd blend into the shadowed stairwell.

His suit was spotlessly black, the same shade of darkness as his immaculately combed hair. The white of his shirt was the only light.

The length and breadth of him was at odds with the cold intelligence in his gray eyes, since such brawn rarely traveled with such brains. He looked as she imagined

St. Ignatius might have: the hard power of a warrior's body joined to the crystalline eyes of a saint.

But the marshal was no saint.

He was stone, as unyielding as granite as he'd attempted to grind her story from her. She'd given him the details he'd needed, but he wanted more. The gleam in his eyes when he'd spoken of taking her to the attack site told her that.

One step and then another. Ten more to go.

His step—heavy, inhumanly steady—behind her.

"Señorita? Are you all right?"

His voice was the only thing not still and dark and menacing about him. It was—

A spike of pain had her stomach twisting. She couldn't think what his voice was, could only note that it did not sound as if it should belong to him.

"Quite." Soon enough, she would be. A few more moments and she'd be alone behind her own bedroom door, could let the nausea rattle her joints, could let the pain drag her down.

And her collar buttons. She could undo those. She reached for the first button and twisted it between her fingers.

Not yet.

She'd survived an actual strangulation. She could manage an imaginary one.

Finally. There was the top step, firm below her foot, more real than whatever she might imagine was at her throat. Only seven steps down the hall and she could be free of him, could shake loose the sensation of him behind her.

"Your room." She flicked a hand toward the open door of it, keeping the motion curt so that her stomach didn't cast up its contents. "I hope it is to your liking. If there's anything you require, please let us know."

Too monotonously recited to be polite, but in a few moments she'd be incapable of speech anyway.

"Thank you."

He moved past her into the room, and she took a step back to avoid him. Too quick—the pain swirled dizzily in her skull and she had to close her eyes to reclaim her equilibrium.

"Are you certain you're all right?"

It took a moment for her poor, pain-battered brain to translate. "Yes." Two more steps back, away from him and toward the safety of her room. "If you'll excuse me."

She didn't wait for his response, hurrying to hide in her bedroom. She sagged against the door as she tore open her collar, one of the buttons clattering angrily to the floor.

She'd survived the first interview with this marshal. He'd given no indication he knew who her mother was, no indication he suspected that Señora Moreno had once been Judge Bannister's sister-in-law—her mother was safe for the moment.

Isabel would survive the trip with him tomorrow, would survive telling her story one more time.

No one had ever died from telling a story.

No one had ever died from being too afraid.

She took a steady breath, pulling the air into her lungs to push away this headache.

Finally, she was alone.

Except for her mother and sister downstairs, no doubt hashing over the entire interview. And the marshal, one wall away, no doubt mulling over his own impressions of her. Or the townspeople, discussing the appearance of the marshal—and telling the story of her attack, over and over and over again.

And McCade, somewhere outside, waiting to grab her by the throat once more.

All of their attention on her and the most terrible moment of her life, the weight of it forcing her to the floor to pant like a dying dog, praying that the next breath would be easier, or the one after, or the one after that.

The pain pulled her into darkness before her prayers were answered.

CHAPTER THREE

WHILE SEBASTIAN DID NOT ENJOY social occasions, he had to admit that a family dinner provided the perfect opportunity to study the Moreno family.

The warm smell of tortillas filled the air as he pushed beans around his plate, trying to give the impression of having eaten some without any actually passing his lips.

He didn't care for beans.

"You and Sheriff Williams made it to Pine Ridge and back all right, then?" Mr. Merrill asked from across the table.

"Yes." He hated idle conversation; of course he'd made it safely back from Pine Ridge, otherwise why would he be sitting at this table?

Señorita Moreno, seated at his left elbow, had not engaged in idle chitchat. He couldn't tell if she too loathed it, or if his mere presence inspired her to keep quiet.

Given the difficulties of their earlier interview, he certainly didn't inspire her to speak.

"How was Joaquin?" That from the youngest sister, Francisca, whose hands and eyes flashed with the speed of her gestures. She moved quick enough at times to make him want to flinch. All that dynamism made him anxious.

"The nurse said he was having a poor day." Better to lay that impression at the nurse's feet rather than admit what he really thought—that Obregon looked as if one bad turn would have him in the grave.

That pushed Señorita Moreno to speak. "I hope your questioning didn't unduly distress Señor Obregon."

"Sheriff Obregon understood the need for it." Or at least Sebastian assumed he had. Not that he had to explain himself to her.

Her only response was the slide of her knife across her plate.

"It really is too awful about Joaquin," Mrs. Merrill put in.

"He is alive." Low and tight, that response from Señorita Moreno.

Interesting, this defense of him from her. Sebastian wondered how the engagement had ended. Unless Obregon's good days were much better than what he'd seen today, the wounded sheriff was in no state to break off an engagement.

Which meant *she* must have.

And yet, she defended him.

Most people's motives were easy enough to read. Greed, power, fear—rarely was something more complicated at the heart of a crime.

But Señorita Moreno's motives eluded him.

He couldn't say he enjoyed being puzzled by her, though the tangle of her motives compelled him to unwind the skein of them.

"Well of course I'm glad he's alive," Mrs. Merrill snapped. "That wasn't what I meant and you know it."

Señorita Moreno pressed two fingers hard to her temple before dropping her hand back into her lap. The headache must still be upon her. He'd seen the signs of it as she'd led him up the stairs—the too-quick flickers of her gaze, the tight lines of her shoulders as she tried to hold the pain within.

"Yes, of course," Señorita Moreno replied.

"Sheriff Obregon is quite lucky," Sebastian said to Mrs. Merrill, trying to draw her attention from her sister, to give Señorita Moreno some space to allow her headache to recede. "And resilient. Few men would have survived."

While he'd intentionally inflicted distress upon Señorita Moreno earlier—and intended to inflict more tomorrow—he found it... *unsettling,* watching another do the same.

Every head at the table nodded solemnly at his words. Except for Señorita Moreno's. She turned to him, their gazes meeting for a moment. The gratitude in her eyes made his heart twitch.

He dropped his gaze back to his plate, grabbing for his knife and fork to saw at his meat.

"Yes, well, let us hope Marshal Espencer apprehends this outlaw soon." Señor Moreno placed his weather-scarred hands flat on the table, as if to declare the subject closed.

The Señor was a thick mustached vaquero who clearly spent more time in the saddle than in a drawing room. The Señora was more refined, the dignified ruler of the household and family.

Both he and the Señora were as Sebastian had expected: specimens of an earlier time, when California had been the furthest outreach of first Spain, then Mexico. They were the living embodiments of the culture of sprawling ranchos, openhanded hospitality, and genteel living. Old California—rather than the glittering, golden promise of the American West it was now.

The senior Morenos and his mother would get on famously—not that they would ever meet.

"We shall pray for his swift and safe capture this evening," the Señora said.

Everyone fell silent as the soft clinks of silver on china floated through the room.

"Tell us, Marshal Spencer," Mrs. Merrill asked with strained joviality, "how is Los Angeles these days? We have cousins there, but it has been too long since we visited them." Her smile was a fishhook, designed to snag in a man's cheek and pull him along in her wake. But then he saw a faint sheen of tears—the smile was purely reflexive. She meant nothing by it.

"Los Angeles grows every day," he said, putting in his own effort at politeness, "with trainloads of refugees from the East coming to escape their drudgery and retire to the indolence and sunshine promised by the boosters."

He perceived, rather than saw, Señorita Moreno's attention turn toward him. Whether she *had* slightly turned, or if it was only his imagination, he could not say, but her regard was a physical thing, more real than the scrub of his clothes against his skin.

He felt as if he'd caught a rare bird in his hand, soft and still, with darting eyes and fast beating heart. One had to be careful with such a thing. He continued on, watching Mrs. Merrill, but addressing her sister. "Indeed, if you have not visited in a year, you would not recognize the place. Streetcars, rail yards, the work on the port." He sketched something rising higher and higher. "And more people. Always more people."

She was listening, he could tell. Some urge, something he'd thought was no longer within him, wanted to lure her, to have her soften and bend toward him. He let his voice drop half a note, gentled it so that she must bring herself closer to hear.

"There are electric streetcars to take you to any part of the city you wish." The rest of the table would take that *you* as a general one, but he meant her and only her. "A line is likely to be completed to Pasadena soon. There are public parks, theaters, universities—anything an intelligent person might wish for."

That hit its mark. She wasn't looking at him—but she was hardly breathing, all of her still as she absorbed his words, her ear tilted ever so slightly toward him.

"You know, Isabel wanted to live in Los Angeles." Franny nodded toward her sister. "I suppose that won't be happening now Joaquin is gone."

Señorita Moreno turned to her sister, allowing him to see the snarl curling her lip and the color highlighting her cheek. "It's Señor Obregon to you. And Marshal Spencer isn't interested in matters of no import."

He didn't allow himself to regret that the moment between them had been shattered.

"You wish to reside in Los Angeles, Señorita Moreno?" he asked. He wasn't ready to release her regard from his cupped palms just yet.

"Señor Obregon and I had plans to move there once we were married." He heard it then, deep under the ice she'd encased her words in—a frisson of pain.

Perhaps that was why the engagement had ended—Obregon could no longer carry her away from here. But such cold calculation was at odds with the hurt in her words.

He'd no assurances to offer her in order to assuage her hurt—he shouldn't wish to assuage it in the first place. But her sadness pricked at him and he could not ignore the sensation. He couldn't promise the renewal of her engagement or that she might make it to Los Angeles regardless—but he could tell her more of the city.

So he did.

"There's a railway that will take you to the top of Mount Lowe," he went on. "It's very popular…"

~~~

He was talking only to her.

Oh, he was looking at her sister, with that practiced smile pasted on her face, but he was talking to *her*. Somehow he managed to bend his voice, to have his words arc straight for her.

For a man of his size, Isabel would have expected his voice to be deep enough to make the earth tremble, but it wasn't. It was golden, mellow, the kind of voice that slipped along and insinuated itself into the small spaces of a person. A pleasant surprise, that voice.

All of him was proving to be a surprise. Now that her headache had faded to a dull throb—and he wasn't interrogating her—she could notice details she'd overlooked earlier.

He was as tailored as a dandy in a novel, his cheeks and upper lip smooth, without a hint of a shadow, in stark contrast to the rest of the men at the table. Every aspect of him seemed specially designed to offset his brutish size.

"Where do you live?" she asked, keeping her gaze lowered. When she'd glanced at him in gratitude after Catarina's comments about Joaquin, that cool gray gaze had held something electric.

She didn't want to be shocked again.

"Just north of downtown, near Rancho Los Feliz."

Ah, that voice.

She couldn't let it cozen her. He was sitting in Joaquin Obregon's place, sent by a man who'd harm her mother if he could—the marshal wanted nothing more from her than the most painful details of her attack.

This trick with his voice, speaking so about Los Angeles—it was all to soften her, to weaken her so that he might breach her defenses.

She wanted Marshal Spencer and his insinuating voice out of Joaquin's chair, and Joaquin in it instead, the two of them still set on their course to leave Cabrillo. She wanted her teaching position back, her privacy returned to her.

She wanted everything to be as it had been before, when her future had been bright, assured—not murkily uncertain.

But that wasn't going to happen. The marshal was here and Joaquin was in the sanatorium. The chances of them switching places were about as high as that of her engagement to Joaquin being restored.

Her and Joaquin's last discussion of the matter made it clear that would never happen. The engagement was over. He'd been insistent, despite her protests. And his condition had prevented her from giving full vent to her objections.

That had been another storm from the gossips to weather, the ending of the engagement and who had severed what. She'd kept the details vague and shouldered most of the blame, given that Joaquin could not answer.

"Do your cousins still live near the city center?" Marshal Spencer asked. He was cutting his meat with the precision of a watchmaker. Such large hands, yet he wielded them with such delicacy.

Then she looked again.

The backs of his hands were netted with scars, the knuckles themselves misshapen from long-healed fractures. He shouldn't be able to use such hands with such grace.

Yet he did.

Was all this practiced? The suit, the smooth-shaven cheek, the voice, the unsettling grace of his movements? His features were unassailably brutish—broad forehead, scarred face, thick neck—yet the rest of him was decidedly not.

What had he asked? Where her cousins lived. "They're... yes, they still live in the same house," she answered.

He cut and cut and cut, the meat dividing into smaller and smaller pieces, until they were fit only for an infant to gum. When there was nothing left to slice, he carefully set his knife and fork aside.

Had he taken a single bite? She couldn't recall the fork ever making its way to his mouth.

"I never could see," Señor Moreno put in, "how Don Enrique could stand to live so enclosed by people."

"Me neither," added Franny.

No, those two wouldn't understand, spending their days out of doors as they did. None of her family would understand, content as they were to remain in Cabrillo.

But Isabel understood. There was something vital, enlivening, about the city, with all those people pressed close, moving and striving so much more quickly than anyone in Cabrillo did. Cabrillo moved at the speed of a grazing cow, while Los Angeles was a veritable stampede. She wanted to run with that stampede, to race toward culture and knowledge and refinement.

"There's something to be said for life in the city," the marshal said dryly. "Electric lights, telephones... sewers."

Her father's mustache lifted in a sneer. "Telephones! What's wrong with the mail service, I ask?"

"Nothing of course, Señor."

The marshal sounded as if he found such things quite commonplace. How extraordinary. But she wouldn't allow herself to ask about them, like some unlettered provincial.

"With so many people," Catarina said, a smile stuck to her face, "it must be quite the social whirl."

His hands froze. "I myself am not particularly sociable, but yes, my mother is always off doing something. Ladies' aid societies. Beautification of... things. Literary societies."

Literary societies. How Isabel's heart ached at those words. She'd been involved in one such society in the valley, an anemic meeting of a few ladies who more often than not hadn't even read the book in question.

"No doubt you have such things here." His tone said that he did doubt it. Who could blame him, coming from a city with electric railways and universities?

"We have sewing circles and barn dances and the like," Catarina said. "There's certainly no lack of amusements."

"The Ladies' Temperance League," Isabel added, not wanting him to think it was all rustic pursuits.

"Oh yes," Catarina said. "Isabel is the president of our local temperance meeting."

"Yes," Franny added. "Isabel ran out the saloon."

As if such a thing had been as easy as herding cattle from one pasture to another.

"Francisca," her mother said gently, "please don't discuss saloons at the table."

Isabel *had* run out the saloon, she and Joaquin's sisters together. They'd been united in friendship and their common cause. The day the saloon had closed had been one of the proudest of her life, knowing that the women and children of Cabrillo were safe from the predations of drunken men.

The Ladies' Temperance League was no more, her friendship with the Obregon sisters ended in the wake of the attack and the dissolution of her engagement to Joaquin.

Once the saloon was gone, there wasn't much for the Temperance League to do, but they'd still met regularly, simply to enjoy each other's company.

"Temperance?" the marshal asked. "That's a very noble cause."

He didn't raise his gaze to hers. Perhaps he'd been as unsettled as she by their earlier glance.

Or perhaps he simply didn't care to look at her, preferred to focus on his meal. Which he wasn't eating.

"You believe in temperance?" In her experience, the men of Cabrillo were undecided on the issue at best. As for the men who had shouted the loudest when the saloon had been shut down—their wives had been the first to thank her.

"I do," he replied. "I've been a teetotaler my entire life. Alcohol has never passed my lips, and never will."

"But what about communion?" As she realized what she'd said, her cheeks exploded with heat, that she would say something so inane.

He leaned toward her and pitched his voice low. "Thanks to the miracle of transubstantiation, it's not truly wine, now is it?"

She bit her lip to keep her mouth from breaking into a grin.

Almost smiling at a joke about the sacrament of communion of all things—thank goodness her parents hadn't heard.

Had it been a jest? He hadn't smiled, hadn't looked to catch her smile in response. Perhaps he'd been entirely serious. And still no food had passed his lips. She didn't even think he'd reached for his water.

Boot heels stomped through the hallway, coming for the dining room. The noise stopped just outside, then the door was swinging toward the wall.

Felipe Ortega, the rancho's overseer, rushed in, still in his clothes from the day. Dusty and wrinkled, his hat upon his head, he clearly hadn't washed for supper.

Franny jumped up. "Where have you been?" she demanded.

"Francisca," her mother warned. As Franny sank into her seat, their mother turned to the overseer. "Felipe," she said repressively, "supper was served quite some time ago. We could wait no longer for you."

"Pardon, Señoras, Señoritas, Señores," he said, slightly out of breath, "but one of the Whitmans' hands just left here."

Her father frowned. "The Whitmans have already begun driving their cattle down the mountain. They sent a hand here?"

Felipe nodded. "They've already driven their herd halfway to the valley. It seems they've lost a considerable amount of food. Stolen by *someone* hiding along the road."

Cold crept across her skin. It couldn't be *him*—there'd been no sign of the outlaw since the attack...

Please let him be dead. Terrible, to pray for a man's death, but she did it anyway.

The marshal half rose from his seat, his chair eerily silent as it slid across the floor. "That's likely him. McCade. He's trying to escape down the mountain."

Don't look out the window. Do not look out the window.

"That's what the Whitmans thought," Felipe said, "so they sent their man to tell us. I'm sorry I missed supper, but I've been speaking with him this entire time."

Isabel's heart thudded dully, echoing in her ears. Her lungs wanted to pant in time with the race of her pulse, but she forced her breaths slow and deep.

He was still alive. He could be peering through that window there, the darkness beyond concealing him and his twisted plans for her...

Stop this. She must remain calm, at least until she could gain the solitude of her room.

"When is your herd leaving for the valley?" Marshal Spencer asked her father.

"Tomorrow at first light."

"I'm coming with you." His eyes were alight with something close to excitement, the most affected expression she'd seen on him yet. "I'll join you on the trail once Señorita Moreno has shown me where they were attacked."

A queer sort of shakiness seized her heart. Lord, could a heart fail a person simply from shock?

But it kept beating, and as long as it did so she would cling to the illusion of calm. Of impassivity.

But her breath slipped past her control, going short and shallow. She released two pants to allow the panic to return to a low simmer.

Enough of this. She'd survived her last trip to that place. She would survive this next.

One last jerking breath, and her lungs were once more under her command.

"As you like, Marshal Spencer." As if she cared not. As if her entire frame didn't feel like it was about to shake to pieces.

His imitation of unyielding stone would be nothing compared to hers tomorrow.

CHAPTER FOUR

Seeing the place again wasn't quite as horrid as Isabel thought it would be.

Lead settled in her stomach at the sight of those sickeningly familiar pines. Her skin went clammy, but the shivers she feared might take hold she kept at bay. For now.

Those pines. They came from behind those pines, closer and closer, hands set on their pistols...

She shook off the images—or tried to. Perhaps she couldn't keep from remembering, but she was still upright. A small victory.

Marshal Spencer stood looking around him, his black suit once again completely untouched by the dust and grime that surrounded everyone else. He looked like an illustration come to life—*Modern Urban Man.*

He stuck his hands on his hips. Her stomach dropped at the sight of his hands so close to those pistols.

He's not here to hurt you.

"So this is the place." He didn't seem to expect an answer, so she kept silent. He slowly turned round and round, eyes narrow as he took in the road and the brush and the pines.

69

It really was a very ordinary stretch of road.

But to tell the story here, all those memories pressing hard upon her...

Lord, it would be like flaying herself to tell it here.

"They came from behind those trees?" Marshal Spencer gestured to the stand of pines.

She straightened and drew a deep breath. "Yes."

"McCade fires," the marshal said to himself, "but he misses."

"No, he hit the horse."

He turned a gimlet stare upon her. "You didn't mention the horse last time."

No, she hadn't. When she'd told the sheriff, he'd gasped at the death of the horse, but had barely flinched when she told of Joaquin's wounding.

She hadn't mentioned the horse again.

And now she must recite all those piercing details, the ones she'd been able to avoid before.

She jerked her gaze away and began to stride down the road, unconcerned with his reaction. She dragged deep breaths into her lungs. In, out. In, out. The tide of her breath began to slowly erode the panic within.

She kept walking. Just a few more feet and she'd turn back, once she'd regained complete command of herself.

Something down the road caught her attention. A thin ribbon of red, growing larger, coming as fast as a man ran.

Her breath arrested in her chest.

The snake stopped. Its red length was half as long as herself, the gray head raised to study her.

She held still as could be, fear soaking her as she willed the snake to turn back.

A large arm curled around her waist, an electric shock running through her. Caught between that arm and a hard wall of chest, with warm breath brushing her ear.

"Is that snake poisonous?"

She gave an abrupt shake of her head, bumping against his chin. A red racer's bite wasn't fatal, but they were famed for their aggression. From the edge of her vision, she saw him slowly lower the pistol she hadn't realized he'd drawn.

"We'll simply wait him out." His arm around her never slackened.

The snake's head weaved as it assessed them with flat black eyes.

Suddenly she saw *his* eyes again—McCade's. Not black like the snake's, but just as flat and pitiless. Saw the buckwheat blossoms explode into a cloud of blood red when his hands brushed past them, reaching for her throat...

The tremors broke free, shaking her like a dog did a rabbit. She gritted her teeth and wrapped her arms around her ribs, trying to push the quaking back inside, but it was too late.

The tremors had hold of her, and she could only ride them out.

Marshal Spencer pulled her tight against him, absorbing the violence as if it were nothing. As if he could take in all her fear and pain, swallow it whole, and leave her free and intact again.

Ridiculous to think so. What had happened couldn't be erased, only endured.

But she'd indulge this once in the solidity of the man behind her and the fantasy that he could repair everything.

A lovely fantasy it was too, that he might always be at her back, that she could trust him as she'd trusted no other. But only a fantasy.

The shaking weakened and she finally regained control of her rebellious body. She slowly stepped forward, his arm falling away, and for a moment she felt much too light.

The snake had disappeared into the brush at some point.

"I apologize for that." She forced that out. Not because she wasn't sorry, but because her throat was too tight to speak normally.

"It wasn't about the snake, was it?"

No, it wasn't about the snake.

She turned back to the site of the attack.

It was past time to do this, to tell the entire story. Perhaps with this telling she might leave some of the pain and terror here, right where it had first been given to her.

She glanced at the marshal, waiting silently by her side, his face intent, but clear of judgment or prurient interest. He met her gaze measure for measure—the first time she'd been looked upon without sympathy or pity or shock since this whole ordeal. That look was as bracing as a drink from a high country spring.

"Before the horse even fell, Joaquin shot both the Carey boys." She marked where they'd been with her outstretched finger. "One, two."

She studied the spot where the Carey rothers had fallen in the road—two useless, wasted lives ended with a shot each.

Such a valiant effort on Joaquin's part, and it wasn't enough to protect them. A wasted effort, in the end.

She paused, trying to sharpen the details of her memories.

"McCade fired then, before Sheriff Obregon could fire at him."

When she tried to move on, to tell the rest, her mind stubbornly repeated that moment, over and over. The shot from McCade, the queer, fleshy thud as the bullet landed, the arc of Joaquin's body as he flew through the air to land in the dust of the road.

"It's no mean feat," the marshal said after a time, "to shoot two men dead with a pistol before they draw."

How had he known that was the aspect her memory wouldn't quit worrying at? "Why didn't he shoot McCade first?" she demanded. "The man killed the horse, for heaven's sake!"

Something sharp twisted just below her breast as she admitted such disloyal thoughts of Joaquin, but she could hold them in no longer.

"He did the easy work first," he said levelly.

The marshal was right; it had been but a moment's work to end those two lives. She was glad Mrs. Carey hadn't been there to see twenty-some years of work on her part snuffed out easier than a candle.

Joaquin should have snuffed out McCade first. Easy to come to that conclusion now, viewing the entire thing in reverse.

She took a deep breath. Halfway there. She was halfway there. Although the second half would be infinitely harder to tell than the first.

"Joaquin kept a rifle under the buggy seat." She pushed out each word as hard and fast as she could, rushing for this last fence. "I pulled it free and fired at McCade, but missed. He made me pay for it."

Tears snagged in her voice, trying to force her words into something undecipherable.

"Señorita Moreno." The marshal's voice had gone deep, tugging at her buried emotions as it dropped. "You don't need to—"

"Oh, but I must." Her smile was sharp against her teeth. She summoned her anger, her rage, needing her weapons and shield, needing to lash out, to strike back as she told this next, even if the marshal was her only target.

"Here is all of it then, every last sordid happening in this sad business." She marched over to where McCade had dragged her. "He pulled the rifle from my hands and threw it aside. Then—then he closed his hands around my throat. Tight."

She rubbed at her throat, but couldn't remove the phantom fingers curled there. "It was much like how you would carry a chicken with a wrung neck." She paused, raised a finger. "One important difference though—I was quite alive."

Her insides knotted at his lack of reaction. Anyone else would have been a bilious green at this point, but not him. No doubt stories of abused and defiled women were quite unexceptional to him. She was simply another victim, one that had the luck of being alive, but in sum not so dissimilar from the rest.

A burning caught hold of her, an urge to make him see her as she really was: not a victim, not a school-marm, not the ugly younger sister of the most beautiful woman in the county.

No, she was a woman of intelligence, ambition, a woman who made plans. She was to be reckoned with.

Her tongue raced to tell the rest. "He threw me down."

Her skull had bounced hard against the packed earth, making stars dance in her vision. Then McCade's leer had filled her sight.

"He held me down by the throat and told me in most lurid detail exactly what violations he meant to inflict on my person." Lord, just the memory... Her stomach sent bile crawling up her throat. She swallowed and sum-moned the anger once more. "Shall I list them for you? For your investigation?"

"That won't be necessary."

The impassivity of his face had bolstered her at the beginning. Now, as she prepared to tell the worst, it en-raged her. Or perhaps she wanted it to enrage her, wanted the fury to give her the strength to tell this most terrible bit. "Truly? But you said—at our first meeting—that I *must* tell you all."

Something sparked in his eyes, reminding her that he was well over a head taller than her and nearly twice as big. She told herself this was what he wanted, while a vicious delight bubbled under her anger. This was the reckoning he had called for—and not even he could remain unmoved under the stones she launched.

"He pulled up my skirt." She bit her lip and forced her muscles to hold as he took a step towards her. She couldn't tell if he meant to halt her—or push her onward.

No matter. She wouldn't stop, not when she was so close to the end. She could *see* the outlaw's hand—the one not wrapped around her neck—as it traveled downward, remembered the heavy sensation as it settled against her thighs.

The vision passed and the marshal's silver eyes and white face filled her sight, the large bulk of him casting her in shadow.

"I flung out my hand, trying to ward him off..."

A thing very like lightning jumped between them as the marshal took yet another step. One more and he would be close enough to snare her.

She ought to be afraid, but...

But he'd held her when the snake had come. If he'd wanted to harm her, he could have done it then. Which meant he was stalking her for some other reason.

"When I flung out my hand, I felt it," she said. "That hard, wooden stock."

She licked her lips, dragging in air as he simply stared, unmoving, his body tense with coiled energy.

It sent shivers through her, to see such power so tightly controlled.

"The rifle." He spoke in a voice so harsh she barely recognized it.

She nodded. "I shot him in the shoulder, just as he was unbuttoning his trousers. He'd had a hand on my neck the entire time, squeezing my life away with each second."

She paused, unable to look away from the endless storm of the marshal's gaze, trying to gather her thoughts for this last. "He cursed me once more, then with his uninjured hand pulled his pistol free and sent it crashing into my temple."

A black buzzing had seized her brain then, a dizzying nausea she'd fought for only a few moments before it pulled her under to darkness.

"You were lucky to survive," he said.

She could clearly see the rise and fall of his chest under the fine suit. He took that last step, the toe of his boot barely half an inch from the hem of her skirt.

"I'm going after him," he promised. "I *will* capture him."

His eyes were deeply sincere, sealing the two of them together in this vow he was making, as sacred as a sacrament. She could scarcely breathe at the intensity between them.

She hadn't sensed her anger and fear ebbing away as he stalked toward her, as his gaze had held her tight. But those sensations were gone, leaving only this strange thing between her and the marshal.

It would be so easy to believe him, to think that because he swore to it, the outlaw's capture was a certain thing.

It would also be a lie. Only fate would decide what happened.

Just as fate had decided her own encounter with McCade.

The strike of hooves coming down the road unlocked their gazes, had them springing apart. He took two quick steps back, pivoting so that she was behind him, protected from whomever was coming.

It was only Franny. "I'm supposed to escort Marshal Spencer to the herd when he's done here," she said.

Isabel could see she was annoyed at being left behind from the drive. It was almost charming, her mulish expression. Franny seemed to have no notion of what this place was—or if she did, she wasn't allowing it to put her off. Franny's normalcy made Isabel feel almost normal herself.

That and having given up her story in its entirety. She remained shaken and sick, but relief was coming up from behind.

"We're finished," the marshal said. His voice was once again mellow, but his eyes remained the color of cold iron. "We can be off as soon as I've retrieved my horse and my things."

Soon. He was leaving soon. Isn't that what she'd wanted from the beginning, the marshal gone and McCade along with him?

"Wait," Isabel called. "I'm coming with both of you."

Her surprise at herself was as strong as the shock on their faces.

"But Isabel," Franny said, "you hate riding."

It was true—she'd always despised long days spent in the saddle and sleeping out of doors. For half a moment, she thought to take her mad impulse back. Her gaze flicked away from the two of them—and landed on that spot, the space where her entire life had been shattered.

No. No more hiding. It was time she left the house. And truly, what could happen to her, surrounded as she would be on the cattle drive? There would be her brother, Felipe, even Franny.

And the marshal, of course.

Foolish, perhaps, to think there was little risk. But as she'd learned, simply leaving her bed each morning carried risk.

It was time she began risking things again. Braving risk was the only way to gain her desires.

She deeply desired the capture of that outlaw. She would endure this one trip, solely to witness McCade brought to justice.

Hadn't she studied harder than any other girl at the teacher's examinations—and placed first for her trouble? Wasn't she a teacher now at the secondary school in the valley, as far from Cabrillo as she could flee? Hadn't she shut down the saloon in this town and rid it of the scourge of liquor?

When she returned, everyone would remember those accomplishments, and not the sad, shrinking thing they thought she'd transformed into.

"A cattle drive is nothing to me," she said, "if I can see this man brought low."

"No," the marshal said slowly, "I'd imagine many things would be as nothing, to a lady like yourself."

There was a faint flicker of something like admiration in his expression.

Heat flooded her cheeks. Silly, to be embarrassed by that mere hint of esteem.

Fortunately, Marshal Spencer left off embarrassing her and went on: "It seems you and I will be traveling together to catch this outlaw."

CHAPTER FIVE

The men—and Franny—were clustered in a circle around a map that Felipe was sketching for the marshal.

Isabel was on the outside, looking in. She'd made such a grand declaration about accompanying them on this hunt... and she couldn't even help with this first step.

When she'd told her mother of her decision, the Señora had searched her face for a long time. Isabel wasn't certain what in her expression had convinced her mother, but she'd given her blessing. And ordered Juan to be Isabel's constant shadow.

Franny was tagging along as usual—her little sister was never far from cattle or cowhands if she could help it.

"From here to the valley is three days," Franny was saying. "Of course, if you're not driving an entire herd down the mountain, it's much quicker."

The marshal studied the route she'd traced, raising a finger to his chin as he pondered it.

Curious. She'd been watching the marshal most of the morning and he rarely made such small gestures. If a movement or a word was unnecessary, he didn't indulge in it.

"Where did the Whitman train notice the missing food?" he asked Felipe.

"Here." Felipe pointed to a place halfway between the first and second night's camp.

"We already searched there," her older brother Juan said in exasperation. "We might not be professionals"— he gave the marshal a brief, sardonic look—"but we know enough to search along the road."

"No one suggested otherwise," the marshal replied mildly. "Is there anything of interest near that spot? A spring, a cave—any reason for a fugitive to linger?"

"There's a ciénaga at the second night's camp," Felipe said.

"A marsh. Fresh water then," the marshal muttered to himself.

"Yes, that's why the second night's camp is there." Franny grinned at the marshal, but his mouth didn't even twitch in response. Franny's smile died. "There's the creek for fresh water as well."

The marshal shook his head. "The road follows the creek too closely. If this ciénaga is as large as the map shows, it offers a better place to hide."

"So he came down the road and now he's camping at the ciénaga?" The incredulousness in Juan's voice came perilously close to petulance. "Of course. That explains why we never found him."

Really. Juan didn't need to be quite that sarcastic.

"Sometimes, when a man is unfamiliar with the terrain," the marshal said, "he might take a meandering, uncertain course that would never occur to a native."

"Why come out now?" Felipe asked.

"Food. Water. Shelter," Marshal Spencer offered.

"Why not head for the valley and the train station right away?" Juan demanded. "He's only a day from it, if he's hiding along the road."

Which meant he might be a day's ride from where she was right now. Or perhaps even closer, creeping silently upon them—

"A man wandering into town with a gunshot wound so soon after a sheriff has been attacked is going to raise quite the alarm," the marshal said. "No, better to wait here until he's healed, then escape by train."

"It's quite a long time for him to be recovering," she put in, not wanting to be entirely superfluous.

Maybe he was dead. Maybe it was a simple fluke, the missing food stolen by some enterprising animal instead of a cold-blooded outlaw.

"If we're lucky," Marshal Spencer mused, "he has wound fever."

If he did, he'd be suffering, his wound alight with pain. She liked the idea of that. It was un-Christian, but she liked it all the same.

The marshal caught the expression on her face, and while he didn't quite smile, his eyebrow quirked up in amusement. "Don't worry—I'm hoping for that as well."

Amusement. He could well afford to be amused or unmoved as he planned his hunt—this was only duty for him.

She pulled her mouth flat. "I was hoping he was dead."

The marshal looked back at the map, his expression smoothing. "Three days to the valley. Two to the ciénaga. Which is where he's most likely to be. Although not guaranteed."

Three days on the trail. Three days surrounded by nothing but pines and open sky and chaparral... and possibly McCade's gaze, trained on her from somewhere she couldn't see, waiting, waiting...

Waiting for what? If he did try to snatch her, every man here would be on him in a flash. McCade appearing before her was the best thing that could happen.

That reassurance didn't stop the fluttering of her pulse.

"Señorita Moreno." Not quite a command from the marshal, but a clear bid for her attention. "I'm taking one of the hunting trails Señor Ortega pointed out. Please stay close to someone at all times."

"Of course." As if she'd be so foolish as to wander off.

She told herself the marshal wandering away from her to search was all for the good—if he captured McCade without her ever coming across the man, so much the better—yet that stitch of unease wouldn't go away.

It lasted the entire morning, mixing with the high anxiety wrapped around her heart, as she searched every bit of brush, every stand of trees, looking for... well, not really anything.

Juan rode on her left, Franny on her right, and the two kept up such a chatter about cattle and this year's beef prices, Isabel had no need to contribute. She suspected they had planned it that way.

But for all that she couldn't stop staring at her surroundings—and for all the irritation Juan and Franny's bickering caused her—she felt surprisingly... even. Not well—she hated riding down the mountain—but closer to it than she'd been in weeks. She was out of doors, exposed and in the open, searching for the man who'd attacked her... and she was still moving forward. There was no hint of a headache building.

And if she couldn't tear her gaze away from the brush... well, she was hunting McCade too.

Although she prayed the marshal would find him first.

Marshal Spencer reappeared just before lunch. Empty handed. An odd relief lightened her—she wouldn't have to face McCade. Not yet.

"I found his camp," the marshal said in greeting.

Her mood deflated. He'd found McCade's camp—but did not have McCade in tow. Her pulse took off at double time, her breath racing to catch up. How could the marshal not have found him?

"Where was it?" Juan demanded.

"Three miles south of here. I found some old bandages, but nothing more."

"So he *is* still out there." There was a grimness to Franny that Isabel had never heard before, her sister's youthfulness deserting her.

"Had you any doubts?" The marshal sent his question not to Franny, but to Isabel.

A warning and a bolstering.

You knew he was alive. Are you prepared to face him again? That's what Marshal Spencer meant by directing the question to her. *Have you any doubts?*

Before she could answer, even if only in her thoughts, the marshal spurred his horse forward, neatly cutting between Isabel and Juan. "I will remain here with Señorita Moreno. You keep watch at the front," he ordered her brother.

Juan's face twisted for half a moment, but then Felipe called out to him and he went off without protest.

Wonderful. Juan had taken a dislike to the marshal, and his temper was mercurial at best. Too bad Catarina wasn't here to keep him in line—he never took Isabel's admonishments seriously.

Isabel found herself sandwiched between her sister and the marshal, all three of them scanning for any sign of what they'd come to find.

The hunt went on.

~~~

Sebastian disliked this landscape. It was too open, too wild—too much space for a man's thoughts to expand. He hated being alone with his thoughts.

Or rather, his emotions—those were not to be trusted.

He scanned the hills yet again. The astringent scent of pines had lessened as they descended, replaced by something much more potent. Sage, perhaps? They did call it sagebrush country. The breeze was sharper here, the call of the birds more cacophonous than in Cabrillo. It all ran against his nerves in the most disconcerting fashion.

He wasn't normally so unnerved by a place. He'd traveled far and wide as he'd hunted men, and nothing had worked under his skin the way these mountains did.

Or perhaps it wasn't the mountains unsettling him. Perhaps it was *her.*

He fixed his gaze on the tall woman riding half a length ahead of him. Señorita Moreno rode with careful consideration, suggesting she'd not been born to ride, but rather mastered the skill against her natural inclinations.

It would not have been so noticeable had her younger sister not been riding alongside. He had the distinct impression the girl was minding them—the two greenhorns pulling up the rear. Now there was a girl born to the saddle. He pondered how two such ladies had been born of the same mother—Señorita Moreno, with her close and controlled manners, and her younger sister, who could be best described as disheveled.

When she'd been reciting her story, tossing it down before him like a gauntlet, Señorita Moreno hadn't even come close to disheveled.

He had been the one upended, watching that proud lady recite her trials, remembering another proud lady who had been bent, but not broken, under life's travails.

His base nature, the one he fought to repress, had roared in response to Señorita Moreno's steely resolve. He'd reminded himself that she was a witness, that he must not touch her, that she and her family might be concealing something.

But such reminders had been ineffective—only the rigid self-control he'd perfected over the years had kept the emotions she inspired from spilling forth.

As it was, he'd been forced to hurriedly scrounge up pen and paper before the cattle drive left so he could set down the sins of that morning.

Admired a lady I ought not to admire. Wanted to kiss that same lady. And find the man who harmed her and make him suffer.

Not quite the same as writing it in his notebooks—he reserved that ritual for the end of the day, safe in the confines of his library in Los Angeles—but it would have to do. The paper had those emotions now.

They would trouble him no more.

Tempt him no more.

He felt nothing more toward Señorita Moreno than his duty demanded. And duty demanded only that he apprehend McCade.

He pulled his stereo field glasses from the pouch hanging from his saddle horn. If McCade had camped nearby, he must have come to the creek at some point for water. Perhaps some footprints or trampled brush remained.

He studied his surroundings, looking over the banks of the creek several times before becoming aware of a presence at his right elbow. A vibrating presence.

The younger sister, since Señorita Moreno was at his left. And she likely never vibrated.

"Would you like to see the field glasses?" he offered.

"Oh, yes please!" She snatched them up, peering this way and that, like a strange kind of owl.

Señorita Moreno watched with a half smile on her face. As much as her elder sister seemed to irritate her, this younger sister seemed to please her.

Had he not seen Señorita Moreno smile so at her sister, he wouldn't have thought such affection possible for her.

"So," Franny said, the glasses never leaving her face, "how long after you apprehend him will he be found guilty and sent off to prison?"

The intricacies of a trial weren't his specialty—his job ended at the courthouse door.

The intricacies of a trial involving the son of one of the most prominent men in California? Well, he was only glad he wouldn't be the prosecutor assigned the case.

"A trial could take several weeks," he hedged.

Señorita Moreno took a sharp, quick inhale. Of course, she would have to testify at that trial. The cross examination was likely to be... brutal.

He didn't let himself dwell on that thought. Such things weren't his concern.

"And once he's found guilty," Franny went on, "how long will he be locked away?"

"*If* he's found guilty," Señorita Moreno put in. "And if he is, he might not be locked away for long. Not for the murder of a greaser. Not Edwin McCade's son."

Her sneer had the hair on his neck rising, irritation blooming too fast for him to squelch it. "I should simply leave now, let him continue to run free? Since it's all useless anyway?"

The surprise on her face brought him crashing back to himself. Too much. He'd let himself show too much. He pulled his expression back to stillness, pulled all of himself back to stillness.

"I never said that." Surprise and indignation mixed. "But our previous sheriff was also gunned down while performing his duty. Do you know how long justice thought his killer should spend atoning for his crime of murdering a Negro?" She fixed him with her fierce stare. "Ten years. I wonder what price justice will place on the attempted murder of a Mexican."

Ah, that fierceness of hers—it pierced his reserve.

"I wouldn't presume to guess; I'm not a judge."

He was only a marshal. He'd do well to remember that in this sparring over justice and punishment. Bringing in this fugitive was all he owed her—or justice. A man with his past had no right to sit in judgment of others.

"Paugh." Even her noises of disgust were controlled. "You must acknowledge that an American who attacks a Mexican, even one wearing a sheriff's star, is likely to be set free by a jury. Is that *your* notion of justice, Marshal Spencer?"

She'd better not be this belligerent at the trial—she'd be clapped in irons for contempt of the court.

"You know it's not. It may be imperfect..." He swallowed, composing himself before going on. His father had taught him too well how *imperfect* the agents of justice could be. But even so... "Justice is all that lies between us and the beast of anarchy."

No tool was perfect, and something was needed to prevent the monsters he hunted from preying on the weak.

"Justice protects some," she answered. "Or rather, the courts protect some. But justice is more than simply what the courts serve."

He wouldn't think on that. For then he might dwell on how his father had served justice so faithfully in his courtroom, but served nothing but evil at home—

No, he would not think on it.

"I serve the courts by delivering criminals for judgment," he said coldly. "Such debates mean nothing while hunting a fugitive."

Her voice went soft. "So you never think of what happens after? If my story will be believed by the jury? If my suffering will hold any weight against the might of the McCade name?"

She'd arrived at the very point he could not contest. He knew full well the power of a father's name, the sins that one could hide beneath the mantle of it. Judge Spencer's name was enough to hide both his and Sebastian's sins—how many more sins could the power of the McCade name hide?

He disliked that—disliked that he could not reassure her and disliked that he had to urge to do so. Thank the Lord he had only a few more days in her company and could leave those sensations behind. Could return to the easy blankness of his life in Los Angeles.

But until then...

"Your suffering matters to me," he offered. A tiny thing, his regard in the vastness of this world, but all he had to give her as reassurance. At least until he captured McCade.

Señorita Moreno's expression eased, which cut deeper than her fierceness had.

Before she could speak, her younger sister shoved the glasses back at him, the way a child would with an unwanted toy.

"It will be all right in the end," she told Señorita Moreno. "You'll see."

Señorita Moreno met her sister's resolved gaze for a moment, then looked back to the scrubby brush surrounding them. "Of course it will," she said, her words quiet with resignation. Or perhaps disbelief.

He put the field glasses to his own eyes, searching once more. He had nothing to offer Señorita Moreno as comfort—nothing more than the capture of this outlaw.

So that was the only thing he'd offer her.

~~~

The night had fallen fast, the thin air of autumn sharp with cold.

Isabel and the marshal were arranged around a campfire for just the two of them, the herd bellowing nearby, the air thick with their scent. The rest of the cowhands were clustered around a larger fire some distance away, but still within sight—propriety must be observed.

There was a palpable sense that she and the marshal did not belong—not that they were unwelcome, but rather a recognition that they would be more comfortable apart from everyone else.

Isabel had to admit the others were correct—she may have volunteered to come along, but she did not want to be here. McCade could be out in that pressing dark, perched in a tree like a mountain lion, watching the scene below, waiting with the unnatural patience of a cat, muscles poised to pounce when the moment was right...

"Does she always sleep like that?"

At the marshal's question, she looked to her sister.

Franny was curled in her blankets, head tilted back and mouth slightly open, her task of minding them finished for the day. She looked so young and fragile, Isabel's heart squeezed.

"Franny's always been completely committed to whatever she does. Riding, roping, sleeping... she does it breakneck or not at all."

His mouth twitched, sending a sliver of warmth down her spine.

How odd.

The last word she would have used to describe the marshal was attractive. Imposing, yes. Infuriating, sometimes. But not attractive. To be honest, something rather dark stirred within her when she saw him, something she named as trepidation.

"I'd imagine it's exhausting being Señorita Franny," he said.

"I can't recommend it."

"I would imagine it's also exhausting being yourself."

Her jaw tightened and her heart fluttered. It *was* exhausting: the sleepless nights, the vivid nightmares—and no peace came during the day, not with the panic and the headaches.

"It can't be easy or pleasant," he continued, "with everyone pestering you for the details of such an ordeal. An ordeal that came with a high personal cost. Even I'm guilty of this."

The fire gave a loud pop, sending a flurry of sparks into the chill night. Staring steadily into it, she carefully folded her hands and tried to swallow down her jitters.

"It hasn't been easy," she finally said. He didn't need to know about the nightmares or the panic—and she didn't want to speak of them in the dark.

He stretched those long legs toward the fire, putting the fine leather of his boots dangerously close to the heat. "You were a schoolteacher?"

"I *am* a schoolteacher."

"My apologies." There might have been an amused glint in his eyes.

"I teach at the secondary level at a school in the valley," she answered. "I was forced to miss this term due to... circumstances."

But not next term. I won't miss that.

"There are teaching positions in Los Angeles if that's truly where you wish to be," he said.

Her eyes flicked up to the innumerable stars that glinted in the cold velvet of the night sky. The stars were somehow sharper, nearer, here in the open country, although she knew logically it was nonsense.

It wasn't only that she'd wanted to be in Los Angeles, more than a simple desire to leave Cabrillo—she and Joaquin had wanted a new life.

"Once we had enough saved," she said, "Sheriff Obregon and I would marry and move to Los Angeles.

We'd planned very carefully, you see." How quickly years of caution and thought had been utterly destroyed.

"Now that Obregon is languishing in a sanatorium, you must immure yourself as well?" A pinch of censure there.

She studied the planes and ridges of his face, turned to sharp relief by the firelight. His cheek was already dark with whiskers; he must have to shave twice a day to keep his jaw as smooth as he did. He stared back, measure for measure, his form arrogantly relaxed, completely unapologetic in his boldness.

"Who would I live with in Los Angeles? I'm not so modern as to live alone," she challenged. Not that her family would have allowed her to do so anyway.

"Who do you live with in the valley during your teaching term?"

"That's different," she said. "I board with families of good reputation who are well known to mine."

"You could live with Don Enrique."

She thought of her foppish cousin and his empty-headed daughters and shuddered.

"No?" His mouth moved not at all, but she had the impression he was smiling. "But Don Enrique is the ideal of a Spanish gentleman, is he not?"

She wasn't entirely sure how she felt about his amusement. Don Enrique was family and a slight to him should be a slight to them all, but he was also the most ridiculous man she'd ever met.

"I thought you only met Don Enrique the once," she retorted.

"I've seen him leading the parade for La Fiesta."

Isabel had never understood the Americans' love of celebrating La Fiesta, or any other of their sad approximations of the "Old Spanish Days." It seemed ghoulish for them to celebrate the very culture they'd smothered on its deathbed.

"You enjoy that sort of thing?" she accused.

"I don't." His voice dropped a quarter tone, just enough for her to hear the change, to know that she'd touched a nerve.

She didn't know what to make of him. He carried an Anglo name, carried himself as an Anglo, only revealed his other half when forced to. Yet when he'd spoken of his mother, there'd been a reverence he'd shown for nothing else.

She stared into the fire. When one wasn't certain how to respond, it was best not to respond at all.

"Tell me what you wish to find in Los Angeles," he offered, "and I'll tell you if it exists there."

She knew exactly how to respond to *that*, but it was one thing to tell him the particulars of her attack, yet another to tell him the particulars of her soul.

Yet he'd spoken so beautifully of the place at supper... against her better judgment, she wanted him to do that again, to weave tales of the city for her.

"I wish to find people who can discuss literature and music, rather than cattle, and the weather, and crops." She paused. "And I wish to find no flies."

He didn't laugh, or smirk, or even smile. He only said, "There are a prodigious number of flies in Cabrillo."

"It's all the cattle."

"We have flies in Los Angeles, Señorita Moreno. Not as many as in Cabrillo, but we still have them. Tell me, which works of literature would you like to discuss in Los Angeles?" He held up a hand. "Wait. I can already guess. *Ramona*."

Her face twisted. Of course he would suggest the story of the doomed love between Ramona and Alessandro, a love ended by Alessandro's murder. It had been a national sensation, bringing hordes of tourists to these mountains in search of the "real Ramona." The novel was a swamp of excess sentiment, Ramona being too saintly for words, and Alessandro—well, she had always despised drunkards.

But it was also about the place and the people that had nurtured her and shaped who she was. How to explain what *Ramona* meant to her? She couldn't explain it to herself. It was much like what Cabrillo meant to her.

She loved and hated it in equal measure—the book and the town.

"I find *Ramona* to be... overly sentimental," she said. She leaned away, telling herself she was overwarm from being too near the fire. That was always the trouble with campfires—your front roasted, while your back froze.

"Truly? Here I thought you'd offer to take me to meet the real Ramona."

He *was* laughing at her, with that arch tone of his.

"And if I told you I was acquainted with the lady who inspired the character?" she challenged.

"Which one? I hear there are five true Ramonas."

"Perhaps there are many ladies who claim to be the real Ramona because their stories are so distressingly frequent. An Indian man gunned down solely on a white man's suspicion, and justice never blinking an eye? Surely you've heard that story before."

He wasn't laughing at her now. Not that his solemn mien had changed the barest fraction—his expression was as flat as ever—but something had changed. His eyes perhaps; they were the only aspect of him that was not fully under his command.

"More times than you could possibly imagine," he admitted. "Don't think I don't feel the injustice of such things any less deeply than you."

She wouldn't allow the sincerity in his eyes to touch her. She simply would not. "Yet you make sport of it.

You claim such stories touch you, but the novel touched you not at all?"

"I've never read it," he confessed. "I don't care for novels."

Of course he didn't. "No doubt you think they contribute to the mental and moral putrefaction of young ladies."

He slowly raised one eyebrow. "I never said such a thing."

"You're right," she said slowly, her gaze caught on that eyebrow. "You never said any such thing. I apologize."

He nodded in acceptance, the firelight and shadows dancing across his face. "So you don't like *Ramona*. That demonstrates good taste on your part. What do you like?"

"*Portrait of a Lady.*"

"Mmm. I have read that. It was very—interior." There was a shudder behind the word *interior* that made it sound like *horrid.* "If you wish to associate and live with those who think as you do, then you must agree with Madame Merle that the exterior of a person and that with which they surround themselves with defines their interior?"

She flicked a hand at his fine clothes. "Haven't you arranged your exterior to suit your interior?"

He rested his palms on his knees, looking as if he were preparing to pounce. "You should not make the mistake of assuming my exterior matches my interior."

She sat still as stone, waiting for him to... well, she did not know precisely *what*.

Rise? Move toward her? *Touch* her?

Suddenly all she could feel was her clothes against her skin—and the lack of his skin against that same space.

Then he shifted, and the moment was shattered. "Do you believe Isabel Archer returned to her husband?" he asked.

"She promised Pansy she would."

"Pansy." He waved the poor girl off. "She couldn't even bestir from that convent to save herself. Why should Isabel Archer sacrifice her happiness for such a spiritless creature?"

"She was dear to her," Isabel pointed out.

The look he sent her pressed the air straight from her lungs. "Sometimes we must sacrifice what is dear in order to save ourselves."

She had the sense he was no longer speaking of the novel, but something nearer to his heart.

What dear thing had he sacrificed to save himself?

And from what?

"No doubt you think she should have returned out of wifely duty." She was deliberately provoking him—she'd not conversed with anyone about books since… since that day in the buggy with Joaquin. They'd been arguing over some serial in a magazine; she forgot exactly which. She hadn't realized how much she missed sharpening her wits in a debate about books. "She's made her bed"—she referred to Isabel Archer—"and now she must lie in it?"

"No," he said, "but I do think Miss Archer chose poorly in marrying Osmond. She had wealth and no need of a husband. I save my pity for those who have no choice." The corners of his mouth dropped and his eyes went stern, shifting into something more severe, even for him. "You had a choice, didn't you? And you took it."

A cold fury settled in her stomach. "You think I threw off Señor Obregon just when he needed me most," she bit off. "Well, it wasn't like that. He was the one who wanted to break off the engagement. He—"

She swallowed hard. She hadn't meant for all that to spill forth, but there it was. Commanding herself not to cry, she plunged on. "We were not in love. It was only to be a marriage of friends, companions."

Yet it had still hurt terribly when he'd ended the engagement against her protests.

"We were clear eyed and saw the world and ourselves as they are," she said. "That is why we're no longer engaged. We didn't love each other, and we knew it, but we did suit one another." She ran a hand around her throat, much as she had done during that terrible moment when Joaquin had ended things. The bruises at her throat hadn't been mere memories under her fingertips—they'd been real enough then.

"Joaquin could not ask a woman who didn't love him to follow him into the life he now leads. For that I am forever grateful." In some ways that hurt worst of all: her gratitude that he had ended it. "He set me free when he could have held me to my duty. I should think that means more than love."

She had gone to visit him for the first time since the attack, her voice a raw scrape against her crushed throat and him... Well, he had been lucky to survive. But survival was all he'd been able to manage.

Joaquin's handsome face had been twisted by his sufferings into something darkly unfamiliar.

"They're sending me to the sanatorium," he'd told her, his eyes dull and his entire self racked with pain.

"For how long?" she'd rasped.

"Forever." Before she could protest, he'd gone on. "Isabel, we don't love one another. At least not deeply."

He'd been correct. They cared for each other, wanted the same things from life, and got on well. It had seemed like a fine foundation for a marriage.

"We have to end this." His words had been flat, final.

Still, she had protested. "I can't leave you now—"

A swipe of Joaquin's hand had cut her off. "What shall we do? Put you in the room next to mine at the sanatorium?"

"You don't have to stay forever." Each word had been painful, both in her throat and in her heart. "When we are well again, both of us, we can resume things."

"I will never be whole again. I'm a cripple, good for nothing but lying in this bed. I can't ask you to follow me into this life. I couldn't ask any woman to, but especially you. You want more and you deserve better."

She'd felt as if her chest were cracking open, cold air rushing in to fill the hollows. "What of what you deserve? To be alone, abandoned in that sanatorium?"

"Deserving has nothing to do with it. How can you share a life with me, when it won't even be a life?"

"But—"

"Please." It was a rough bark. "Just go."

The defeat in his voice—that had finally convinced her. That and his turning away from her with a groan. She'd never seen him like that before.

Voices had come from the next room. More townspeople, more and more, always wanting to hear the story, always prying, prying, prying. Wanting to see just how low Joaquin had been brought.

How low they both had been brought.

"Very well," she'd said to the knot of his back. "If that is what you wish."

The raggedness of her words hadn't been solely due to the wounds at her throat.

She'd resolved to tell no one any more than that their engagement had ended. Let them think that she had ended it, that she was the heartless one. It was the least she could do for him, after the sacrifice he'd made to protect her, to keep her safe, the hole in his belly a permanent reminder of that sacrifice. What right had any of them to the details?

But now there were few details in this sad, painful business that the marshal did not know.

The marshal had heard every aching detail unflinchingly. The great bulk of him appeared as if it could take all the pain she had to give.

He now picked up a dried pine needle from the ground, then idly flicked it into the fire.

"I know nothing of love," he said. "In fact, I try to know nothing of any deep emotion. It clouds the brain and makes my duties more difficult. I'll simply have to take your word on the matter."

"You're a liar." The words tumbled from her mouth without thought, yet as they left, she knew they were true. His reserve was an impressive thing, nearly impregnable—but she could push him out of it. At times.

Slowly, torturously, he turned his head toward her, and she sensed that a dark, dangerous thing within him was poised to leap at her. A most delicious thrill snaked through her, a thing that terrified and enthralled her all at once.

"Whatever do you mean?" The words were low, all hint of mellowness gone. The deep rasp of it fit his brutish looks.

She had no doubt the menace was quite real. Yet the fear she felt was somehow not real, more like the chilling shock felt when someone jumped out from a dark corner.

She knew real fear, had felt it at McCade's hands, and this was not it.

She held his gaze. "I've seen you in the grip of a strong emotion twice. Once, when I was showing you the site of the attack. And now you're in the grip of that same emotion. Considering we've known one another only two days, that's a considerable number of times for you to be overcome."

To her surprise, he relaxed at that, his body unwinding. "I hope for you never to see me *overcome* by emotion," he said mildly. But he kept his gaze averted. "In point of fact, I'm certain that will never happen, since I've made it a practice never to let emotion rule me."

She ought to agree with him—to tell him she also never let emotion rule her, to compliment him on his eminently sensible way of handling sentiment.

But only one word sprang to her lips: "Why?"

He stared into the fire for a time, his expression pensive, rather than impassive. She found she liked that look on him. Still quiet, still grave—but not so empty as the one he usually assumed.

"When a man is ruled by emotion, he becomes no better than a beast." He addressed the fire, and spoke in generalities, but she sensed something deeply personal lurking beneath.

"Then it is well you exercise such impressive restraint," she offered. "If more men followed such a philosophy, the innocents of the world would suffer less."

He didn't answer. Simply kept gazing at the fire.

Silence pressed upon them, sharp with chill and the piercing starlight. And out there, somewhere, McCade.

If he were caught, that would not be the end. There was the trial—and if he was set free, he might come after her. She would never be free of the lurking specter of him then.

"The trial is unlikely to be successful, isn't it?" she asked.

She could not convince herself it would be. She wanted to discuss it rationally, without sentiment—and the marshal was unlikely to offer her platitudes.

He gave her a measured look. "I won't lie—Edwin McCade will be a formidable opponent. But you have a stronger ally than you think—Judge Bannister."

She warned herself not to overreact. "I read the papers. I know exactly how Judge Bannister feels about our people. Why would he help me?"

And why do you work for him?

She didn't ask, not wanting to distract him.

"Judge Bannister has a special interest in the case. A personal one."

She waited for him to elaborate, but he didn't.

"You can't say what that is?" she demanded. "Don't you think I ought to know, seeing that I'm trapped in the middle?"

A muscle in his jaw ticked once, twice, and she sensed him struggling with something, weighing it behind those gray eyes. He flicked another pine needle into the fire.

"McCade Senior owns a controlling interest in the Water Company of Los Angeles," he said finally. "He wants to keep the water source for the city private. The city government wants to control it themselves." He rattled that off rather reluctantly.

"He sent you because of water rights?" She could almost believe it—water was a precious resource.

"McCade also owns a controlling interest in the electric railway. More importantly, he owns the entire Santa Gertrudis valley. He runs water to that valley and a rail line, and he stands to make a great deal of money when he subdivides it."

"It's about money?" Her mouth tasted as if she'd licked a coin.

"No, power. With money comes power. He wants to sit in the governor's mansion. Wealth—and seeding the Santa Gertrudis valley with his constituents—is a way to get there. He has dreams of being grander than even Stanford or Huntington."

"And the judge doesn't want him to?"

"It offends Judge Bannister's sense of justice to have any one man be too far above his equals. No one should stand taller than he, you see." He shrugged. "He also personally dislikes McCade. He'll do everything he can to see Edwin McCade's son brought low, to strike at the man himself. If this trial can't be used to embarrass Edwin McCade, Judge Bannister will find some other means."

"For this, marshals are sent forth to do what should have been done regardless?" she mused.

His gaze was intense, almost passionate. She felt the force of it right in the center of her chest, as if he had laid his hand there. "Understand, Señorita Moreno, those are not my reasons for hunting this man. Let them play politics in Los Angeles. I'm here now. I will find him and deliver him to the courts for justice."

He really did believe the courts would dispense justice. How could he work with a man like Judge Bannister and still believe that? She'd seen what happened to her people—*their* people—when they faced American justice.

But the thought of this outlaw running free, ready to strike at any moment, made a leaden dread drip through her bones. The marshal might be certain he could capture this man, but capturing him wouldn't bring an end to her nightmares.

She'd begun to fear that nothing could.

CHAPTER SIX

HE WAS STRANGLING HER AGAIN.

Only this time he wasn't a man—he was a tentacled monster. When she pulled one of his arms free, another took its place to wrap around her throat, each one tighter than the last. They constricted until she saw stars, then gray.

Until at last everything turned black.

Isabel opened her eyes to darkness, her throat closing with panic. She sat up in her bedroll, her lungs burning with the speed of her breathing, her heart climbing up her rib cage.

It was only a dream. He wasn't here, didn't have his hands at her throat. She repeated the words again and again, until her heart came back under her command and slowed its futile race to nowhere.

She looked into the blackness surrounding her, the fire having dimmed to coals hours ago.

He was out there, somewhere.

Her entire body went cold, ice creeping under her scalp. She was ready for him. This time she would not miss. Because if he caught her again, it would mean her death.

Your hands are still shaking. You missed last time because your hands were shaking.

She curled her hands into fists. They would not shake. She would not allow it.

"Can't sleep?"

The voice from the other side of the fire made her start, a whimper escaping her throat.

"It's only me," the voice assured.

"Marshal Spencer," she breathed. "You're awake."

His form slowly coalesced in the darkness as her eyes adjusted, revealing him perched across from her, some great beast come to warm by the fire as they slept.

She blinked to clear her head. He was not a beast or a monster. The only monster was the one they were tracking.

"Try to sleep," he said softly.

Oh Lord, she wanted to. She wanted to sleep as she once had, free of nightmares chasing her from dusk until dawn, to wake without her throat aching as though phantom hands had encircled it all night long.

"Are you going to sit up all night?" she asked.

"Mmm," he answered. "I won't allow anything to happen to you. Go to sleep."

His assurance was quite solid in the unreality of her half-awake, post-nightmare state. She lay back at his command, ordering her heart to slow and her jitters to still. The sky was heavy with stars and she began to pick out familiar constellations. She didn't know many, but she could find the Dippers—and there was Orion.

"You're not sleeping." A hint of gray annoyance crept into his voice.

"How can you tell?" she demanded.

"I can hear you thinking."

"One can't hear a person's thoughts."

He sighed. "You've a gift for attributing words to me I didn't say. I don't know *what* you are thinking, only that you are. The air fairly hums with it."

She smiled into the dark. "I have to be precise with you, don't I?"

"You don't require precise handling?"

She couldn't stop smiling, although no one other than herself would consider such a thing a compliment.

"Go to sleep, Señorita," he urged.

She did as he said.

~~~

They had reached the second night's camp. And were within sight of the ciénaga, although the twilight wasn't quite enough to see it clearly.

There was no sign of McCade.

Isabel sighed and rubbed at her lower back. Riding down a steep trail for days at a time always set her back and legs to aching.

The cattlemen of Cabrillo had constructed a corral and shelter here to function as a stop on their annual fall cattle drives. Even now, the herd was penned in the corral and everyone was busy preparing for nightfall, taking advantage of the twilight while it lasted.

If McCade was somewhere on this road, she had only tonight and tomorrow to witness his capture. The marshal would continue to look for the outlaw—however long that might take—but she would return to Cabrillo. She couldn't very well hunt with Marshal Spencer, even if she wanted to.

Every step they'd taken closer to this spot had been a rivet in her spine, until she was nothing but anxious stiffness, clinging to her horse to keep from falling to the ground like a wooden dummy.

Marshal Spencer had disappeared into the brush at times during the day, investigating likely hiding spots. At one point he'd found a pile of bullet casings that appeared recent, but nothing else. Each time he disappeared, she'd prayed that he would return with McCade—and that he himself would return whole and intact.

She dreaded the thought of facing McCade again, the anticipation a heavy ball of poison in her belly. What would she do if she came face to face with him again? Would she spit in his eye? Would she want to shoot him again?

Or worst of all, would she weep?

She didn't have to find out—the marshal returned empty-handed each time. And she only had to grapple with a mixture of disappointment and relief—disappointment that McCade hadn't been found, and relief that the marshal returned safely.

She rubbed her back with one hand and her temple with the other. Her spectacles dug into her ears, heavy on her face, and a headache beat a distant drum against her skull, coming closer and closer with each hit.

If only she and Joaquin hadn't gone for that drive. If only, if only, if only...

"Is your back hurting?"

She turned, letting her hands fall. Was he truly that quiet when he walked, or was she too distracted?

The marshal was watching her with something quite like concern. Although if she took him at his word, he didn't feel things such as *concern*.

"A bit," she allowed.

His expression went much darker than mere concern. She swallowed hard and licked her lips, his eyes darting to her mouth to follow the path of her tongue.

"Are you—are you leaving for the ciénaga?" she asked, the merest quiver threading through her voice.

If McCade was there, he was not more than half a mile away. Perhaps closer if the noises of camp had lured him in, hoping to steal more food.

If he'd seen her, was he waiting to grab her, instead of provisions? A shaking began in her shoulders, her hips, stealing throughout her limbs until—

"Will you be all right here?" The doubt in his question had her snapping back to herself.

She motioned to the people moving about the camp, catching Juan's gaze as she did. "I'm hardly alone."

There were half a dozen men surrounding her— McCade was impulsive, but not stupid. Nothing could harm her here.

"Of course not. How ridiculous of me."

Guilt pinched her at his words, although he'd said them as calmly, as unreproachfully, as he said everything else.

He went to his saddlebag and prepared for war.

At least it appeared that way. Most of the men of her acquaintance carried at most a rifle in a saddle holster, so to see the marshal check and load not one, but two rifles, holster two pistols at his hips, and slide a Bowie knife into his boot—well, it was quite unusual.

Seeing a hard man ready to do violence on her behalf evoked a most interesting sensation in her bosom.

Yes, that was what she would name that sensation. Interesting.

He turned to her, the beginnings of a beard thick on his cheek, his body bristling with weapons—the epitome of the word *dangerous.* Her heart quailed at the sight of him.

Oh, just let McCade try him. The outlaw would come out the loser, of that she was sure.

"Stay in camp," he warned, his voice low and thrilling.

No need for the warning; if she stepped into the brush surrounding them, the paralytic fear would be upon her. It was a tickling in her joints, waiting to seize her should she leave the safety of camp.

She wasn't stupid—she wasn't going anywhere.

At her nod, he walked off into the dusk, and she watched him until he faded into the twilight. Even when she could no longer see him, she kept staring at the spot where he'd disappeared, her breathing shallow and her heart thudding.

She was safe. She was protected. The marshal's presence wasn't necessary to ensure that.

"Isabel?"

She didn't turn toward the voice at her elbow. "Yes, Franny?"

"Did the marshal go to the ciénaga?"

"He did." She felt curiously light, as if her insides had disappeared.

"Want me to sit with you?" Franny asked. "I expect you don't want to watch the boys practice their roping."

Isabel didn't, although it was clear Franny did. "Yes, please sit with me," she said. She couldn't be alone just now, no matter how it inconvenienced her sister.

They settled side by side on a log by the campfire, a pot of beans smoking above it.

Isabel arranged the schoolbook in her lap. Might as well use the light for as long as she could and plan lessons for next school term. Opening to the chapter on the geography of Brazil, she looked down at the page and began reading.

Brazil. A republic, formerly a Portuguese colony, capital was Rio de Janeiro... Her thoughts trailed into nothingness. How many minutes passed, she could not say. It felt like several, though she still hadn't turned the page, her mind everywhere except on the geography of Brazil.

Franny sighed deeply, setting her chin in her hands and looking as though she'd like to be anywhere else.

"Would you like a book?" Isabel asked her, although she knew what the answer would be.

Franny simply shook her head and buried her chin deeper in her palms.

Isabel returned to her reading, trying not to smile at Franny's exaggerated slump of boredom.

A crackling came from deep within the brush. The plants were inky sketches on the dark gray of their surroundings, all detail lost in the twilight. Every part of her went taut as she waited and waited for something to appear.

It didn't.

"Did you hear that?" she asked Franny.

"Hear what?"

She listened for a moment more. Only silence reflected back from the brush.

"Nothing," she said.

She took a quick glance behind her. Felipe was watching them, and when he dropped his gaze, Juan looked their way.

Nothing to fear—the men would make certain they were safe, watching as closely as they were. She forced her gaze back to her book. No more ridiculousness. There was nothing out there.

Brazil. The Amazon river, the jungle, flesh-eating fish... Her thoughts trailed away again, the words becoming a jangle of letters before her eyes.

A rustling came from her right and her heart skittered. She rose, peering this way and that, telling herself there was no need to investigate further. There was nothing in the brush. At least nothing that shouldn't be there.

"What are you looking for?" Franny had risen as well, and was frowning at her.

"I heard something. I definitely heard something." An ache began to ring within her skull like a bell. A headache coming on, no doubt because she was working her-self into a state.

"Maybe a rabbit?" Franny offered. Her loose stance made it clear she thought Isabel was making too much of the whole affair.

And she was. These were the mountains; there were any number of creatures mucking about in the gathering darkness.

"I'll go see what it is." Franny began to march off into the brush.

"Francisca, no!" She was too late in grabbing for her sister's skirt. "Come here! You can't leave either."

"I'm not leaving," Franny tossed back. "I won't go more than a foot or two into the brush."

"Francisca!" Panic splintered the last syllable.

Franny stopped, turned. "I'm going to prove to you that it's nothing. You were always so fearless." She drew her hands into fists. "I want you to be fearless again," she pleaded.

Oh, Franny. The panic ebbed, but the need to weep remained. "You're the fearless one," she said softly.

Franny held out her hand. "It's only a rabbit."

Isabel set her hand in her sister's and allowed herself to be led to the edge of the clearing, where the firelight thinned into darkness. Because she found herself agree-ing with Franny—she wanted to be fearless again too. So she kept putting one foot in front of the other, let the pressure of Franny's hand compel her forward—as a rising urge to flee, to hide, to do anything but advance toward that noise built in her veins.

As they reached the edge of the clearing, the buckwheat reaching out to scratch at her skirts, a rabbit burst out, white tail flashing, wildly zig-zagging as it raced for shelter.

Manic laughter burst from her lips, the chortles bubbling out against her will, choking her as they tried to become sobs.

Franny had been right—it had only been a rabbit. While she wasn't quite feeling fearless, triumphant might fit. And a little mad, the laughs changing into heaving breaths that she couldn't even begin to control.

"See?" Franny's smile was wide, the spark in her eyes one of victory. "Let's get back to the fire."

Her sister marched away, clearly intending for Isabel to follow. Which she'd do with some haste—Isabel had no intention of remaining in the shadows, no matter that it had only been a rabbit.

She raised her heel, her knee bending as she shifted her weight forward, preparing to take that first step—

A hand snaked out from the brush to wrap round her ankle and stop her dead.

~~~

Goddamn this brush.

Sebastian dragged himself past yet another redshank bush higher than his head, wishing this hunt could have been easier. He had no clear line of sight anywhere, the brush was more difficult to move through than downtown at quitting time, and his witness would not cease unsettling him.

Not that it was her fault. He was the one at fault, the one who had to rein in the unruly sensations she evoked in him. God, if only she weren't so resolute, so unflinching... He'd find it harder to admire a woman who was softer.

She'd spent all day in a state of high agitation—he'd seen the evidence in the set of her shoulders, the stiffness of her back, the way she'd rubbed her temple—and still she'd snapped at him when he'd asked if she'd be all right in camp. For half a moment, he'd wanted to remain right where he was and let her sharpen her tongue on him all she liked.

Then he'd remembered himself and shoved that malignancy deep within, to be swallowed by the darkness there. And reminded himself to the do the same whenever she provoked a similar response.

Soon enough he would be back in Los Angeles, among his familiar things, in his trusted routine, and all this emotional nonsense would fall out.

He stopped short before he ran into a stand of cacti almost as prickly as a certain lady he knew. He pushed aside another buckwheat bush, the spines tearing at his coat.

After this trip, he would have to burn this suit. It was a shame; he rather liked it.

He briefly considered taking his frustrations out on McCade when he found him. A fist to the jaw, a boot to his rib cage—Sebastian would think of Señorita Moreno the entire time, her fierce expression as she'd detailed what McCade had done to her—and every blow would be pure deliciousness.

He stopped dead.

No. No, he mustn't think such things.

He wasn't that kind of man any longer. He wrapped a hand around the spiny buckwheat, pressing until he felt the flesh give against the spines. Not enough to wound, just enough to call back his reserve.

After several cool breaths, he felt recovered enough to release the spines. He went forward, but only traveled a few feet before his boots caught in something, squelching wetly when he tried to pull them free.

He'd walked into a marsh—he must be close to the ciénaga.

Now these boots were ruined too.

No time to mourn them. He crouched low, his every sense taut with anticipation. No more fruitless introspection—it was time to do what he did best.

He crept along the edge of the marsh. If McCade wanted to be as far from the road as possible, he'd be on the southern end of the ciénaga. That was where Sebastian would begin, and then work his way back toward camp.

The colors of the day had dissolved into gray in the fading light, making his search that much harder. Only something light in color would stand out, although the breeze might catch some bit of fabric the fugitive had left behind and draw his eye with the motion of it.

As he came into a small clearing on the far southern side—with a no doubt fine view of the road from the treetops—he spied a long white square of fabric flapping in the wind. Likely a sheet stolen from some housewife's line, it was draped across a tree branch to form a rather pathetic shelter.

He pulled his pistol free, the heft of it as familiar to his hand as a pen was to a scholar's.

"US marshal," he called. "Come out unarmed and with your hands in the air."

No answer except the snap of the sheet in the wind.

He tried again. "McCade, I know you're in there."

Still nothing. Either the fugitive was waiting for him in that tent, or else was somewhere in the brush, ready to put a bullet in him.

Or he wasn't there.

The hair on his nape rose as he consciously slowed his breathing. Time to take a risk and see if it paid off.

If it didn't, he'd end up with a bullet for his trouble.

He tore down the sheet in one quick rip to find...

Nothing.

Oh, there was a bedroll, and the remains of some food. But no fugitive. Judging by the unspoiled state of the food, he had been here recently. Which meant he could return soon.

But if he had food, why leave?

McCade could have seen their arrival. He might even now be at the edge of camp, watching, waiting. Wanting to seize Señorita Moreno once more.

Sebastian shook off his chills. He could not be distracted by her, not now. She was perfectly secure, in a camp with a dozen other men for protection, one of them her own brother.

But he remained uneasy. He'd promised to keep her safe.

The best way to do that is capture McCade. Not by playing lovesick swain in camp.

Sebastian looked up at the tree overhead, judging how high he could climb without falling and breaking his neck. Fairly far up, if the thickness of the branches was true to their strength. He could place the sheet back, then climb into the tree to await the outlaw's return.

Of course, if McCade saw him first, the outlaw could shoot him right out of the tree. The ground was quite a ways from the first branch—it would hurt when that dirt caught him, to make no mention of whatever hole McCade might punch into him.

He had to decide. He couldn't stand here all night thinking; that was a certain way to get shot.

He looked north, to the camp so far away, then back to the tree.

The tree it was. It would be an uncomfortable night, but if the saints were smiling, McCade would return to his hovel before too long.

He jumped to grab a low branch, the bark tearing at the skin of his palms. He braced his feet against the trunk and began to lift himself up.

Shouts.

He distinctly heard them, faint as they were, drifting from the camp. Much too high pitched to be a man's— they must have come from either Señorita Moreno or her sister.

He paused, his ears straining to hear more.

There they were again. Louder this time, and definitely female.

McCade was there. He'd seen them, he'd been watching camp—those shouts were Señorita Moreno's, perhaps crying for help.

God, he shouldn't have left, should have stayed hard by her side, duty or no. He dropped from the tree, running as soon as his feet touched the ground, gooseflesh rising to slide against the fabric of his clothes.

More shouts now, distinctly male. McCade or the cowboys? He couldn't tell.

He ran as fast as he could, praying his promise to keep her safe hadn't been made in vain.

CHAPTER SEVEN

THE HAND ROUND ISABEL'S ANKLE tightened painfully, a thumb digging into the tendon. She attempted to jerk it free, some instinct still operating in her poor fear-fogged brain.

"Don't."

She'd never forget that voice. It haunted her nightmares, echoed in her skull when she was in the grip of a headache—sometimes she even imagined it in the whisper of the wind through the pines.

McCade had found her.

She could still bolt free—he only had her ankle, all she had to do was pull hard enough, scream, and she'd—

A pistol cocked behind her. "I'm aiming for her," he said, low and easy.

Franny. Dear Lord, he wanted to hurt Franny. She was walking to the campfire, so sure that her fearless sister was following close behind.

Isabel set her trapped heel to the ground, signaling her surrender.

"Good. You know enough to keep quiet. Take two steps backward." A relaxed command. He already knew she would obey.

She did, her knees trembling with each step. The sounds of the night were sharp in her ears, the air too hard against her skin, all of her at a heightened pitch as she stepped back into darkness.

As she completed the second step, she was jerked backward and down, a weight coming over her—a familiar weight. Panic bloomed, a choking, endless void, leaving her only a pinprick in the midst of it. Her limbs were no longer hers, were simply dead weight in the limbo she was trapped in—

"Isabel?"

Franny's voice pierced her panic, brought her back from madness. Her sister had noticed she was gone.

Please, Franny, don't come here, go get Juan, or Felipe, or anyone. Don't come here.

"You better not answer her." His voice might have been casual, but his expression wasn't. Hard, grim—loathing was written in the set of his features.

She'd wondered how she would react when she came face to face with this man once more, when she confronted this creature who'd shattered nearly everything of hers. The paralytic fear had been her greatest worry, that she would be rendered insensate, useless at the sight of him—and he would have her again.

He did have her again—but the fear wasn't foremost. She was *angry*. Livid. Furious.

"I don't have to," she said. "She's going to get the men right now. Can you kill me in time?"

He wrapped his hand around her throat and squeezed. "Probably. But I'd rather drag you someplace private to do it. Dispose of your corpse where it won't be found—and then I'm free. No witnesses without you."

A savage pleasure rose within her fury—he'd miscalculated, the fool. "I'm not the only witness," she hissed.

His fingers tightened, dark spots dancing before her eyes—whether due to the pressure at her throat, or the panic rising once more, she couldn't say. It was too close to her nightmares to be gripped like this, pinned like an animal for the slaughter, for her to hold off the panic much longer.

"I shot that sheriff in the gut. He's dead." McCade drew out the word *dead* like the name of a lover.

"But he's not," she gasped. "He lived."

The moonlight spilled across McCade's teeth as he bared them, looking as vicious as she knew him to be.

"Goddamn it." He stared at her, contemplating her the way a cat did a wounded bit of prey. "But that won't save you."

In the half second before his hands tightened around her throat, she heard them—the men coming closer, their voices floating over them as they searched for her.

That half second was her moment to act.

"Juan!" She feared her throat might split like an over-cooked sausage, so hard did she yell. "He's here! Juan, he's here!"

The hand clamped hard on her neck, harder than it ever had before, tissue giving way with a crackling sensation that traveled to the very end of her spine. True blackness came closing in, not the false blackness of her panics. This was the darkness of the void from which no one escaped.

McCade meant to send her there.

Just as the last light slipped from her vision, the pressure eased, then ceased, the weight pinning her suddenly gone. As her senses returned, she registered only chaos, blows and curses falling onto someone nearby, bodies boiling up all around her, an arm around her shoulder, another at her waist lifting her. A familiar voice asking if she were all right, to please for the love of God answer.

Franny. Franny's arms were around her, Franny was begging her to answer.

"I'm all right." Her throat was aflame, but her voice was surprisingly intact. When she'd heard the crunch as he'd borne down, she'd thought her voice lost forever.

The chaos slowly ebbed, became simply a gaggle of men once more, their voices rising in time with a heavy thudding. There was a flurry of motion a few feet away, grunts rising from the melee—Juan had McCade facedown in the dirt and was raining his back with blows, each connection between Juan's fist and the other man's flesh forcing a groan from McCade.

"It wasn't just a rabbit," Franny breathed. "It was him. Oh Isabel, I'm so, so, so sorry—"

Isabel held up a hand, an ache rising behind her eyes. "It doesn't matter." Rather froglike, her voice. But still recognizably hers. "He's caught."

Watching Juan smash McCade into the dirt wasn't satisfying. There was only a creeping, chilled numbness, as if McCade had smashed her in the head again.

"Juan, Juan, Juan!" Felipe called as he jogged up to the two men. "That's enough. He's down."

Her brother stepped back, but not before giving the fugitive one last kick.

The men formed a circle around McCade, all watching as he kicked and writhed upon the ground, the way children might watch a worm wriggle in its death throes. There was an empty quality to the atmosphere surrounding them, as though everyone were deciding exactly what it should be filled with.

Franny gave voice to what they all were thinking. "What now?"

Isabel's numbness slid away, leaving only naked fear behind, freezing up her joints, her skin feeling as if it were coated in frost.

She couldn't understand this, how the terror could be so much more potent *after* he'd been captured and was no longer a threat.

Two of the men hauled him upright, hanging onto his arms on either side, while Juan watched with predatory intent. Blood trickled from a cut on McCade's lip, and the redness high on his left cheek would soon turn to a purple-black bruise. In every aspect, he was defeated—collapsed, even.

So why did her stomach continue to turn in on itself? She closed her eyes and raised a hand to her brow, the skin clammy under her shaking fingers.

"Shoot him."

Her eyes flew open at her brother's words, tossed off so carelessly.

No. That was the word her lips wanted to say. But why should she give this man that consideration? He certainly hadn't given it to Joaquin or herself. If he were dead, there would be no need for trial. He would simply disappear—and she could resume her life without the specter of him lurking over her.

"You could end up in jail yourself," Felipe warned.

A hand settled lightly on her arm, the fingers hot against her shivering skin. Franny. "We shouldn't let Juan do this."

We. She meant that *Isabel* shouldn't let Juan do this. Isabel didn't think she could stand for much longer, much less stop their brother. The ache in her head turned into a nauseating throb, a sick headache coming on faster than she'd ever experienced.

"We'll say he was trying to escape," Juan said.

"You'll have to shoot him in the back to make that story work," Felipe countered. "Could you shoot an unarmed man in the back? I couldn't."

McCade struggled briefly. "You can't shoot me. That's murder—you'll hang."

A few men canted backwards at the word *murder,* their expressions saying they wanted no part in such a thing.

Murder. No, she didn't think she wanted any part of that either.

"You'd know all about that, I'd reckon," her brother said to McCade. He turned back to Felipe. "He hurt Isabel. He shot Obregon in the gut. It'd be no more than he deserves."

The men who'd been undecided before—their expressions hardened. Juan was no orator, but his words were convincing them all the same. As he gazed at each man in turn, he knew he was winning them—it was there in the grim half-smile he wore.

Except for Felipe—he wasn't convinced. He looked as Isabel felt: wary, watchful. Uneasy. Juan wouldn't convince him as easily as the others.

But perhaps Juan had no intention of persuading Felipe. One man would stand no chance at stopping the rest should they decide vigilante justice must be served.

"If it was your sister," Juan demanded of Felipe, "what would you do?"

Felipe averted his face, Juan's harsh blow landing just as he'd intended it to. Because Felipe never would truly know what he might do if it were his sister—all his sisters were in the grave.

Isabel had allowed McCade to seize hold of her rather than risk her sister—and she'd do the same all over again.

"The boys will back up any story we come up with, won't you, boys?" Juan asked.

The crowd's will leaned toward Juan. They were ready to follow him.

"We ought to hand him over to the marshal," Felipe said, still battling for the moral choice.

"Where the hell is he?" Juan gestured to indicate his absence. "As usual, when we need them, the law is nowhere to be found."

The marshal had sworn that she'd be safe. Had insisted that he would capture McCade. He'd been wrong about both.

The crowd's will moved a little closer to Juan. A little closer toward acting on their own, without his go-ahead.

A different kind of cold began to seep through her, one tinged with an unyielding horror. They could string McCade up—and she might have to stand by and watch. For all that she hated McCade, she didn't want to see her brother kill him.

She began to make her way toward Juan, skirting the ring of men and the captive in the center of them, Franny following close behind.

"We caught him—we decide what to do with him," Juan declared.

With that, Juan had the men completely on his side. The shifting of their feet, the hardening set of their expressions, the squaring of their shoulders—they looked like men preparing for a hog butchering, steeling themselves for the squealing and blood and entrails about to follow.

"Juan," Felipe tried once more, "you should not do this."

Isabel arrived at Juan's side then, ready to take up Felipe's entreaties—only close in Juan's ear, so that no one would hear her plead for the life of the man who'd tried to kill her.

"Fine," Juan spat. "Let's ask Isabel." His gaze, sharp with antipathy, met hers. "What do you want us to do?"

What did she want done with him?

Suddenly, when Juan shoved the decision before her, wanted her to declare herself before everyone, uncertainty crept in like a thief and made off with her resolve. Her head throbbed and every joint wobbled. If only she had a bit of quiet to think, some solitude in which to reflect and pray, to know what the answer should be...

But she knew.

She couldn't ask her brother to shoot a man in the back, no matter what the outlaw had done. Juan's blood was running hot—he would do it without hesitation if she gave the word—but she couldn't put that on her brother's soul, even if he was willing to take it on.

Yet, if McCade were dead... She could regain her peace of mind for the price of a man's death. Such an evil whisper that, sneaking in the cracks of her carefully reasoned morality. Seductive in its simplicity, its wrongness.

"Isabel?" Juan prompted. "What do you want?"

She licked at her suddenly too-dry lips, her throat closing as if McCade's hands were circling it again. "I—"

"Step away from him." The voice was polite, pleasant even, but commanding nevertheless.

The marshal came into the clearing, the pistol in his hand pointed straight at her brother.

Anger flared in her. *You're late. And I wasn't safe, not at all.*

Juan didn't move. He stared right back, his stance challenging. "You could just head away from here," her brother suggested. "Pretend you didn't see anything."

"I don't think so." The pistol was as steady as his voice. She'd no doubt that he'd fire on Juan if he thought it necessary.

"There's a dozen of us and only one of you. How do you propose to stop us?"

The marshal released a sigh that seemed to say, *You idiot.* The gun remained fixed. Every eye was fastened to that deadly length of metal as it pointed right for her brother. Her heart shuddered as though the pistol were aimed at her instead.

"We ought to let the marshal do his job," Felipe said. Always the peacemaker, Felipe. He turned to her, his expression pleading. "Don't you think, Isabel?"

Her head rang savagely with her headache. She could hardly think for the pain. She rubbed at her temple, trying to find a glimmer of clarity in the muddle of her thoughts.

She'd told them what she'd decided, hadn't she? She'd spoke clear at one point, saying—

The thread of that thought was snipped by sharp pain. She couldn't remember what she'd decided. The pain had washed it away.

No. No, she knew.

She let her hand fall back to her side.

"Felipe's right," she called so that all could hear. "Let the marshal have him."

Juan's mouth twisted in disgust as he glared at the marshal. She prayed that her brother's temper wouldn't rule him, just this once. Prayed for him to accede to her wishes.

She held her breath as Juan continued to stare, but eventually he stepped away. Relief and gratitude blunted the knife's edge of her headache for a moment.

"If that's really what you want," Juan said. He motioned to the two men holding the outlaw to release him.

The marshal set his pistol back in the holster before stepping forward with a pair of handcuffs. "Your wrists, please."

McCade held them out as docilely as a child proving he'd washed his hands, his bloodied lips twisting in a mocking grin. "Come to take me home, then?"

The metallic scrape of the cuffs closing echoed in the silence, rubbed rough against her ears. The marshal checked that the bonds were secure, then turned to her.

"Did he harm you?" the marshal asked darkly.

She shook her head, her brain feeling as though it were swimming in her skull.

"Move. I want you far away from her." He gave McCade a rough shove to get him going.

"Wait," she called. "I want to ask him something."

"You don't want to do that," the marshal warned, continuing to herd McCade away.

"Please." Marshal Spencer paused, glanced back at her. "Please," she pressed on.

His impassive expression flickered for half a moment. He pulled McCade to a halt. "Quickly. You won't like his answers, I assure you."

"Why did you do it?"

He might not give her answers, but she had to try. She wanted to understand—to find some order, no matter how malignant, in the chaos he had unleashed on her life.

"Your man was going to kill me." McCade's eyes were flat, as dead as a snake's. Perhaps more so, since a snake had its low nature as an excuse for its pitilessness and he had none.

"No, he wasn't, you—"

"Stop." The marshal's command was as harshly grating as the snap of the handcuffs had been. "I told you, you wouldn't like his answers."

"Oh, she'll like it even less when I have these men tried for assaulting me." The assurance in McCade's voice was a terrible thing. He might be handcuffed, but the outlaw carried himself as if he were the victor in all this, his bruised state making his statement all the more damning.

Juan might go to prison.

She pressed her fist hard into her belly. Yet another member of her family endangered by this. Lord, when would it all end?

McCade went on, "First the sheriff tries to kill me, his woman shoots me, and you rubes try a third time." He shook his head. "I might even press charges against *her*." His gaze landed on her, the stark promise within bringing bile to her throat.

He wanted to harm her. Very, very badly. "She'd be in prison then, too. No more than the bitch deserves—"

His words were stopped by the marshal's fist landing on his jaw. Before she could even gasp, McCade was falling to the ground, Marshal Spencer's fist following him, landing again and again and again, each thud echoing through the dark.

Everyone stared in shock at the violence erupting from the marshal. He'd always been so controlled, so contained—she could hardly believe such ferocity could be coming from *him*.

After several hits, the marshal pulled back from the bloody work he'd done, his chest heaving and his gaze on the man at his feet. McCade rolled to his side and spit what appeared to be a tooth onto the ground.

Her stomach rolled and she scrambled backwards. She couldn't have been more horrified if a grizzly had wandered into camp and begun mauling men.

"Now we can blame me for your injuries," the marshal ground out. "Not even *your* father can threaten a marshal, now can he?"

He jerked McCade to his feet. "Bring a rope," he said to no one in particular.

Even if Isabel had a rope, she wouldn't have dared to approach Marshal Spencer, not with the state he was in. Where had such fury come from?

Franny was the only one brave enough to obey him, her rope coiled in her hands as she moved toward him. Felipe took a step forward as if to stop her—but only the one.

The three figures moved off to an oak tree not thirty feet away.

"Is he going to hang him?" Juan asked.

"No," Isabel answered. She wasn't sure what he was doing, but she knew it wasn't that. She watched in silence as he tied the outlaw to the tree, wincing when he bore down on the knots with his considerable strength, leaving McCade held fast like some kind of pagan sacrifice.

When he was done, he stalked back, Franny at his heels. The violence had not quite left his frame, his muscles trembling with it. His face was tense, his eyes coldly burning.

"Don't you all have something else you should be doing?" he growled.

The crowd dispersed with alacrity. Except for her.

"He won't get loose," he said. His expression gentled, going softer than she would have thought possible. "By tomorrow, we'll be on the train for Los Angeles."

She ought to thank him, to give some gesture of appreciation for what he'd done. Instead, she said, "You weren't here. He came, and I was all alone."

She realized then how much she'd needed him to be there, that for once she wouldn't have been alone in this.

Just once.

He went still, and with a nearly audible click, his mask slid fully into place, his expression slipping into that hateful impassivity. "No," he said. "I wasn't."

There was no apology in the words.

She swallowed hard, trying to make sense of the emotions surging through her despite the pain slicing across her head. She had just been granted her greatest wish: her attacker had been captured. The fear that he would seize her in an unguarded moment should be dissipating.

So why did she feel so bereft? She wanted to drop to the ground and weep.

The marshal continued on. "I wasn't here, but he's caught now and you're safe." His words were bracing, almost crisp. "You won't have to see him again until the trial."

"Until the trial." The words were numb on her tongue.

"Yes," he said. "You're the only witness. Unless some miracle occurs with Obregon, it will be your word against McCade's."

She pinched the bridge of her nose, fingers resting on the wire of her spectacles, that slender bit keeping the whole together.

Her word against his. And only hers. Alone again, with Joaquin—and the entire town—looking to her to send McCade to prison. To see that justice was served.

To attempt such a thing with Edwin McCade's son... it would be David against Goliath, and she hadn't even a sling.

There was nothing for it. She looked at the marshal, at his unreadable features. "I know that. I will be prepared, I assure you."

She took a deep breath and held out her hand. No sense holding him responsible for being absent when McCade had come—foolish of her to be upset by it.

"Thank you very much for capturing him," she said stiffly. "You carried out your duties admirably."

He studied her for a long moment, her hand held out between them.

"I apologize for any distress I caused you," he said finally, regret tempering his tone. "It was always in service of a higher goal."

With that, he captured her hand. Instead of shaking it, he brought it to those unsmiling lips. His breath fanned across her skin, followed by the brush of his lips. Gooseflesh broke out in a chilled flush along her entire length at the touch of his mouth.

"Perhaps we shall meet again, Señorita." The words, spoken in that beautiful Spanish of his, stroked warmly against her, even more caressing than the kiss had been. She wanted to curl her fingers and capture that breath, to keep it close to her.

Such an intimate farewell. Or perhaps her own addled state was misconstruing it. The marshal she'd known until now would never have offered such courtly gestures.

"Perhaps. At the trial, of course. But beyond... Only fate will tell."

"Indeed." There was no sadness in him, only acceptance. "If you'll excuse me, I must sit with my prisoner. I recommend you stay far away."

As if she would want to come close to McCade. "I'll see you in the morning, then."

"No," he said, "you won't. I'm leaving before the sun comes up. It will be better that way."

So this was the end. A stitch tugged her heart toward her breastbone. A few days ago, she couldn't wait to see the back of this man, but now... sadness wasn't quite the word for what was lodged in her breast, but perhaps regret would fit.

"I wish you the best of luck," she said.

"I wish the same for you." He was so solemn, she found herself wanting to offer to sit with him through the night, to not leave him alone with that outlaw.

But that was foolishness.

She turned and left for the safety of the others, telling herself that this was the outcome she had always wanted.

CHAPTER EIGHT

HAVING HIS WRISTS SHACKLED TOGETHER didn't seem to bother McCade. Nor did being hauled back to Los Angeles as a captured fugitive.

Still wearing the soiled clothes he'd been captured in, he sprawled shamelessly in his seat across from Sebastian, the two of them alone in the train compartment. A few souls had come through the sliding door, seen the handcuffed man and Sebastian's stern expression—and promptly left again.

"Spencer," McCade said musingly. He tapped his forearms against his thighs. "I think I've heard of you."

Perhaps he had. Although Sebastian's crimes were over a decade old.

"You haven't." Sebastian sent the other man his most implacable stare.

McCade wasn't put off. "No, I've heard rumors about you. About the things you did when you were young."

Sebastian's stomach turned to think of what McCade might have heard.

"I've heard rumors about you as well," he said, pushing the other man into speaking of his own crimes.

153

If they continued down the path of Sebastian's past, his control could slip. McCade might learn how deeply the past was still rooted within Sebastian.

"Don't think that because you prey on the weak, the oppressed, that no one hears of your violations," Sebastian went on. "Your father must hear of them—else why would he wash his hands of you every few months?"

Sebastian didn't seek out such stories—Judge Bannister relayed each new rumor of father-son estrangement with glee. "Working on a ranch, being this far out from Los Angeles—you were out of favor again, weren't you?" he asked. "I wonder how your father will view this little escapade."

"Once he hears the truth—that a vicious band of Mexicans targeted me, no doubt thinking they'd gain some of my father's wealth by threatening me—he'll see to it that the guilty are punished." McCade's smile was sickeningly triumphant. "And the guilty parties won't include me."

It was cunning, Sebastian had to admit. With a good lawyer, a jury might be convinced by it.

"Let's not split hairs," he said, tired of sparring over falsehoods. "We both know you did it. This wasn't the first of your crimes."

"And you've no crimes on your conscience?" McCade asked.

He did. Terrible ones. Sebastian had used the same things McCade would—his father's name and the anonymity of his victims—to escape his deserved punishment.

Sebastian would spend the remainder of his life in penance and repentance for the evil he'd inflicted as a callow youth, as he'd raged against his absent father. Justice hadn't punished Sebastian, so he would punish himself.

McCade shifted indolently as his stare grew more aggressive. He'd no idea of the silt he churned from the bottom of Sebastian's soul.

"If this is an attempt to force a confession," the outlaw drawled, "you'll have to do better than that."

No, it wasn't an attempt at a confession. McCade wasn't intimidated by his bulk, his silence, the badge on his chest.

This was a *study*. Of a man who'd had a gentleman's education, had every opportunity to live a life of purpose, to better others through his efforts. Or at the very least, take his money and education and live a life of leisure. And McCade had chosen the exact opposite. Chosen to heedlessly toss chaos and despair into the world, destroying one life after another and counting on his father's name and the powerlessness of his victims to spare him from punishment.

Sebastian was also such a man. Or had been.

His father's actions may have forced violence upon him, but he'd chosen it for himself as well, time and time again.

Until that fateful day at seventeen, when he'd chosen differently. And set onto a path away from the empty, violent waste of a man he'd been. It took rigid self-control to keep to the path, and he'd been compelled to abandon much of his interior life in the effort—but he had saved himself.

"No confessions," Sebastian said. McCade wouldn't understand such things as confession and penance—they'd be lost on him. "I suppose you had to put those marks on Miss Moreno's neck in self-defense. Both times, that is."

"Might not have been me. Mexicans tend to get violent with their women. She strikes me as a woman who needs a lot of correcting." McCade sounded as if he'd enjoy *correcting* Señorita Moreno.

Sebastian caught the rage that threatened to snap out of him just in time, shoving it hard behind his reserve. A man's race couldn't predict if he was likely to brutalize a woman.

Judge Spencer was an Anglo, and his wife had been punished with more viciousness than the criminals brought before him.

"Really?" Sebastian allowed his voice to slip deep, needing that slight escape for his rage in order to keep the remainder caged.

"Oh yes." McCade's smile was obscenely polite. "She says something she ought not to"—he raised his hands to encircle an imaginary neck, slim enough to fit in the space there—"and all a man has to do is squeeze to teach her to know better."

Sebastian's rage slid into nausea. "I know what it looks like when a man strangles a woman."

McCade dropped his hands. "Well, then, I don't need to explain to you what might have happened to her." He shrugged. "Might have, of course. *I* didn't do it, so I couldn't say."

"Of course you didn't," Sebastian replied. And allowed himself to imagine striking McCade until the man went down and then striking and striking again and again, until his knuckles were bloodied and broken, until McCade ceased to scream for mercy... just as Sebastian had done before.

He shoved the images away before the viciousness of them could sicken him. He began to silently recite the Stoics, words carefully chosen to remind himself that he was a man, with a man's control—and not some mindless beast.

And that he must never surrender to such bloodlust again.

~~~

It still broke Isabel's heart to see Joaquin like this.

He sat up in bed, his face pale and drawn. It had been a month since the attack—a week since the marshal had hauled McCade away—yet Joaquin was not improving. Beneath the smell of the caustic chemicals the nurses used, there lurked a thread of corruption—a faint whiff of the unhealing wound in Joaquin's torso.

Isabel puttered about his room, trying to hide her dismay. A twitch of the curtains, an adjustment of a vase, then she felt ready to face him again.

"You look…" She didn't want to lie, but *well* was not how he looked. He looked tired, ill. Crumpled.

Compared to how dapper he used to be, how confident, how handsome, the man before her seemed an entirely different being.

His smile was tight, lacking the brilliance it once had. "If I look as I feel, then it must be quite bad."

"It's not… bad." And it wasn't. In those early days, he'd looked as if death's shadow had passed over him—likely because it had. There had been definite improvement since then, his skin regaining some color, his frame recovering some flesh. "But you have looked better."

"Honest Isabel," he said in a low voice with a keen edge. "The only one who will look me in the eye and speak the truth."

He, who'd always welcomed the truth from her before, sounded as though he despised her for it.

He was in a mood today.

She sank into the chair next to the bed, suppressing a sigh. She knew that before she left, they would exchange harsh words. Again.

They'd never exchanged harsh words during their engagement, a thing that had delighted her, had made her believe that she'd chosen oh so wisely. But their engagement was ended, and their accord had ended with it.

She looked at the newspapers scattered across his little table. All from Los Angeles.

She stared at a headline that prominently featured both her and Joaquin's names. "Did you read this?" she asked.

He flicked a fingernail at the paper. "Yes," he said. "I never thought to find myself being impugned in print for doing my duty. Have you read it?"

She shook her head.

"Don't," he ordered flatly. "You don't want to see what they printed about you."

Which of course set curiosity to burning within her, to see exactly what insults they'd written.

She'd regret it as soon as she did it though, so she turned back to her satchel instead.

"I've brought you a book. Much better than a newspaper, I should think." She pulled it from her bag like a conjurer pulling a trick.

"*Travels in West Africa*," he read. The air of disinterest as he set it aside abraded her nerves. She'd chosen it with such care.

"I thought you would enjoy a tale of someplace far away," she said as cheerily as she could. "A place far from here."

Tales of exotic places had always interested him before. They'd talked of such books for hours. She'd thought the gift might reignite that spark within him, but she'd been wrong. He was perfectly content to sink into despair here. Or perhaps not content. Perhaps he was simply too enervated to do more.

She raised a hand to her aching temple.

"I'm sure I will enjoy it. Thank you." His dark eyes were as flat as his thanks. "But we also have adventure here in the sanatorium."

"Really?" She raised an eyebrow, trying to insert some levity. Trying and failing.

"Yes. Just this week I was assigned a new nurse."

A new nurse? High excitement, indeed. "Oh?" she said. "Old as the hills? Stout as a battle ax?"

His face pinched into a considering sort of frown. "She *is* stout, but not old. She's terrifyingly efficient. Whips in, whips out."

"She's treating you well?"

"Oh, yes." He drew the words out almost to the breaking point. "Everyone here gets treated well. It's a most luxurious captivity."

She glanced about this "cage" of his, taking note of the indifferent painting hanging on the wall, the curtains drawn over the window. Her gaze lingered on the window a moment longer than she would have liked, an old habit she no longer needed.

The marshal had hauled McCade away.

She pulled her gaze back to Joaquin, the paper within her satchel crinkling as she shifted in her chair.

The telegram. The reason she was here.

She drummed her fingers on the chair arm, worrying at her lower lip, wondering how to broach this next issue.

"The marshal sent a telegram," she said baldly. "The trial begins in a few days and I leave for Los Angeles tomorrow."

The marshal's summons crinkled once more as her arm twitched against the satchel with the drumming of her fingers.

Joaquin looked away to the wall. "I won't be able to go," he said.

Her mind may have known, but her heart had still hoped—hoped she wouldn't have to be alone in the ordeal.

"I know," she forced out. "The marshal said that this—this McCade"—her tongue stumbled over having to say that name to Joaquin—"is the son of a powerful man."

Joaquin's mouth curled in a sneer. "The marshal. The hero of the day."

She stiffened. "And what you did wasn't heroic?"

"Oh yes, I'm quite the hero. I can't even testify at the trial for *my* attempted murder." Never had he spoken so caustically to her.

She absorbed that for a moment. "I will fight for both of us," she assured him.

"It doesn't matter," he said dully. "Even if he's convicted, the son of a prominent man won't serve long for the attempted murder of a Mexican."

Her heart began to knock against her chest. He was correct—and yet...

"What would you have me do?" she snapped. "Not testify? I thought you cared about justice." Now she was sneering back at him. Really, what did he think her choices were in this? She had none.

"A courtroom isn't like a schoolroom." His voice rose with agitation. "You can't command everyone to believe you through sheer force of authority."

Such words from him were like a strike from his open palm. He'd always believed her to be extraordinary, had taken pride in her air of command, her steady self-containment.

"I can only be myself," she said tightly. She'd no choice in that, either. "I'm no dissembler. I haven't been trained in the finer points of legal misdirection."

"Well, you're going to become well acquainted with it soon." Such bitter sarcasm from him shocked her. "You'll likely find yourself questioned by some of the finest lawyers money can buy. Playing the teacher with them won't win the day."

He thought she'd come out the loser in such a match, did he?

Lord, if even Joaquin thought this beyond her...

"Money can't buy the truth," she said. A silly, childish sentiment, but his air of defeat, his pessimistic assessment of the coming trial—it *hurt*. Why couldn't he bolster her, instead of tearing her down?

"It can make it look remarkably like lies," he threw out, before his face twisted savagely.

Her shoulders sagged as she rushed to his side, regretting that she'd met his ill temper with some of her own.

He'd told her once that the pain came and went in swells like the tide of the ocean: sometimes high, sometimes low, but always present. He must be having a surge, his fist pressed tight against the wound in his belly, all of him curling around it.

"Do you want me to call for the nurse?" she asked softly.

"No." The word was pushed from between his clenched teeth. "It will pass."

She took his hand, wishing there was more she could do. Slowly, over a period that felt like eons, but must have only been a few minutes, his face relaxed.

"Better now?" she asked.

He nodded, his eyes still closed. He sighed deeply, opened them again. "You should go. You have a long drive back home. And a long trip tomorrow."

Yes. A long trip, the end of which would find her alone against the best legal prowess in Los Angeles.

The marshal might be there, watching the trial. Watching her.

He'd be clean shaven once more, his suit pressed, the dust and dishevelment of the trail gone. But the bulk of him would be as impressive as always, his eyes still that unsettling gray...

She gave herself a shake. She ought not to be wishing for the marshal; he might have Judge Bannister with him. If Judge Bannister happened to see her mother, if he realized that the woman who'd evaded him for decades was right in front of him, finally within striking distance...

Yet another tangle she must navigate during her time there.

"I'll see you when I return." She brushed a kiss across his cheek, the gesture born of habit now rather than affection. The texture of his unshorn skin had her halting for a half a moment of surprise. Joaquin had always been so fastidious about his appearance—spending the day with a quarter inch of stubble on his face would have been abhorrent to him. The nurse must not be shaving him as often as she should.

She took one last look around the room, the drawn curtains throwing gloom across the book abandoned on the side table and the man slumped in the bed. Perhaps... perhaps if she returned with news of McCade's conviction, it would impel Joaquin to rise from that bed. To more actively seek his own recovery.

One more reason she must be victorious in Los Angeles.

Isabel left with heavy heart and shuffling feet, nearly crashing into a nurse in the hallway.

"Excuse me," she said as she caught herself.

The nurse's smile was strained. "My fault." She was short, with pale hair and skin, and an air that clearly said she wanted to get on with her duties.

"Are you Sheriff Obregon's nurse?"

"I am." Her eyes went a little flinty, although the smile didn't leave her face. "You must be his fiancée."

Isabel didn't bother to correct her. The dislike in the nurse's gaze made her feel as prickly as a hedgehog.

"Is there anything he needs?" she asked briskly. "Anything I can bring him?"

"Between his family and the nurses here, he doesn't lack for anything." A neat dismissal.

The nurse glanced down the hall. "And here come his sisters now," she announced.

Sure enough, Teresa and Ines were coming down the hall, slowing when they caught sight of Isabel. A sticky awkwardness entangled the three of them, weighting Isabel's limbs. The little nurse disappeared, clearly happy to leave them to themselves and return to her duties.

"Teresa. Ines." She nodded a greeting.

"Señorita Moreno," Teresa said, her expression solemn, the lines of her face taut.

It had once been first names only between them.

Silence fell, and Isabel could sense all of them searching for something to say.

She'd spent many a productive afternoon in the Obregon sisters' company, sewing, planning the next action of the temperance meeting, discussing her coming marriage to Joaquin.

Although they knew that Joaquin had ended the engagement, they behaved as if they held Isabel responsible for its demise, speaking to her as little as possible when they did happen to meet.

She'd lost more than a fiancé when Joaquin had severed things between them—she'd lost friendships as well.

"We hear you're leaving tomorrow for the trial," Teresa offered.

"I am," Isabel replied, not allowing her trepidation purchase within her words.

"We don't have to tell you how vital it is that this man is punished," Ines said severely.

No, they didn't. After Joaquin's lecture, she didn't need *their* reminders.

"I know what's expected of me." She'd meant to be crisply assuring, but she only sounded cold.

"Good," Teresa said, more warning than approving. "We'd hate for this trial to fail because of you."

Easy enough for Teresa to be so archly nasty—she wasn't the one about to face down her attacker in a courtroom.

"I'm glad I meet with your approval," Isabel said, keeping her voice cold.

Their expressions shuttered. Good. Let them feel some shame for trying to badger her.

"We only meant that—"

"I know exactly what you meant." Isabel cut Ines off without a bit of remorse. "Joaquin and I already discussed this."

Teresa's expression softened. "How is he today?"

The concern in her question softened Isabel as well. "Better than usual. I left him a book; perhaps he'd like one of you to read it to him."

The awkwardness crept back in like a fog, and Isabel sensed that the sisters wanted to end this conversation as desperately as she did.

"I must be off," she said with a short wave of farewell.

The sisters only nodded in return.

Isabel didn't look back as she left. She'd find no comfort from that quarter.

~~~

McCade looked entirely different.

Head lowered contritely, with a fresh haircut and finely cut suit, he looked exactly as he was—a gentleman's son. Sebastian might not have believed the transformation had he not seen it for himself here at the bail hearing.

Of course appearances weren't everything. Beneath that fine suit and innocent expression, McCade was still a criminal.

"Tell me, Mr. Alder," Judge Hess was saying to McCade's lawyer, "why shouldn't I refuse to set bail for Mr. McCade? He's accused of trying to murder two people."

"There are no other witnesses to the attack other than the alleged victims," Alder pointed out smartly. "Mr. McCade has never been charged with a crime before."

Brisk. Earnest. As if Alder actually believed in McCade's innocence.

In the week since he'd returned, Sebastian had spent the time looking more closely into McCade's illegal activities. A beating here, a theft there. Few witnesses, none willing to testify, and no evidence that could be presented in court.

McCade had been smart with his crimes, targeting the lower elements of society—Negros, the Chinese—people the law cared little about and often actively persecuted. Just the sight of his badge had gotten more than one door slammed in Sebastian's face in Chinatown; the memories of the Massacre of '71 hadn't yet faded.

But he'd done nothing so brash as shooting a lawman before. McCade was becoming more daring the longer he went unpunished.

If McCade wasn't convicted, if he knew he could escape justice even after nearly killing a sheriff—what might he try next?

McCade might even threaten Señorita Moreno again. Sebastian suppressed his reaction to that, focusing again on the scene before him.

"Perhaps Mr. McCade hasn't been charged before," the judge allowed. "But he did run after the alleged attack."

"Your honor," Alder said in appeal, "this sheriff murdered two men himself. That's certainly not in dispute. Mr. McCade feared for his life after being attacked by the sheriff. No one in that town would have believed in my client's innocence. He had to run, to save his life."

"Hmm," Hess said. "Mr. Halstead," he called to the prosecutor. "Do you have anything you'd like to add?"

Halstead merely shook his head. It was clear he did not want to argue this case. What man with hopes of a civic career in Los Angeles would *want* to argue against Edwin McCade's son?

Edwin McCade. He was in the courtroom, watching the proceedings with a melancholy air, his mouth turned down. But he didn't appear in the least bit defeated—an air of wealth, of command, clung tightly to him.

And resolve. A terrific resolve lit his gaze.

That worried Sebastian. If McCade meant to fight to the utmost for his son—hiring Alder on as a lawyer indicated that he did—things would not go well for the prosecution.

Especially if Halstead decided to roll over and show his belly to preserve his own future interests.

"Very well," Hess said. "Given Mr. McCade's previous flight from authority, bail is not granted. He will remain in custody." The judge snapped the gavel down as he rendered his decision.

For half a moment, Edwin McCade's features twisted into something savage. A man didn't become that powerful by being pleased when thwarted.

Halstead looked as if someone had walked over his grave, taking no joy in his victory.

The only one who did look pleased was Cole McCade, a queer little smile twisting his lips as he was led away.

A chill ran through Sebastian at the man's uncaring air. It was unnatural, that smile of McCade's.

Sebastian put that last image of the man from his mind. Time to inform Judge Bannister of what had happened.

Judge Bannister's chambers were only a few floors above the courtroom, and Sebastian made the journey in less than five minutes.

"I still can't quite believe how you brought him in without a hitch," the judge said as Sebastian settled into a chair across from his desk.

Still trim well into his sixth decade, in a suit of blue wool, with a close-cropped white beard, Judge Bannister carried his air of prominence as securely as Edwin McCade had.

"After all these years of slipping through our grasp"—the man squeezed his fist for effect—"we finally got him. What happened at the hearing?"

"No bail," Sebastian said, allowing himself a small bit of pleasure. A small bit couldn't hurt.

"The witness, this Mexican girl, she's coming today?"

"Not Mexican—she is of old Spanish stock. And yes, she is." Why he'd corrected the judge, he couldn't say. He'd never yet met an Anglo who could distinguish between a Spaniard, a Californio, or a Mexican. Or least one who bothered to attempt the distinction.

"Spaniards," the judge grumbled, thumping a newspaper on his desk. "All I read of in the papers these days is the arrogance of Spaniards. They won't make peace, though we handily won the war, and there's talk of abandoning the Philippines. Those poor people need our civilizing influence. It would be un-Christian to leave."

Sebastian forced himself to blink, rather than roll his eyes. All this hand wringing over the Philippines was infuriating. Or would have been, had he allowed himself to care—fury was too dangerous an emotion for him to allow it purchase.

He sat still as stone, his face carefully blank, waiting for the judge to return to the matter at hand.

Bannister thumped the paper one last time and harrumphed. "Spaniards," he muttered again. "A Spanish woman murdered my brother, you know."

Sebastian did know. All of Spanish California knew that story, although he suspected the one he'd heard at his mother's knee would be quite different from the one Judge Bannister might tell about the Black Widow Alvarado.

But they were here to discuss Señorita Moreno, not old stories. "You were asking about the witness?" he prompted.

The judge shifted in his chair. "This girl is the entirety of the case. She folds and McCade walks free." He sent Sebastian a probing look. "Do you think she will?"

Sebastian remembered the steel in her spine, and a curious sensation tugged at his chest. No, she wouldn't fold.

"She went with me to apprehend him and didn't flinch once."

She'd been like the warrior queen California had taken its name from—fierce, resolved... compelling.

"I can't imagine that a courtroom will frighten her," he finished.

If anything, she would be too controlled, too strong in front of the jury. A more... *pliant* lady would play on their sympathies better.

Sebastian had been thinking of her often. Remembering her throwing her story right in his teeth, remembering her by the fire at night, talking of novels—and remembering her in those final moments, holding her fear at bay and standing tall before McCade.

Only, he didn't want to be thinking of her. He'd been so certain that once he was back in the city, among his familiar things, she would fade from his mind. His notebooks were full of memories of her, full of the sensations she evoked that he was trying desperately to eradicate.

Trying, and so far failing.

As for the dreams... She came to him at night, forced him to admit that he desired her, that his emotions ran deeper than simply admiration—and then demanded that he act on those emotions.

He wasn't certain what to do about the dreams. Thoughts of her he put into his notebook, since he ought to be able to stop thinking of her—but the dreams...

He'd no control over his dreams. Was it a sin even when one didn't intend to sin?

He gripped the arms of the chair tightly, bringing himself back to the matter at hand.

"Hanging this entire case on one girl makes me uneasy," the judge admitted. He rubbed a thumb across his chin. "The sheriff—the one who was shot—are you certain we can't bring him here?"

"The doctor advised very strongly against it." Given Obregon's state when Sebastian had seen him, he'd no doubt the trip was likely to kill the sheriff.

"I suppose if the doctor said no..." The judge didn't look at all perturbed by the thought of a man dying for his pet case. What was one crippled sheriff against bringing down the son of a man the judge thought too powerful for the public good?

Of course, the judge wouldn't actually risk Obregon's life. His previous skirmishes with Edwin McCade had never involved anything extralegal. If Cole McCade was found not guilty, Bannister and McCade would return their fight to the pages of the newspapers, gallons of ink spilled rather than blood in their battle to be the most prominent man in Los Angeles.

Not that it would be of much comfort to Señorita Moreno if McCade walked free.

"The lady will do quite well," he assured the judge.

Bannister fell silent at that, but Sebastian sensed he wasn't finished. The older man fingered a scrap of paper on the desk, gazing at it thoughtfully.

"I suppose she looks like her sister," the judge finally said.

Why would Bannister assume that?

"No," Sebastian said, "she doesn't."

Her sister's beauty had been of a sly sort, the kind she wanted you to stop and take notice of. Señorita Moreno's features, on the other hand...

He sighed, resisting the urge to rub his hand across his face. He *must* stop thinking of her.

Sebastian caught sight of what the judge was looking at.

A wedding photograph, his son and daughter-in-law standing stiff and formal for the camera. None of the vitality, the affection of the couple, had made it to the picture, all of it pressed flat by the eye of the camera.

Sebastian didn't think a camera would fail to capture all of him—he already felt quite two-dimensional at times.

"I suppose you saw my son while you were there," the judge said with false carelessness.

"I did." Sebastian looked into the blue eyes so like Mr. Merrill's, speaking of resemblances. "He owns a ranch in Cabrillo."

The judge's lip curled. "A ranch. I give the boy every advantage, and he runs off to play in the dirt. And marries a Mexican to boot." He peered more closely at the photograph. "She looks a bit familiar, actually."

Do we all look alike to you?

"If only he'd been like you," the older man continued, "stayed in Los Angeles, had a law career..." He stared off at some imagined reality, then back at Sebastian. "Now, you, you're a son a man could be proud of."

Sebastian's waistcoat tightened about his ribs, but he said nothing. The Bible might command children to honor their parents, but Sebastian's father had earned nothing from his son, not even the appearance of respect.

Besides, Judge Bannister's continuing devotion to Judge Spencer was why the man more often than not chose Sebastian as his appointed marshal. When Bannister needed a man he could trust, who better than the son of the man he'd trusted the most?

So Sebastian ignored Bannister's praise of his father and concentrated on his duties. As long as Sebastian served justice, what did it matter whose hands he served it at?

Justice is more than simply what the courts serve.

There she was again, intruding into his thoughts. Making him question his path in life.

It would not stand. He must work harder to eradicate such wayward thoughts.

"I still miss him, you know," the judge mused. "Other than myself, he was the finest judge in Los Angeles. Lady Justice lost an exceptional defender all those years ago."

Sebastian's hand twitched before he could still it. His father may have defended justice all those years ago, but who had defended his mother and him from his father?

Sebastian realized Bannister was waiting for him to say something appropriately reverent about the late Judge Spencer.

"He did love being a judge." That at least was true.

"We'll not see his like again," the judge said.

Sebastian sincerely hoped not, as the arms of the chair pressed hard against him, trapping him.

"But I always know I can count on you," Bannister said fondly. "Just as I counted on your father."

Suddenly everything was closing in on him, his waistcoat, his tie, his chair...

He snapped to his feet, sending the chair screeching across the floor.

"I'll just get back to my duties then." He clenched at his hat, reminding himself not to crush the damn thing. "If you'll excuse me."

The older man's smile was warm, as if he had bestowed a great compliment by comparing Sebastian to his father, instead of the gravest insult. "Keep an eye on this witness while she's here. We wouldn't want anything to happen to her."

A chill seized him. He already thought too much of her; spending more time with her would no doubt prove dangerous to his hard-won equilibrium. But what could he say? Protecting witnesses was part of his duties as a marshal.

"No," he said, "we wouldn't want that." God help him, he meant it. Deeply meant it.

Sebastian couldn't leave fast enough.

CHAPTER NINE

ISABEL HAD LOVED LOS ANGELES from the very first time she'd seen it—it was more alive with people and horses and noise than dusty little Cabrillo could ever hope to be.

Her legs itched to pace the aisle of the train, but her mother's staid posture in the seat next to her commanded her to sit as still and calm as Señora Moreno.

But the thought of being in the city electrified Isabel's anxiety, made her muscles twitch.

Every revolution of the wheels brought her closer to McCade.

And the marshal.

Any lady might wish to pace when faced with such a prospect.

They were off the train, through the depot, and onto the streetcar with hardly any time for Isabel to take in their surroundings. But once they were settled on the streetcar, the familiar urge she always had in the city—to be active, exciting, smart—took hold of her.

People were crowded into the streetcar, the sidewalks more so, a cacophony of voices, wheels, and the rattling cough of a consumptive ebbing and flowing

179

around her. She pressed her heels hard against the floor to push it into going faster.

"Isabel," her mother chided, "stop fidgeting."

Isabel pulled herself to stillness. A grimness had stolen over her mother the closer they had come to Los Angeles. No doubt she was thinking of Judge Bannister and how best to keep evading the vengeance he might take upon her for murdering his brother.

It was clear from her mother's description of her first marriage that if she'd not shot her husband, he would have murdered her.

The coroner's inquest had agreed with her mother's view and cleared her of all charges.

Judge Bannister—although he'd not been a judge then, only a young man—had not seen it that way.

"You don't have to attend the trial with me," Isabel assured her mother in an undertone.

"Of course I won't," the Señora replied evenly. Her breathing was unnaturally steady, the product of a concerted effort.

The night after the first attack, nightmares had plagued Isabel, her broken throat trying to force out an endless scream. As a consolation, her mother had told Isabel the story of her first marriage—a story Isabel had heard before, but never suspected involved her own mother.

Her mother had been heiress to the Rancho Alvarado in the days of Mexican California. When the Americans had come to California, the Bannister family seized the rancho as their own, her mother married to the eldest Bannister son in an attempt to join the two families' claims to the same stretch of land.

But the eldest Bannister son had been cruel, so cruel, bloodying and beating her mother, breaking her bones. Her mother had no choice, no other means of escape—except to shoot him.

Isabel knew the story, of course—everyone born into the Alvarado family did—but the identity of the Alvarado heiress had been mysterious, concealed.

Because her mother was still hiding from Judge Bannister.

Her mother had offered Isabel that story as both a comfort and a bolstering. For if her mother had survived such a thing, surely Isabel could survive what had happened to her.

They had always been close, Isabel and her mother, sharing more than a few traits. But that story had forged a new bond born of their shared suffering.

Just as Isabel feared to face her enemy in Los Angeles, so did her mother. Only Isabel had no choice in the matter—she *had* to attend the trial, had to see McCade again.

At least the marshal might be present.

Isabel sighed and stared at the passing scenery. Her gaze caught on a man in the crowd, the curve of his arm, the set of his head sending a sickening bolt of recognition through her, making her heart seize. She dropped her gaze to the floor, all of her wanting to follow along behind, to sink beneath the seat and hide from whom she thought she'd seen.

Look again. Make certain. She forced her head up.

There he was again... and he was nothing like McCade. Same age, same hair color, but there the resemblance ended. She dipped her head, let her breath release. It wasn't him.

Besides, shouldn't McCade be in jail? Wouldn't he be held there until the trial? She wasn't certain, and she wished she'd thought to ask the marshal.

Only... the marshal had done his duty in bringing in McCade—which meant she would no longer be of interest to him.

Eventually they arrived at their stop, the pressure under her heels releasing to launch her off into the street.

The paved street. With actual sidewalks.

The crowds pressed all about them, her mother following as Isabel led them forward. The energy of the people pressed close on the sidewalk pushed out all thoughts of the marshal and the trial.

After a few blocks, they arrived at Cousin Enrique's home, a multistory structure covered with carvings and curlicues painted the most sober shade of lavender. The strip of green in front was a riot of blowsy colors and scents, as Cousin Pilar's roses expended themselves in one last bloom before winter came.

Isabel had always envied those roses, but Catarina refused to plant anything that took so much effort for no return in edibility.

When Isabel had a house of her own, she would surround it with rose bushes—and pay someone handsomely to care for them.

The entire Jaramillo family came out to greet them. First Cousin Enrique himself: still short, still round, and still dressed like a don of old by way of a peacock. The amount of gray in his hair surprised her, although she'd seen him at Caterina's wedding. Someone as effusive as the Don ought never to look so old.

"Cousin Maria! Cousin Isabel!" Don Enrique spread his arms wide to embrace them. For all that the little man was quite ridiculous, he kept to the old ways of hospitality, and no one left his house without feeling the full warmth of his regard.

Her mother's smile was cordial, but restrained. Don Enrique might think it perfectly fine to embrace in the street, but she held herself to a higher standard. As did Isabel.

"Cousin. We are most glad to see you." Her mother sighed. "I do wish our trip were for a happier purpose."

Isabel stiffened. Their questions about the trial were certain to come next.

Don Enrique flapped his hands. "A terrible business to be sure, but let's not speak of it here."

Her throat prickled with relief. A reprieve—at least until they reached the parlor.

"Come in, please." Don Enrique gestured for them to enter.

His three daughters followed behind, their dresses bedecked with as much folderol as the house. No work dresses for these ladies; they lived the life of refinement and ease Isabel had always dreamed of.

Too bad the three of them put together had no more sense than God gave a goose. Perhaps less, since geese knew to fly south for the winter, but the Alvarado girls didn't have the brains to come in from the cold.

Thank goodness it never froze in Los Angeles.

They swarmed Isabel in the entry, assaulting her with embraces, kisses, and questions until her head throbbed from the warmth of their welcome.

"Girls!" her mother said with a sharp clap of her hands. "We're here all week. Please let us get through the door."

They scattered to the parlor.

Once Isabel and her mother had washed the travel dust from their faces, they found their way to the front parlor, where the table was set for tea and the air was thick with the scent of roses.

Isabel breathed deeply before settling on a sofa next to Pilar. Pilar was the middle of the sisters and tended to be the one most likely to speak sensibly. Sometimes.

It also gave her a clear view of the windows, with none at her back.

Her mother and the Don sat themselves in a far corner of the room, no doubt to discuss things the children shouldn't hear.

Dolores, the eldest girl and *de facto* mistress of the house since her mother had passed, handed Isabel a dainty cup with enviable grace. "Do tell us how you are faring, Cousin Isabel."

"Well enough." They knew why she was here; hopefully they would take that answer as a warning not to discuss the details further. She took a sip of her tea. Much too weak for her taste and already a touch cold.

The pleasantries out of the way, Pilar leaned forward, an absurdly excited look on her face. "I have the most shocking news about Rosa Verdugo. You remember Rosa."

"Faintly." No doubt they were related in some convoluted way and they'd met once, briefly, at some family function.

"She..." Pilar paused for effect. "Is marrying..." Another pause. "A *Scotsman*."

That last was hissed so low, the S seemed to go on forever.

"A Scotsman?" Isabel searched her mind for something that could be shocking about a Scotsman. "Does he wear a kilt like Waverley?"

Daria gasped. "No. Do you think he might one day? And we'll see his *bare legs*?" She mouthed the last two words to escape the attention of the Señora and the Don.

"I should die if I saw a man's bare legs," Dolores whispered.

"That bodes ill for your marriage," Isabel murmured behind her teacup.

Pilar flapped her hands. "Forget about his legs. He's a Presbyterian! And there's something even worse."

"Worse than being a Presbyterian?" This Isabel had to hear. Did he have cloven hooves instead of feet?

Daria compressed her lips, then bravely went forward. "His hair is... *orange*."

Isabel blinked as Pilar nodded solemnly. "Yes. It looks like he has carrot peelings atop his head."

"I couldn't look at such hair for the rest of my life," Dolores said, bringing her hand to her breast. "It would hurt my eyes so."

Isabel studied the tray of food. She preferred to speak of books or something similarly elevating—or at the very least, people she actually knew.

She reached for a plate. There were some dainty tortas, the cilantro topping them greenly fragrant, and little pastel cafes as well, sprinkled with cinnamon and studded with pecans.

She glanced up to catch Dolores sliding her a sly look. "I know one man who has fine, dark hair," her cousin said archly.

Her scalp prickled. They could not possibly be speaking of...

"Marshal Spencer!" Dolores finished triumphantly. The volume of her voice made Isabel flinch. "We hear he apprehended your outlaw." Her cousin tried for serious, but spoiled the effect with a titter. "Isn't he utterly too much?"

"Too much of what?" Isabel asked coolly.

"So thrilling," Pilar went on, "how he captured that man! Tell me, did he appear quite savage when he did it? Because he appeared quite savage the time we saw him."

Savage? If anything, he was remarkably controlled. It was only his size that made him appear savage.

That and his shocking attack on McCade. Then he'd appeared savage indeed.

She took a sip of tea as she gathered her thoughts. What to say about the marshal?

"Well?" Dolores demanded.

Her mother sent them a quelling look from across the room. "Well-bred young ladies should not be discussing a gentleman in a familiar manner."

Pilar and Dolores had the grace to blush, but Daria never removed the simper from her face.

Isabel leaned toward her cousins and pitched her voice a little lower, a dash of heat blooming under her skin. She hoped she hadn't an answering flush across her cheeks. "You're familiar with the marshal?"

Her mother might disapprove, but curiosity burned a hole in her stomach, right through her morals.

"Of course we are," Pilar answered. The three tittered again, ignoring the Señora's stern expression. "His mother is a Vasquez."

"Cousin Enrique," the Señora said, a bit too loudly, "please, tell us all about the La Fiesta parade."

She was clearly announcing that the children should stop speaking.

The Don smiled brightly and clasped his hands together. "I was Grand Marshal last year. Of course, this year it was cancelled, thanks to this terrible war, but never fear. Next year it will go on once more and I'm certain to be Grand Marshal again. They say I give an authentic feel to the festivities."

"How lovely," the Señora murmured.

Isabel turned back to her cousins. "What do you know of the marshal?" she whispered. The girls were terrible gossips, which she normally frowned upon, but such information could only aid her in dealings with the marshal.

Her curiosity wasn't a bit prurient.

The three leaned in close, almost knocking their heads together.

"We don't see him much," Dolores said. "His mother visits occasionally, but he's only accompanied her once."

"He was very stern." Daria shuddered theatrically.

Isabel pressed her lips together. She already knew all of that. Was that the best these three had? *Is he worse than that Scotsman?* she wanted to ask.

Pilar said in the barest whisper, "They say his father drank himself to *death*."

Isabel sat back in shock. Now *that* was something new. She remembered his pronouncement that he never touched alcohol. His fervency made perfect sense now.

"Who are *they*?" she whispered back.

Pilar shrugged, obviously uninterested in the source—true or false, it was too salacious not to repeat.

"He's quite well off," Dolores said.

"Yes, it's a shame he's not married by now," Daria added.

The three sisters exchanged a look.

"What?" Isabel asked. "What was that about?"

"Papa says the marshal would make a fine match for one of us," Pilar said.

"But…" said Daria.

"He's too stern," Dolores finished.

"Too brutish," Pilar offered.

"Too… *much*," Daria said.

Her cousins were correct; a few years of marriage to the marshal would turn one of these three to dust. Isabel could hardly imagine the marshal married to anyone, really. No lady would want those cold gray eyes trained on her for a lifetime.

But then she remembered his lips on the back of her hand, her fingers trying to curl round the warmth of his breath…

A lady might like a lifetime of that. *She* might like a lifetime of that.

A knock at the front door sent every neck craning toward the hallway. The patter of the maid's feet came as she hurried to answer.

"My daughters, were we expecting another visitor today?" the Don asked.

All three girls shook their heads.

The door gave a whining squeal as it opened. The heavy tread of booted feet approached, accompanied by a rapid swishing.

She knew who it was. She recognized that step, remembered it behind her on the stairs at their very first meeting. Something bloomed deep within her at the knowledge—lush, blood red, thorny. She didn't even try to force it to wilt.

Isabel slowly raised her gaze to find him in the doorway, immaculate as ever in a perfectly fitting black suit. The sight of the marshal sent her stomach tripping up to her throat, her heart jumping to join it.

She didn't care that he was too stern, too brutish, too much—she craved the sight of him. Seeing him there, so still and solemn, as unmoving as the mountains—everything might be all right now.

Irrational, yes, but her reason was gravely listing with this unexpected visit from him.

On his arm was a tiny doll of a woman, in a dress a decade out of fashion, pearl gray to match her upswept hair. She was about the same age as Isabel's mother, but with a kind, painfully open smile. A smile her mother had never and would never wear.

This must be Marshal Spencer's mother. How did a woman with a smile so open produce a son so guarded?

Don Enrique practically fluttered as he rose to greet them. "Señora Vasquez! What a lovely surprise." He craned his neck to look up at the marshal. "You've brought your son. How... unexpected."

"My son wished to pay his respects to Señora and Señorita Moreno. I thought I might accompany him to visit you and your lovely daughters." Señora Vasquez's voice was as sweet and delicate as the rest of her. After carefully settling herself across from Isabel's mother, Señora Vasquez accepted a cup of tea with a hand as fine as the china cup itself.

But there was something amiss. Señora Vasquez's ring finger stuck out at an odd, painful angle, and a fine network of scars was patterned like lace across the back of her hand. Her gaze rising to the lady's face, Isabel found more evidence of violence written on her—a bump on the bridge of her nose, more scars climbing out of her high collar to twine up her neck.

And the marshal, looming over his mother: his hands bore the same scars. She could suddenly see nothing else.

It all clicked into place.

She had seen this innumerable times in her students. It began with a bruise or a cut, which soon enough faded. Then the bruises and cuts began to pile atop one another as the students slowly shrank in on themselves. The mother often bore the same signs.

Always the same thing was whispered about the father: he was a drunkard.

She'd witnessed too often the wages of violence and alcohol in her students—every bruise, every cut, every ashamed flinch sickened her. The innocent should never suffer for the weakness of men.

She guessed that the marshal and his mother had paid those wages personally.

She looked up at him and her breath caught. As he waved away Pilar's offer of tea, his gaze locked onto her in the most unsettling manner, searching her face. He lifted his eyebrow the barest fraction, as if he knew what she was thinking.

She swallowed hard, dropping her gaze.

Of course he couldn't read her thoughts. He'd said as much before.

"Señora Vasquez," Don Enrique said, "allow me to introduce my cousin, Señora Maria Dolores Alvarado Jaramillo de Moreno, and her daughter, Isabel." The marshal's mother nodded to each of them in turn. "Of course, they are both already familiar with your son."

Every head in the room turned to the marshal, and Isabel almost laughed at the discomfort twisting his mouth, the spark of unease lightening his eyes. He hadn't been lying when he said he wasn't sociable. His clothes might be fit for a drawing room, but it was plain to see he did not like being the center of attention in one.

"I had the pleasure of meeting these fine ladies in Cabrillo," the marshal responded, "and when I heard they would be arriving in Los Angeles, I wished to pay my respects." Those eyes drilled into her again. "And to introduce them to my mother."

Her cousins looked as though he'd announced some sort of romantic expectation. How absurd. His interest in her was solely one of obligation.

"How kind of you to check up on us," Isabel said coolly. "Don't worry, Marshal Spencer. I fully intend to do my duty."

"What my daughter means to say," her mother cut in with a sharp look toward her, "is that while testifying in this trial may be difficult, she is eager for the opportunity to put this outlaw in jail."

Difficult. Her stomach twisted at the reminder of the ordeal she still had to face, the real reason why the marshal was here: the trial.

"Indeed," said Señora Vasquez. "Señorita Isabel is most brave to testify at that trial. I think not one girl in ten could have such fortitude."

She sent Isabel a smile so sympathetic, so true, the blood rushed to Isabel's cheeks that she had attempted to be rude to her son.

"Señorita Moreno's bravery would not be found in one in a hundred girls," he agreed.

Now she was truly mortified, heat flaming across her face. She hated this—being embarrassed, being the center of attention, receiving compliments from the marshal—she had to stop it.

"You needn't skulk like Mr. Darcy," she said. "There are plenty of seats for everyone."

She thought he'd be confused by the reference or, worse, annoyed. Instead, the corners of his mouth twitched slightly and he went round the sofa to sit right next to her. Which might have been worse than complimenting her.

"You're quite correct, Señorita," he murmured. "I needn't behave like an arrogant oaf. Especially since I haven't the wealth or social standing for it. But you, however, do have a very fine pair of eyes."

As his own very fine pair of eyes stared into hers, something quite fierce clutched at her insides, stealing her breath.

He was so closed, so reserved, he must have truly meant what he said.

He's only interested in justice, and you are merely a tool in that quest. Fine eyes or not.

"Ladies," he said to her cousins, "would you permit Señorita Moreno and I a few private moments? So that we might discuss the trial?"

The three of them were up in a flash. Her cousins moved away to the piano in the corner, all three crowding onto the bench together.

The marshal angled himself so that he and she formed a cozy *T*, the two of them like half-opened bookends.

"The bail hearing was this morning," he said in an undertone, canting his head toward hers.

She was grateful for his attempt to keep this between them, even as her skin prickled at his nearness. "And?" she prompted.

"No bail. He's to remain in custody."

A quiver of relief shimmied to her very toes. "Oh. Oh, that is good news. Thank you."

His throat bobbed as he swallowed. "I had nothing to do with it. I'm only the bearer."

"The bearer of good news also deserves gratitude."

His expression tilted toward discomfort before he recovered. "I'll bring the prosecutor by tomorrow," he said briskly. "He'll help to prepare you for the trial, which will begin the day after."

That was worse news—no doubt the prosecutor would want a piercingly detailed dissection of her story.

"I'll remain with you throughout the day to ensure your safety," he finished.

She blinked at him in shock. "But you said... He's going to remain in custody." Her chest heaved. "What is there to fear?"

"Nothing," he admitted. "Simply a precaution."

She watched him for a long moment, especially studying his eyes, since those often escaped the hard mask he set his features into. She found nothing but firm assurance.

"I meant what I said. About your eyes."

Such a thing, spoke so steadily—never had a man's words flustered her more.

"Thank you," she said, wishing she had Caterina's trick of graciously accepting compliments. "Shall we move on to discussing some other novel you've never read?"

His eyes gleamed quicksilver. "What novels do you think I haven't read?"

She, who read with a passion each and every day, found her mind curiously blank of even a single title. She seized on the first name to float free. "*Waverley!*"

He closed his eyes in a moment of disgust. "If you mean to turn my taste toward novels, choosing a tasteless romance set in a place I've no desire to visit is not the way to do it." The corner of his mouth ticked up. "A well-read lady like yourself can do better than that."

Was he actually... flirting with her?

She didn't have enough experience to tell, not with him or with men in general. Aside from Joaquin, no man had ever paid her any considered attention. Joaquin preferred practicality to flowery speech, and had rarely complimented her. If asked, she would have said she, too, preferred practicality, yet she found herself unacceptably pleased by the marshal's attention.

"You don't read novels." He opened his mouth and she quieted him with a shake of her finger. She placed that same finger against her lips as she studied him. "You strike me as a philosophical sort of man."

"I have read some philosophy." Now the quicksilver was in his voice as well. It tickled her, that change in his voice.

"Theology as well, I'd imagine," she said.

"You'd imagine correctly."

"I would guess that you've read St. Augustine."

"I confess to that one."

She pressed her lips hard together to keep the smile from them. "And Cardinal Newman?"

"Of course. I thought you were going to make this difficult, Señorita."

She thought back to her first impression of him. "And St. Ignatius?"

His eyes flashed some deep emotion, painful to see, guttering like a candle before being snuffed out. "Yes."

He went to utter stillness, the teasing air doused.

He'd exposed himself, and when she'd touched a sensitive spot, he'd withdrawn. There was a code to the marshal, if one took the trouble to decipher it.

She wasn't one to shy from a difficult task.

Time to change the subject and allow him his retreat. "Tell me, what really brings you here on this visit?" she asked. "You yourself said you don't pay many social calls."

"Am I not allowed to pay social calls?"

She passed a plate to him. He picked up one of the tortas and examined it the way a butterfly collector might inspect an inferior specimen before he set it back uneaten.

"You are clearly very devoted to your duty," she answered, "and your notion of justice."

"You mean to say that I am driven?" She nodded in response. "Indeed I am, but the same could be said of you. You graduated at the top of your class and scored high marks on each one of your certifying exams. You teach at a secondary school in the valley rather than a small rural school close to home."

She flicked a glance over at her cousins before turning back to whisper accusingly, "You've been interrogating my relatives about me."

"No, I asked my mother what your cousins had said about you when she visited." His words were as mild as cream. "They're very proud of your achievements, you know."

Irritation itched beneath her skin, that he should have investigated her before she'd come. He wanted to pry all these details from her, yet gave nothing away of himself.

"I suppose your mother has an infallible memory as well," she said tartly.

He glanced at his mother, his expression going fond as he did. "No," he said softly. "I don't take after my mother."

Which meant he took after his drunken father? But that wasn't correct either. The marshal was no drunkard.

"When will the trial begin?" Best to drive the conversation to the business between them, leave behind this personal nonsense.

"In two days." He was all business again himself. "You'll need fortitude to go through with this. You mustn't wilt the first time you see McCade staring you down across that courtroom."

Then came a pitiless stare that no doubt *was* meant to wilt her.

"I can assure you, Marshal, I do not wilt." Anger prickled on her tongue. "Did I wilt when I shot that outlaw?"

His mouth pursed as he assessed her, making her stomach swoop. "No, you didn't." He leaned toward her, dropped his voice. "I still regret I wasn't there to spare you from his second assault. I think often of it."

He'd been thinking of her all this time—as she'd been thinking of him. The unexpected weight of that made her drop her gaze.

She traced a finger down the bow of the cup handle, cold and smooth. "You shouldn't worry about it. I survived."

She kept her eyes on her cup, bringing her fingertip in an arc back to the top.

"I promised," he said softly.

"You promised I would remain unharmed." Her finger slid slowly along the cold ceramic. "And here I am. Unharmed."

"That wasn't what I meant." Soft. Almost... fervent. He was close enough that his warm breath brushed against her cheek.

Her heart seized as currents danced across her skin. He shouldn't be so near—but she didn't want him to pull away.

"You..." She paused, tried again. "You mustn't even think of it."

His hand slid across his thigh, came close to her own. "I can think of nothing else. If you had been harmed—"

At his sharp inhale, she raised her eyes to his.

They soaked for a moment in that silence filled with his regret and her disquiet, her body remembering all the places he'd touched. Her waist had known his arm, her back, his chest. And her hand, his lips.

A teacup clattered in a saucer, reminding her of exactly where they were and who was watching.

He said a little too loudly, "Are you planning on any sightseeing?"

She swallowed down her agitation, trying not to glance at their mothers, praying they hadn't seen.

"No," she said just as loudly. "I'm afraid there won't be any time, with the trial."

"You don't have to attend every day, you know." This in his more usual tones.

"But I do. After all, that is what I'm here for." To correct the wrong done to herself, Joaquin, her family—the entire town, really. All of them waiting at home, waiting for her to deal justice to McCade.

"Yes." He looked down at his hands. "That is what you are here for." He clenched them into fists, once, twice, the joints blanching with the force of it. A slow exhale, and then he was setting aside his untouched plate as he rose.

"Mother," he called, "perhaps we should take our leave? I'm sure that the Señora and Señorita are quite fatigued from their journey."

"But you only just arrived," protested Don Enrique.

Señora Vasquez sighed, but rose to obey her son.

"Please don't leave on my account," Isabel urged. "I feel quite all right." As agitated as their exchange had made her, she didn't want him to leave. Beneath the eddies of anxiety there was a deep, swift current of calm that hadn't been there before his appearance.

"Yes, please stay," her mother said. "It's so rare to find someone to talk with about the old days."

The marshal remained standing, forcing her face nearly parallel with the ceiling so she could look up at him. "We really should let you rest," he said. "Señora, Señoritas, Don Enrique." He nodded to each in turn, offered a black-clad arm to his mother. "Shall we, Mama?"

"Thank you for your hospitality, Don Enrique," Señora Vasquez said. "It was a pleasure to meet you, Señora Moreno, Señorita Isabel. I certainly hope we have a chance to visit again before you leave Los Angeles." She moved to take her son's arm, and he protectively tucked hers within his own. "Señorita Moreno, I hope to see more of you as well." She slanted a glance up at her son's impassive face. "We both do."

As they took their leave, Isabel was left to ponder exactly what Señora Vasquez could mean by that.

~~~

"She seemed very nice," his mother said as they drove back home.

Sebastian went as still as he could, knowing exactly who she was referring to. "Nice?"

"Well, perhaps not nice," she amended. "Interesting. Or I should say: *You* found her interesting."

He knew where she was going with this, but he had no idea how to stop her. And why should he want to stop her? Isabel was of old Spanish blood, he was of old Spanish blood—what could be more natural and correct than for the two of them to court?

He wished he could drop the reins and fix his cuffs. One was a hair higher than the other, and he could feel the hives breaking out beneath.

"She's a witness in this trial, Mama."

But that hadn't stopped him from complimenting her on her eyes—twice!—and talking amusedly of books with her. Damn it all, he had been *flirting*. He would have shaken his head at his foolishness if his mother weren't watching.

He'd been close enough to Señorita Moreno to catch her scent. At first he'd thought it some kind of citrus, sweetly tart, yet as he'd inched closer, it had turned dense and dark in a way citrus never could. For some reason, it put him in mind of a pomegranate—a perfectly lovely shade of rose on the outside, but when it split open, one found the lush, juicy red hidden within.

"Oh, yes, of course I know that." His mother's tone was unconvincingly bland. "But she's still interesting."

His hands tightened on the reins, the leather biting deep.

Interesting. His mother was correct in that. Interesting. Intelligent. Señorita Moreno wasn't the least intimidated by him. And the way her finger had slid along the handle of her tea cup...

He summoned his control once more. Señorita Moreno might be *interesting*—both to him and his mother—but he couldn't permit *interesting* to expand further into something like affection.

The contagion he'd inherited from his father meant he could never marry—and would never pass it on to his children.

But he couldn't say that to his mother. She thought him wholly reformed, a complete man again. He couldn't shatter her illusion.

"She is interesting," he allowed. "She's also returning home in a few days."

"They don't have mail service in the mountains? How extraordinary."

Amusement tickled him. When her persistence was so charming, it was hard to be annoyed.

"I will protect her while she's here," he said, pulling the team into a right turn, "and when she leaves, that will be the end of it. Find a lady closer to home, Mama."

Preferably one who wasn't likely to stumble onto the truth of him. When Señorita Moreno had mentioned St Ignatius, a cold horror had crept along his skin. He'd done his best to mask his reaction.

After all, many people practiced the saint's spiritual exercises. It wasn't anything remarkable.

He darted a glance over to his mother. Her expression was resigned, as if she knew her machinations were for naught but she still had to try.

Lord, he wished he could be a better son to her, to give her the daughter-in-law and grandchildren she deserved. But his state now—alone, contained, controlled—was the best he could achieve.

Better was not in the cards for him.

"Oh, Sebastian," she said with a sigh. "I'm running out of ladies here."

"You'll simply have to keep looking then," he said lightly. *And put Isabel Moreno out of your mind.*

Which was exactly what he himself had been desperately trying to do. He shuddered to think what his dreams tonight would be like after seeing her today.

His other cuff began to irritate him, a burning prickling setting up under the skin of his wrist.

"I only want you to be happy," his mother said. She looked up at him and the naked pleading on her face opened a fissure in his chest. "Are you happy?"

I cannot allow myself such a thing.

He turned the question to her. "Are you happy?"

They never spoke of the old days. Of life under his father's rule. Of Sebastian's madness after his death.

Did she think of them as constantly as he did? He doubted it—her air of charm, of happiness, would not have been possible if she did.

She'd earned the right to forget those years, to forge contentment from her life.

"My happiness would be complete," she answered, "if you were happy."

"I am content." He couldn't lie, not even to soothe her.

His mother's steady gaze made him itch with exposure. "You might be happy with Señorita Moreno," she said. "If you tried. You must admit, you paid her considered attention. Which she repaid."

Again, the lies wouldn't come. "I am a most... particular kind of man. Few ladies would be happy to accommodate such things for a lifetime."

Señorita Moreno struck him as having her own brand of particulars. The two of them might be drawn to one another, but he didn't think they would make each other *happy*. She struck him as too exacting, too prickly to be satisfied with mere happiness. And he could not offer her more of himself than he already had.

"You still deserve happiness," his mother insisted.

Her words fell harder than any of his father's blows ever had, his bones aching with a thousand remembered hurts.

He tightened his hands on the reins and let her comment slip past him.

"Oh, Sebastian," she sighed at his continuing silence.

But the despondency in her voice wasn't enough to crack his reserve, to change his mind about Señorita Moreno and her *interesting* character.

His mother might believe he deserved happiness—but he knew better.

CHAPTER TEN

THE PROSECUTOR WAS NOT INSPIRING confidence in Isabel.

A wisp of a man, with his pink scalp peeping through the patches in his colorless hair, tufts of which waved in the breeze coming from the open window—no, Mr. Halstead did not cut a confident figure. As he'd searched through his papers—for well over five minutes now; she'd timed it—his bleary eyes watered as if he were about to have a sneezing fit.

She couldn't imagine this man convincing a jury of anything.

"Found it," he muttered to his briefcase, pulling a paper from the mess.

Marshal Spencer watched with his usual lack of affect. He'd brought the prosecutor here, introduced them, then gone to sit in the corner and watch.

He didn't appear annoyed at the time it took for the man to hunt down that paper. He left all the annoyance to her.

"The marshal's report," the prosecutor explained, with a nod toward the man himself. "Have you read this, Miss Moreno?"

She'd only been the one to give him the story written in it. "Of course."

"Good, good. This report covers most of the questions I'll have for you in the courtroom." He shoved the paper back into the case. "Do you have any questions for me?"

There was an air of dismissal about him—he clearly wanted her to say no, and then he'd wish her a good day.

"I don't understand," she said. "Shouldn't you be preparing me for the trial?"

His bleary eyes sharpened. "Didn't you tell the marshal the truth?"

"Of course." If she had lied, why would she ever admit it? Why wouldn't she simply go on lying?

This was the man meant to prosecute the case? Yes, definitely uninspiring.

Mr. Halstead's smile was relieved. "Then you're prepared."

"What of the cross examination?"

His smile fell. "I can't predict what the other lawyer might ask. Just be honest and you should be fine."

There was more to testifying than that—she'd no experience with a courtroom and even she knew that. This prosecutor was expecting her to fail—he was even preparing her to do so!

She caught Marshal Spencer's movement from the corner of her eye—a slight flick of his hand, no more.

But enough to tell her that the lawyer's words had agitated him.

"I am always honest, Mr. Halstead." She let her tone imply that he might not be.

He was unmoved. "Excellent." He snapped his briefcase shut. "I'll see you tomorrow then."

By the time the maid escorted Mr. Halstead to the front door, Isabel was in a towering rage, pacing the length of the parlor.

"That couldn't possibly be the correct way to prepare a witness for a trial," she fumed.

Marshal Spencer reached for a book on the table next to him, thumbing through it. "I'm not a lawyer," he said mildly.

She slowed her steps, her anger beginning to burn out. There was no point in this display of temper. It certainly wasn't helping her to prepare.

How *was* she to prepare?

She'd told Joaquin that she had the truth on her side, but it seemed a poor shield in the face of the lawyer's clear disinterest. If this was the man who was supposed to be *helping* her...

Victory would be much more difficult than she'd thought.

She sank to the sofa and contemplated her hands. She mustn't admit defeat before she'd taken the field. These lawyers would be crafty and cunning, but her intellect was second to none. And she spoke the truth. She had to believe that counted for something.

She took up a newspaper, intending to occupy her mind with something other than her situation. She flipped to the social calendar first—a concert at a park, a lecture at the library from a famed naturalist, a meeting of the local Shakespearean society discussing *Julius Caesar*. She'd have been delighted to attend any one of those events.

After the trial. She'd find time for one of them after the trial, after she was victorious.

She came to the end of the social calendar and sighed. A meeting of the Ladies' Temperance Union. It would be a large meeting of ladies—certainly more than three women gathered in the family parlor—all impassioned, all devoted to halting the scourge of liquor.

It would have been wondrous.

She lowered the paper, no longer interested in tormenting herself with events she couldn't attend, and looked over at the marshal.

He was still engrossed in his book, in the exact same position as when she'd taken up the newspaper.

"Is that interesting?" she asked.

"Not particularly," he responded. "It's a novel, and you know how I feel about those."

She almost smiled. Perhaps she didn't need to regret being stuck in the house—she could needle him instead. "Shall I read to you from the paper?"

"If you like." He didn't put down the book.

She looked over the front page of the *Herald*. "Here's an interesting piece on Judge Bannister." Spoken as if she had no particular interest at all in the man. "Much better than the last one he was quoted in—that was the 'greaser menace' story, which you must have seen."

A flicker of his jaw was his only response.

"In this article," she went on, keeping her tone indifferent, "he speaks very convincingly of the need to keep the city water supply under municipal control. 'Water must not be made scarce—it is required for the growth of the city and it must be provided cheaply for those too poor to pay the exorbitant rates Mr. McCade would charge.' I must agree with him there."

He dropped the book. "I don't want to hear that story."

Oh ho ho, a hint of irritation there. She set aside the *Herald*, picked up the *Star*. And swallowed hard at the first story. "Well, there's this one," she said stiffly. "It tells of how Joaquin and I—my *lover*, they don't use anything so genteel as fiancé—planned to rob and murder Mr. McCade." She didn't want to go on—the joke had lost its allure—but she kept reading out of sheer perversity. "Apparently the entire town was in on the scheme. I am an adventuress, a Jezebel, no better than the rest of my race—"

He pulled the newspaper from her hands, the newsprint grittier than sandpaper as it slipped from her grip. "I don't want to hear that either."

His expression was his usual impassive one as he loomed over her—but his eyes burned.

"How long have the papers been running such stories?" she demanded.

"Since I arrived back with McCade. The *Star* has always been partial to Edwin McCade's politics and agendas." He let the paper drop to the floor.

"So all of Los Angeles has been reading such lies about me?" She'd thought the truth would save her—but the papers were spinning their own version of the truth. And serving it to the entire city.

"Yes." The marshal didn't move to reassure or distract her—he simply let her absorb that, and she was grateful for it.

She stared at the paper for long moments. She'd never thought they could use the newspapers against her. There was only one opportunity for her to strike back—on the witness stand.

"You'll have to help me prepare," she said finally. "For the trial."

He straightened. "I told you before, I'm not a lawyer."

"But you interrogate people."

"That's different. Lawyers manipulate emotions—of the witnesses and the jury. I merely extract the information I need."

"*Extract.* That's what a dentist does with a rotten tooth." She wouldn't let him unsettle her with such macabre terms.

"Many of the people I track are quite rotten."

She'd no doubt of that; certainly McCade was corrupted to his very core. "Then treat me like one of them." She leaned forward, let her voice tilt toward imploring. "Treat it like one of your worst interrogations. So I can be at least a little prepared."

He sighed, then rose and grabbed a chair, setting it in the center of the room. He gestured for her to come over to him. He indicated that she should sit in the chair, not quite moving quickly enough out of her way, so that his pant leg brushed against her skirts, pressing her petticoats against the length of her legs. A caress that wasn't a caress, which made her shiver.

An accident, no more.

She sat and watched him pace before her.

"A trial such as this, with a witness unable to testify and the tangled politics involved—I've never witnessed such a thing," he warned. "I don't know what the defense attorney might ask—or what the judge will allow him to ask. You can't count on Halstead to object if the defense attorney asks something he shouldn't."

"What will they ask about? Besides what happened during the attack?" Despite what the newspapers had printed, she'd lived an unobjectionable life.

"How you met Sheriff Obregon," he ticked off, "what your plans were for marrying, what happened at the fight at the dance, how Obregon carried out his duties, what role your family played in all this..." He took a deep breath. "Any number of things."

"They'll ask about my family?" There wouldn't ask about her mother, no way that they would know...

"What might the rest of your family not want brought up in court?" He was suddenly tense. He stopped pacing, set his hand upon his thigh. The light trailed across the scars there as he flexed his hand.

"It just seems odd they would ask about my family," she said as carelessly as she dared. "They had nothing to do with any of this."

"Lawyers don't always care about the straight progression of facts. They'll meander if it means they'll win the jury over." He hesitated. "It might help some if you were less..."

"Less what?" she demanded.

"Less strident." Was that actually a hint of color in his cheeks? "More... yielding."

"You mean put on a simper and flutter my eyelashes?" Something that felt remarkably close to betrayal turned in her stomach. "Tell the truth, but lie about my basic nature as I do?"

He tugged at his cuffs, adjusted his collar. "Juries tend to like people they can pity. With your demeanor, it's difficult to pity you."

"Good. I don't want anyone's pity."

But his words placed a worm inside her skull, turning and turning with what he'd said. She thought of Joaquin, lying there in his bed, grievously wounded, waiting for her to bring him news of the trial.

She so wanted it to be good news.

What did it matter if she put on a show for the jury? If she played the fluttering, helpless female for once? If they won the case—if McCade was punished—wouldn't that justify some playacting on the witness stand?

There was one small problem: She'd never in her life attempted to simper or flutter or any of that nonsense.

"I know you don't want pity," he was saying, "but perhaps think on what I've said."

She would. She had a brief thought of practicing her simpers with him—but that would go over about as well as this courtroom playacting had.

Besides, she didn't want to simper for him. She wanted to be her usual reserved, private, prickly self. And sharpen her tongue on him as often as she liked, while he watched her with those quicksilver eyes...

He'd stopped speaking and was staring intently at her. She had the strangest thought that he was imagining her sharpening her tongue on him.

Nonsense. He was merely waiting for her to reply.

"I shall think on it, thank you," she said briskly. "I find it hard to believe this is anything like one of your worst interrogations. What do you do when you want to break a man? Shove a kitten in his lap?"

The marshal actually allowed his lips to twitch. "I don't *want* to interrogate you."

"It's only playacting. Exactly what you wish me to do on the stand."

"When I interrogate someone, I'm not pretending. To pretend to inflict hurt upon you"—he adjusted his collar again—"is beyond my abilities."

She studied him as he began to pull at his cuffs, staring quite intently at them as he did. Her own wrists began to itch.

"You're right," she said slowly, "you don't make a very good lawyer. This was a foolish idea of mine. I won't trouble you further about it."

She rose, lifted the chair—and froze when his hand settled over hers.

"I can carry it," he said gently.

She held on to the chair for a moment too long, the feel of his hand over hers something she didn't want to give up.

But of course she must.

She released the chair and stalked back to the sofa, picking up a newspaper to hide behind.

"You'll do just fine during the trial," he called after her. "There's no need for nerves."

She snapped off the couch, her temper flaring. Before, he'd said that she must be flattering, false—and now he said she'd do just fine?

She didn't want this counterfeit assurance from him—she'd prefer his impassivity.

"I know that," she retorted. "I know that it's all up to me, that I mustn't be nervous or I might fail. I know all that." She clenched her fists, letting her feet carry her back and forth.

His look was long and considering, his hands heavy on the chair back. "You are a magnificently difficult woman, Señorita Moreno."

A laugh burst from her throat, just the one. "You give the most unusual compliments, Marshal Spencer."

"You deserve the most unusual compliments."

Did he really mean to compliment her or was he only trying to calm her? After all, a man might speak sweet nothings to even a horse to calm it.

But it had worked—she wanted to sink down on that chair he was holding, pull him down next to her, to feel the solid bulk of him against her side. Not that the two of them would fit on that chair. She'd have to sit on his lap...

His eyes caught hers and held—and she knew he meant it as a compliment. The seconds stretched into minutes as her heart thrummed slowly, echoing in her ears until there was only his gaze and the sound of her heart between them.

Just as she was ready to move toward him, to reach for him, he blinked.

They both looked away, trying to make space for what had happened. She laced her hands together and squeezed, willing her composure to return. Somehow his presence turned her temper mercurial. It was the strangest thing.

He cleared his throat. "My mother enjoyed meeting you yesterday. And your mother as well."

She sank onto the sofa, her anticipation ebbing. "My mother enjoyed it too. It was very kind of you to bring her. I know you dislike social occasions."

"It was no difficulty."

"It's clear you're very protective of her." She meant it as a compliment, but his eyes flickered the barest fraction and she knew she'd hit a soft spot. Again.

"What son isn't protective of his mother?" He drew it out as if to put an edge on it. One to warn her away.

He'd have to do better than that to unsettle her. "Of course," she allowed. "Yet you also claim to be unsentimental."

"Shouldn't a man care for his mother in her elder years?"

"Yes. But it's more than that, and I think you know it." She wouldn't allow him to hide his affection for his mother behind aloofness—he could confess something to *her* for once.

He didn't answer, only stared her down. She waited him out, a trick she'd learned from him.

Eventually he sighed and she swore she heard the cracking of his reserve in it. "I don't know why you think you are entitled to the information"—his mouth went blade-flat—"or why I am even telling you, but yes, I am exceptionally protective of my mother. Nothing else in this world commands that same force of feeling. I have seen nothing yet in this life that deserves it, except her."

Something sharp twisted in her chest. "She deserves it because of your father? Because of how he treated the two of you?"

She couldn't quite believe she'd done that, but she couldn't snatch it back.

His face sagged, a wash of pale green coming across it, and nausea rose sympathetically in her own stomach.

"What do you know about him?" His voice was deep, harsh, and he was rising then, his length unwinding over her—the brute had returned.

"I—" She licked at her lips. "I don't know anything, really." Her cousins' gossip of yesterday seemed obscene in light of his reaction. "You and your mother—you both have scars. I've seen that before... in my students." She took a shaky breath, wanting to flee—both from him and to him.

He closed his eyes, and she could see him reaching for that reserve of his, shrugging his shoulders into the mantle of it.

"Of course," he murmured. "Of course you would see it." His eyes opened, and for half a moment she feared he might sway—but that was ridiculous. He was always still and strong and uncaring, wasn't he?

"She deserves this... this regard," he said roughly, "because she is good and kind and true. But most especially because of my father. A lady as great as she deserved so much better."

Melancholy flowed through her, making her seasick with the roll of it, knowing that whatever his father had done to make him this way, it must have been terrible.

"Didn't you deserve better, as well?"

His mouth twisted. "Whatever I've received in this life, it's been more than I deserved." She wanted to protest at the bitterness there, but he kept on. "So now you have my secret."

Yes, she did. But she'd never dreamed that prying a confidence from him would be so painful. For both of them.

"You have many secrets of mine," she pointed out. "You know that I didn't love Joaquin, and I've never told anyone else as many details of the attack."

He walked over to the window, giving her only his back to study. "It's a strange sort of intimacy that's been forced upon us, isn't it?" He linked his fingers behind him, clamping them together.

"I am sorry." She'd hurt him with her probing—the agitation in his fingers proved that. "This wasn't my choice; none of it was."

He crossed to her then, capturing one of her hands within both of his. They were so large, so encompassing. And so gentle as well.

"You misunderstand me. I esteem you greatly, perhaps second only to my mother." The flash of his smile was brief enough for her to have imagined it. "I understand that you wish to see only the back of me. To have no further reminders of what happened. To forget that you were ever humbled and vulnerable. But I wish only to see you safe." His fingers flexed, drawing her hand closer into the embrace of his. "I know that my presence distresses you, but it's only for a little while longer."

She blinked dazedly, that smile still flashing behind her eyelids. "It doesn't distress me," she got out. "Your presence."

"You certainly give that impression."

"I am frustrated," she confessed. "And angry. I do wish to leave all this behind. You, unfortunately, are the easiest target for my ill feelings."

But she didn't feel ill just now, with her hand in his and his gaze so intent on hers.

She felt unsettled, peculiar, but not distressed.

"I'm glad to hear it. I'm always happy to be a target for such a worthy lady."

He released her hand and she clasped hers together, trying to hold in the sensation of his skin on hers.

He did nothing so foolishly sentimental, reaching instead for his pocket watch. "Your family ought to be back soon."

If she needed more evidence that he was unaffected by what had transpired, it was there in his prosaic tone.

The sounds of a carriage came from the front of the house, both of them looking toward it.

"That must be them," she said.

"Shall we go see?" It sounded as if he wanted something to occupy him. Something other than sparring with her.

"Yes, let's." She could use a moment away from the strange tension in this room herself.

They went side by side through the hall, their shoulders almost brushing in the small passage. Yet she didn't feel crowded by him. Rather, he took up exactly the right amount of space—the space right next to her. Foolish, such thoughts. But they wouldn't be chased away.

When they opened the door, there was no carriage out front. She stepped just outside the door, looking about. "I suppose it wasn't them."

He came out as well, maneuvering himself so that he was between her and the street. "No, it wasn't. We'll have to head back inside."

She took a step backward, the better to turn toward the house, but his expression arrested her. It was expectant, as if he were waiting for her to declare something. Or waiting for himself to come to some conclusion.

She was puzzling over this so deeply it took a moment for her senses to register the first gunshot.

CHAPTER ELEVEN

SEBASTIAN ACTED ENTIRELY ON IMPULSE, without the barest moment of conscious thought.

Before the second shot was fired, he had her on the ground, safely pinned beneath him. Something strong moved within him as the second bullet whistled overhead. The thing traveled with the force of an ocean wave, but he pushed it away before he could give it a name. Now was not the time to lose control of himself.

The sounds of the others on the street running for cover were dim to his ears. His focus was solely on her, her limbs tangled with his, her chest moving beneath him, the wash of her breath into his neck. After the space of ten breaths without any more gunfire, he slowly raised his head to see her face.

Her expression was stiff as a mask, her breathing unnaturally regular, and deep within her eyes he saw a flicker of panic. But only a flicker.

He had to admire her resolve. Given what she'd been through, she had more cause than most to fall apart—but she never allowed those lesser emotions through.

If he were a better man, he might let that admiration bloom into something deeper, something like...

He didn't dare finish that thought. She was a witness, and someone had just tried to kill her. That was all that mattered now—that and his duty to her.

Her silence was an implicit affirmation of her trust in him. Lord, but he prayed he could live up to that trust, that he would see her safely through this, unlike the last time she'd been in danger.

Her hair brushed against his cheek as he leaned into her ear. "When I let you up, duck your head and run into the house. As fast as you can."

She gave a quick nod and tensed beneath him as she prepared to run. He didn't bother telling her to keep away from the windows. She was quick enough to know that.

He levered himself off her, twisting to face the street, trying to glimpse the gunman as he did.

Señorita Moreno was up and in the house quick as a flash, obeying him to the letter. He sighed as the weight of her safety lifted from him.

Using the brick gatepost for cover, he scanned the street carefully, making pass after pass with narrowed eyes, looking for anything suspicious.

Only rattled pedestrians and spooked horses. Nothing sinister. Nothing that could have harmed her.

"What was that?" a heavyset man called to him, no doubt thinking the badge on Sebastian's chest meant he had some answers.

"Gunshots," he answered. "Did anyone see who fired?"

He searched the faces turned to him, looking for any flicker of guilt.

No one replied.

Stupid of him, to linger with her on the doorstep like a lovesick suitor. Stupid, stupid, stupid.

One last searching look, and then he was turning back to Don Enrique's house.

He ought to be thinking of going to the police or of heading out to search for the gunman. But all his mind could summon was that flicker of panic in her eyes. The image drove him into the house in search of her, in search of reassurance.

He found her in the parlor, pacing in front of the hearth.

At the sight of her arms wrapped so tightly about her, that tidal wave of sensation hit him once again, almost driving him to his knees. He stumbled forward under it and did something he hadn't done in ages—he caught her up in his arms.

Her head nestled just under his chin, her breath sending eddies of heat washing along his neck. She placed her hands between them, set against his chest, on either side of his heart. Strange to hold a woman again after all this time, to wrap his arms around another being simply for the physical pleasure of it.

No, not pleasure. This wasn't like any embrace he'd shared with a woman before. This was for comfort, re-assurance.

He allowed himself to relax. She was safe, nestled here with him. The sensation rose again, and this time he allowed it, the first time he'd *felt* something without trying to suppress it in over thirteen years. The emotion surged fast and sharp as a flood, filling him up to his throat. He couldn't name it, but namelessness didn't prevent it from existing.

After a few moments tucked into him like that, she lifted her head, her eyes clear, a question curled within them.

If he were any other man, this would be the moment when he kissed her.

But no matter how grateful he was she was safe, no matter how he trusted her with some of the secrets of his past, no matter how he might *smile* at her, he must not kiss her.

He could only allow himself one small indulgence.

Lifting a hand to her jaw, he caressed the line of it, the softness of her cheeks. How long had it been since he'd touched a woman like this? Thirteen years now, when he'd been a stupid, lost boy of seventeen. Before he'd gone on the path to repentance.

He'd forgotten how yielding a woman's skin could be, how her breath could caress as it moved over his hand. Or perhaps he'd never truly experienced anything quite so exquisite as this in his youth.

Because it was exquisite, her fine dark eyes following his, her breath going deeper, slower, with each sweep of his hand. And her hands, still framing his heart as it began to speed at her touch.

Because it was exquisite, he knew he could never go further than this. This here was the boundary of what could be between them, this far and no further. Exquisite things were delicate, easily damaged.

He was very good at damaging things.

Reluctantly he pulled away, even as his heart thudded in protest. He took a deep breath, trying to school himself back to his usual state.

"Are you all right?" he asked.

She set a hand to her hair, then to her cheek. "Yes."

Her steady regard was a hard rap to his aching conscience. His failures today would take some time to put into the notebooks tonight.

"Pack your bags," he said.

"Pardon?" She hadn't been expecting that.

"Someone may or may not be trying to kill you." She flinched, but kept her chin high. "Pack your bags," he repeated. "It's not safe for you here, so you're coming home with me."

She'd be safest there, under his roof, where he could always watch her. Night and day.

"Right now?" she asked.

"Yes. I'll send for your mother later, when she returns."

She gasped. "You don't think my mother is in danger?"

"I don't know." He couldn't lie and say no, even to spare her pain.

She raised a hand to her mouth, her fingers trembling. "But... but McCade is in jail. Who else would have done it?"

His gut twisted at the thought of who might have sent the gunman. "Perhaps his father," he admitted. If one of the most powerful men in Los Angeles wanted her dead... "I want you where no one will find you."

She pondered that for a moment, her eyes wide. She tapped her fingers against her lips, slowly, one, two, three. Four.

"Yes, well, I suppose I should go to your house." She spoke through her fingers. "So that my cousins are out of danger."

She let her hand fall, all fierceness gone from her stance. He missed that fierceness with a deep ache.

"You won't be captive," he assured her. "And I have a very fine library."

She would be delighted by that. She might even break into one of her rare smiles.

"You don't read novels." A tremor shook the words, even as she pushed for levelness. "How fine could it be?"

"Well, now you can correct my taste in reading."

His effort was rewarded by the tiniest of smiles from her. "Let me fetch my things, then."

As she left the room, the full weight of what he'd done crashed upon him.

He was taking her into his house. She would eat with him, would sleep near him, would always be within reach.

He didn't know if he could stop himself from reaching for her if she were always near.

But he had to keep her safe. Not only as part of his duties, but also for himself. Some part of him, a part he'd thought long dead, would wither if she were not in this world.

Having her under his roof might be the greatest trial of his life.

~~~

So this was where the marshal lived.

Isabel took in the stately parlor, which matched the house's imposing exterior. The furnishings were far from ornate—sparse even—yet of the most luxurious quality. The entire effect was one of calm, clearly intended to produce a contemplative state.

Except for the flowers.

An arrangement sat next to the sofa, and what an arrangement it was: the roses in it practically erupted, reaching higher than her head and spreading wider than both her arms outstretched. It was a wild abandonment, a burst of floral chaos in this Spartan room.

The flowers must have been his mother's addition.

The marshal paced in front of the fireplace, his feet moving in time with the ticking of the clock on the mantel. He'd been agitated since the shooting, although she wasn't certain if it was because of the gunfire or because he had embraced her.

Both events had certainly left their impression upon her. The sensation of his hand lingered on her jaw, a heavy tingling that refused to be rubbed away.

When she'd heard the shot, the paralytic fear came hard and fast upon her, until she was only a stuttering heartbeat and ragged breath. But then the marshal's arms were around her, his heart under her palms—the weight of him over her as he shielded her with himself...

The marshal had been there this time. He'd not failed her.

"Would you like to sit down?" she asked.

He raised his head and lightning sparked from his eyes. He didn't answer, merely turned and set to pacing again, snagging her heart in the process and pulling it painfully against her ribs.

"The trial begins tomorrow," he said suddenly. "Until it ends, you will remain in this house"—he pointed to the floor between his feet—"except for when you're in court. You mustn't even go to the door."

"I know." He needn't be so stern. She was happy enough to remain in this cage, secure from any more attempts on her life. And as far as cages went, this one was impressively gilded.

She studied the pictures on the walls. A few were photographs of the marshal and his mother, but the largest was a painting of Señora Vasquez as a young lady. Her smile was shy, her eyes downcast, almost as if she were painfully embarrassed to be subjected to the viewer's gaze.

A girl with eyes like that would never have stood a chance against a violent drunk.

There were no pictures of his father, and the earliest ones of Sebastian were as a young man, already guarded and tense. Whatever had happened to make him as he was must have occurred when he was no more than twenty.

"It's a good likeness, isn't it?" he asked. He'd followed her gaze to a photograph of him, looking younger and grimmer.

"It's a photograph. It's meant to be a good likeness," she said. For comparison, she looked him up and down, taking in his suit, his black hair and gray eyes. If it weren't for the warm tones of his skin, he would be as colorless as that piece of paper on the wall. "But no, it doesn't truly capture you."

He tilted his head, as if changing the angle of his gaze might change the contents of the photograph. "I suppose a camera can't capture a person's interior."

She stilled at the second reference he'd made to his interior.

"What should it have shown?" she asked carefully.

He didn't answer, at least not directly. "There are many men in this world who claim to be models of justice and morality, yet their private actions betray them for what they truly are."

"You can't possibly be describing yourself."

"No, but what of the opposite?" He gestured toward the picture. "A man who struggles with the evil inside himself, and strives for the good. Does the darkness of his interior negate the good he accomplishes in the world?"

Was that how he saw himself? As rotten inside? But why? Did such a view explain his unnatural reserve?

"Aren't most of us struggling against our own sinful natures?" She'd certainly spent her fair share of time in confession.

He turned to her, holding her gaze for a moment, hands tight against his thighs. "Some of us struggle more than most."

He looked so isolated, so solitary—her heart strained at the sight.

"I don't believe you have a sinful nature." As comfort, it was a poor effort, but she didn't dare reach out to touch him.

"How can you say that? You saw what I did to McCade when he insulted you."

Oh, she remembered that shocking burst of violence, all the more surprising given how contained he usually was.

"Why did you do that?" she asked. "He wasn't resisting."

He released a harsh breath. "I wasn't there to stop him when he seized you. Then he insulted you. Threatened you."

He'd done it for her. "You were protecting me," she said wonderingly. "Defending me."

His gaze caught hers as every line of him went tight, his suit straining with it. Something shifted between them, something dark and feral. Anticipation began to drip between them, coating her skin and lungs with every inhale.

"You think I'm protecting you?" he asked harshly.

"You are." Her voice was as breathless as his was harsh.

He took a heavy step toward her, and her ears thrilled to the solid beat of his heel against the floor. "You thought I was defending you?"

"You were."

Another step toward her. Another thrill dancing along her nerve ends.

One more step and they would touch.

"You don't believe I'm evil?" he asked.

She lifted her face to him. "No, I don't."

He took that last step, his chest barely touching hers, as faint as the brush of fog against her skin. She saw the scars crossing his face and her belly clenched.

She knew then she would kiss him, because she wanted to comfort him, to remind him that he was not alone, to tell him that he wasn't evil.

But most of all, because she wanted to, with an urge that pained her with every unsteady heartbeat.

"Do you really believe that?" he asked.

Before she could say yes or no, or even think *yes* or *no*, his hand came around the back of her head, anchoring her in place before his lips caught hers.

She was no shrinking virgin—she and Joaquin had ensured that they would be entirely compatible, including in intimate matters.

But this kiss was nothing like any she'd shared with her former fiancé.

From the first, his lips forced hers open, his tongue entering her mouth without hesitation or apology. She held still under the onslaught, shocked temporarily into submission.

The taste of him filled her mouth as his tongue caressed the deepest recesses, a taste surprisingly warm and penetrating for a man so cold and reserved. The scent of his skin was dense, musky, the thin hint of soap clinging to it vainly attempting to mask it.

She let the sensation of his nearness, his need, wash over her for a moment, savoring the heavy drag of his hand at her nape.

Then she acted.

She slid a hand around his neck, trying to tangle her fingers in the hair at his nape, but it was too short to find purchase. She raised her other hand to his shoulder, attempting to clutch at his jacket, but there was nothing on him for her to cling to, nothing to grab at but pure muscle and sinew.

So much muscle and sinew. She greedily ran her hands along his upper arms, his shoulders, his upper back, as he strained to get closer to her.

To invade her.

Her knees went weak at the thought, because she just might let him.

She pulled him as near as her strength allowed, her tongue slipping into his mouth to taste and tangle with his. His hand on her neck tightened, and the kiss became a struggle. Not for dominion of one over the other, but rather against their own physical limits, a climb to transcend the realities of lips and hands and bodies and somehow merge together.

He was the first to break away, those gray eyes alight as they'd never been before. She bit back a groan at the loss of his mouth, wanting more, again, but knowing it wouldn't happen. He was sure to slam down that reserve of his.

She slid a hand down his chest and felt the hammering of his heart under her palm. She smiled, her lips raw.

He *did* experience intense emotions. And she could make him do so.

But the power was not all hers. Even now the clasp of her corset was tight against her breasts, her thighs pressed together against the ache between them.

He'd plucked her, and still she hummed.

A look of perfect horror crossed his face, eyes and mouth widening with it. "I never—"

She stopped him right there—she couldn't bear to hear him apologize. Not for that kiss.

"You said that I was safe from any improprieties," she teased.

She thought his eyes would gleam at that. Or he might even smile.

But he did something extraordinary.

He laughed.

Unlike his voice, it was neither mellow nor pleasant; it was the word *rusty* reborn as a laugh. For all that it was as harmonious as metal against metal, she liked it. Wanted to hear it again.

He grew serious after a moment. "I should not have done that. Not to you."

She stiffened. "Why? Because of the attack? McCade didn't claim ownership of me or ruin me. My affection is still my own to bestow."

He smoothed his face back to its usual impassiveness. "No, not because of that. But because *I* have no affection to bestow."

Ice crept under her skin. How could he kiss her so passionately and then say something so... cruel?

"You must be exhausted," he went on. "You should lie down and rest."

She was being dismissed then.

"Tomorrow will be just as taxing," he said, "and you'll need all your strength."

Tomorrow.

Her heart kicked sickeningly. She wasn't ready—after today, her nerves were sharp and thin, rending her reserve to ribbons. The courtroom, the lawyers... *McCade...*

He was correct: she would need strength.

She pulled her own reserve about her, straightening away from him.

"If you could show me to my room?" As haughtily as her namesake, a woman who'd conquered all of Spain.

"I'll call one of the maids." He went for the door almost eagerly.

One of the maids. Of course, he would have more than one maid. A house like this would require such a thing. And a housekeeper, too.

And he'd neatly avoided having to escort her to her room.

Her head began to throb again.

CHAPTER TWELVE

ISABEL WONDERED ANEW AT HOW Señora Vasquez had come by her openhearted, sweet nature. Especially given how uncaring her son was.

Her mother had arrived that afternoon, as close to fretful as Isabel had ever seen. Señora Vasquez had taken pains to set them both at ease and was continuing to do so over dinner.

That shy girl in the painting hadn't been obliterated by her husband—she'd blossomed instead.

Her son, on the other hand, was clearly ill at ease. He'd actually *fidgeted* over dinner: shifting in his seat, grabbing his utensils only to set them back, never allowing a single bite to pass his lips, and tapping his fingers impatiently on the table.

His mother watched all this with a slight smile, which she would occasionally send Isabel's way. As if they were conspirators in something.

Isabel would have returned it out of sheer politeness—not out of any sense of collusion—only she didn't, because she was as twitchy inside as the marshal was on the outside. His every unnecessary motion, each adjustment he made to the silverware or his cuffs, was like the flick of a whip across her nerve endings.

She'd never realized how calming his demeanor was to her until he'd lost it.

"Will you be escorting the ladies to the trial tomorrow?" his mother was asking him.

"I won't be going," Isabel's mother said.

The tumble of Señora Moreno's words snapped Marshal Spencer into alertness.

"No?" He let that sit, let the silence stretch after.

He was playing the marshal again, only with her mother this time.

Isabel's simmering anxiety threatened to boil over. Would he truly interrogate her mother at the table? Her mother would never confess her identity, no matter what he might do—but Isabel feared what would come next anyway.

Señora Vasquez darted an uncertain gaze from her son to Isabel's mother and back again. "If Señora Moreno doesn't wish to go to the courthouse," she said, "then she can spend the day with me."

Clearly an attempt to diffuse the situation. Would her son heed her unspoken admonition?

Isabel watched him closely, his eyes narrow, his shoulders tense. His mouth pursed, as though he meant to question her mother further.

But then his gaze slid toward his mother, touched on her for a long moment—and he relaxed once more.

"As you like, Mother," he said, with no hint of his earlier tautness.

His mother's smile was too wide, too relieved. As if she'd been more alarmed by the marshal's sudden tension than she'd let on. "Wonderful," she announced. "The Señora and I can visit the Jaramillos again—and the citrus exhibition, we must see that. We should show her something of the city while she's here."

Isabel wouldn't see anything of the city. At least nothing outside of the journey between here and the courthouse. What a lowering thought.

Señora Moreno's aspect of severe diffidence had never slipped, and she continued to wear it as she answered, "As long as we return before Isabel does."

"But Sebastian will be with her the entire time," his mother offered.

Her tone was so blandly innocent, it made Isabel's cheeks prickle with heat. Surely she couldn't be thinking of matchmaking?

What would it be like to be married to him? She'd be the mistress of this house, with two maids of her own and as many rose bushes as would fit in the yard.

She'd be the mistress of him, with his fiery kisses and icy reserve.

She glanced over at the marshal, wondering if he suspected as well. He didn't smile—of course he wouldn't—but he did flick his eyes heavenward.

She dropped her gaze to her plate and bit her lip to stifle a wild giggle at his unexpected humor. Now they were the ones in a conspiracy.

A strange conspiracy—his every tiny movement, whether of agitation or amusement, sparked a heightened response from her.

He plucked her, and she hummed.

Clearing the laughter from her throat, she said, "Truly, Mother, I'll be fine on my own. No doubt the marshal has business to attend to, and I'll... I'll spend the remainder of the day reading." She slanted him a glance. "The marshal did promise to allow me to correct his taste in novels."

"But, Sebastian," his mother said, sweetly chiding, "you don't care for novels."

"The Señorita means to change that," he said.

His fingers left his knife as his eyes met hers. Every bit of her broke out in gooseflesh as he held her there with only his gaze.

Señora Moreno's eyes narrowed, no doubt catching the current running between them. She studied the two of them, her mouth parting a hair, as if to sigh, but nothing came forth.

After a moment she said, "I suppose you will be safe enough here. With the marshal."

Isabel knew what that cost her mother, to admit her daughter might be safe with this man—the battle that must have occurred against her hard-earned suspicions! Saving her daughter from a gunman must have weighed more heavily in her mother's consideration of the marshal than his working for Judge Bannister.

"Sebastian will see to it that Señorita Moreno is entertained," his mother said. "Won't you?"

He was playing with his fork again, turning it over and over in his scarred hands. He set it beside the plate before saying, "Certainly, Mother."

"Don't worry, Marshal Spencer," Isabel said, something wicked within her wanting to poke at him. "I won't bother you."

But, oh, she wanted to. The urge was a powerful tightness in her breast.

Several hours alone with him. Perhaps an entire afternoon. She swallowed hard, the sound loud to her own ears.

"Oh, please, do call him Sebastian," his mother said. "'Marshal Spencer' sounds much too fearsome."

His expression was wry—and a touch sad. "I don't believe that anyone finds me fearsome. Not anymore."

Isabel had thought him fearsome at the beginning—or at least menacing. But now... No, *fear* wasn't this odd, churning buoyancy he inspired in her.

His mother drooped slightly, her smile dissolving. "You were never fearsome. Only misguided."

He reached across the table to clasp at his mother's hand, a silent apology that made Isabel's heart wrench. She desperately wanted to know what he was apologizing for. A man that closed off, that tightly wrapped within himself—what could he possibly have done?

He gave his mother's hand one last squeeze, then rose from the table.

"I'm going to retire to the library," he announced with a bow to each of them, "before my fearsome reputation suffers any more blows."

"Oh, yes, go to the library and sulk," his mother said, her smile back in place. "If you'll excuse me, I shall say good night to you all here."

Her mother rose to join Señora Vasquez. "It's past time for us to retire, as well. Are you coming, Isabel?"

"Perhaps I could see the library first?" She looked at the marshal—*Sebastian*—towering over them all, his knuckles set hard against the table as he heard her request. He gave no indication if he wanted her to stay—or to go. "If that's where I'm to spend the day tomorrow."

He only inclined his head in agreement.

"Not too late, Isabel," her mother warned, as through she were still a child.

Then she and Señora Vasquez retired, leaving Isabel alone. Alone with Sebastian.

~~~

He should have told her no, to leave him alone, to go to bed before she awakened within him something so strong he could not repress it.

So strong he could not control it.

But how could he have said all that to a simple request to see the library?

The library had always been a bittersweet place for Sebastian, home to some of the best and worst memories of his childhood. He chose to focus on the good these days, rather than the bad, so he could still enjoy the place.

And the library was where he kept his notebooks.

He walked down the hallway to the paneled doors, knowing she was following behind.

"There is a dog," he warned. "He keeps close to my mother—he shouldn't bother you. I'll lock him in the garden during the day."

"I'm not afraid of dogs," she said.

She would be of this one. Junius wasn't anyone's pet—he took his duties guarding Sebastian's mother very seriously. Perhaps too seriously. But he was devoted to her, and that was all that mattered.

Junius would be in his mother's room; he always was this time of night. Sebastian would lock him outside first thing tomorrow. Señorita Moreno would never encounter the dog.

He pushed the library doors open, then punched the switch on the wall, filling the room with the buzzing yellow light peculiar to electric lamps.

Suddenly, a memory flashed through him. His father, in this very room, breath thick with liquor, red-faced, those same lights buzzing indifferently above his raised fist.

Sebastian closed his eyes, nearly stumbling under the image. As his eyelashes met his cheeks the memory eased its hold, but behind his eyelids the image of his father echoed, ghastly in its insubstantiality.

His father was dead, but Sebastian could not rid himself of his memories of the man, of what Judge Spencer had done to his mother, to him, a spreading corruption pressing all about him—

Except for the presence at his back. The corruption did not reach her.

Isabel was right behind him. He could feel her, as clearly as if she were draped across the bared skin of his back. He forced his eyes open, his vision clearing, took a moment to resettle his composure, and stepped away from her.

The sensation of her along his back persisted.

"Here it is," he announced.

She looked like he'd presented her with a cave full of treasures, her eyes going wide, her mouth parting as she put a hand to her breast.

It wasn't much, as far as libraries went. Truth be told, it was a bit of a mess just now, with newspapers and books littering the tables and the chairs. He'd run out of space on the shelves a while ago, and since his mother only entered infrequently, the maids mostly left it as it was.

She rummaged through a pile of newspapers, her fingers flying. "You must take every newspaper in the state."

"Hardly. I take a few California papers, some from back East, and two from Mexico," he said. She triumphantly held up one from the stack. "I see you've found *Alta California.*"

She rustled through it, then dug back into the stack.

"So," she said, "I'm to call you Sebastian." His skin tightened at the sound of his name on her lips. She looked up, her eyes curious behind her spectacles. "How many people call you by your given name?"

"My mother," he said. "And now you."

It was a temporary intimacy. She would leave after the trial—and take the sound of his name on her lips with her.

Her brows drew together. "Not very many."

It wasn't, but he wanted to tell her that only the people he esteemed in this world called him Sebastian.

Instead, he said, "Not very many at all, Isabel."

He drew her name out, a three-syllable poem he savored.

Isabel.

Her name was a sigh, meant to be whispered in a lover's ear at the moment of final possession...

He gave himself a shake.

Her cheeks were flushed and her breathing erratic. If she kept looking at him like that, he might kiss her again.

No, he might *want* to kiss her again, but he certainly wouldn't do it.

"I'm glad I am one of them," she said softly.

"As am I," he said just as softly.

She picked up another paper, hugging it to her bosom.

He never imagined he'd be envious of a newspaper.

"How do you find time to read them all?" she asked.

"I read quickly." He gestured to the paper round her chest. "You can take that to your room, if you like."

The paper crinkled as she squeezed it closer.

A snapping, a snarling—and a mass of gray fur rushed toward her before he could even blink.

The dog.

"Junius!" he roared, his hand reaching for the dog's collar, but finding nothing. "Down!" His voice vibrated with the urgency of the command—and the fear that it wouldn't be enough.

Thankfully, the dog subsided mere inches from her. But he kept his teeth bared, the fur of his back standing in stark warning to the woman in front of him.

Heart racing, Sebastian grabbed the collar and pulled the dog away, Junius straining against his hold.

She was pinned against the door, her eyes wide and her face drawn. But no marks on her skin or tears in her dress. She was whole.

Sebastian exhaled sharply. The dog hadn't harmed her, only scared her. If he'd known Junius was here... The dog didn't usually have such a severe reaction to strangers.

"It's all right," he said. "The dog won't hurt you now." Although if he hadn't been here, he shuddered to think what might have happened. "You said you weren't afraid of dogs."

"I'm not," she snapped, never moving from the door. "I *am* wary of dogs who want to eat me."

As if to prove her point, Junius lunged, the leather of his collar folding into Sebastian's palm.

"Sit," Sebastian snapped. "Down."

What had gotten into the beast?

The dog came to lie at Sebastian's heels, but kept a baleful eye on Isabel.

"He'll be locked outside from now on, I promise." Sebastian wished he could reassure her the dog meant no harm, but it wouldn't be true. Junius had been bred to be aggressive and protective—and he was. Sebastian could go about his day with an easy mind, knowing the dog was there to protect his mother.

She continued to watch the dog with equal parts suspicion and fear.

"I swear to you," Sebastian said, "the dog won't hurt you. I won't allow it."

Her back finally came away from the door.

Junius growled.

"Junius," he warned. "Perhaps you should go," he told her. "Tomorrow he will be properly secured."

She bent to pick up the paper she had dropped, and the dog bared his teeth.

"Good night." She opened the door enough to slide through, then disappeared.

Sebastian stared at the door, although he knew she wouldn't return.

Junius shifted at Sebastian's feet, claws squealing against the floor.

Sebastian frowned down at the dog. He could ask it what the hell it had been thinking, but the dog couldn't answer. And Sebastian already knew.

The dog was only doing what it was supposed to do.

What's bred in the bone will come out in the blood.

There was nothing to do but to lock the dog away to keep him from doing any damage.

Sebastian sighed and moved to the far wall, to the shelves where row upon row of unmarked black spines marched along.

Time to ensure that what was in his bones stayed there.

He flicked a fingernail along the notebooks, marveling at how many there were. He hadn't taken inventory of them in years. Amazing how many sheets of paper it took to tame a man. There would be fewer and fewer new ones in the years to come, as his mastery over his emotions grew ever more complete.

Someday, he might not have to add any new ones at all.

But not today. With the entrance of Señorita Moreno—*Isabel*—into his home, today's entry would be longer than usual.

A kiss was a very large sin to do penance for. Not to mention all the sensations she had stirred within him that he would have to account for.

Idle curiosity had him pulling out the very first notebook. The one from that terrible day when he realized he was becoming an even worse monster than his father.

He flipped to the first page. A smear of dried blood stained the words he'd scrawled.

The blood that day had been up to his forearms—he'd scoured them for what seemed like hours. He'd never been able to scrub it clean.

He ran a fingertip along the words there, written in the emotional scrawl of a seventeen-year-old. So much rage, so much violence in those words. His broken knuckles had barely allowed him to hold the pen, making the words nearly indecipherable.

But he knew what was written there.

He'd been a perfect terror that day, thinking there was no escape from his father's curse, that he would break his mother's heart as surely as his father had. In desperation, he'd turned to the notebook, not knowing what else to do.

He wrote not to recall his base impulses—nothing was ever erased from his memory—but rather to elide them from his heart. To scrub the sin from his soul, as best he could. To prevent him from sinning again.

The notebooks had taken some trial and error, of course. Recording only that which was evil and vulgar within himself wasn't enough. The good, the pleasurable had to go as well.

After all, when contagion entered a house, everything had to be fed to the fire, reduced to barest ash, no matter how innocuous.

Every sensation he experienced in a day—each time he gritted his teeth, every urge to smile—all went in the notebook. When he shut it, those emotions were gone. The paper could swallow up any sin he submitted, never retching it back up.

There was very little to erase these days. Even the strictest priest wouldn't demand penance for the trifles he recorded now.

The image of McCade spitting out one of his teeth flashed through his mind.

He snatched his hand back from the book as though it had burst into flame.

He'd reacted as instinctively as the dog had, attacking without thought or reason. All because the outlaw had insulted Isabel.

Isabel.

He'd never once been tempted by alcohol and had no desire to roll in the aisles at a tent revival, but he would do nearly anything for another sip at her sanctified lips.

He ran a hand through his hair, tugging at it. He only had to keep his feelings chained for the duration of this trial. Then she would go, and he could return to normalcy. He had enormous reserves of self-control. The next few days would hardly be enough to tap them. No matter how he ached when he imagined holding her again.

Enough. Time to erase these unwanted sensations.

He pulled the current notebook from the shelf. He wrote quickly, leaving nothing behind. His panic at the shooting, the feel of her in his arms afterward... and the kiss. He paused, the pen poised above the word *kiss*.

He shut the notebook with some force.

Done.

Gone.

He set it back and pondered the wall of black spines. Pages and pages of his sins, set down in blackest ink.

Perhaps he ought to move them if she would be here. A curious lady might look in them and discover all his secrets.

He decided to leave them as they were. There was nothing about these books that would catch her eye, especially given all the titles surrounding them.

Before Sebastian retired for the night, he made certain the dog was securely locked outside.

Nothing in this house must harm her.

CHAPTER THIRTEEN

THE BRICK FAÇADE OF THE COURTHOUSE spoke to strength and rightness. The courtroom was a wood-paneled temple to justice and order. The rows of chairs in the spectators' section were worshipfully arranged around the high altar where the judge sat, as the lawyers prepared their offerings to him—all of it constructed to appear as though God himself had assembled it and His own angels ran the proceedings within.

Isabel had only to look at the judge, heavy-lidded as a frog, the lawyers, slick as snakes, and McCade himself, a wolf put into sheep's clothing for the occasion, to re-member that this whole edifice had been constructed by men.

There was nothing celestial here.

Despite her unease, she kept her hands folded in a neat deception of calm, the bench beneath her as rigid as her spine. The judge was going on about the charges and all the other legal folderol that accompanied any gather-ing of lawyers, but she couldn't force her ears to attend to what he was saying.

She didn't have to force her gaze to hold to McCade's back—it clung there entirely against her will. His pomaded hair gleamed as he turned toward his lawyer, his cheek bare and his suit expertly tailored.

Today the outlaw was as carefully put together as... well, as carefully as the marshal himself. But while Sebastian's studied appearance was reassuring, a thing that spoke to his care and consideration, McCade's spoke to something filthy swept under a fine rug.

Each time he turned to his lawyer, the light catching on his hair, the curve of his ear, her heart flinched.

He never once glanced at her.

Everyone else had, though. She'd met more than a few penetrating stares, their owners not even having the courtesy to drop their eyes when their gazes met. Thanks to the charming illustrations the papers had run of her—where they got the photographs to draw from she'd no idea—she was instantly recognizable to anyone following the case. The spectators were determined to look their fill of her, now she'd appeared in the flesh.

No matter. Stares were simply that—stares.

The great Edwin McCade was attending as well, wearing a mane of iron-gray hair and a sadly imploring expression. A lion come to beg for his cub's life. Still powerful, but supplicating himself before the court.

If the man hadn't sent someone to murder her yesterday—and hadn't produced such a foul creature as his son—she might have been moved by the picture he made.

The judge continued on to the matters of true import—the testimonies.

McCade testified first.

He settled loosely into the witness stand with a kind of blank assurance, as if all this were a mere formality and he could return to his life of mayhem any moment.

She stared at those hard eyes across the room. How dare he sit there so loose-limbed, when he'd left Joaquin a twisted wreck who couldn't rise from his bed?

Bile rose in her throat and she tightened her stomach to keep it down. The phantom pains in her throat, the headaches that attacked her, the fear that paralyzed her—he could see none of that. That animal would never know how he still affected her. She clamped her hands together, pressing them hard against her thighs.

The commotion of a spectator arriving late was only a dim happening in her periphery. Until a weighted heat settled at her left shoulder, spread along her back—someone's gaze.

She turned to see who was staring at her so.

Marshal Spencer.

He'd left her at the courtroom door, apologizing for the duties that claimed his attention. His presence on the journey to the courtroom had been so steady, so silent—she'd found the space to bolster herself for the coming ordeal in that quiet.

He'd said nothing of returning, so she'd assumed he wouldn't, that she would be entirely alone.

But he'd come back.

His collar was high and tight, his tie forming a perfect right angle to it, his waistcoat free of any embellishment. He looked a perfect gentleman, even as large and scarred as he was. He set his hat on one knee, his gaze never leaving hers.

Something tight unwound within her. Her hands unclamped and her chest eased.

She wasn't alone—Sebastian was here.

The lawyer was already speaking by the time she turned back, asking the outlaw why he'd been in Cabrillo, where he'd met the Careys—questions that didn't interest her.

"On the day of the alleged attack, what were you doing on the road?"

That question from the prosecutor snared her attention and held it fast.

The man wasn't any more inspiring in front of the court than he'd been at Don Enrique's house, his suit carelessly pressed and his manners hesitant. But the jury—all men wearing stern expressions of utmost respectability—attended his words quite closely.

In spite of her efforts, she began to breathe much too quickly, her stomach twisting as her heart raced. She concentrated on forcing the air in and out.

Stone. She was made of stone.

"We were out for a ride," McCade said.

"You were riding with your friends, the Carey brothers?"

"Yes." His voice was as flat as his eyes.

"And you came across Obregon and the woman on the road?"

Her hands tightened into fists. She had a name, and Joaquin was Sheriff Obregon to the likes of them. Not that anyone else here noted the slight—the only glances she received when he mentioned her were unsympathetic.

"We did."

"What happened then?"

"Obregon said we were up to no good, that he had his eye on us." McCade's tone went affronted, that he should be treated so. "But we weren't up to any trouble."

That last was spoken with bright innocence—and it was a lie. Her head began to throb as if someone had taken a chisel to it.

Or the butt of a pistol.

McCade leaned forward, concern knitting his brow. "Then Obregon pulled his gun on us."

She blinked hard. Her protests clogged her throat, trapping the breath in her lungs. She'd known he was going to lie, but hearing the falsehoods spoken so easily, McCade's gaze coming every so often to rest upon her without a hint of shame—it was more difficult to absorb than she'd expected.

What happened to you doesn't matter. I have an endless store of lies—you only have the truth. And no one here cares.

That was what McCade was telling her with every careless untruth he tossed off.

"You're saying that the sheriff drew first?" the lawyer asked.

"He certainly did." Aggrieved now. "Pulled his gun without warning and started firing."

The jurors' expressions shifted to match his indignant tone.

She nearly leapt out of her chair. Lies, lies, lies. She concentrated on keeping her thighs on the chair, her hands in her lap—her body hummed with the effort toward stillness.

The men in the jurors' box were nodding, faces open, considering. She ground her teeth together at their stupidity.

She'd refute all this rubbish later, when she took the stand.

"You returned fire at that point?" the lawyer asked.

"Yes, sir." The outlaw's eyes widened earnestly. "That woman of his started firing too."

Her breath left her in a rush as he stared straight at her, the spark within his eyes dark, menacing. After only a moment of those eyes boring into her, her nerve broke like a frayed rope and she had to look away, cursing herself as a coward as she did. Almost without thought, she sought out the marshal.

There he was, the large black bulk of him a steadying presence. He was watching McCade the way a cat might watch a mouse hole, patiently waiting for any excuse to strike.

She found the courage then to look back at the witness stand.

Stone. She was made of stone.

"What happened after the sheriff began shooting?" the lawyer asked.

"Well, he killed both of the Carey boys straight off. They never even fired." The regret in his voice was as shallow as a drought-dry stream. "I was frightened for my own life, so I fired at the sheriff. I was hoping to only scare him off, but I accidentally shot him."

Accident? It had been no accident. The outlaw's eyes had sparked with deadly intent as he'd leveled that gun at Joaquin, the only time they hadn't been as flat as river stones. Like when he'd reached for her...

It was coming. The part she dreaded the most.

The blood-red explosion of the buckwheat blossoms. Thousands upon thousands of his fingers wrapping around her throat. The gray blur creeping at the edge of her vision as she realized this was it. She was about to die.

The cold, hard stock of the rifle under her fingers.

Her gaze found the marshal again. Her heart leapt when she saw he was looking directly at her, so steady, so sure.

She knew that if he were close enough, he would take her hand and give it a squeeze, just as he had yesterday after the shooting.

But he couldn't. So he gave her his gaze instead. And it was enough.

She took a steadying breath and turned to face the worst.

McCade went on. "Then that woman"—he pointed straight at her—"shot me. Right in the shoulder." His expression was the same as when he'd reached for her throat, no longer pretending at blamelessness.

Lord, she was going to be sick, she couldn't hold it in any longer, had no more control over her body—

He looked away before she embarrassed herself, the sourness coating her tongue a reminder of her near miss.

"I hid out in the mountains after that," McCade went on. "I figured those folks would lynch me for defending myself against the sheriff. They nearly would have too, when they caught me, if the marshal hadn't warned them off."

She was sure she looked a fool, with her mouth hanging open, but she could hardly believe what she'd just heard.

He wasn't going to mention his assault on her. Nothing about dragging her off that wagon seat, lifting her by her throat and carrying her to the brush, nothing about the rapine intent of his hands as they'd clasped her thighs. Nothing about the pistol whipping he'd given her.

The throb in her head became a full-on wave of pain, swamping every one of her senses.

He'd lied about everything else—why not that as well?

You don't matter.

Some of the jurors were nodding along as McCade told of the planned lynching, and her heart sank. She swallowed down a bit more pain, a little more bile, and set her jaw. It wasn't over yet.

McCade moved on to describing his capture. "They tried their best to kill me when they caught me." He looked at someone in the spectators' gallery and put on a chilling half-smile. "But the marshal saved me."

Marshal Spencer stared back impassively, his stillness perhaps the most menacing thing she'd ever seen. The darkness within him was bearing down on the man in the witness stand.

The image of him pummeling McCade bloomed in her mind. Her ears recalled the sound of his fist landing on the outlaw's jaw, flesh and bone crunching wetly.

He'd done that for her.

She was snapped out of her reverie by a strange choking noise coming from the judge's bench.

The judge leapt up in a flurry of black robes, running to the spittoon with a hand across his mouth.

The sound of retching erupted from him, followed closely by the horrified gasps rising from the spectators.

~~~

Judge Bannister was not pleased.

Not that the judge was ever truly pleased, Sebastian thought, but he was especially displeased at the moment, rigidly sitting behind his desk, his fingers worrying at a pen.

"I understand the trial's been delayed three days because of Hess's stomach upset," Bannister said, with a cruel twist to *stomach upset*. It was clear he would have simply vomited on McCade in the witness stand and then gone on with the trial.

Not everyone could be made of such sternly vindictive stuff.

"Hess claims he ate some bad fish." Sebastian was unruffled, going calmer, stiller, with each fidget of the judge's.

Bannister raised an eyebrow. "Fond of fish, is he?"

Sebastian shrugged. "It does happen."

"You don't believe that." Halfway toward a question.

"A random shooting one day, a violently ill judge the next? No, I don't believe it was coincidence." Neither did

Bannister, but he'd never admit that. No, he would force Sebastian to voice the suspicions he wouldn't, to preserve his facade of impartiality.

"Mmm." Bannister scratched his chin before bringing up what he'd obviously wanted to all along. "Edwin McCade has turned another councilman. One more vote, and the city water supply stays in private hands. His hands."

The business of water and politics was beyond him, so Sebastian kept quiet. He'd done his duty in bringing in McCade; he was sheltering Señorita Moreno in his own home. Giving his opinion on the water supply wasn't part of those duties.

"I got a look at your girl today," Bannister went on.

She's not my girl.

Even if he was forced to kiss her when she used honorable words such as *protect* and *defend* when describing him—it didn't give him ownership of her.

If she knew half the things he'd done, she wouldn't use those words. But for now, she thought him only an ordinary sinner and didn't hesitate to say so.

He took the opportunity to adjust his collar, the edges of it razor sharp against his neck.

"She's entirely unsympathetic looking, isn't she?" the judge asked.

Sebastian ground his teeth together, the rasp of it echoing in his ears. "Am I supposed to make her look different somehow?"

The other man laughed. "Not unless you have hidden talents!"

Sebastian resisted the urge to flex his fists. He hadn't always found the judge this irritating—usually he could shrug off his political obsessions as being of no concern to himself.

But this particular obsession concerned Isabel—and anything involving her was proving difficult to treat with indifference.

Today in the courtroom, watching her suffer McCade's lies—he'd been a hair's breadth away from vaulting out of his seat and removing a few more of McCade's teeth.

Having her so close was making him wax dangerous. But he could—*would*—control these violent urges. He'd been practicing exactly that for over a dozen years.

He rolled his shoulders, trying to drain away the tension. "As I said before, she'll do quite well on the witness stand."

"She'd better. With the way his testimony's going, it'll be his word against hers." The judge's voice hardened. "In fact, his story is a fair sight different from hers. You don't think she's lying, do you?"

"Obregon's story matches hers." At least the parts the wounded man had remembered. "And we know McCade's been involved in other crimes, even if he can't be brought up on charges. He never mentioned attacking her, but someone did. She had the marks at her throat and temple to prove it."

"Did the prosecutor bring that up in cross-examination?"

"No. Judge Hess took ill before he could."

The judge's eyes were sharp. "What did the jury think?"

Sebastian hesitated. "They believed McCade," he admitted. "But she has yet to tell her story."

"Well, if you believe her, then," Bannister said. "It's hopeless to expect any more help from the prosecutor. You've got three days—make sure no one harms her. And try to soften her up. That surly puss of hers is going to look terrible on the witness stand."

Sebastian squeezed the arms of the chair, enjoying the creak of the wood, before rising with a quick nod and heading for the door.

He didn't bother admitting he liked her hard edges. They matched his own so well.

CHAPTER FOURTEEN

AS SOON AS SHE AWOKE, Isabel knew there would be no library for her that day. The evidence was in the dull pressure building in her skull, the push of an enormous hand from inside out that would eventually develop into bewildering, blinding pain.

It was to be expected after the tensions of yesterday—hearing McCade lie so easily about everything, followed by the collapse of Judge Hess. Fortitude under such conditions would exact a price in the end, which would be a vicious headache.

It remained merely a light pressure at breakfast, allowing her to hide it from her mother.

"Are you certain you won't be too lonesome?" her mother asked.

Isabel pushed a bit of egg into a triangle of toast, her stomach rebelling at the thought of putting it into her mouth.

"I'm certain I'll be fine," she told her mother.

She wouldn't be—this headache would have her bedridden soon. But she desperately craved solitude, even if she would be forced to suffer alone when the attack hit.

273

"Sebastian is here," Señora Vasquez pointed out. By *here*, she did not mean the table—apparently supper was the only meal that he pretended to eat at. "He will make certain Isabel is well taken care of."

Doubtful, since she'd be spending most of the day in her room.

"The library will provide more than enough stimulation," she said with a smile to Señora Vasquez. "The marshal won't need to exert himself for me."

"It will be no exertion."

She held back her instinct to flinch at his voice behind her. And the impulse to turn to him. Held them back just as he'd restrained that dog of his.

"See?" Señora Vasquez's smile was wide and true. "It's no bother."

Isabel rose, setting her napkin by her untouched plate.

"You two enjoy your day out and about," she said to her mother. "I'll be fine."

She purposefully did not meet the marshal's eyes as she passed him, but the great black hulk of him could not be missed. The hairs on her arms lifted as she passed, as if reaching out for him.

She escaped to her room, where a shelf full of books waited for her. Remarkable, that this house had not only a fine library, but books in the bedrooms as well.

It was about two hours later, as she was reading with the door open, that the staves round her head tightened to painfulness.

She set aside the newspaper, the crinkling of it almost unbearably loud, closed her eyes, and concentrated on her breathing. With each exhale the pain receded, but every inhale brought the pain flowing back in.

The light. It was too much, stabbing against her eyes. She stumbled toward the curtains, her ears filling with the piercing pure tones of pain. Her stomach rolled hard, nausea flowing throughout her, until it seemed her very joints might cast up their accounts. Oh Lord, she mustn't vomit, how would she explain such a thing?

She went for the floor, setting her jaw to keep the sickness inside her, her fingers finding the cool hardness before she set her forehead there. She rolled her forehead back and forth—yes, just that. She needed that. The wood soaked up some of the pain, just enough to allow the nausea to retreat into her belly.

Back and forth, back and forth, so blessedly cool and firm.

Her knees came to her stomach, her palms flat against the floor, and she waited. Waited to be something more than pain and nausea.

She moaned when someone's hands slid under her arms, lifted her up from the floor.

"Shh, shh," a voice murmured as she was cradled in strong arms. "I have you."

Oh, *his voice*. It was bright as gold, soft as fur. She wanted to drape herself in it. The scratch of his woolen suit was nearly unbearable against her cheek, but thank God he smelled of nothing. Her stomach for certain would have turned inside out if he'd been wearing cologne. Or pomade. She kept her eyes shut tight as he gently set her on the bed.

He ran a hand along her hair. She caught it up and pressed it hard against her eyes.

Oh, heaven, the heavy weight and coolness of that.

He tugged his hand free and she whimpered, turning in search of it.

"Shh. I'm only going to close the drapes. I'll return," he assured her.

Thank the Lord—he wasn't leaving her alone in this.

Darkness. Sweet, sweet darkness, once the curtains were closed.

She was dimly aware of him moving through the room. The bed sagged after a time, her poor brain spinning into vertigo with the motion. A cool, damp cloth was placed on her forehead. Utter, utter bliss. A fingertip trailed along her cheek.

She reached blindly for that hand, her palm striking something hard, knobby. A wrist. She seized it and set his hand hard against her temple.

Cooling, weighted bliss.

"I cannot bear this." His low voice barely penetrated through the pain muffling her ears. "I want to ease your pain."

Twin spots of pressure pushed against the skin between her eyes. *His thumbs.* His fingers came to rest at her temples, his hands cupping her brow and the ache there. His blunt fingertips began to draw slow, deep circles, while his luxuriant voice murmured soothing nonsense.

His fingers pushed the pain away, his words wrapping her in comfort, reminding her that there was something beyond this agony.

The pain went to low tide, finally allowing her to curl up on the shore and sleep.

~~~

Two hours.

For two hours he'd been watching over her as she slept. After the first fifteen minutes, he'd removed the cloth so she wouldn't catch a chill. And kept his hands from her forehead.

He stayed. The door was open, the maid was puttering about down the hall—it wasn't terribly improper, as far as things went.

Watching a woman he admired as she slept was something he shouldn't be doing. He shouldn't even admire her.

But the distance between *what ought to be* and *what was*—it was too far for him to traverse any longer.

He'd been on his way to his own room, passing her open door as he did. When he'd seen her lying on the floor like that in such obvious agony—his entire world stopped.

Once he'd assured himself that she wasn't bleeding, that she hadn't been shot, the agony in his chest shifted as his mind stuttered forth memories of another lady, weeping and broken on the floor exactly so.

He'd shoved the recollections away and gone to help Isabel. He recognized it as a migraine from the symptoms.

Close the curtains, keep noise to a minimum, a cool compress, and rest. Simple things to help her, her sigh of relief as she'd slipped into sleep telling him her pain had eased.

It was the other things he'd done that worried him. Carrying her to the bed had been necessary, but now his arms could never forget the feel of her there. Running a finger down her cheek—that had been entirely unnecessary.

Two hours by her bedside, watching the rise and fall of her chest, listening to the soft noises she made as she dreamed, inhaling the scent clinging to her—that was beyond unnecessary.

It was madness.

He'd fought madness before. The evil kind, composed of smoke and fury, that left only ash in its wake.

This kind of madness was sweet and all the more dangerous for it.

She curled in on herself as she slept. Those dark eyes were hidden, but she couldn't hide her thin nose or sharp cheeks. Another man might not have found anything to linger on in her face, but *his* gaze could not be pulled away.

He'd seen the resolve she carried with her, as sturdy and shining as a shield. He'd seen her deploy it fearlessly in even the worst of conditions, even when a man who'd violated her without mercy lied about it without shame, almost to her very face.

Another man might take a fleeting glance at her face and never think to linger to find the fierceness behind it.

But it was her hair that called to Sebastian. Darker than the River Lethe it was. He could imagine running his fingers through it, the great wave of it spreading all about him. How long was it? Did it fall to her shoulders, her back, her flanks?

Slowly, he reached for that enticing darkness. It was pinned up, but a few strands had escaped. He set a fingertip—only a fingertip—against one of those free strands.

After a few moments, he drew it back ruefully. It was soft, yes, and invited a man to linger—but the touch of it didn't bring forgetfulness, didn't wash away his memories or his sins.

He turned away from her, focused his attention on the wall, and marshaled his thoughts toward more appropriate subjects. His notebooks, for example. He'd be with them for hours tonight, cataloguing all of this.

He'd dreamed of her last night, standing before him as he knelt, naked and bound, as she forced him to confess the dark truth of himself. She'd listened with unblinking regard, as unresponsive as a sphinx.

When he was finished, she'd shoved him down, straddled him, and clawed a shame-filled climax from him.

He'd awoken as hard and hot as a blacksmith's hammer. Pulling his belt from the dresser, he'd wrapped it tightly around his hand, once, twice, until his fingers went white and tingling.

His father had liked to do the same, wrap the end of his belt round his hand like that. No matter how drunk Judge Spencer was, his hands never shook as he twined the leather around his palm.

Sebastian had clenched his fist tight and paced the room, quoting Marcus Aurelius until he'd once more mastered himself. By that point, the belt had rubbed his hand raw, the leather clinging to the wound it had made. He'd slowly peeled it away, bandaged his hand, and gone back to bed.

The wound was now only a line of pink along his palm. He'd always healed quickly.

A soft sigh and a rustling from the bed brought him back from his undimmed memories. He allowed himself to turn back to her.

She was blinking sleep from those fine dark eyes of hers, soft in every aspect, such as he'd never seen from her. Her eyes widened a hair when she saw him.

"How long have I been asleep?" Her sleep-rumpled voice scraped pleasantly along his ears. "A quarter of an hour?"

He shook his head. "More like two."

She darted a glance to the open door, but did not ask the obvious question as to why he'd remained while she'd slept. Lucky for him, since he couldn't have answered it anyhow.

"I—" She rubbed at her forehead. "Where are my spectacles?"

He handed them to her. "Are you feeling better?"

"Yes." She slid the frames up her nose, her gaze taking on its more usual sharpness. "Although I always feel a bit cotton-headed after an attack. There's no pain—my head just doesn't feel quite right." Her face tilted toward the bed. "Thank you for your assistance."

"It was nothing."

That was a lie. It had been everything to help her through her misery. He should go now that she was more herself, before he succumbed to the lure of destruction she presented.

But his will wouldn't hold. It became slippery as a thrashing eel, fighting free each time he tried to grab it. So he allowed it to slither away.

"Would you like me to read to you?" he asked.

Her eyes went wide behind her spectacles. She watched him as if weighing his intentions. Or perhaps her own. "I wouldn't want to torment you with any novels."

He ducked his head. "I don't mind when you torment me."

The dream bloomed in his mind, her above him, wreaking the most delicious havoc. He took a slow breath.

"I believe I can find something that would suit the both of us," he said.

Once he was in the library, he forced himself to look at his notebooks to remind himself what was at stake. When he sinned, it wasn't venial—it was catastrophic, mortal.

The blood in the first notebook attested to that.

Finding the volume he wanted was easy, slim as it was, bound in blue, sitting between *La Commedia* and *Paradise Lost*.

When he returned to her room, she was sitting up in bed, her hair smoothed back to perfection, hands folded in her lap. She watched in silence as he sat in the chair next to the bed.

He opened the volume, the pages smooth beneath his fingers.

"*Yo soy un hombre sincero, de donde crece las palmas...*"

He didn't really need the book—he had Martí's poems memorized. But it gave him something to hang on to as he watched her face. She lifted it like a bloom to the sun, as if his voice was her source of light and life. When he reached the bit about "*mi pecho bravo*—my brave heart" her eyes slipped closed and she mouthed the last few stanzas with him.

When he finished, she sat in a kind of pained rapture. Or perhaps the pain was all on his side, witnessing how such simple verses transported her.

"Are you a sincere man?" she asked after a time.

Now *that* was painful. Because if he were truly sincere with her, told her of the dark heart of him—

"No." He shut the book and stared at his hands. So many scars there. All of them self-inflicted. "I am the dark night. Mortal deception, sublime pain," he quoted from the poem.

Her mouth twisted. "Which makes me what? A comely woman? Divine beauty?"

"No. You are the diamond." He couldn't help but offer that compliment. "And I am the coal," he finished. He meant it as a warning—he hoped she'd heed it.

She laid a hand on his arm. For a moment, it appeared as if the pale length of it would be swallowed by the darkness of his suit.

"We are both coal, I think," she said with soft wryness. "But coal has its own luster. In certain lights, it gleams."

You gleam to me. Not just in certain lights—in all lights.

He could never say such a thing to her. She'd find no luster in the darkness within him if she knew the depths of it. He wasn't coal; he was the dank, hot mine from which it was torn, swallowing men whole.

She removed her hand. "You don't agree." She linked her fingers together. "What have you done that is so terrible?"

An icy fist gripped his heart.

"To me, at least?" she continued, and the fist released.

"When I kissed you—" He stopped, brought his voice back under his control. "You are a guest under my roof. It was ill done."

"I kissed you as much as you were kissing me. It was done together." She brought a hand to the hollow of her throat, hidden by her high collar. "What that man did to me—that was ill done. Never put what we share into the same drawer as what he did."

Theft, assault, attempted murder—if he dared detail them to her, the catalogue of his crimes would look much like McCade's. Some of them were worse. And that last sin, trapped in his first notebook...

If he could dip that notebook into the River Lethe and wash away his sins along with the ink—then and only then could he think of reaching for this woman.

He stared at the slim volume in his hand. He must keep holding the book. He must never reach for her, must never even think—

"Sebastian."

The steel she put into his name made his blood run hot. He raised his gaze to hers.

"Yes?" With that one word, he all but begged her to do it again. Even as he feared she would.

"In the courtroom yesterday," she asked, "you wanted to harm McCade, didn't you?"

She'd no idea of the harm he could inflict.

"I did," he said slowly.

"Yet, you held back. You did not give in. I don't believe that outlaw would have done such a thing. I know exactly what he's capable of."

"You've no idea what *I'm* capable of."

She only shook her head as if his attempts to warn her off were pitiable. "My collar." She raised a hand to it. "I have to wear it as high as I can now. For the sense of protection it provides."

He nodded. Wasn't his suit, his sober mien, his own kind of armor?

"But it pains me." Her voice went low. "I feel as if I am strangling all over again, with this collar tight round my neck."

He understood. By the end of the day his fine suit was rougher than a hair shirt. He was always surprised to see his skin smooth and unblemished beneath, so violently did he imagine his clothes rubbed against him.

She took his hand, the one wrapped around the book, and pried it free. Slowly, slowly, she lifted it to the first button at her neck.

What did she mean by this? He'd warned her, he couldn't have said more clearly how dangerous he was...

"Isabel, I—I cannot dishonor you."

If she commanded him to, he would, though. He'd always bend before the steel within her.

"You wouldn't dishonor me," she said softly. "I am asking you."

Asking. A request from her was as good as a command, as addled as he was.

He heard the maid moving in the next room, the door wide open on the iniquity he was about to perform. He pinched the button between his thumb and forefinger, the hole pulling wide as he did.

Just like that, it was free.

"More," she said.

One by one he eased each button free, both of them breathing shakily. When he was done, he set his hand next to her thigh and simply watched her. Her eyes were wide, her chest jerking with her breaths. A mirror to the anxiety twisting within him.

"Isabel, are you all right?" Perhaps he shouldn't have done this, no matter that she'd asked.

She nodded. "And you?"

"It wasn't like this. Before." Their kiss had been fervent, frantic—this was trembling, halting.

"No, it wasn't. Today"—she grabbed his hand again—"today we are not playing at love. Today, we are testing each other."

He wanted to pass this test of hers—to never fail her again.

She set his hand against her thigh. "Here. Here is where he set his hand, and told me all the foul things he'd inflict on me." She pressed his fingers hard into her thigh, trapping them between her urgency and her soft flesh. "Is that what you would do if you could?"

"Never."

You *would hold* me *down and detail the things I must do to please you. I'd do them all, every last one, to have a kind word or caress from you when I'd finished.*

She pressed again. "You claim to be a monster, that you are coal, neverending night. Yet you unbutton me to the waist, I shove your hand against my thigh..." She watched him, then moved his hand to her waist. "Where is this monster?"

He closed his eyes tight. He wished he had the fortitude to tell her everything, so that she would end this dangerous trial.

Her hand came to his cheek, her fingers rubbing. Didn't she feel the stubble there? Didn't it burn her palm the way it did his?

"One thing I have wondered about you," she mused.

He stiffened. If she asked again what he'd done, he might not be able to refuse her.

"Do you have to shave more than once a day?" She punctuated that with another sweep of her fingers along his cheek.

His lungs released in a great rush, the closest to a laugh he'd allow. "When I can."

She set her hand back in her lap, the shy smile she gave him recompense for the loss of her touch. "Would you read more?"

He took up and read, until the clatter of the front door signaled the return of their mothers. The shadows in the room were long, the light wearing the dark gold of evening as it fell across Isabel's face while she buttoned herself back up, hiding her throat once more.

When their mothers appeared in the open doorway, the scene they presented—her sedate in bed, him reading to her from across the room—was entirely unobjectionable. But something tight passed over Señora Moreno's expression, even as his mother's opened.

Señora Moreno was right to be anxious—her daughter hammered at his control like no other.

"Good evening, Señora. Mother." Serene as a swan gliding across a lake, Isabel was. "I had a headache earlier and the marshal offered to read to me once it had passed."

He daren't look at any of them, so kept his gaze on the book in his hand, his finger pinched between the pages to keep his spot.

"How kind of Sebastian," his mother offered, "to keep you company."

Would his mother never cease to think him extraordinary? Worthy? The love he had for her threatened to crack his chest open.

"Yes," Señora Moreno said. "How kind." Suspicion flavored her words.

"He is," Isabel said firmly. "You know how my attacks are."

He cleared his throat. No more compliments for him—he couldn't take any more. "How was your day out?"

"Wonderful," his mother said. "We're quite ready for supper."

He looked to Isabel in the bed, still paler than he'd like. "Would you like to come down? Or should we send up a tray?"

The frank gratitude in her gaze made him ache. "Perhaps it's best that I take a tray here. And retire early."

He nodded and went for the door, commanding his will to hold and not look back at her as he passed both their mothers.

CHAPTER FIFTEEN

AN ENTIRE DAY SPENT READING wasn't quite as enjoyable as Isabel had imagined.

The trouble was, nothing was keeping her attention.

The Señoras had left right after breakfast and Sebastian, for all his promises to entertain her, hadn't been seen. No poetry from him today. She looked at the clock on the mantel—noon. She'd had four hours alone.

She'd idly flipped through the papers for an hour before they lost their charm. But she had carefully read the article in the *Herald* on "The Water Issue," which had prominently featured Mr. Edwin McCade. There had been a short, neutral mention of his son's trial within—and thankfully nothing about her.

After, she'd flicked the electric lights on and off, enjoying the buzz. She'd look a perfect rube if she were caught, but she'd risked it for the pure enjoyment.

Then she'd spent a half an hour deciding on a novel to read, before settling on *Middlemarch*. She found herself only able to skim until the Reverend Casaubon exited the stage. She liked to imagine a different ending— Dorothea living alone in Europe, enjoying herself with the wealth the Reverend had left to her.

Isabel tossed aside the novel, the thunk of it as it bounced along the sofa oddly appealing. Time for something new.

She rose and sidled over to the north window. The curtains had been drawn this morning, and when the maid had come to open them, Isabel had done her best to ignore what might be beyond those windows.

Enough cowardice. McCade wasn't there—he was in jail.

Taking a deep breath, she stepped in front of the windows, exposing herself to whomever might be watching, expecting there would be no one.

Only there was someone.

She jerked and stumbled backward into the shelves, bruising her calves as she did.

Away. She had to get away.

Her fingertips trailed along the unyielding spines as she inched her way to the sofa, one small step for every other shuddering breath she drew.

The man, there on the street, watching the library window—he'd stared straight at her. He was watching still, she just knew—

If I can't see him, he can't see me.

She chanted it in time with the beat of her heart, the words melting into a frantic muddle as she sagged toward the floor, commanding her weak legs to move.

Away. She had to get away, to hide—

The library door swung open.

Ah God, the man had come into the house somehow and—

She blinked, looked again.

Sebastian had come.

He looked her over, halfway toward collapsing to the floor, and went for the window.

"Don't," she begged. "He'll see you."

"That man?" He leaned further into the window frame. "I want him to see me. To let him know I know what he's about." He stared out a few moments longer. "That ought to do it. He's leaving now."

He sighed when he turned and caught sight of her. "It was only some man passing by," he said.

"You don't know that," she accused. She tried her knees, found them still too weak to hold her.

"No, I don't. But I'm here, and Junius is in the garden." He slowly walked toward her, wariness in his steps. "Even if he meant harm, he'd never get past either of us." He took her hand, pulled her up. "Come. Sit."

She looked at that hand enclosing hers so completely, warm with just a hint of roughness. It was only a hand, touching only her hand, but she felt the pull of it all the way to her belly.

He led her over to the sofa, her calves aching with each step. He tucked her next to him—and kept hold of her hand.

Yesterday, when she'd pressed that hand to her neck, her thigh, it had trembled as much as her own. She'd learned then that Sebastian was not a man to touch a woman lightly.

"What do you think he wanted?" she asked.

His fingers tightened on hers. "Don't worry about him," he said. "That's my job."

Hardly an answer.

She wet her dry lips. It wasn't only the man outside dragging along her nerves. She'd dreamed last night of the judge vomiting up blood and viscera instead of his breakfast. Of being forced to scrub the floor clean of it while McCade watched with his cold half-smile.

But now Sebastian was here and he was holding her hand.

She squeezed her fingers against his, feeling the strength there.

"I would never allow him to harm you," he said.

"I know." The fervency in his tone burned away her uncertainty, had her pulse slowing.

Something very like a smile touched his eyes, even as his mouth remained firm. It had felt soft under her lips, though.

"Better?" he asked.

"I am, thank you."

And she was. As she studied the smile in his eyes, she realized she wanted to kiss him again. Badly. It was a smolder at the center of her, this urge to taste him again.

Her kisses with Joaquin had been pleasant, but never entrancing enough to make her forget herself. She'd taken comfort in the knowledge she was not a woman at the mercy of her baser natures.

But she'd been wrong. With the right man—with *Sebastian*—her baser natures were powerful enough to run her into the worst irrationality.

What a dreadful time for this realization.

Her heart echoed in her ears, her entire world shrunk to that sound and her desire.

She'd kissed him after being shot at, she'd pressed his hands to the very places where she'd been wounded, she'd told him over and over he was no monster—it was madness, her reaction to him. A madness she wanted to taste again and again.

Such madness did not touch him, judging by his protests after their kiss. He was here only to protect her, to ensure she made it to that witness stand.

A smart rap to her heart, that.

But he made things better. Always, he made her feel better. She wanted to do more than kiss him. She wanted to unlock him, to get a close look at the gears that made him run.

"Isabel?" Such steady concern in his voice. "Are you certain you're all right?"

No. She thought it had only been her orderly existence that McCade had tipped off its axis with a flick of his trigger finger.

But she herself was upended as well.

"I'm fine." She pulled her hand from his, but the heat of his touch lingered. "A little bored, I'm ashamed to admit." She waved weakly to the books surrounding them. "I certainly have enough to choose from."

"Did you find something to your taste?"

"I thought I might read *Middlemarch* again, but I find myself unable to."

"Hmmm. We shall have to find something to hold your attention, then."

The smolder in her belly flamed as she thought of one particular activity that would hold her attention.

A crease formed between his brows as he pondered how to entertain her. She wanted to touch that furrow with the tips of her fingers, to get the texture of it under her skin—

"Isabel?"

"Pardon?" She blinked hard. She'd been staring so intently at him she hadn't registered his words.

"I asked, do you play chess?" That smile was back in his eyes.

"No." She'd always wanted to learn, though. "We'll have to find something else to occupy us."

"I can teach you. If you'd like."

Ah, those words and what they did to her insides. He wanted to teach her. No one had offered to teach her anything since... well, since she had become a teacher.

"Yes. Please." She smiled at him with all the gratitude she felt.

Some time later, he set the board for their second game. "So," he said, "you lead the local temperance meeting."

"Yes. We've had some successes—the saloon shut down last year." For all that she and the Obregon sisters would likely never join in such a cause again, it remained a proud moment.

"Really?" He adjusted one last piece on the board. "I won't go easy on you this time."

"I'll still win."

"Doubtful. How did you get the saloon shut down?"

She made her first move. "Well, it took months of work. The saloon owner, unsurprisingly, was most resistant to our appeals. So I went to speak to James Harper."

"He's one of the most prominent men in town, isn't he?"

She nodded. "He's also a teetotaler." Her voice strengthened as she went on—he was listening with the most gratifying attentiveness. "After some carefully reasoned arguments on my part, appealing to his moral nature, he spoke with the man who owned the building housing the saloon. The saloonkeeper was told to look for new accommodations, and he chose to leave Cabrillo."

She left out their previous efforts to convince the other men in town to stop frequenting the saloon, efforts that had failed. And there was no need to speak of the anger those men had directed at her once the saloon was gone.

"What did your fiancé think of your efforts?" He kept his eyes firmly on the board, but there was hint of something—disapproval?—in his voice.

"Oh, Joaquin was most supportive. A town without a saloon is one with fewer disturbances."

He nodded abstractedly at the board. "That is very true."

"It hasn't all been victories," she admitted. She deployed her castle, seeing an opportunity to capture his bishop and harass his king. "My efforts in the valley to organize a temperance meeting haven't been as fruitful. And in Cabrillo... well, the Larsens still sell liquor out of their living room on Saturday nights and provide whiskey at the barn dances. Not even the ax incident halted that."

His eyes were quicksilver with surprise. "The ax incident?"

Heat crawled under her cheeks. She wasn't particularly proud of that story.

"At one dance the men were imbibing much more heavily than usual. I'm not certain why. It doesn't excuse the violence of my response, but one particular man—Mr. Kern—his wife was only a month away from delivering their fourth child and he was near to falling down with drink. It made me angry that she must suffer his drunken attentions, his loss of control, while in such a vulnerable state."

"So you went for an ax?"

Her face felt as if the noonday sun were burning it. "No, not then. I saw my sister with…" She sighed. "With Billy Carey, of all people." Her ears buzzed to hear herself say his name. "He was trying to get her alone, rather roughly, and she was resisting. He pinched her, hard enough to make her scream. She managed to throw him off and ran back to the barn. So I found an ax and smashed every last bottle of whiskey I found."

She kept her eyes firmly on the board, pretending to ponder her next move, but in truth not wanting to see censure in his gaze.

"You did the right thing."

Her gaze snapped to his. No one had thought her action that night to be correct—the town had laughed about it behind her back.

"It was very immoderate of me," she pointed out.

"And the drunkards there weren't behaving immoderately?" He drew an edge on the question.

She wasn't quite sure what to say to that. Even Joaquin had disapproved of what she'd done. She'd never told Catarina that she'd seen Billy's assault on her, that the entire incident had been to avenge her sister. No doubt because her initial impulse had been so reprehensible—she'd heard her sister's scream and thought, *Catarina shouldn't have gone off with him like that.*

But of course her sister had never deserved such treatment.

He slid his knight across the board, not waiting for her answer. "So, you took up the cause of temperance for your sister?" he asked.

"No, for my students. My father never touches strong spirits, so it was in my students where I first saw the damage a drunken father can do to a family."

She'd seen her students going hungry because their father had spent the grocery money at the saloon the weekend before, their mothers swelling with yet another baby they couldn't house because their fathers couldn't control their animal urges—and then there were the bruises...

Being confronted with the damage to her pupils, knowing there was little she could do to prevent it—if ridding a town of liquor spared those children, she'd smash every bottle herself.

He pinched a rook between his fingers much too tightly, the skin going red and white with the force he was applying. "I see."

She swallowed hard, debating how far she should take this conversation. Unease was written in his shoulders, in the too-hard grip of his fingers. She wanted to soothe that unease, to give him the comfort he'd offered so often to her, rather than make things worse.

But he *had* brought the subject up. "I made it my mission to save those innocents—the wives, the children— from that. Why should those who are most powerless pay the price for a man's weakness?"

He set the rook back on the board almost too carefully, never looking up. "Innocents always pay the price. You would have to overturn the entire world to change that."

You paid that price, didn't you? You and your mother.

"Even so, we must try. Even if our efforts are doomed to failure, the struggle is still worthwhile," she urged.

He continued scrutinizing the board, although it wasn't his move. She sensed him struggling with something within—not the darkness she sometimes saw, but something deeply melancholic.

When they'd discussed justice before, her arguments had slid right off that reserve of his. But she'd touched a buried nerve this time.

"If you think the struggle is useless," she asked gently, "why become a marshal?"

"I don't believe the struggle is useless, only that..." He gave a wave of his hand, the futility in the gesture squeezing at her heart. "I became a marshal because I do believe in justice. But I know it's not always served."

She pushed further. "So you *do* consider what happens after you deliver a man to the courts?"

He closed his eyes for a moment. "I try not to. What you do, fighting for temperance, losing as often as you win... The directness of being a marshal suits me."

It pained him to speak of this—and an answering echo of that pain moved through her.

"Yes," she said slowly. "It does suit you." Studying him for a moment, taking in the melancholy weighing on him, she pondered her next words. "You say that you could not do as I do, fighting for temperance... well, I could not do what you do, protecting the innocent from the criminal. We each of us have our own fight, and none is less consequential than another."

His face, when he lifted it from the board, was suffused with a gratitude that pained her to see. His gaze held hers for a long moment, and then his expression twisted, mirrored her own ache, and he looked away.

He said nothing, simply breathed into the silence, his hunched shoulders speaking of a need to conceal himself.

Enough. She couldn't allow his torment to continue.

"Shall we finish?" she asked with studied calm.

He straightened, inhaled deeply, and slipped back into impassivity once more. But his next question betrayed his clouded thoughts. "Finish what?"

She gestured to the board.

He frowned down at it. "But you won. Again."

The pique in his voice had her biting back a smile. "Another game?"

An hour later, he was staring at the board in the most delightful state of bafflement. She was only two moves from checkmate—again—and he was dreadfully perturbed.

She watched him considering his options as he studied the pieces, his frown deepening as he discarded one possibility after another. And then, his eyes never leaving the board, he raised his thumb to his mouth and sank his white teeth deep into it, holding tightly.

She nearly gasped. He had never before done anything so... *abandoned.* She could imagine her own teeth sinking into that exact same spot, his skin yielding to the firmness of her mouth, his eyes fluttering closed in sur-render—it made her shudder to her very toes.

"You won. Again." Close to a growl.

She blinked hard to clear her mind. "Do you regret teaching me the rules now?"

His mouth twisted. "Yes, I do."

She busied herself with the board, trying to ignore the persistent quivering in her belly. "Don't like to lose, do you?"

"No. I thought the first two games were sheer chance, but this third?" His eyes narrowed, giving the quivers new life. "Were you by chance lying when you said you didn't know how to play?"

She snorted at the slur to her honor. "Certainly not. I'm simply better at this game than you are."

"No more chess, please. Let's find a game you're not good at."

"It doesn't exist. I never would have expected you to be so put out by losing." She wagged a finger at him. "You'd best be careful, or I'll have all your secrets soon."

His gaze dropped, his limbs tightened—and the at-mosphere turned oppressive.

"I certainly hope not," he said quietly.

She swallowed and tried for levity. "Why, are you afraid I'll stumble across your mad wife in some locked room?"

His gaze slid over her, leaving gooseflesh in its wake. "Hardly. And you are not poor, plain, or obscure."

Well, well, so he *was* familiar with *Jane Eyre*. And *Pride and Prejudice* and *Portrait of a Lady* and *Ramona* and likely scores more she had yet to mention.

"You do read novels!"

"I never said I didn't read novels. I said I didn't care for them."

"You seem to have read quite a few for someone who doesn't like them."

"I read them to my mother." His voice was soft, almost regretful, as he looked off at nothing. "She was... blinded in her right eye and can't read for long periods. It gives her a headache. So I read to her. And once I read a passage, I remember it. Always."

Her lungs emptied in a rush, as if he'd worked her like a bellows. "Oh." She searched for a response. "I didn't notice. About your mother."

He continued to ponder something she couldn't see. "There were a great many things no one noticed."

She laid a hand on his arm, her skin starkly white against his suit. Had any other man told her he read novels to his mother, she would have thought it unremarkable.

In him, she thought it extraordinary.

"I shall pray for you," she offered. "The both of you."

He shook his head. "My mother is… She doesn't need those prayers any longer. But me?" His voice was harsh, low. "I do. I most certainly do."

"Then I will pray for you." Pray that his torment might cease, that he might find a measure of peace.

He turned to her, his expression bleak, and her heart rent at the sight.

She wanted to offer him something, some assurance that he wasn't alone—but he already had all of her secrets. Knew how deeply she herself had suffered.

But she *did* have something to offer him—it wasn't her own secret, but it might ease his pain.

"My mother," she began, "she was married before. He—he hurt her." Isabel's heart hammered with anxiety. Perhaps she ought not to be sharing this, perhaps she ought to have kept this last secret to herself—she prayed she wasn't miscalculating.

His expression remained bleak. "Such a story is all too common. There's nothing unusual in it."

She recognized the impulse behind those words; he didn't think himself deserving of sympathy.

"There's more to the story. You've heard of the Alvarado heiress, I'm sure. The one who… who shot Judge Bannister's brother." She couldn't say *murder*, couldn't say the word *husband*.

"Of course." Puzzlement creased his brow. "Bannister men murdered her brother, supposedly. She disappeared after killing her husband. But the judge had nothing to do with that—he was a very young man at the time."

Time to confess the last. There was no going back. "My mother was as well. But not too young to be married."

Comprehension had his face sagging. "That's why... That's what the three of you were hiding, at our first meeting. You thought I might betray her to Judge Bannister."

"You won't, will you?" Dear Lord, let her not have misjudged him, to have gambled and lost...

"Of course not." His voice vibrated with conviction. "I could never betray a person you loved. Not your own mother." He went still for a moment. "That's why she abandoned you at the trial."

Unease twisted through her insides. "She didn't *abandon* me."

Not at all. Her mother had only been protecting herself. She knew Isabel was strong enough to survive such a thing alone.

And he had been there, in the end.

"The judge cannot know she's here," she continued. "If he somehow realizes who she is, asks you to confirm his suspicions—what will you say?"

It was irrational, she knew—how would the judge find out?—but the threat to her mother made her irrational.

"I will lie to him," he said simply.

"You would?" Surprise chased away the last of her unease, warmth spreading in its wake.

"Isabel." His expression softened. "Don't you know by now that I would do a great many things for you? To keep you and yours safe?"

The weight of that assurance stilled her lips to silence. Held her heart to quietude.

"I know what it is to see your mother cowering in terror because of a man," he went on. "I would never inflict such a thing on you. You believe me, don't you?"

He wanted proof of her faith. Well, she would give it to him.

She kissed him.

He was still, only the rush of his breath indicating he was not a statue under her lips. For a brief moment she wanted to snatch herself back, to undo the press of her lips against his. But it was too late.

He was pushing her beyond the wall of his reserve again, before this kiss had even begun.

Just as she was about to pull away, he sighed into the kiss, into her, and she was warmed all over.

As harsh and frantic as their first embrace had been, this was soft, leisurely. They had an eternity to explore each other's lips, to find the entirety of the universe within, and they would take the time they'd been given.

He lifted her onto his lap, draping her legs across his thighs as he removed her spectacles, sliding the frames from her face with aching care. Once she was secured, he settled kisses all along her forehead, her temples, and at the corners of her eyes.

For all the hardness of his thighs under her legs, the unyielding expanse of his chest under her hands, the brush of his lips against her skin was only slightly more substantial than the touch of a breeze.

There was a reverence at work there. Each contact said, *You are precious, you are cherished.*

A monster would never—could never—kiss so.

He made his way along her cheek, coming to the edge of her jaw, and she stilled. His mouth remained along that boundary, not once heading over.

"I wouldn't ever touch your neck," he whispered.

Tears burned in her eyes.

"I want to," he continued against her ear. "I want to so badly, my hand shakes with it. But"—he pulled back to gaze at her—"I never would."

She longed to give him permission, to let him place his lips there, where her pulse throbbed with want for him, but she couldn't. Not even for him.

"You've been wounded worse than I have," she said. "Where can I touch you?"

"Anywhere." A teasing spark lit his expression. "Everywhere."

Their next kiss was hotter, more insistent. She ran her hands anywhere she could reach, wishing she could peel the black fabric away to find the warm skin hidden beneath.

He pressed kisses against the lace-covered expanse between her neck and her bosom, the fever of his breath traveling right through the thin fabric to caress her skin. Once, twice, he lifted his hands to the buttons running down her shirtwaist. Both times he let them fall.

"Give me leave, Isabel," he said. "Permit me."

She lifted her own unsteady hands and eased the buttons free herself. He watched as though she were unwrapping a prophecy, as if he might see his future written on her skin.

When the last button came free, he lifted his hand without hurry to that bare strip of skin, running the backs of his fingers across it. Eddies of sensation followed in their wake, swirling through her like smoke curls, dancing around the smolder building between her legs.

His fingers brushed lower, trailing across her chemise, then her corset. Her breasts tightened, silently asking for his touch.

He didn't answer. Instead, he put his hands to her hair. His touch was light, yet her scalp tingled.

"I want to see it. May I?" He tugged at one of the pins.

"My hair?" He had her unbuttoned to the waist and he wanted to see her hair?

No man had ever seen her hair unbound, the fall of it reaching past her flanks. For *him* to see it thus, his scarred hands running through it...

She nodded and he snatched out the pins, the mass of her hair kicking free of the simple twist she favored to fall across her back. He combed through it, his fingers massaging her scalp as he spread her tresses about her. She almost moaned with pleasure at the heavy kneading of his hands.

"I can see now why the Turks keep their ladies strictly covered." His voice was so deep, so harsh, so close to her ear, she shuddered with it. "You would tempt a saint to sin looking as you do."

His face was taut with desire and she could almost believe him, could almost believe she could tempt *him* to sin.

He lowered his chin to the top of her head and breathed deeply. "You smell like books."

She swallowed a shaky chuckle. "You mean dry and dusty?"

He shook his head, his jaw rubbing across her hair. "No, more like a sunny afternoon spent lost among the pages. You smell like... escape. Anticipation."

Something quite beyond desire or comfort filled her at his words. Something that only just fit within her frame; any larger and she would burst with it.

His fingers in her scalp stilled. "Is this where he hit you?"

"Yes."

He gently probed the scar he'd found. "Does it hurt?"

"Not any longer. There are the headaches, but the scar itself doesn't pain me."

He ran his fingers across it one last time, then caught up her hand and pressed a hot kiss into her palm. "I'm sorry he marked you."

She tugged his hand toward her. "You have your own marks."

She kissed the scars on his knuckles, feeling the thin ridges of them against her lips, wondering if they pained him.

"Don't." He pulled his hand away abruptly, her fingers closing on emptiness as he did. "I deserve those. And more."

She looked him up and down, knowing that under his fine clothes were more scars, more than any man deserved.

"You said I could touch you." She put a dare into those words.

His eyes were wary, as if he sensed her purpose. "So I did. Shall I let down my hair for you?"

She reached up to run a hand through his hair. "You hardly have enough to grasp, much less let down." She'd noticed that although he never wore pomade, his hair was never out of place. "It's so short as to be unfashionable."

"I don't care for fashion."

She raised an eyebrow. "Oh, really? Then you won't mind if I do this."

She popped a button clean off his shirt, enjoying the gap she'd made. She and Joaquin had never played such games, had never thought to—but she was enjoying it, silly as it was.

"You could just ask me to disrobe." His words were arid, the undercurrent of heat licking at her.

She settled her hands primly in her lap. "Disrobe. Please."

He wrestled out of his jacket and waistcoat with one hand, while the other pulled free his necktie and collar. Such clever fingers he had. Her skin tingled at the thought of those clever fingers going to work on her.

"If you want me to disrobe completely," he said as he finished, "you should remember our mothers will return at any moment. You might wish to begin to compose a likely explanation for them."

She pretended to ponder that. "Very well. Unbutton only your shirt. Then we'll be equally unclothed."

Slowly he did so, watching her as she watched him. One button free—and then a pause, the anticipation building. Another button free, each breath they released adding to the swell of tension. And then the last button was loose and the teasing was entirely finished.

She slid her hand beneath the linen and shuddered at that first brush of hot male skin against her fingertips. The rise and fall of his chest moved the dark hair ticklishly under her palm.

She inched her way along the plane of muscle to his shoulder—and halted at something raised and hard.

A scar, nearly as wide as her finger, and who knew how long.

He caught at her hand, trapping it flat against the unmarred part of him.

"Did your father do this?" What kind of a father would leave such a mark on his son?

"No." With no further explanation, he claimed her mouth again, this time with urgent intent. Her blood pulsed with the promise of it.

She shifted on his lap, trying to crowd closer while also exploring every inch of what was under his shirt. His hands pulled her deeper, her hip jutting against his lower belly.

Finding one of his nipples—finally—she plucked and pinched, avoiding the scar lying only an inch away. His mouth grew ever more demanding and his hips turned in a licentious rhythm, each roll sending a pulse straight through the pit of her belly. She shifted again, partly to relieve the ache building there, and partly to reach more of him, mewling when she couldn't quite manage either.

He lifted her to settle her astride him, her skirts shoved nearly to her waist. Her hair formed a curtain all about them as she retook his mouth, her hands free to do whatever they pleased.

His hips moved against hers in earnest and she moved with him, craving the sweet friction as they rocked and kissed together.

He yanked down her shirtwaist to expose a shoulder, all the while pressing love bites against her lower lip. She'd never dreamed the sting of his teeth could be so sweet.

He moved to her collarbone, sucking and biting as her own hands moved ever lower. The trail of hair that led from his navel was coarse, curling round her fingers as if begging her to explore what was hidden under his waistband, that hard length pressed between her legs.

He groaned hotly against her shoulder when she found the fastening of his trousers, the muscles of his belly quivering under her fingers. She bit her lip as she struggled with the fabric and her own trembling hands. Only a little more work and...

The clatter of the front door brought her crashing back from where she'd been flying. Her heart skittered at the murmur of voices from beyond the library door.

Sebastian pulled away slightly, but made no move to set himself to rights. Instead, he cocked one ear toward the door, listening for a moment, then turned back to jolt her with those storm-cloud eyes.

The voices began to move toward the library.

His mouth began to travel toward hers.

The voices grew closer and closer, clearly now those of the Señoras.

His mouth moved closer and closer, clearly intent on a kiss.

The voices were right outside the door and his mouth was hot against hers, the danger of exposure making the pleasure that much more heady. He pulled her tight against him, driving their bodies against one another as their tongues tangled.

Nervousness danced in her stomach as her heart pounded with his, waiting for their mothers to open the door and discover them...

The voices moved on, receding as they went on to the rest of the house.

"Lupe, how long until dinner?" she heard.

The exhilaration suddenly emptied, leaving her sagged against him. He kept his hands at her hips, anchoring her against him in a most carnal manner.

Her rational mind told her to pull away before they were caught, but she wasn't particularly interested in listening.

They stared at one another, intent as two fighters in a ring.

"I won't apologize." He was being neither aggressive nor regretful, merely stating a fact.

"Neither will I." She had nothing to be sorry for.

"I would say that this has been a mistake, but I've never wanted to repeat a mistake so much in my entire life."

She smiled, but couldn't bring herself to admit she, too, wanted to repeat this, as soon as possible. "I suppose we should refasten our clothes."

He gave her one last kiss, pulling away much too soon. "Yes, I suppose so."

He kept her on his lap as they buttoned one another up, the backs of her thighs tingling at the feel of him under them. He helped her repair her hair, their fingers tangling together as they did the best they could without a brush and a looking glass.

By the time the soft rap came at the door, they both looked respectable once more.

"Sebastian?" his mother called. "Are you there?"

"Yes, Mother," he said.

Señora Vasquez opened the door, Isabel's mother right behind her. Both of them looked about, sharpishly.

Isabel licked her stinging lips, innocently she hoped.

"We've been playing chess." He gestured to the board, set for a new game.

"Chess," her mother repeated slowly, disbelief written in the crease between her eyes. "I didn't know Isabel knew how to play."

"Sebastian taught me today."

Señora Vasquez's smile was tipped with mischief. "You're quite good," she said to her son. "Is it too much to hope Señorita Moreno won at least one game?"

"The Señorita has a natural gift. She won more than a few games." When his gaze met hers, she had to look away before she blushed.

She caught her mother's eye as she did. Her mother raised a brow. "It must have been difficult to see the board without your spectacles, Isabel."

Isabel's blush burned from her scalp all the way to her toes.

~~~

Sebastian carried with him the strangest sensation for the remainder of the evening. A tingling lightness in his chest that made him feel as though his heels were a fraction of an inch off the ground.

When she'd first set her lips to his, he'd meant to refuse her. Gently of course, but a refusal nonetheless. Then something shifted within him and he realized he could not.

After yesterday, she had only to give the command—or simply a request—and he would follow her anywhere.

In the end, it had been the greatest relief, not to hold himself in and assume his usual mask. To abandon his reserve, if only for a moment.

He had simply been Sebastian in those moments, playing at love with a lady he cared for.

Dinner was a storm of ambivalence from the Señoras, with Señora Moreno sending him repressive looks every chance she had, while his mother sent him approving looks every chance she had.

They couldn't know for certain what had happened in the library, but they certainly suspected.

Señora Moreno's suspicion he would weather. His mother's, tinged as it was with triumph, would be harder to disregard.

Isabel, for her part, appeared to have that same effervescence lodged in her chest. He imagined kissing her until they both burst with it.

After the last bite was consumed, before her fork hit the plate, Señora Moreno herded her daughter to the safety of their bedrooms.

He stared at the door for a long moment after they disappeared, the soda water sensation in him flattening as he realized he wouldn't see her again until tomorrow.

"Sebastian."

He knew what was coming next. The lilt of his mother's voice was a dead giveaway.

"Nothing improper occurred," he said, guilt twitching in him.

It was true, if you counted only the act of penetration as improper—and nothing else.

"Hmm," she said.

He didn't respond. He rolled his knuckles against the table, watching as the skin went as white as the scars crossing them.

His mother wasn't deterred. "I know you would do nothing truly dishonorable."

She knew no such thing. In fact, she knew exactly how dishonorable he could be. He hadn't been able to hide all of his crimes from her.

"There can be nothing of permanence between me and the Señorita," he reminded her. "When the trial is done, she's going back from where she came. Don't begin planning the wedding."

He thought she might argue, say something witty about how a lady could live just as well in Los Angeles as Cabrillo, but she didn't.

She did something much worse.

"He's been gone for fifteen years," she said, her voice heavy with entreaty. "You've been redeemed for nearly as long. Isn't it time you began to act as such?"

It shouldn't have hurt as much as it did; he'd finished with his father years ago. Even so, his clothes became unbearable against his skin, his collar too tight, the chair trapping him in its embrace.

"Is he really gone?" Sharper than he'd intended. "Because every day in that courthouse, I hear of what a great man he was, what a loss we suffered when he died. They speak of him as some kind of hero, when all the while he was beating you until he could no longer raise his arm. Whether he was drunk, whether he was sober, whether you looked sideways at him, or didn't look at all—"

He shook his head. His mother had been there for all of it—she didn't need it repeated.

"I don't want to speak of what he did to us." She waved a small hand, the same one his father had broken so badly the doctor had been shocked at the damage. "I wish to speak of what you'll do now. Because I've seen you, Sebastian. You *look* at her. With an openness, a hope, I've never seen before."

Hope. The room spun sickeningly. He gripped the edge of the table tightly, clutching for some kind of anchor.

"I do not," he spat through his clenched jaw.

His mother sighed. "What you did at the beginning, as a cure? It was necessary. I know that. But now... it's too much, too severe. You must unbend, or you will break."

He gripped the table tighter and tighter, his fingers aching with the effort of keeping himself right there, not to fly off into who knew where. He couldn't answer her, could barely breathe. All he could do was hang on for dear life.

After a time, she rose and left.

And still he gripped the table.

Slowly, minutes or hours later—he wasn't certain—he pried his stiff, cramped fingers from the table and went for the safety of the library.

Only it wasn't safe any longer. *She* had been there.

A lone hairpin crunched under his boot as crossed the room. He picked it up and studied the twisted shape, bent beyond repair by his clumsiness.

He contemplated that little reminder of what happened when he grew careless.

Things ended up bent, broken.

Destroyed.

He carefully placed the pin on a side table for Isabel to find tomorrow, then pulled down his notebook and sat on the sofa.

Before he began to catalogue the day's sins—and there were many—he leaned his head back, letting his jaw sag, remembering what he'd done with her in this exact spot not a few hours earlier.

He raised a hand to sketch her: the slope of her jaw, her breasts which curved just so, the swell of her hip coming to hand. And finally her hair, the great dark fall of it, enough to shield the both of them from the rest of the world.

He could write an entire novel of what they'd done that day, of everything still running through him at the thought of her, but really, the one sentence would do.

He picked up his pen and set it down in ink.

Quiero chingar Isabel Moreno.

The word looked so rude, hissing and guttural all at once. He wrote it out in English as well, for good measure.

I want to fuck Isabel Moreno.

Strange that the English words should be so different, yet still hold the same rasp, the same thrust, as the Spanish.

He put it down in French, in Italian, in Latin, in every language he knew. He wanted to set his hands and mouth to her until her cries were beyond any language either of them knew—

He slammed the book shut.

Done.

Gone.

But it wasn't. The urge to grab hold of her, to bury himself—all of himself—within her still crept under his skin. It would take a surgeon to remove it at this point.

She was invading all the small parts of him, just as he'd feared.

There wasn't room for her within him; his years of self-denial had made sure of that. She would burrow her way in and then, in her quest for space, would shatter the shell of him from the inside out.

There was no way to stop it. He could only hope to survive until she left.

He set the notebook back on the shelf, and before he retired for the night made certain the dog was securely locked outside of the house—and well away from Isabel.

CHAPTER SIXTEEN

ISABEL SPENT THE MORNING BEING interrogated by her mother.

The experience was a novel one for her. She'd seen that look of the Señora's before—the pinched mouth, the narrowed eyes—but it had never been directed toward her. She was the good child, the one who never put a foot wrong.

She supposed she should be experiencing something like shame—clearly her mother thought so—but the best she could summon was a sort of abashed bemusement. She sat with folded hands on the edge of her bed, awaiting her mother's scolding.

"I always expected something like this from Catarina," her mother began, "but never from you."

"Because I'm not beautiful?" So keen was the edge of her mother's words against her pride that she spoke without thought.

"Because you are too intelligent," her mother snapped. She'd utter no false compliments about Isabel's beauty. "You've never let a man turn your head. You were so methodical, so sure, with Joaquin—I never had to be concerned about *your* choices."

Her mother studied her as if trying to puzzle out what was happening in Isabel's head. Isabel wasn't quite sure what was happening there herself.

"Was I wrong?" her mother demanded.

Before today, she would have agreed with her mother. She had chosen Joaquin with deliberation and a lack of sentiment she'd thought would serve them both well. But now?

Now all she could think of was the marshal's hands on her, his mouth tangling with hers, the pure need he awakened within her. She wasn't sure if she liked this, this burning on her tongue, in her throat, a burning that ran throughout her entire body when she tried to ignore it.

"No, you weren't wrong."

At least not when it came to what Isabel had been before. Before, she'd never been the kind of girl who kissed a man with her spectacles off and her hair down.

"I've learned some very disturbing things about the marshal's father from Cousin Enrique," her mother said. "He told me when we were out, the day the shooting occurred, but I thought it best not to mention. Not with what you had to face the next day."

The next day had been the trial. And the judge's collapse.

Tangles upon tangles—would she ever feel unknotted again?

"What did he say?" Isabel ventured.

"That Judge Spencer was overly fond of drink and it killed him."

Which wasn't even half of what Isabel suspected had happened. "The marshal is a teetotaler," was all she said.

"These things do run in families."

"So we are to condemn the marshal with the sins of his father?" Isabel retorted.

If only her mother had seen Sebastian's reaction whenever his father was mentioned, she would not say such things.

Her mother hadn't heard Sebastian's confessions about his father, about what the man had done to Señora Vasquez—and Isabel wouldn't share those with her mother. That intimacy was hers and Sebastian's alone.

As for Isabel's own confession about her mother's first husband—that too she'd keep between him and her.

"I thought—well, never mind what I thought yesterday," her mother said. "You are not to be alone with him."

For the very first time in her life, Isabel was ready to disobey her mother. "Am I confined to my room?" she challenged.

Her mother's face softened. "No. I'll be here, to act as a chaperone. You may go to the library, as long as he's not there."

Señora Moreno was wrong about Sebastian. Isabel wouldn't allow her mother's prejudice to keep him from her, even if she had little hope of convincing her mother of her error.

Isabel pondered how to give the appearance of agreeing with her mother without actually doing so. Deceit did not come easily to her, but she couldn't promise. She nodded once, quickly, and hoped it would be enough.

Her mother relaxed at Isabel's seeming acquiescence. "I will be sewing in the parlor with Señora Vasquez. Will you join us?"

Here then already was a test. She could sit quietly with the ladies, avoiding temptation, or—

"May I go to the library?"

Her mother's expression hardened, but she only motioned Isabel toward the door.

In the end, temptation—and her mother—had nothing to fear, since Sebastian wasn't in the library.

Now, she had only the task of finding something to read.

But first... she sidled up to the window. A tilt of her head, and a sliver of the street came into view.

A little further tilt, a little more street. Her neck stretched, her gaze searching inch by inch...

She fell onto the shelves behind her. He wasn't there today. He wasn't there.

She rubbed at her temple, wishing her nerves would give her some rest, would let her look at such things rationally, instead of through a haze of terror. Telling which dangers were real and which were phantoms was impossible when her anxiety insisted that it was all real, that danger was just outside every window.

She knew it wasn't—she only wished to be able to tell the difference again.

She tilted her head back, the twist of her hair dragging along the books behind her as her gaze fell on the far shelves.

Row upon row of unmarked black spines—their very blankness sparked her curiosity. She walked over, looked more closely. She'd wondered before what they were, deciding they must be journals or diaries of some sort and therefore not for her perusal.

Only, what if they weren't?

She ran a fingertip along the spines as though the contents would seep through the pages into her skin, the ink coiling through her to sink into her mind.

What was in them?

There must have been at least twenty, all bound in the same black leather, all the same size. Perfectly matched books, marching along like grim soldiers.

Likely they were only household accounts or something equally prosaic, a tally of all the odds and ends that summed up a household.

It certainly wouldn't be a tally of Sebastian's odds and ends, the bits that summed up to the whole of him.

A deep tug of inquisitiveness had her choosing one at random and pulling. It slid halfway free then stuck, as if to ask, *Are you certain?*

He hadn't said she couldn't look at them. He hadn't forbidden her anything.

The notebook came completely free of its neighbors with a soft sigh of surrender. She opened it to a random page.

26th January, 1892—Took pleasure in the sunset. Angered by a lawyer's questions.

Neat, intent script—no excess flourishes or blots. The paper under her fingers was nearly as smooth as the sheets she'd slept on last night. What a strange thing to record, those moments of pleasure and of anger. She flipped through the rest of the book.

Wished to strike the judge.

Had carnal thoughts about a lady on the street.

Almost smiled at a child playing with a dog.

No actions, no deeds—only sensations. Thoughts. Impulses. Not every day—certain dates had no entries at all. Did that mean he'd felt nothing important enough to record on those days?

Or had felt nothing at all?

She slid the book back, her hand trembling. She looked them over again, all twenty-some of them. Her curiosity was a flame, fed by the strangeness of what she'd seen. Were they all like this?

She noticed three volumes at the very bottom of the shelves, tucked into a corner, and crouched to see them better.

Touching each one with a fingertip, she read off the titles. *The Spiritual Exercises of St. Ignatius. The Works of Seneca the Younger. The Meditations of Marcus Aurelius.*

Nothing exceptional there. If there ever was a man inclined to the philosophy of the Stoics, it was Sebastian.

There weren't only books there; a slip of thick paper peeped out from between Marcus Aurelius and Seneca. The photograph came free with the slightest of tugs, much easier than the notebook had.

She recognized his father at once, despite never having seen him before. Where Sebastian carried his heft like a possession he didn't want, this man sat with his bulk on proud display, his mouth concealed by a beard, the gaze beneath his heavy brow direct, intent. As if he could rise from the photograph and bend one to his will.

She slid the photograph back in its hiding place, her fingertips feeling unclean. She pulled out the last notebook, the one closest to her, and flipped to the most recent entry.

What she saw set her aflame.

He had written this just last night. While she had been in her bed, dreaming of all the dark, sensual things she wanted to do with him, he was writing *this*.

Her skin sizzled as she read the words again and again. She ought to be repelled by the crudity of it, but it excited her. A shameful urge took root between her legs.

She shut the book with an echoing thump, trying to slow her wild breath, to will away this dizzy heat that made her ache.

She was wrong. She *had* found a tally of him, the bits and pieces he tried to hide from the world.

His entire emotional life was right here, locked away behind these black spines.

But why? Why must everything be imprisoned here? Why wouldn't he allow himself to experience these emotions?

Frowning as she did so, she pulled down the very first notebook and set to find out.

~~~

So she had found them.

Sebastian looked at Isabel sitting on the floor of the library, notebooks pinning down the circle of her skirts. She was so engrossed, she hadn't glanced up as he entered.

Or perhaps she couldn't bear to look at him after what she'd read there.

Her expression was indecipherable, as flat and blank as when he'd first met her. He told himself it was better than disgust, even as his hands began to shake.

The same dizziness that had taken hold of him last night jolted him again, and he knew if he didn't grab on to something, he would spin out into nothingness.

But there was nothing to grab hold of except for her. And she would never allow him to touch her again.

Not if she'd read the notebooks.

"I see you found them," he said, when he trusted his voice not to shake.

"Yes." She didn't look up, and he was grateful to be spared her gaze. "But you wanted me to look in them. Didn't you?"

She turned another page.

Had he? He'd every opportunity to remove them— and he never had. "I suppose I did."

His heart throbbed painfully as he watched her for a moment more. As he etched in his infallible memory the silk of her hair as the afternoon light caught it, the curve of her jaw as she ever so faintly mouthed the words, the sweep of her lashes as her eyes ran across the pages.

This might be the only time he could look on her like this, without others watching. Without her turning from him.

The last thing he wanted to do was speak, to ask the question that would send them hurtling to their inevitable end.

He steeled his nerve anyway.

"Did you read them all?" His words were splintered, but he'd no control at this moment. No control at all.

"Is that your way of asking if I know *all* your secrets?"

He swore that her gaze, unflinching as it was, burned a hole straight through his center. He raised his hand to rub at the scorch marks that must be there, the fabric of his waistcoat as rough as a hair shirt.

"Your way of asking if I now know that you beat a man to death with your bare hands?" she finished.

He was more stunned by her tone than her words.

She'd said it baldly, as if it weren't a terrible deed, as if his soul weren't forever stained by it. Perhaps she was still in shock from what she'd read. Because if she knew, if she *truly* knew, she'd not be so calm. So... so *serene*.

He noticed then that she had the notebook open to the very first entry, the start of what was to become the rest of his life. Her fingers idly traced the smear of rust red on the page.

"Don't." His voice cracked.

"Why?" It was more demand than question.

There was a wealth of meaning behind it. Why have her stop tracing the visceral evidence of his crime? Why did he have all these notebooks? Why had he done what he had all those years ago?

He began with the easiest part. "My father, he... he brutalized us. For years." It wasn't an excuse, but it was an explanation. "Rage was his constant companion and he set that rage upon us when the mood struck him. Which was often. The liquor fed the rage." Rage had been Sebastian's constant companion then as well, an impotent fury desiring the destruction of all he encountered. "I couldn't intervene when he set upon my mother—that only made it worse. And he was always so much bigger than me, no matter how I grew."

She closed the book and looked up at him. God, why wasn't she running away? Her composure stung more than her hand across his face would have.

He swallowed, moving on to the difficult part. "Finally, after years of wishing for it, when I was fifteen, he died. I was packed with dynamite by then and his death lit the match." He sighed softly. "I went mad."

Still no reaction. He suspected she could be staring at the very mouth of Hell and would wear that unsettling blankness on her face.

"If I could fight it, I did. If I could fuck it, I did." His gut twisted in rebellion that he should have to admit this to her, but there was worse to come, and she knew it. "There was no limit to the evil a young man with a bit of money could do in this town, especially with the company I kept."

"Liquor?" Sharp—she expected him to say yes.

"No." He shuddered. "After watching him die the way he did… He was yellow by the end, as if he were turning to wax." He gave a violent shake of his head. "No, never that. Everything but that."

"And your mother?"

"She was frantic, of course. She had no idea what to do with me. She'd only just buried the man who'd made her life a prison, and now her son was traveling the same path. I would come home bloody, bruised, after a night of depravity—or was carried home, in the worst cases." Even now, the thought of how badly he'd wounded his mother, just as surely as his father had, made his throat clog. His nostrils flared, catching the faint scent of smoke in the air. "She never tried to stop me, though. She'd learned that lesson with my father—never try to stop us when we're in a rage."

She tapped the cover of the book, the sound echoing through the room. "When did this occur?"

Her tone was as implacable as any judge's, demanding a full and true accounting of his crimes. Of course, he knew what would happen after the confession.

The punishment.

"I was seventeen," he said.

"So, not old." She speared him with her gaze. "But not young." She held the book in her palm, weighing it, watching him as if she were weighing his very heart. He prayed she should not find it wanting and toss it to the waiting jackals.

But his heart *was* wanting. It had been forever blackened at seventeen.

No, he couldn't claim youth as an excuse. Now he had only to confess the very worst of it—the very worst of him—and alienate her forever.

"He was a young man, about my age, out for trouble, just as I was. We dared the other to strike. Two stupid young cocks trying to sharpen their spurs on each other." The bitterness of the memory seeped into his tone.

He rubbed at his forehead, at the memory of what fools the both of them had been. "I struck him until he went down, until he went still. But... it wasn't enough. The rage, it just grew hotter with each swing of my arm. So I kept striking him. Even when he wouldn't move. I struck him until his face was nothing more than fragments of bone and bits of brain." At the memory, his knuckles ached, but not as much the hollow space behind his breastbone. "After, without a thought, without a care for him, I went home."

He'd no idea what had become of the young man— whether he had family who keened their sorrow at his demise, whether he had a sweetheart left bereft at the loss of him—he didn't even know his name.

Sebastian looked at the knuckles that had done that terrible thing, watching the scars stretch and pull as he flexed his fingers.

He'd never again see those hands fasten on her flesh, would never hear her soft sighs as he ran those hands along her skin.

Because these were the hands of a murderer.

Easier to look at those hands rather than her expression, coward that he was.

"My mother was entertaining one of her friends, Mrs. Hathaway, when I returned," he went on. "I overheard them discussing my wildness and my mother's worries, and Mrs. Hathaway said very clearly, 'Well, Sebastian's blood is finally showing.'" He tried to swallow past the dryness in his throat, feeling as if he'd eaten a full bucket of ash. "I knew what she meant. She meant my Mexican blood, that I was only living up to the heritage of our people."

He tried to swallow again, but it was too much, his throat too tight.

He distinctly remembered his mother's reaction to those words, the way her chin had dipped low—dragged down by the weight of him and his madness.

"She was right," he said. The words were coming with difficulty now, each one pulled from somewhere far past his throat.

He hadn't been free to comfort his mother—because he was covered to his forearms in another man's blood.

"She was right," he repeated, "but not in the way she thought. It was my *father's* blood that was showing, not that of my mother."

What's bred in the bone will come out in the blood.

The rest came in a rush, his throat somehow un-stopped. "I was killing my mother, just as my father had, only with my wickedness rather than my fists. I resolved then and there to spend the rest of my life doing pen-ance for it. And for every evil thing I'd done before then."

Her eyes, her posture, the very essence of her was still and solemn. There wasn't a hint of give in her frame. She ought to be running screaming from the room to hide behind her mother's skirts, especially after what that animal McCade had done to her.

But she remained. She was so quiet, so somber, as he bared the worst of himself to her, as he flayed himself before her.

"I didn't know how, at first... how to eradicate the evil within me." He gestured to the books surrounding her. "That's where the notebooks came from. Each time I had any kind of sensation, good or bad, I put it in there. Eventually, I stopped experiencing most sensations."

"I noticed that. From the entries."

Had he imagined the softening of her voice? He must have. She wouldn't show mercy to a murderer like him.

She was rising, the books falling from her skirts like so many dead leaves as she came toward him.

Knowing she would have to sweep past him as she made for the door, he held himself stiff to keep from reaching out to her.

But she didn't leave.

She wrapped her arms around him instead.

He stood rigid in her embrace, not daring to believe this was real, that she could be doing such a thing after everything he'd told her.

The scent of her surrounding him, the press of her chest against him, the bands of her arms along his back, the silk of her hair against his neck—it was all the product of his fevered brain.

It couldn't be real. He didn't *deserve* it to be real.

"Sebastian," she said quietly, and he ached to hear her say his name, "you said that only two people use your given name. How many people touch you?"

He closed his eyes against the sweet pain of that. "None."

"Well, now there is one person who touches you. Me." Tender enough to slice straight to his heart.

He'd been correct at their first meeting. She would draw his blood, but he'd had no way of knowing it would be his heart's blood, that she would set him to inwardly bleeding with her softness.

Her forgiveness.

He put an arm around her, pulling her deeper as he tipped her face toward his, her skin yielding, supple.

"Why?" he asked. "What I've done…" He faltered under the press of her against him, the knowledge she had not left. "It's a mortal sin."

"It is. You will have to do penance your entire life for it." She raised her little hand to his cheek, the weight of it surprisingly heavy. "And you *will* do penance. You already have. You are even now. An evil man would never go to such lengths to make amends for what he'd done. An evil man wouldn't deserve this."

She raised herself to brush her lips to his.

He closed his eyes against the unfamiliar burning there, a prickling he hadn't felt since before his father died. Her mouth was whisper-soft against his as her hand cupped his cheek.

Something wetly hot traveled down his face to graze her fingers.

Sebastian wouldn't have been more surprised had rain fallen from a clear, blue sky.

He set his forehead to hers, his breath stuttering through his chest. "I don't deserve this."

"None of us do." Tinged with exquisite sadness. "That's the beauty of forgiveness."

Forgiveness. He didn't deserve it. Yet he found, as with her kiss, he could not refuse what she offered. Could not refuse her.

Perhaps his mother was right. Perhaps the time to unbend had come. To unbend to Isabel.

He could already feel himself doing so, the core of him leaning into her. Violence had made him what he was, violence had set her in his path.

Yet perhaps there was hope. Was this sensation hope, this lightness? This wonder within him that bent him toward her? He wasn't certain.

He only knew he could no longer suppress any emotion she called forth from him.

CHAPTER SEVENTEEN

ISABEL LAY WITH THE SHEETS twisted round her waist, listening in the dark as the clock struck two.

Her mind was too much occupied to sleep, but she didn't dare leave her room. She knew, just knew her mother was listening from the room next door.

She also knew Sebastian was awake, somewhere in the house.

The air fairly hums with it.

The air around her was humming right now, snapping and crackling against her skin. Her legs ached with the urge to find him. She kicked the sheet away in frustration, the cool of night washing across her skin as the nightgown bunched at the tops of her thighs.

Those notebooks had been revelatory. His confession had been heartbreaking.

He might look as she imagined St. Ignatius did, but it was St. Augustine's words that echoed as she read those books.

I confess.

The words written there had been both penance and confession, as he worked to make amends for what he had done. It didn't lessen the severity of his crime—

343

which was severe, make no mistake—but the effort behind those amends!

All those pages and pages as he eradicated his emotions, his very self. She wanted to weep again at the
memory. She'd held her tears until after she left the library, not wanting him to see and think they were
meant as censure of him.

He had censured himself more than enough.

She wept for him, for the young man whose life he'd
ended, for his mother, and finally for herself.

Because tomorrow the trial would resume. She'd play
the part she'd been assigned in all this, play it as best she
could, then return to Cabrillo.

She'd never wished so hard that things could have
been different. She could have met him years ago, on a
trip to visit her cousins, met him quite naturally. They
could have courted as normal people did, as she and
Joaquin had. Such a meeting wouldn't have been choked
with these forced confessions and this strained intimacy.

But without that force, would either of them have
cracked?

And, oh Lord, when he cracked...

I want.

It was only the smallest part of what he'd written in
that last entry, the one that sent a fire through her, but it
was the only part she could whisper, even in the privacy
of her thoughts.

If she imagined the rest of it, those crude words would bring to mind in stark detail all the carnal things she wanted to do with him in the dead of night, and she would melt right into this bed.

She threw her head back into the pillow as she imagined finding him tonight, undressed as she was and aching, aching for him. The pleasure that hit her was so sharp, she rolled her fist into her belly for relief.

Lord, grant me chastity and continence. But not yet.

More words of St. Augustine's. But the saint had been a coward compared to Sebastian. The marshal hadn't asked for continence—he had seized it himself, with both hands, holding it as tightly as...

As tightly as she wanted him to hold her.

Lord, grant me chastity and continence.

But not yet.

She kicked her legs over the side of the bed. The floor was cold and hard under her feet as she slipped as quietly as she could from her room, her ears straining for any sound.

She hardly breathed as she went past the bedroom doors, her lungs burning and her ears near to bursting with the silence. When she made it to the stairs without incident, she sucked in sweet, cool air as a reward.

I want, I want.

The beat of it drove her all the way to the library doors.

Where she stopped.

He was there, she knew—his vitality, his bulk, radiated through the very walls. If she put her hand to the door, the wood itself would breathe with him.

She held up her own hands for inspection, spreading the fingers wide. Thin and long, too stretched to be dainty or ladylike, the skin there smooth.

His hands were large, scarred—the hands of a murderer.

She wanted those hands over every inch of her skin.

She'd had a murderer's hands on her before. Hands bent on murdering *her*.

Her entire self, every atom of her rebelled at the memory, fought to throw off the phantom image of McCade's hands on her.

Yet at the thought of Sebastian's hands on her, those same atoms arched towards the door, toward him, bowing her back as they did. His hands had never brought her pain—only pleasure. And comfort.

Always, comfort.

After what had happened to her, after what she'd learned of him today, what did it mean to desire Sebastian so fiercely?

It meant... nothing.

Nothing at all. She hadn't been damaged or broken by McCade's assault. Wounded, yes, and she might always shy from hands at her throat, but she was still intact. She was hanging by her heels, but she was still herself.

Sebastian, no matter what his offenses, was no McCade. Hadn't she known from the very first, no matter what darkness peered out from within him, that she had nothing to fear?

There was no fear between them—only desire.

Now she would finish turning *him* upside down.

The door swung in with only the slightest pressure, as if it had been waiting for her fingertips all along.

He was there, as she had known he'd be, sprawled in a chair in the most shocking state of undress. He wore nothing but trousers and a shirt unbuttoned to the waist, his hair in disarray, as if he'd been running his fingers through it while waiting for her.

Lounging there, with his chest and feet bare, he looked a perfect beast. Every erg of power in him was openly, nakedly, displayed for her.

She shivered at the sight of him, but not with fear. Never with fear.

His eyes were silver with hesitation, rather than dark with certainty. For all of the brutishness he was parading before her, he was undecided still.

Well, she would have to convince him, now wouldn't she?

Time for one more confession from him.

"What you wrote in your last entry," she said, heat flooding her cheeks as the words danced before her. "Did you mean it?"

He shifted in the chair, spreading his legs wide as he leaned forward. "Yes." His voice was all rasp and file now, not a hint of gold left in it. He crooked one heavy finger at her. "Come here."

She gazed at him sitting there, crouched like some great beast about to devour her. The illusion held until she saw his eyes.

Those eyes never would obey him—and now they betrayed his unease at this flaunting of himself.

"No." She lifted her chin. "You come here."

His smile was all the more wicked for being so unexpected. "You are magnificently difficult."

He rose from the chair, the heat of him buffeting her as he reduced the distance between them to mere inches.

The silver of his eyes had gone to pewter, but they could be darker yet.

"What now?" he asked. "Shall I kneel before you?"

Desire moved low in her belly, sharp, insistent, at the thought of him on his knees before her. "Yes," she breathed.

He lowered himself before her, his hands gripping her thighs for balance, staring up at her in near-worshipful reverence. His eyes were onyx now, glitteringly black in the paleness of his face.

Her head spun with the sensation of having this man supplicant before her. This must have been how the great Queen Isabel felt after the last battle of the Reconquista, as her general knelt before her and informed her all Spain was hers to command.

But she, Isabel Moreno, had something much better than Spain under her command.

She had *him*.

She sunk her fingers into his hair, watching his eyes slip closed as she did. He was so beautiful, the male power of him in thrall to her, gentled only by the thread of her hand through the silk of his hair.

"Take off your shirt," she ordered.

He released her to do so and she swayed; he'd been bracing her as much as she had been him. With a flick and a shrug his shirt was gone, the entirety of his torso bare to her. His hands came back to clasp at her thighs and she sighed at the rightness, the surety, of his touch.

She took in his unclothed chest, unable to do anything but look for long moments. He might fancy himself a Stoic, but his form was pure barbarian, hirsute and scarred.

The scar she had found but not seen lay stark before her eyes, running all the way from his left shoulder to carve around his rib cage, halting on the right side of his navel. She let her hand hover above it, waiting for him to stop her—because while she was in command, he had the right to refuse.

Her fingertips settled on the ridge of it, his hands remaining firm on her legs.

"How did this happen?" she asked.

"A knife fight."

She shook her head as she followed the line of it down his torso. Only an inch more to the right and he wouldn't be here. Her fingers tingled at the potential loss of him from under them. He gasped as she reached the end of the scar, the muscles of his belly pulling into tight relief.

"I feel I should warn you—" He cleared his throat in an odd manner. "I should inform you it has been quite some time..."

She frowned. "Quite some time?" Comprehension dawned. "Ah. How long is *quite some time?*"

"I haven't been... *intimate* with a lady since I was seventeen."

She blinked. Of course, she should have known that, since it would have been in the notebooks if he had, but even so. Over a decade of chastity made him practically a virgin once more.

"Don't worry," she said, "I'll be gentle." Her smile turned sharp. "This first time."

He smiled with his entire face at that, and her heart seized. She would give anything to possess all this man's smiles.

"Well, then," he said, "let's finish this. Because I want to get to the part where you turn fierce."

I want.

The words sank into her very bones, until she was nothing more than want herself.

"Kiss me," she ordered.

He did, putting his mouth right on the quivering skin of her belly, a tongue-slick caress that made her knees crumble, even with the barrier of her gown between them. But his hands were there, holding her oh so tight and keeping her upright. She leaned her head back, closing her eyes to savor the press of him against her, his hot mouth sending shockwaves to buffet her from head to toe. Most especially in the core of her, right under that wicked mouth of his...

One of his hands traveled down her leg, sliding through the ticklish hollow at the back of her knee, curving around the line of her calf, before halting at her ankle and seizing a fistful of nightgown.

"May I?" he asked against her.

She ran a hand through his hair, savoring the sleek pull of it between her fingers. So polite.

Such politeness should be rewarded.

"Yes."

He drew the fabric up her body with exquisite slowness, as if he were unveiling a priceless statue and wanted to prolong every drop of revelation.

She raised her arms to allow him to pull it over her head, after which he dropped it carelessly to the floor. His entire length was drawn taut with hunger.

He moved to grab her.

She held up a hand. "Wait."

He stopped dead and his breathing went harsh. He was enjoying this game immensely, she realized, the lines of his neck and shoulder stark with anticipation rather than frustration.

"Take off your trousers," she said, her voice nearly as rough as his. She licked her lips as he obeyed her, hungering for every inch he revealed. It was quite a few inches.

The core of her shook with her need for him. He was muscle and sinew, molded into a man, living, breathing brawn. She went to him, lifting her hands to run them over his shoulders, down his arms, across his chest, her skin crackling at the nearness of him. They both gasped when his erect member brushed against her belly.

She wrapped her fingers around it, his breath hissing at her touch. It was silky smooth, yet hard at the core.

He closed his eyes, his nostrils flaring as if he were in agony.

She knew he wasn't—it was being held so intimately by her that made him so. She stroked him from root to tip, the thrust of him against her hand making her belly clench and her breasts tighten.

She caught up one of his hands with her free one and set it against her breast, her nipple hardening at the rough press of his fingers.

All she had to do was give permission, and he went to work pleasuring her. His thumb rubbed in slow circles, the sensations spiraling out from that one point to drive her hips into his, trapping her hand, still wrapped around his member, in the heated skin between them.

He lowered his lips to hover above her breasts before whispering, "May I?"

"Yes."

He planted an open-mouthed kiss on her bosom, sighing as he did so. When he tugged her nipple into his mouth, it was her turn to sigh. His tongue darted out to circle and taste as he kissed and nipped, before lavishing her other breast with the same attention.

She swayed against him, her legs threatening to give out. But he was ready, scooping her up and carrying her with gratifying ease to the sofa, the corded muscles of his arms tight around her, so tight she knew he would never drop her.

He set her down gently, the fabric rough against her sensitized skin as she sank into the cushions. His hands roamed every inch of her as his mouth trailed down her torso, pausing to kiss and bite around her navel, making the center of her pull toward him, seeking... something.

"Precious Isabel mine," he whispered, the words a brand against her skin. "Tell me what you want."

She threw her head back and lifted her hips. "Kiss me..."

Her words failed her. She had no name for the place begging for him, knew it only as a dark seething need at the center of her. She lifted her hips again and whimpered, reaching for some name, any name, so he would release her from this jagged peak.

"Here?" he asked as he cupped her between her legs.

The pleasure that exploded nearly made her sob. "Yes, oh yes."

He arranged her, kneeling between her legs, and then his mouth was upon her. It was both relief and torment, easing her ache even as he drove it higher.

He was hesitant at first, but she directed him with her sighs and moans, and finally her words, where and how to lick and kiss and suckle, until she was at the very peak, and just one more touch...

She came undone with a cry, pleasure singeing her to her toes.

When she came to herself again, she looked down at him, still kneeling between her thighs, his power hers to command, and his eyes darker than the blackest part of night.

"Now," she said.

~~~

He would do anything for her.

Her limbs were languid with her climax and the musky taste of her was sharp in his mouth. Yet she was as regal, as imperial as ever.

When she said, "Now," he knew exactly what she wanted.

When she commanded, it was his pleasure to obey.

He lifted her from the sofa, switching their positions so she was astride him. Her knees sunk into the cushions as the velvet of her inner thighs slid along his. The curtain of her hair brushed his knees. The head of his member was at the very gate of her, her soft folds slick with her desire and his loving.

He gripped her hips, holding her and himself in this moment, thanking God he would remember it always.

She rolled her sex against him, gripped his arms, and said again, "Now."

He thrust home, giving them what they both needed. She was tight, yet yielding, so, so slick, and just... *right*. Almost too *right* to bear.

He took a shuddering breath—too close. He was too close.

He searched for his self-control, that iron grip that had taken so many years to perfect, but she moved against him, and it slipped right past his fingertips.

He drove himself to the hilt, her head falling back as he did, a moan leaving her beautiful lips.

My heart.

He withdrew, inch by torturous inch, savoring the slide of their most intimate parts against each other, before thrusting home again.

My love.

One last thrust and his climax was upon him, his member pulsing as he spilled his seed within her.

"My Isabel."

He let his forehead fall against hers, savoring the aftermath of release for just a moment. The entanglement of their flesh, for just a moment. The painful pleasure stretching his heart—for just a moment. A moment was all he needed to remember, forever.

He lay back, pulling her close, wishing there were something at hand to cover himself with. He must appear a perfect ape to her, covered in hair and scars, better seen through the bars of a cage.

He ran his hands through the fall of her hair, still awed by the length and amount. However did she manage to pin it up as she did? It was more than enough to cover the both of them.

Setting his chin on her head, he closed his eyes, reveled in the feel of her against him. He was wrung out, shipwrecked on some strange shore, sputtering water and trying to find his bearings.

After all those years of avoiding emotions, to spend a night luxuriating in some of the strongest ones was nearly overwhelming.

He held back a yawn, forced open his eyes. Overwhelming and exhausting.

He didn't dare sleep. He had to return her to her room. They were risking discovery.

If he were a normal man, a better man, he could marry her and spend the rest of his days—and nights—by her side. Exactly like this, her limbs twined with his, her hair covering them, their hearts sounding in the same rhythm.

Such a wondrous image.

But he wasn't a better man. This was the best he could achieve and it still wasn't good enough.

He could never have her for the rest of his days; tonight would have to suffice for a lifetime. Tonight was a sin, yes—but a small one compared to shackling her to a man such as himself.

No matter how carefully he controlled it, the blackness at the core of him, the darkness that had been a gift from his father, never went away. He could hide it—and had hidden it for thirteen years—but it was always there. Waiting for him to stumble.

It waited even now, coiled around his heart, slithering in his ear. *Let them come, let them discover you—then she will be yours.*

He mustn't listen—he'd stumbled enough tonight. It had been a transcendent, freeing experience, but there were always consequences when he let his self-control lapse. If he left behind his iron reserve, let himself walk into the sunlight of her affection—how long until he found himself in the darkness once more?

He savored the scent of her, the catch of her hair against his chin, her ear against his heart, for one more moment. "Isabel," he called softly. "You must return to bed. Tomorrow... the trial..."

"Getting rid of me so soon?" The gentle amusement in her voice made him want to weep.

He didn't tell her that surrendering control to her had been the greatest relief. Relief and release all at once. He could simply experience each sensation and not worry if it were right or wrong.

"We have to get you to bed," he said again. Or else he might keep her here all night. "Remember tomorrow. Remember to be soft." He ran his hand down her back. "Supple." Another stroke. "Pliant."

"So I'm to be a willow now, bending and weeping with the breeze?" Her usual sharpness was creeping back.

She was no willow. She was more like a mesquite tree, slender and smooth in all its parts and searing in its brilliance when it bloomed.

"No." He couldn't ask her to be what she was not. Couldn't ask her to hide what he loved most about her. But McCade could not be allowed to escape. "Remember, you're playing to the jury, not winning a game of chess. Terrifying brilliance won't serve you well there."

She stroked her hand down his chest as if she enjoyed it, as if there weren't scars marring the journey. He felt each and every collision as her fingers met the evidence of his nature.

"You think me terrifyingly brilliant?" she asked.

He did. He wanted to gaze on her brilliance for the rest of his days, until he was blind from it.

Blind. His mother was half-blind, and all because of his father.

After the events of tonight, he could be a father…

His blood reversed course, his heart straining from it.

That could not happen—that *must* not happen. He shoved the thought of a child away, along with his feelings for her, forcing his frigid calm to descend upon him once more. It took several breaths, but his reserve still came when it was called. Just barely.

"You know how intelligent you are," he answered severely. "Now put on your nightgown and go back to bed."

She reared back, studied him.

He held himself steady, refusing to flinch, even as her expression closed.

"I see," she said, acid etching the words. "Sebastian is gone, and the marshal has returned to take his place."

"I am always the marshal. I have to be." Almost as coldly spoken as he felt.

He rose, setting her on her feet. Refused to give in to the urge of his fingers to clasp her close again.

She sent him a slicing look, then pulled on her nightgown.

His iron self-control rattled against his heart as she walked to the door without a word, then shut it quietly behind her.

Rattled hard, but held.

CHAPTER EIGHTEEN

ISABEL HADN'T YET TESTIFIED, AND things were already going terribly wrong.

She hadn't even left the house.

Sebastian was leading her down the hallway, having found her at the breakfast table. Not that she had been able to do more than prod her eggs into her toast and back again. Even when she'd been afflicted with the grippe, her stomach had never rolled so queasily.

"Where are we going?" she asked, the question only slightly louder than their footfalls on the carpet.

There was something different about him. It wasn't simply that she knew now what lay beneath that fine suit, the wildness he hid beneath it. He was as still as ever, but it was the stillness of wire strung too tight.

If she plucked him, he might snap.

Or it could be her own tension pulling her nerves to unnatural thinness. She was certainly carrying enough anxiety for the both of them.

"To the library." His voice at least was as mellow as ever. "We must ensure the dog won't attack you."

"What?" Her stomach rolled as she stopped dead in the hallway. She was about to sit in that witness box, in front of twelve hostile men, and convince them she was telling the truth—and he wanted her to face that dog?

He must have gone mad.

"No, I don't need to be introduced to the dog again."

She peered at him more closely. His expression had gone beyond impassive, all the way to drawn, the color of his skin matching that of his eyes, the lines around his mouth deeply grooved.

"Did you sleep at all last night?" she asked.

"No. Of course not." Impatience sharpened the words.

She might have felt sorry for him, considering how terrible he looked, but it was no less than he deserved. He should be regretting how summarily he'd dismissed her after... well, after everything they'd shared.

And yet her heart panged at the sight of his distress. It evidently was not quite as put out with him as her rational mind was.

They'd reached the library, and he turned away to open the door.

She placed a hand on his forearm. It stood pale against the darkness of his suit as he held himself in wait before the door. She noticed a small speck of lint, just to the side of her hand—the tiniest mote marring the perfection of his sleeve.

This was not good.

"Sebastian."

He turned to her slightly, but kept his gaze averted.

This was bad.

Perhaps she should not have been so eager to turn him upside down. Perhaps he couldn't handle hanging from his heels as well as she could. Perhaps he was unable to prevent all the things he kept inside from falling out.

Or perhaps she was placing her own anxiety on him. It was only a speck of lint. But it produced a most perfect horror in her, as if his very skin had been marred.

His unnatural demeanor today, the speck on his normally spotless suit—she feared he was coming undone, and she so desperately needed him to be whole.

Mother of God, she must regain control of herself.

"Why do I need to see the dog again?" She forced her voice into pliancy, but kept her hand upon his arm.

He took a ragged breath before looking at her with haunted eyes. "Junius must come inside today since our mothers will be alone. I can't have him hurting you."

That was reasonable. The dog was inside, as it usually was, and Sebastian was going to ensure the dog knew she was no threat. Then the dog would be no threat to her.

It was all *so* reasonable—so why was she having such a time convincing herself? Perhaps because she kept seeing that gaping mouth snapping toward her, the teeth attempting to sink into her flesh, the savage surprise of it...

She plucked the lint from his sleeve, flicking it to the floor as quick as she could, hating the fibrous pebble of it between her fingers.

"Thank you," he said gravely.

She inhaled deeply, reaching for steadiness. If she couldn't handle seeing a dog, no matter how vicious, she'd never handle the jury.

"Very well," she said. "Let's say good morning to Junius."

When they entered the library, Junius was stretched before the fire, looking like a rather ugly rug. He thumped his tail at Sebastian's approach, but made no move to rise.

"Junius." At Sebastian's call, the dog came to his side. "Hold a fist out to him," he prompted Isabel.

She didn't want to. The dog was peaceful enough, watching her with soft eyes as he sat next to his master— but what if he transformed before her, turned savage again?

"He won't hurt you," Sebastian said. "I promise." His gaze was pleading—as if nothing mattered more to him than that she should make peace with the dog.

She curled her fingers into her palm and offered her fist, her trembling held within her grip.

Junius stretched his head forward, his nose brushing gently across her skin as he sniffed. His breath was hot, his exhales forceful. After a few moments of investigation, he drew his head back...

And thumped his tail on the floor. He opened his jaws, gave her hand one quick lick, then lay back at Sebastian's feet.

He hadn't hurt her. He'd even... *licked* her.

All of her tension drained straight away. She'd faced the dog dead-on—and been perfectly fine. What a bit of fuss for nothing.

Her relief was reflected in Sebastian's expression. "Of course he didn't snap at you," he said. "Of course he didn't."

He sounded as if he didn't quite believe it, though.

She set her hand on his sleeve once more, right over where the bit of lint had been. "Are you reassured now?"

He put his hand over hers—such a heavy, comforting weight. "Yes. And now we must get you to your next trial."

Perhaps... perhaps after all this, once the trial was finished, they might look anew at what was growing between them. Perhaps, once the weight of the circumstances surrounding them was lifted... perhaps there was a chance for something more.

But such questions must wait until after the trial. The rest of her life must wait until after the trial.

"I'm ready," she said.

~~~

Isabel held her hands stiffly in her lap on the witness stand, resisting the impulse to wipe them on her skirt like a sticky-fingered child. She drew careful, shallow breaths, willing her face into a mask of serenity as she watched the prosecutor in front of her.

She hadn't felt this nervous on her first day of teaching.

She'd just turned eighteen then. Butterflies had fluttered through her as she looked out at the young faces she was meant to instruct, the stick of chalk gritty in her clammy hand. Every face had been turned toward her, watching, waiting, expectant. She hadn't been certain she was up to the task.

She wasn't certain she was up to the task now—if she'd had a piece of chalk in her fist, it would crumble to dust.

The faces of the jurors looking back at her were hardened in a way her pupils' never had been. Skepticism narrowed the men's eyes and pinched their mouths.

She had to erase that skepticism, much as she'd clean a blackboard. Only then could she write the truth upon it.

One last steadying breath and she was ready to answer the prosecutor.

"Sheriff Obregon and I were out for a drive that Sunday. He was my fiancé," she explained.

Mr. Halstead was rifling through some papers, obviously uninterested in her answer. "And what happened then?" he asked the stack in his hands.

"The Carey brothers and Mr. McCade came out from behind a stand of trees. They had their pistols drawn." *Be soft*, she reminded herself as the muscles surrounding her spine tensed against her will. *Supple. Pliant.*

She only just kept herself from glancing over at Sebastian.

"Mr. McCade said he was going to teach Sheriff Obregon a lesson." She decided to leave out the part about punishing Joaquin for being Mexican. The jurors didn't look as if they'd be very sympathetic to her people. "Mr. McCade fired first and killed the horse."

She braced herself for the gasp she knew was coming, the one she always hated.

The spectators gave her exactly what she expected. She knew that they wouldn't be gasping when she came to Joaquin's shooting and her own attack. Not if they'd read the graphic details the papers had printed.

She paused. This next bit was rather damaging to Joaquin, but there was no way to avoid it. "Sheriff Obregon shot both the Carey brothers. Then Mr. McCade shot him."

The prosecutor hadn't looked up once.

What was the point of telling all this if he wasn't even paying attention? The muscles around her spine tightened another notch and she used an old school-teacher trick to get his attention.

She kept silent.

Finally, blinking like he'd just awoken, the prosecutor turned to her.

"Uh, what happened after that?" he asked.

"After what?" she said, letting anger color her question.

"Uh—" He tapped the stack of papers against his palm. "After Obregon shot McCade."

"You must mean after *McCade* shot *Obregon*."

"Oh, yes. After that," he muttered.

"Mr. McCade pulled me off the seat of the buggy and carried me to the brush." Her heart thudded heavily in her chest and her head began to ache in time with it. She plunged forward despite the foul taste flooding her mouth. "He threatened..."

She faltered, her view of the prosecutor's back no help.

Sebastian. She wanted to see him.

Her gaze found him, still and solemn as always, sitting among the sea of spectators. Still, solemn, and reassuring.

Yet there was torment in his eyes. He'd worn that same expression when she'd told him this story the first time, on that terrible stretch of road where it had happened.

He at least was listening. He at least cared. She pulled her shoulders back, set her jaw. If she could tell Sebastian the entire story *there*, she could tell it now, here.

"Mr. McCade threatened my virtue. In vulgar detail." Nothing about those words was soft or yielding. And neither was she.

"Did he—"

"No." She cut off the prosecutor before he could finish asking if McCade had been successful. That was all anyone ever wanted to know of her story—if she'd been thoroughly ruined. Well, they weren't getting that satisfaction from her. "He began to strangle me, my wits going black under the force. I found a rifle on the ground next to me. I shot him in the shoulder and he clubbed me in the head with his pistol. I remember nothing after."

She sat back without losing a bit of the steel in her spine. She was finished; it was done. And every word had been the truth.

She looked to the jurors. A few—the ones who would meet her gaze—looked sympathetic. Pitying.

Perhaps they had believed her.

Perhaps there was still hope.

She glanced at McCade. His gaze was ruthless, un-blinking. He hadn't liked that she'd told the truth, had he?

"No further questions," the prosecutor said to his papers.

McCade's attorney leapt up, clasping his hands as though he'd like to rub them together in anticipation. The steel in her spine went cold at the sight.

"You were out for a drive, you say?" His oily tone made her ears itch with the drip of it.

She nearly nodded before catching herself. Everything here must be spoken for the record.

"We were."

"Obregon had announced his intention to harass Mr. McCade before that, had he not?"

"Harass?" Her entire mouth went tight, jaw and teeth and tongue turning to iron. "*Sheriff* Obregon suspected the man of murdering someone in the valley. Simple prudence dictated he keep a close watch on Mr. McCade, not harass him."

"Yet there was no real evidence Mr. McCade had done such a thing, was there?" He cocked an eyebrow for the jury, displaying his skepticism to them. "Only rumors."

She knew what he was trying to do, but couldn't see a clear way to defeat him. "No," she said, "the sheriff found no evidence of a crime, as far as I knew. But it was his duty to investigate such matters."

"If he found nothing, why keep harassing my client?" The attorney went on before she could answer. "The sheriff also had a vendetta against the Carey brothers, did he not?"

He was putting this all on Joaquin then, painting him as some obsessed lunatic who'd randomly opened fire on three innocent men.

But she could certainly speak to the true character of the Carey brothers. "There was no vendetta," she said, contempt sharp on her lips. "Those brothers were worthless through and through."

The attorney raised his eyebrows as if he'd never before heard of young men being shiftless. "How were they worthless? What could they have possibly done to deserve being shot down?"

She'd heard a lifetime of the Careys' foolishness: drunken pranks, fights with the neighbor boys, and manhandling of girls at dances—and heard again her sister's scream as Billy pinched her.

She supposed it truly was all inconsequential next to the finality of murder.

But they *had* meant to commit murder that day, she was certain of it. How could she convince the jury of that?

"They drank to excess." The titters from the jurors made her shoulders snap back. They might think it was amusing, but it was a serious matter. "When they did so, they fought with anything that moved. They were... too familiar with the ladies."

The lawyer leered at her. "Were they familiar with you?"

She drew back in shock. "Certainly not."

He turned to the jurors and raised an eyebrow.

She nearly closed her eyes in frustration. Her story was slipping away from her, this stupid, mugging lawyer turning everything around. She was smarter than this, smarter than him—she ought to be able to outwit him.

"Miss Moreno, what dealings did you have with Judge Bannister before this?" the lawyer asked.

She blinked, almost shaking her head. "None. I have never met Judge Bannister."

"Never met him?" The contrived surprise in his voice grated on her. "Isn't his son married to your sister?"

Sebastian had warned her the judge's vendetta was at the heart of this. But to have it brought up during her testimony... she'd never expected this.

"Yes, his son is married to my sister." She was as careful as a mule picking its way up a steep trail. "But Judge Bannister did not attend the wedding, nor has he ever visited, as far as I'm aware."

"Hmm." The lawyer scratched at the few wisps of hair he'd obviously very carefully coaxed from his upper lip. "Such an... *intimate* connection between your families, yet you've never met him."

"No." Firm, ringing. She'd rather discuss the attack than this probing of familial connections. She certainly wished to make no claim of kinship to Judge Bannister. "He and his son are estranged."

"Interesting. Yet, Judge Bannister sent a marshal to Cabrillo at his son's request. That doesn't sound estranged to me." The lawyer didn't wait for her protest. "So you had no idea Judge Bannister is currently engaged in a battle with Mr. McCade's father over the city's water supply? No idea the judge has stooped before to using slander in an attempt to win this battle?"

"I—" She knew now, thanks to Sebastian telling her, but she hadn't known before the attack. "Marshal Spencer mentioned something to me about the water supply, yes."

The lawyer was staring at the floor, one hand behind his back, and the ease of his stance scared her more than his leers had. "What dealings did you have with Marshal Spencer before this?"

He looked up then, and the triumph in his eyes made her stomach turn inside out.

He knew.

So this was the trap they'd set for her. Nothing so in-elegant as a random shooting—oh no, they had laid a cunning snare and she and Sebastian had walked right in and pulled it tight round their ankles.

No one here cared what had happened to her, or what had happened to Joaquin.

Her role wasn't to tell the truth. It was to be too in-timately linked to a man who had a political stake in all this, no matter how she might claim she'd never met Judge Bannister. Her word was suspect before she'd even opened her mouth.

And now she was much too intimately linked with the man sent to bring in Edwin McCade's son.

They'd used the newspapers to lay the trail and then sent that man to watch her. What that man might have seen from the library window—it would have been tak-en as evidence that she and Sebastian were... well, were in cahoots. Evidence that proved she was nothing more than a lying Jezebel.

"Before when?" She didn't know if she could success-fully bluff her way out of this, but she had to try. Sebas-tian was wrong—it *was* a chess game, but she feared she was already too close to checkmate to escape.

The lawyer turned to face her fully, his mouth twitching with self-satisfaction. "Well, let us start before the supposed attack, and we can work forward from there."

Their chairs creaked as the jurors leaned toward her, their gazes intent, hard. Every eye drilled on her, stuck in this chair, and if she squinted, she could see their ears twitching.

"Before the attack, I didn't know Marshal Spencer at all," she declared.

The lawyer sent a sardonic glance skyward. "Just like Judge Bannister. And after the attack?"

"After, he was sent by the judge to apprehend Mr. McCade." Her heart began to race, because it sounded so damning, even to her own ears.

If not for Mr. Merrill's request to his father, Sebastian would never have come. If not for the judge's vendetta, he would never have sent Sebastian.

Power and the governor's mansion. That's what this had always been about. Never justice.

You don't matter. Your suffering, Joaquin's suffering—it is nothing to people like these.

"You helped him track down Mr. McCade, did you not?" the lawyer was asking.

She nodded.

"Miss Moreno, you must speak your answer," the judge reminded her.

"Yes," she said, louder than she might have liked.

"If you aided him in his capture of Mr. McCade, wouldn't that make you more than passing acquaintances?" the lawyer asked. "In fact, Marshal Spencer visited you the day you arrived in Los Angeles. You're residing with him now, are you not?"

All those questions from the lawyer, when he already knew the answers, dragging her into his performance for the jury.

Although it was the worst kind of folly, she could resist no longer.

She searched out Sebastian.

He was furious.

He knew exactly what the lawyer was doing, and the darkness within him wasn't just peeping out—it was glaring at that lawyer. Violence lurked in the set of his jaw, the tension in his shoulders.

For the first time, she was afraid of the darkness within him. Not for herself, but for what he might do if it were unleashed.

"Miss Moreno?" the judge prompted. "Can you answer the question?"

She remembered Sebastian's words of last night. *Supple. Pliant.* The smooth sweeps of his hand down her bared back.

Supple and *pliant* could not save this—nothing could. But she could keep Sebastian from doing something he would regret, like knocking out this lawyer's teeth. He liked her fierce. Well, she would be all tooth and claw, for the both of them.

She stared straight at McCade, who looked back with murder in his eyes. Exactly how he'd looked just after she'd shot him.

"Yes, I am residing with the marshal while I am staying in Los Angeles. *Someone* attempted to murder me."

The outlaw gave her a half smile. A conspiracy between them, that smile—one that would end badly for her.

He would punish her for telling the truth, if he were free. That's what that smile promised.

"Miss Moreno," the lawyer said condescendingly, "Los Angeles is a large city and occasionally dangerous. What makes you think the shooter wasn't some common drunk? You might not be used to such things in your little town."

"Not used to such things?" She kept staring at McCade, until the corner of his mouth dropped. "I remind you I was pistol-whipped and nearly strangled to death in *my little town*."

The lawyer halted before the witness stand, placing one hand upon it to steady himself, puzzlement crossing his face. He wasn't expecting this from her.

"Yet we only have your word on it," he said, a shadow of uncertainty darkening the words.

"I have a scar at my temple," she reminded him.

"Which could be from anything," the lawyer countered, regaining his composure.

She nodded toward McCade. "You only have his word on it as well." She sent him her best schoolteacher glare, the same one that had wrung innumerable confessions from her pupils. "Whose word would you believe?"

"Well," the lawyer sputtered, "likely not the word of a woman who claims to have no relationship with the men known to have a vendetta against Mr. McCade, yet is related by marriage to one and is residing with the other!" He puffed his chest out and paced before the jury box. "I don't know about *your people*, but decent folks consider an unmarried lady residing with an unmarried man to be immoral."

He made it sound as if she were something he'd cross the street to avoid stepping in.

She was as indignant as he pretended to be. "My mother is there as well," she insisted. "There's nothing improper about it."

And then her memory—her foolish, tricky memory— brought forth an image of just how *improper* she and Sebastian had been. And then her body—her foolish, tricky body—betrayed her, as guilty heat flooded her cheeks and buzzed in her ears.

The lawyer, catching the blush spreading over her, let a small smirk play at his mouth. "Your mother, hmm? Yet you're blushing like—"

The judge snapped down his gavel. "That's enough."

The lawyer stared at her for a moment more, then waved a dismissive hand. "No further questions."

She didn't dare to look at the jury as she walked back to her seat, her face still aflame and her eyes burning. But she did allow herself a look at Sebastian.

He wasn't watching her—his gaze was for the jurors. A grim gaze too, with those narrowed eyes and a tight jaw.

She had written that blackness upon his expression with her poor performance.

She had failed.

Her head throbbed as she sank down into her seat in the gallery, utterly alone. Eyes open. Spine straight. To sit here was all she had to do now, and even so, she could hardly accomplish it. Thank goodness the judge was dismissing them for the day.

Tomorrow would be the day of reckoning, the day the verdict was returned.

She rose mechanically, following the spectators as they filed out of the courtroom, ignoring everyone's stares. Despair wrapped its tight hand round her chest.

No, no, she must remain upright and not give in. She could collapse when she found the privacy of her room, but not a moment before.

She sensed Sebastian at her elbow, just behind her. Her entire self yearned to reach out for him, to seek the comfort of his touch, but to do so would give truth to those claims in the courtroom.

She didn't dare even speak to him in public now.

Instead, she kept her head down, blindly following the crowd while her every sense was trained on the man behind her, the man she could not turn to, no matter what.

So intent was she, she failed to notice the man blocking her path until she'd almost smashed into him.

She jerked her head up when he didn't move aside, only to find an older version of her brother-in-law staring her down, a man as ruthless looking as she'd always imagined.

Judge Bannister.

He simply stared, never saying a word.

At least she thought he was silent, because her ears had stopped working for some reason, the pain constricting about her head all she could hear, see, taste—

Sebastian was there, lifting the judge clear off the ground as he growled something, but the pain wouldn't allow her to translate. Was he speaking Spanish or English? She could no longer tell.

The pain receded for a brief moment, and a devastating clarity came over her as she took in the entirety of the scene before her.

She had to stop Sebastian. Striking McCade was one thing—striking the judge was quite another. Seeing the open mouths of everyone watching, she realized that was exactly what they were waiting for. No one was inclined to step in, not even the bailiff.

She sighed deeply before condemning them both to scandal.

"Marshal Spencer." She laid her hand on his forearm, stark white against the black of his suit.

He gave no indication he'd heard her. Instead, his fists tightened on the judge's lapels until his knuckles were as pale as the scars covering them.

"Sebastian," she said, a little louder this time, loud enough for everyone to hear. It was too late to worry about exposing herself.

The muscles of his arm tensed, gathering up their strength. She pressed her fingers deeper, reminding him that she was here, to come back to himself.

The tautness under her hand slipped, then eased, Sebastian finally releasing the judge. The spectators stared at her as if she'd charmed a grizzly into eating from her hand. Slowly, every one of their expressions hardened, and she knew what they were thinking.

That she'd lied on the stand.

That she was nothing more than a pawn in Judge Bannister's hands and a whore in Sebastian's bed.

A knife twist to her gut and a hammer blow to her aching head, those condemning expressions. Somehow, she found the strength to speak to Sebastian.

"We should leave now."

His jaw was clenched tight, the muscles standing in stark relief, but he managed to nod.

Isabel pulled him away, as Judge Bannister's stupefied gaze followed them. She ignored him, thinking only to escape.

It had all gone so terribly, spectacularly wrong, but at least she could still flee the wreckage.

CHAPTER NINETEEN

SEBASTIAN WAS... UNWELL.

He was choking on sensation, on everything he'd done since she'd come to him last night. There wasn't room for anything else—there was hardly room for the air in his lungs.

As soon as he'd arrived home, he'd bathed, the water hot enough to make his skin red with irritation.

After, he'd carefully laid out his shaving kit, every piece in its precise place. He'd slid the blade across the strop, back and forth, until it was sharp enough to split hairs.

His father, when he'd been too fuddled with drink to find his belt, had occasionally gone for the strop.

Of course, this strop wasn't his father's. Sebastian had burned that one, along with most everything else of Judge Spencer's, reducing as much as he could of the man to ash.

When the blade was ready, he'd scraped it across his skin, swirling it in the bowl every so often, the dark hairs looking like drowned ants in the scummy water. He forced himself to set the blade aside once his cheeks were bare and not give in to the urge to keep sliding the cold metal across his face. He'd done that once before, pulling the razor in long sweeps until the skin beneath was weeping with it.

He had more control now.

Once the shaving kit was clean and packed away, he'd taken out a new suit, brushing and brushing and brushing until he was certain everything foreign had been removed. Then he carefully dressed, the fabric making his skin scream with the touch of it, before looking himself over in the mirror.

He looked like himself, every inch the marshal.

So he sat in the chair in his room and did not move. He was waiting for...

For her?

No. No, she wasn't coming. After the disaster of today, after his rejection of her last night... she was most certainly not coming.

His gaze fell on the belt on the dresser, and for a brief moment he entertained a vision of it wrapping round his hand, biting deep into his palm as he paced the floor.

He imagined Isabel finding him like that.

She'd not be pleased. In fact, she'd likely scold him for it.

So he left the belt as it was and sat in silence.

His heart had been so foolishly buoyant this morning. The dog had sniffed her hand and thumped his tail, no bared teeth or raised fur this time. He'd thought to himself, *Well, this is a fine thing.*

He'd begun to hope.

Then he'd let himself trust: trust in her brilliance and trust that the jury would be blinded by it as well. He'd imagined them celebrating her wondrous performance tonight, first with their mothers, and then later, alone...

He'd chosen a solitary walk to arrive at the courthouse, in order to give space and time to the sensations within him to stretch and settle. When he'd passed a druggist on the way, he'd slipped inside, feeling like a green idiot, but doing it anyway.

But green was the scent of hope, the color of perhaps, and it was those very things driving him to the counter with a packet of preventatives in his hand. He'd been as dazed as any other young buck with a posy for his blushing miss, that tin burning a square into his jacket pocket.

Because of course, his lady love would win the day, and after she would demand tribute from him, wouldn't she?

He dragged a hand through his hair, the ends prickling against his palm. What a fool he'd been. Instructing her to be yielding on the stand, as if a simper and a smile from her would have changed anything—she'd been a skeptic from their very first meeting, and she'd been proven correct.

He'd exposed her and he'd been her downfall in the end. When she'd flushed so deeply on the stand, he'd known exactly what she'd been thinking, since he was remembering the same thing. Only he was too shameless to blush over it.

Dear God, he had nearly struck Judge Bannister today.

He closed his eyes, craving the darkness behind them. All the judge had done was to stare at her—but it had frightened her, and Sebastian's last thread of control had snapped.

But then there was her hand on him, her soft voice speaking his name—and she called him back from the darkness.

Cementing every suspicion raised in that courtroom in the process.

By morning, it would be in the papers and it wouldn't look good for any of them—not him, not the judge, and especially not her. He'd have to hide the papers, but he wouldn't be able to hide the verdict from her, which was certain to be not guilty.

He'd be more concerned about her reaction if he weren't so worried about his own. Because he knew if McCade looked at her sideways, he'd kill the man. Putting this suit on hadn't restored calm to his soul—it was only the thinnest veneer over the wildness churning within him.

He could not have another death upon his soul. He could not.

His mother had told him to unbend or he would break. Well, he was unbending and he was still breaking—the fissures deepening as darkness oozed from them.

He'd opened himself to Isabel and now he was coming undone.

The clock chimed two, the exact same hour she'd come to him last night.

She wasn't coming. She'd never come to him again.

Pain speared him, and without thought he rubbed at his sternum to soothe it. But his shirt rubbed like nettles against his chest.

He couldn't go to his notebooks and risk finding her in the library. So he remained in his room, still and suffering, listening hard for the footfalls that never came.

But even as he tried to convince himself it was better she was not there, he never looked away from the door.

When the handle finally turned, he thought it only a figment of his imagination. It moved excruciatingly slowly as it revolved toward releasing the door.

He stopped breathing. It could not be her.

But it was. She was barefoot, wrapped in a dressing gown entirely too thick for the mild autumn night. Armor was what it was.

Armor against him.

If she thought that gown could erase from his memory the image of her naked and astride him, she was wrong.

"You should not be here," he said. Heavy with warning.

She cocked her head, studying him. "No," she said, "I shouldn't. I shouldn't have been in the library last night either, but you didn't protest then."

Heat curled in his gut and his member twitched at the reminder. "What do you want?"

He needed to drive her from this room soon, or he would certainly lay her on that bed and use it.

She wasn't put off by him—she never was. Instead she came closer, her bare toes peeping out from her nightgown with each step. "Are you well?"

Was he *well*? He was so far from *well*, he didn't remember what it looked like.

"No," he rasped. "I am not well. I almost struck a judge today. In that courtroom, I had to sit and watch as you... as you..."

"Failed?" She threw the word at him.

"No, as you were slandered."

She swallowed, pink crawling up her cheeks. "He knew about us."

Us.

There wasn't going to be an *us.*

His reaction to the judge had proven he could never unbend where she was concerned. He set his jaw. "So you think all this was an elaborate plan to entrap McCade?" he asked. "That you were only a pawn?"

"I believe I was only a pawn to Judge Bannister and to McCade's father. No one in that courtroom cared about what happened to me. They had already made up their minds."

She'd said nothing about him. He shouldn't want to know, should be shoving her out the door, but something deep within him, something beyond the darkness that lurked there, needed to know. He sent his plea to her from that place. "And me?"

"You." She sighed. "You make everything better."

No one had ever said such a thing to him—he'd only ever made things worse.

He couldn't deny any sensation she called forth in him, and he certainly couldn't resist the one she'd summoned with those words.

He rose, the force of her words driving him to her, lifting her up and claiming her mouth before he laid her across the bed. He stretched out next to her, smoothing back the hair that had escaped her braid and wishing he could simply close his eyes and rest. To gather her close and know the peace of sleeping next to her.

He would never know that peace.

Her fingers traced the edge of his jaw, sliding along his freshly shaven skin until she found a small nick. It stung faintly under her touch.

"Did you do this to yourself?" she asked softly.

"No," he replied as quietly. "That one was an accident."

Her fingers traced over the faintly pink lines still crossing his palm. Of course she knew. She saw all of him.

"Does it help?" she asked.

"Yes." He didn't attempt to explain it further—he wasn't certain if he could, not without appearing mad.

"Do you aspire to sainthood?" Her finger ran up the lines and back again.

"No." Men such as he didn't become saints.

"Would you stop?" Not at all a command—a plea. "If I asked?"

She pressed a kiss to his palm.

"I won't ever do it again," he swore. He wouldn't, not when she treated his flesh so worshipfully. He couldn't harm something she loved.

They lay like that for several moments, her fingers caressing any bare skin of his she could find, while he simply breathed into her hair.

"Promise me you won't read the papers tomorrow," he said, adjusting their positions so he could gaze at her face.

"Do you truly think it will be so bad?" As if she were trying to convince herself it wouldn't be.

"It certainly won't be pleasant."

She blinked rapidly, but no tears fell. Her eyes squeezed shut, and the pain that lanced through him at the sight made his breath rasp. He wished she'd never taken that fateful drive that Sunday long ago. She would be safe, in her little mountain town, her insipid fiancé at her side, her life plans still intact.

And he would never have hurt her as he was now.

But time only marched forward, never backward. Erasing the past wasn't possible, so he needed to find some other means of soothing her.

He kissed her.

He wasn't entirely certain if the kiss would help, but it was what she usually did when he was overset. Just a simple brush of his lips against hers, accompanied by a stroke of her beautiful hair, but it jolted him right to his very bones.

He pulled away to see if it had had the intended effect. Her eyes were clear, with a sardonic spark.

"Isn't that exactly the kind of thing the papers will assume we're doing?" Her voice was as dry as her eyes.

He suppressed his laugh, but he did allow himself a small smile before growing serious again. "I am sorry I've exposed you to this."

"I'm just as much at fault." She closed her eyes, a soft breath passing her lips. "I never thought I would be so happy at the thought of going back to Cabrillo. Los Angeles was my dream for so many years, and now I never want to see it again."

He knew to expect this, that she would leave and not wish to return, but he still felt as if there were a hot poker pressed against his breastbone.

"You'll be safe there." He pressed another kiss against her mouth and she opened for him with a sigh. "None of this will follow you," he said against her lips.

"They'll still know I failed here," she murmured. He kissed his way along her jaw. "I'll have to face them all knowing that I let that man walk free."

"You didn't let him walk free," he insisted. "Don't think that."

She didn't seem to have heard him. "The way he looked at me on the stand..."

"He'll never hurt you," he rumbled, his mood going dangerous. "I swear it."

She didn't answer and he sensed her slipping from him, already traveling back in her mind to Cabrillo.

"I'll have to tell Joaquin I failed." She stared into the distance bleakly, no doubt already imagining that conversation.

Bitterness cut at his tongue at the thought of her erstwhile fiancé. He knew it wasn't fair—the man could hardly walk—but damn it, twice now he'd left Isabel alone to fight this outlaw. Had Obregon been here to take the stand, everything might have been different.

Sebastian growled as he flicked open the buttons of her nightgown. "Don't worry about that."

He slid his hand in to seize her breast, to remind her that he, Sebastian, was here and had been at her side through the entire ordeal.

She raised an eyebrow as if to ask, *Did I say you could do that?* but didn't stop him. "How can I not? Everything is so completely ruined. Thanks to the papers, tomorrow all of Los Angeles will think me an immoral jade." She arched into his hold as his thumb rubbed across her nipple. "And they will think that because of exactly what we are doing at this moment."

He swallowed hard, guilt clenching at his heart. He'd been just as immoral as she, but Los Angeles society wouldn't slam its doors in his face as it would hers.

Her family would still receive her, but polite society—Anglo society—would think her tarnished beyond repair. To return to Cabrillo seemed the best solution—people she'd known her entire life wouldn't believe the lies the newspapers had printed. But God, he wished there were another way.

One that kept her by his side.

Even if he couldn't have that, even if it was beyond rash, he would take tonight. It was all he could have— even if he didn't deserve it.

He grabbed a fistful of her nightgown just above her knees and began to drag it up. She writhed against him.

"Do what you did last night," she ordered. "Only, use your hand instead."

Desire pulsed through him at the command and at the thought of her coming undone under his fingers. He stroked the silk of her inner thigh, the heat from the center of her maddeningly tempting. He would part those folds soon, lingering in her slickness until they were both ready to go up in flames.

But first... "Were you sore today? Did I hurt you last night?"

She frowned. "No, of course not."

He'd heard a lady's first time was painful, but apparently that wasn't always true. Good, because if this night was all he had left with her, he wanted to use it to its fullest. Use them both to their fullest.

"Well?" she asked breathlessly, and lifted her hips in demand.

His mouth tipped in the smallest of smiles as he set his hand against the very center of her. Greedy, demanding woman.

Lord, but he loved her like this.

Her sex was soft, slick, aflame—the slide of it against his fingertips made his head spin. The liquid of her desire coated his hand and the scent of it filled the air as he stroked and circled just as she'd shown him last night. He watched her reactions closely, each breathy moan from her lips, every licentious roll of her hips a reward for his efforts, rewards that sent the lightning stitch of lust through him.

Her moans began to shift to something more urgent, more keening, the arching of her hips becoming thrusts against his hand, and with one last cry that she held deep in her throat, she climaxed against him.

Her nightgown had bunched up about her waist. He settled along her side, pressed his face into the silken warmth of her belly, savored the smell and sound of her as she rode the last peaks of her pleasure.

He found the edges of her gown and tugged upward in a question. "May I look at you? Touch you? May I take down your hair?"

She slid a hand through his hair, her nails scraping his scalp as she pulled his head up to look at her. When their eyes met, she gave him a smile so soft, so fond, his belly clenched with it, clenched with the need to keep such a smile on her face forever.

"Yes," she said. "You may do whatever you like. After, I'm going to touch you. Taste you."

"Whatever *you* like." Kneeling beside her, he pulled the gown over her head, then released her hair from its braid, spreading it all about her shoulders. She lay back again, her fond smile turning satisfied, and he found he had not the words to describe how she looked to him then. She was female desire incarnate, everything he'd ever lusted after, every carnal fantasy he'd tried to erase.

Everything his heart could never have.

He ran a hand along her shoulders, her breasts, and down her torso, encountering the silk of her hair every so often. Against the pale slenderness of her form, his hand was brutish—ugly, scarred. And yet she still curled into his touch.

She lifted her arms to wrap round his shoulders, pulling him down for a kiss. She tasted of hope and desire, their tongues tangling just as the rest of their bodies were.

As her hands ran along the fabric of his jacket, he realized he was still fully clothed. He pulled back from the enticement of her mouth to tug off his jacket and toss it to the floor. His fingers went to the buttons of his waistcoat, when her hand caught his wrist.

He looked at her in question, her eyes heavy lidded, smoldering with anticipation.

"Just the jacket," she said. "Leave the rest. I want to see you as the marshal"—she ran her hand down his waistcoat—"and as Sebastian"—her hand ran down his cheek—"both at the same time."

An odd sensation shimmered through him, equal parts anxiety and excitement. "But I am always both."

"No," she replied. "You aren't. You are either one or the other. I want to see you as both."

He went to protest again and she laid a finger across his lips. "Are you arguing?"

The words sent a thrill through him, every stern schoolmarm who'd visited him in unruly dreams coming to life in her.

He shook his head.

"Good." Her praise gave him an even deeper thrill. "Your turn."

She pushed him to stand next to the bed, then settled herself between his legs. The sight of her, naked as Eve while he was fully clothed, was more erotic than he could express. Her hands went to his trouser fastenings, her hair sliding across her shoulders as she did. The sight of all that dark luxury moving against the moonlight of her skin distracted him from the fact she was pulling his member free.

His penis appeared rude, nearly obscene, standing straight at attention, red and thick against the dark of his clothes. She ran her hand from head to root and the slide of her palm against him made him close his eyes.

"Sebastian."

His eyes snapped open.

"You will watch me." Her hand moved along his length, and the pleasure that flowed nearly forced his eyes closed again, but he kept them open. For her. Because giving her pleasure was his only reason for being in this moment.

She lowered her mouth. The first touch of her tongue against him pulled a moan from deep in his chest. Her mouth was so hot, so wet along his skin. Her hair caught on his trousers, onyx on midnight, as she took him deeper. He settled his hands on her shoulders to keep himself upright under the sweet slide of her tongue along his length.

His belly clenched and his thighs went tight as he kept his eyes open and on her, the rose of her lips against the crimson of his skin almost more than he could bear. Against his will, he thrust forward, once, the painful ache of his desire too much to bear any longer.

Her eyes flicked up toward his, the depths of them fathomless. Never looking away, she cupped his scrotum and took him as deeply as she could.

He did close his eyes at that, lest they roll back in his head.

Just as he was about to warn her of his imminent climax, she pulled away, clutching at his arms to drag him to the bed and over her.

"I'll crush you," he protested.

"Yes." She writhed against him. "Exactly."

At those words, he realized that *was* what he wanted to do: crush her into that bed with the weight of him, abrade her skin with the rasp of his clothes, have his buttons bite into her as he drove her right into the headboard with his urgency.

Some last stutter of rational thought had him reaching into his jacket, pulling out the preventatives—the events of the day hadn't been enough to completely obliterate that green shoot of hope—and sliding one down his penis.

With one fierce thrust, he buried himself within her to the hilt. Her eyes closed, her breasts rising to meet his chest as her back bowed. He thrust again and her legs came up to twine round his hips.

He was a beast now, pure feral impulse, as he thrust again and again, the jiggle of her flesh and her inchoate murmurs maddening him until all that was left was instinct and sensation. Then the sensation burst, drowning out even instinct, as his climax hit and he poured himself into her.

He fell onto her, her legs still locked around him, her body shuddering in time with his.

"I've hurt you," he muttered as he rolled over, pulling her atop him.

"No. Never." Her eyes were closed, her head against his shoulder, peacefully curled against him as she swept a hand along his jaw.

His body had stopped shaking, but his mind was shuddering in the aftermath, his heart quivering with every beat. If only he could keep her here, stop time and have her always next to him in his bed. In his life.

But tomorrow was still coming, bringing with it potential injustice and certain scandal. She would leave tomorrow and there was no way to keep her.

Only there was a way.

It was a path through a dark wood, choked with the specters of everything he feared most in this world, but it existed. She could be his.

He wet his dry lips. "Isabel, after last night you could... you could be with child."

His blood went as slow and cold as an Arctic river, but he kept his expression blank, his voice steady. She didn't need to know how he dreaded that very prospect.

For her part, she raised her head and merely blinked. "It was only the once."

"It only takes the once. Do you understand? We would have to marry then." God, to have her forever... but not like that. Not snared like prey. "No matter what happens tomorrow."

She turned away, reaching for her nightgown.

"The chance is small." She'd put on her schoolmarm tone once more. "We can discuss that if it actually happens."

She tugged the gown over her head, covering all her loveliness, then wrapped her dressing gown around herself.

He pulled her back down to him, unable to release her just yet. If this was their only night together, she could stay until the dawn. He could have at least that many more hours to hold her.

"At least we used a preventative tonight," she mused.

He cocked his head. "Preventative?" What did she, a virgin as of yesterday, know of preventatives? Come to think of it, she hadn't asked any questions when he'd pulled out the tin and covered himself...

The realization hit him in a horrifying rush of nausea and bitterness and his hand went tight against her thigh, his fingers sinking into the soft flesh.

Obregon.

She had been intimate with Obregon.

Sebastian, who'd been by her side through this entire ordeal, wanted to be by her side always, got only two nights with her, while Obregon, that unworthy...

How many nights had *he* gotten?

A black cloud of rage surrounded Sebastian's heart, filled his mouth, clouded his mind. The taste of it was sharp, metallic, like a dagger against his tongue and as familiar as the give of flesh under his fist. He pushed himself off the bed to stand over her.

"Where did you learn about preventatives?"

She sat up then, no fear at all on her lovely face, only annoyance. It enraged him, his blood going to flame as it roared along his veins.

"Did you learn about them from Obregon?" he growled, his voice low enough to crawl upon the floor.

Isabel stared at him for a moment with wide eyes... and then her lip curled.

"This is about Joaquin?" she asked scornfully.

When he couldn't answer, she scrambled off the bed, clutching the dressing gown about her, glaring at him as she did.

She seemed entirely unaffected by the smoke filling his vision, the ash piling in his mouth.

"I'm not going to remain to hear such things," she sniffed. She swept out as regal as a queen, never once looking back at him.

And that was it. His last chance to be intimate with her, to feel the press of her against him, to find relief and release with her. Perhaps even his last chance to see her. His temper had driven her out, yet still it ran hot and thick in his blood, this rage, transforming him into nothing more than smoldering wrath.

His fingers felt no more substantial than smoke, yet somehow they found the edge of the dresser in the corner of the room. His muscles were as hot and formless as lava, yet somehow they flexed.

The dresser fell right over, shattered glass and splinters spewing from it like poisonous ash from a volcano.

~~~

Isabel froze in the hallway at the terrific crash from Sebastian's room.

What on earth had he done?

She couldn't move forward and she couldn't go back, her heart hammering in her ears, her muscles stiff with indecision.

She ought to check on him, to ensure he was unharmed, but her mother would be awake and out of her room at any moment. Both of their mothers would be. She must not be caught in his room.

If she wanted not to be caught out of bed, she needed to race to her own room immediately.

Instead, she remained right where she was, caught in sticky uncertainty.

Her mother came down the hall first. Wonderful.

"What was that?" she demanded. "Why are you out of bed?"

Before Isabel could answer, Señora Vasquez came toward them, Junius at her heels.

"What has happened?" Her tones were more measured than Isabel's mother's. "Are you all right?"

"I'm fine," Isabel answered. "But..."

She gestured toward Sebastian's door. All three of them turned to stare at it.

Señora Vasquez's face went tight with trepidation—a feeling Isabel shared—even as she squared her shoulders and pushed open the door. Isabel and her mother followed close behind.

A chest of drawers was tipped over, the shards of the mirror spread in a halo of destruction.

Had he pulled it over in his anger? Every inch of her skin prickled at the thought.

Sebastian himself was staring down at the massive piece of furniture, his brow furrowed as if he couldn't quite discern how it had happened.

"Sebastian?" his mother asked quietly, seemingly afraid to rouse him.

He didn't look up.

"Sebastian?" she tried again, just as timorously. "What has happened?"

He sighed and pinched the bridge of his nose, his shoulders slumping.

His mother crouched down, reached for a shard of mirror. "I'll just call the maids to come clean this."

"No." The word was harsh, low, and it froze his mother in place. "Don't call them."

Isabel's mother stepped forward. "What happened here?" Her voice crackled with authority.

"It was an accident," Señora Vasquez said. "He didn't mean it."

Isabel closed her eyes as the words echoed, echoed with all the times Señora Vasquez had obviously said the exact same words, only to a different man, in hopes of appeasing him, of limiting the damage.

If Isabel gave in to that impossible dream in her heart, the dream of her and Sebastian somehow together in the future, would those words be echoing from *her* mouth one day?

She shuddered as her lips formed those phantom words against her will.

No. Her eyes flew open. Señora Vasquez's fate, her mother's fate—a violent marriage—that was not *her* fate.

"Marshal Espencer," her mother said, her jaw tight and her fingers clenching in her skirt as if reaching for a pistol that wasn't there, "I ask you again—what has happened here?"

He looked up, and her heart stopped at the stricken expression on his face. Never before, not even in the throes of passion, had emotion been written so starkly upon him.

"I pulled it over. It was no accident," he confessed.

Isabel knew that was what had happened, knew before he spoke, but hearing it from his own lips... She caught the sob in her throat before it could escape.

She'd cracked his reserve and this was what had come out. This senseless destruction.

A sad sort of triumph passed over her mother's face at his words, but he missed it as he bent to help his mother up.

"Please," he said softly, "I'll clean it up. It's my fault."

"I ask you then—what are your intentions toward my daughter?"

Isabel did gasp at that, at the baldness of her mother's demand.

Sebastian looked past her mother, straight at her, his eyes as clear and cold as the winter sky. "I wish nothing for your daughter but happiness and a long life." He released a slow breath and she swore she could see it in the air, so cold was she. "Therefore, I have no intentions toward your daughter. None at all."

She stumbled backward under the weight of those words, under the storm of his gaze. She only just kept from clutching at her face to pull off that weight, to allow herself to breathe.

"No." His mother rose from the floor, the shard of mirror falling from her hand, a fragment of light released from her fingers. "It *was* an accident." She turned to her son, her face nakedly pleading. "Sebastian, you are not like your father."

"Of course not," he said softly, but his eyes said that he lied. "Please, Mother, let me clean this up and you return to bed." He looked at Isabel and his face was impassive once more. "Please, everyone go back to bed."

That was it then. He was finished with her.

She ought to be grateful, given what he'd just done, but she was... *empty.*

"Mother," Isabel called, her voice unnaturally high. "It doesn't matter. We're leaving tomorrow."

Her mother sighed. "I suppose you're right."

Both the Señoras went for the door, Isabel waiting for them to pass before following. She paused, unable to leave without one last glance at Sebastian.

He might be finished with her, but she wasn't quite finished with him.

He was staring at the shattered mirror with that puzzled expression again. When she walked out, he would be completely alone with whatever he was wrestling with.

This could be the very last time she saw him.

"Isabel," her mother prompted, "come along."

The shard of mirror in his hand flashed white at her for half a moment, before she saw the red smeared across it and his fingers.

She shivered at the sight, shivered as the memory of each and every time he'd let his emotions slip their leash rose in her mind, the blood on his fingers, the blood the outlaw had spit from his mouth after being struck, the blood thundering in her ears as he spewed his jealousy at her former fiancé…

She turned and followed her mother from the room.

CHAPTER TWENTY

Isabel walked slowly behind her mother, her feet moving against the weight pulling her heart under.

The white of her mother's nightgown disappeared into the gloom, leaving only darkness surrounding her.

Isabel halted.

He was all alone now. She imagined him picking up every last piece of that mirror, his brow knit with that strangely puzzled expression of his... and her heart wrenched with it.

No. She couldn't let this image of him, deserted, with only his own agitation for company, be her last one.

"Isabel," her mother called, nothing more than a voice in the dark, "what are you doing?"

"Nothing." She couldn't leave him like this, no matter what her mother insisted. "You go on."

"Isabel, I am not leaving you alone with that man." Her footsteps came toward Isabel.

"Yes, you are," she insisted. The footsteps ceased, her mother no doubt shocked by her impertinence. "I'll be perfectly safe. Give me just five minutes. That's all I ask."

"I don't know..."

"You said you trusted my judgment. Please trust me now."

Silence, as her mother pondered that. "Five minutes only. If I hear anything else—"

"Of course."

She heard her mother move away as she turned back to his room.

The door was still ajar, allowing her to slip in with little noise. He was crouched by the shattered mirror, looking nothing like the beast he thought he was.

He looked as vulnerable as he must have been when he'd been a boy and cowering under his father's rule.

But he wasn't a boy anymore. He was a man, and men of reason did not destroy the furniture when piqued.

When he finally lifted his head, he looked as though he found her presence as puzzling as the broken mirror.

"You shouldn't be here." He'd said that before, and he was correct—then and now. But here she was.

"Why?" She gestured to the mess on the floor, but meant so much more. This surely could not have all been for her actions with Joaquin.

He looked from her to the mirror, then back again. "Because I was... angry."

As his words sank into her, dripping to her very bones with the weight of them, she realized he could not handle this—this connection between them. The closed-off, entrapped manner in which he had been living before was the only way he could be without falling back into violence.

Like Pandora, she'd opened something better left closed.

~~~

The horror and shock on her face was hardening now into something close to contempt, Sebastian saw.

"Because you weren't my first? You were angry about *that?* You were no virgin."

When she said it in such a manner, he realized how ridiculous it was, to be jealous of her life before she'd met him. She wasn't a sweet to be hoarded. His reaction had been madness.

Yet he couldn't undo what he'd done.

It hadn't done a damn thing to make him feel better. When he'd been seventeen, destroying something in a rage had left at least a hint of satisfaction when he was finished, but now he only felt ridiculous.

And a little angry.

Foolish, but he resented that he would only ever have these few days with her, while Obregon might have had more.

But it wasn't only Obregon. *You are leaving me. Forever.* A ragged cry from his heart, one that he couldn't allow to pass his lips.

He *must* let her go.

"Yes," he said heavily. "I was jealous. Jealous of a man who can hardly leave his bed."

He shook his head at his pettiness. What a fool he was. That was the problem with emotions—once they were loose, it was damned difficult to lock them away again. Especially the emotions she inspired in him.

"This is how you react? Like a... like a... a seventeen-year-old boy?" she snapped. She was finding some anger of her own now.

He *had* reacted just as he would have at seventeen, yet the aftermath didn't feel the same at all. He needed her to understand that.

"Isabel, I... I am sorry for this. It won't happen again."

Her frown went from angry to confused. "We're leaving tomorrow. It doesn't matter what you promise."

Tomorrow. His heart strained at the word. Why had she come back? Why couldn't she have stayed away, have left the two of them sundered?

But she had come back—and he had to let her go once more. Oh God, how could he release her? If she left, he couldn't return to what he'd been before, not without his entire self irrevocably breaking. He didn't know how to shove all of these emotions back within himself—and if they continued to run loose like this, more damage would be done.

Stay, he wanted to tell her. *Give me some time to learn to live with these sensations again, more than a few days.*

If he could learn to live with sensation again, he could learn to live with her. But to unbend after only a few days—it was too much. It had taken over a decade to reach this point; it would take some time to reach a new equilibrium.

Perhaps it was better if she was absent during the process. After a few months, perhaps a year, he would re-master himself, become a new man for her. And then they could be together, and to hell with what the good people of Los Angeles thought.

"What your mother said tonight"—her voice seemed to flow from around a stone lodged in her throat—"I don't ever want to have those words come from my mouth, because you've smashed some furnishings, or struck someone, or harmed... harmed *me*."

"No." The word was torn from the deepest part of his soul, the part beyond the darkness, that part that would shatter without her. "That would never happen. I would die before I hurt you."

Her face crumpled, but no tears fell. "I want to believe that." Low, fervent. "I want to believe it so badly."

"You must believe it." He took a step toward her, but she held up a hand to stop him. "Please, Isabel. Please believe me."

He would go down on his knees for her, beg her to understand that he could never harm anything so precious to him, beg her to know that he needed her...

He opened his mouth to tell her so, to ask for just a bit of time to right himself—wasn't a man entitled to that when a woman tipped his world upside down?

She must have seen his intentions in his eyes, because her hand turned from halting to beckoning and he could see in her expression her need to believe him, and he knew, just knew, when he had explained it all, they would find a way to make this work...

"Isabel," he pleaded, "I know I am unworthy. Only say the word and I will—"

A snapping. A snarling. Something rushing toward her.

Junius attacked.

Sebastian hadn't seen the dog come in with his mother, so it took him a moment to realize what had launched itself at Isabel.

A moment too late.

His hand snagged the collar without thought, the dog's teeth sinking into the fabric of her nightgown. She instinctively stumbled back and the fabric gave with a painful rip.

He yanked the dog away, his entire body pulling the animal back as it continued to lunge for her. His heart took off like a bolting horse.

"Are you all right?" *Please God, let her be unharmed.*

Her eyes were wide in her white face, but he thankfully saw no blood. She stared for a moment before her expression crumpled. Then she did something he had never seen her do before.

She wept.

In every trial he had seen her endure—and there had been many—she had never once cried. Not once. But she wept now. Tears ran freely down her cheeks to fall to the floor, her breath coming in rending sobs. He couldn't even comfort her, since he could not release the dog.

It was all too much like it had been thirteen years ago—the edge of that memory slicing him to the bone. His mother's tears, his hands covered in blood, his helplessness before the horror of his nature...

What's bred in the bone will come out in the blood.

He'd thought Junius would be safe around her.

He was wrong.

He thought that he, Sebastian, could find some way to live with her and not release the darkness within him.

He was wrong.

She would be the one to pay the price for his errors and arrogance someday. He had already become the best man he could before she'd come into his life—better was not within his reach.

He had to let her go to save her from himself.

He took all of the pain, the sheer agony that welled within him at the thought of never seeing her again, honed it to a knife's edge, and put that edge to the words he had to say to her.

"You thought that I needed redemption." His own ears bled under the words, but he kept on. For her. "You thought that being oh so clever, you could unlock me, redeem me for yourself." His tongue felt forked as it moved against his teeth. "You were wrong."

A sobbing moan left her lips and she wrapped her arms around her midsection, folding over them. He almost broke then, under the weight of her despair, almost went to her and confessed his lies, but Junius lunged again, reminding him of what he must do.

"I don't need you to redeem me—*I have already redeemed myself.*"

She straightened and he could see it in her eyes—she was turning from him. So he finished it, for the both of them.

"There is no happy ending for us."

She blinked the last of her tears away and left the room without a word, taking with her the only part of him that hadn't shattered at what he'd just done.

CHAPTER TWENTY-ONE

ISABEL KNEW IT WAS COMING, yet she'd still been surprised.

Not guilty.

She laid a dress in her travel trunk, carefully smoothing out the fabric, thankful her hands had finally stopped trembling. That had been her only reaction to the fall of those two words against her ear, a faint nervousness working through her fingers lasting until... now.

Sebastian hadn't been there in court to witness her stoicism. He was off somewhere—where she knew not—and she didn't care.

The words clanged mendaciously in the hollows of her thoughts.

She and her mother were catching a train in a few hours. She'd likely never see him again, not in this life. Her final memory of him would always be that terrible scene from last night.

To become jealous over Joaquin of all things, especially given the stains of his past—it was beyond absurd.

It was *infuriating.*

Before the dog had lunged, his expression had been so beseeching—as if he were about to beg her for something.

She'd never know what he might have asked her for. Nor what her answer might have been.

Her hands were smashing the folded dress into the trunk, wrinkling what she had so carefully smoothed. She stared at the imprint left in the fabric, stress lines radiating out from the impressions of her fingers.

Rather like how the fragments of mirror had radiated out from the overturned dresser last night.

A small wet spot appeared on the fabric, then another, and another, until she was hunting for her handkerchief. She curled around the open trunk, holding the little square of fabric to her mouth to catch her sobs. Just a dainty wisp of lace, nowhere near large enough to soak up all her grief. The tears shuddered through her, her ribs heaving until she feared they would crack.

But they didn't crack, and slowly the storm passed. She was left hanging onto the trunk as if it were her lifeline in a thrashing sea, with only the throb of yet another headache left as wreckage.

The edge of the trunk bit against her palms as she straightened to her knees. Methodically, she smoothed the dress yet again, unable to erase the sea salt drops of her tears from it. No matter. It would dry, given enough time.

She, too, would survive.

Given enough time.

She had disobeyed him this morning—*disobeyed*, as if she were his wife!—and looked over the papers. The *Star* had a truly astonishing illustration of her as a harpy, complete with spectacles, holding Mr. Edwin McCade in one claw, his son Cole in another.

If she had looked half as fearsome in the courtroom as she did in that illustration, the verdict might have been very different.

She laid a chemise into the trunk—the same one she'd worn that first day in the library, the one Sebastian had seen her in. The lace edging was almost painfully rough between her fingers. An image of her fingers flicking that chemise into a fire rose in her mind, but she pushed it away. Burning it would be too ridiculous, would give entirely too much weight to the matter.

She would leave this city, never to return, and that would be the end of it.

Once in back in Cabrillo, she would...

Her hands stilled on the brush she was nestling into the trunk.

What *would* she do when she returned home? She'd always had some goal to work for, some height to strive to.

Before all this, it had been to reach Los Angeles.

After the attack, it had been to track down McCade and to see justice done.

She had failed at all of those, fallen so miserably far she felt as though her nose were in the dirt.

Staying in Cabrillo wouldn't be wise. After the verdict had been read, McCade had finished shaking hands with his lawyer, then those flat eyes found her among the spectators.

There had been a promise in that gaze, a promise that if he got hold of her, he'd finish what he'd begun.

Her throat had throbbed, closing so tightly she saw gray, but she'd held his gaze as steadily as gravity held her to the earth, not needing the false promise of Sebastian's security to find the nerve to do so.

But stares wouldn't keep her safe if McCade did decide to come after her. The windows... Passing any window would be a severe trial. Not to mention leaving the house. She'd have to ask Juan for a pistol to carry when she returned home.

No. No, she'd purchase her own pistol, with her own funds. And not some silly ladies' pistol. She'd get a real one, a long-barreled Colt with six shots. It would be the first thing she did upon returning home.

Pain rolled between her temples, the wash from it sending nausea all throughout her. She could not begin to imagine speaking of what had happened at the trial—especially with Joaquin. She did not think her lips would be able to form the words. It would be a contortion beyond their ability.

But she would have to find a way.

She released her hold on the brush and looked about the room one last time. The bed, the table, the dresser—all were painfully empty, her pitiful few days here erased as though they'd never occurred.

Sebastian would clear his mind of her as easily as she'd cleared this room. He'd put every memory, every sensation of her, into those notebooks of his and shut them tight. She'd be forever trapped on those pages, never to escape. While he went on with a mind as serene and smooth as a blank page.

Cold moved across her skin, bringing gooseflesh with it. She didn't want to be in those books, didn't want to be a memory he could not forget but chose never to revisit.

He'd made it plain last night that was all he wanted her to be.

Truly, if loving her meant he could no longer control the wildness within him, who was she to break him open?

It was better—safer—for everyone if she left.

Of all the failures she had accomplished, her failure with Sebastian hurt the worst because it had held the most promise. He thought her *magnificently difficult.* He thought her *terrifyingly brilliant.*

Where would she ever meet his like again? Certainly not in Cabrillo.

She brought down the trunk lid with a thunk that echoed softly throughout the room.

The door opened and her mother looked in.

"Good. You've finished packing." Her mother spoke rapidly, as if the pace of her words could speed them from this place.

"Yes." She rose, her knees holding onto their ache from the floor.

"The driver will carry your trunk to the carriage."

"Is he here already?" She paused, uncertain if she should risk the next question. "Have you seen—"

"No," her mother snapped, "and I don't care to see that man ever again. No better than his father, it seems." Her mother drew a shaky breath. "That is exactly the kind of man I feared you and your sisters might find yourselves married to."

Yes, her mother would fear that, given her history. But her mother didn't know Sebastian's history.

"I told him who you are." A stark confession, out before Isabel had even decided to confess.

"What?" A stunned release of breath from her mother.

"I told him who you were." More defiant than she'd ever dared before. "He knew and he never betrayed us."

"That was not your story to tell," her mother snapped.

"You gave it to me for comfort," she said. "And I gave it to him for the same." She clasped her hands to her breast. "Mother, he said he'd never betray someone I loved, that he would die before he harmed me—"

"Isabel."

Quietly spoken—her mother never needed to raise her voice to instantly gain her children's attention.

"He pulled over a dresser," her mother said, every syllable distinct. A marked warning for her daughter to reclaim her sense. "I would rather he told my secret to Judge Bannister, hauled me before the man himself, than to ever have you in danger from him."

An inarguable point. He *had* pulled over a heavy piece of furniture out of base jealousy. Of course her mother wanted to keep her safe.

Sebastian had promised to keep her safe.

She did not think she'd ever felt quite so adrift in her life. Her knees softened, the bed meeting her thighs as she sank down. She could only contemplate her linked hands for long moments, her mother watching silently.

And then: "Isabel." Her mother clasped her hand, a rare touch from her. "It's time to leave."

Leave Sebastian, her mother meant.

"Once we're home, you can put this marshal from your mind," her mother went on. "None of what happened is your fault. Remember that, when everyone asks about the outcome."

Of course. She'd been repeating that to herself since the very beginning, with every recitation of her tale.

But fate clearly didn't care who was at fault here.

Neither did justice.

"Now come," her mother urged, "wipe that expression from your face and splash some water on your cheeks. You don't want anyone to see you like that."

How like her mother—always a reminder to sit up straight, to never let them see one flinch—even in the things she offered as comfort.

"Yes, of course," Isabel answered. Because her mother was correct—she didn't want to be seen like this. Didn't really want to be seen by anyone ever again.

"Come down to the carriage," her mother said, motioning to the door. "We are finished here."

~~~

The apology had been wooden, even to Sebastian's ears, but seemed to have been successful.

Judge Bannister's expression held a hint of wariness as he looked across the expanse of his desk, but it wasn't openly hostile.

"Well, I can understand you were overwrought in the moment," the judge was saying stiffly, "losing the case like that."

He blinked thoughtfully, perhaps remembering that he'd never seen Sebastian so much as perturbed before.

"Yes," Sebastian said, before Bannister could comment further. "Exactly so."

It was true, in a sense. If the judge assumed he was overset because of the trial, so much the better. Best for everyone if Bannister believed the lawyer's insinuations were nothing more than that.

His gaze flicked to the clock behind the desk, solemnly ticking off the seconds that would make up the remainder of his life. Only two hours and five minutes until Isabel's train left.

He'd cleaned up every last shard of glass last night, slicing his fingers a few times in the process. He'd been injured worse before, had bled more, but every glimpse he'd caught of those red smudges made his heart stutter.

When his heart resumed its usual rhythm, he had reminded himself this was why he could not unbend.

Things were destroyed when he unbent.

People bled.

This morning, he'd left the house with the false dawn, the temptation of her too much for his battered resolve. If he saw her again, he might yet say those words he'd wanted to say last night, foolish words of love and marriage and second chances.

So he'd run as soon as he could, trusting the rail company to do what he could not—to take her from him.

Judge Bannister drummed his fingers on the desk, considering. "Well, there are always other ways to stop this water business."

Sebastian didn't care to know. He wanted only to be done with this interview so he could slink home to his notebooks.

He would put every last bit of her within them and shut her away. His iron self-control would return then, he knew it. He could sense it hovering just near his fingers, waiting only for the specter of her to fade before it would come near enough for him to seize it again.

"If we keep an eye out, we're likely to catch McCade in something criminal again." The judge's face clouded. "This time we'll be certain the case doesn't rest on an uncertain witness."

The darkness within Sebastian rolled and snapped. Oh, he would watch McCade very closely. If a legal means to see him hang presented itself, Sebastian would pursue it to its bitterest end.

He'd already set a man to watch McCade—if the outlaw made a move to go after her, Sebastian would be right behind him. McCade would make that move someday. Sebastian was certain of it.

But if Bannister thought they would ever find a witness more certain, more brave than Señorita Moreno, he was dead wrong.

She had only cried the once...

"If the jury had known you," the judge was saying, "they wouldn't have fallen for that nonsense of an improper association."

Sebastian swallowed hard. It hadn't been nonsense at all. Even now, his skin heated at the memory of their *association*.

He shoved the memory away, thought of ice, of winter, of nothingness stretching cold and far and forever.

Bannister shook his head. "Why, you don't have any associations, much less improper ones."

Sebastian was struck by how this man had known him since he was a boy, yet knew him not at all. Bannister thought him to be simply *the marshal*, an instrument to be used when he pleased, as well as the son of a man worthy of admiration.

Isabel had known the truth of him—known his father was a monster, known there was more behind his façade of nothingness than merely empty, echoing darkness.

He looked at the clock again. One hour and fifty-five minutes until her train left. He only had to restrain himself for that length of time and she would be safe from his weakness. Because if he let them, his legs would run to her, his mouth would kiss her, and his heart would claim her.

Instead, he gripped the arms of his chair and tried to attend to what the judge was saying.

"No, sir," he answered. "There is no association between us."

"Well, of course not," Bannister said with a wave that expressed how foolish the idea was. "We lost this case, but there's always the next."

Sebastian didn't care. What did it matter if he brought in another criminal? He'd thought there'd been meaning in what he did as a marshal, that his actions tipped the balance toward justice. That his efforts, small as they were, were a means to make amends for his own crimes.

He'd brought in McCade, set him before a judge—and now the man would never answer for what he'd done to Isabel.

"I'm certain Cole McCade will do something criminal," the judge went on. "He can't seem to help it."

"I've set a man to watch him," Sebastian said.

Bannister stiffened. "I never told you to do that."

"I'm paying the man. It's entirely unofficial."

"Well." The judge blinked uncertainly. "That's commendable foresight, I suppose."

Sebastian hadn't done it for the judge—he'd done it for *her*.

A knock came at the door, the judge's clerk poking his head in. "A boy just delivered a note for Marshal Spencer."

Sebastian rose, took the slip of paper. As he read it, a roaring moved through his ears and he set his teeth together hard to keep it from escaping his mouth.

He snatched up his hat, his fingers numb upon it. He glanced at the clock. One hour and fifty minutes before her train left. Could he arrive in time?

If he didn't...

He'd promised to protect her.

Always.

He *must* arrive in time.

"What's happened?" Bannister asked.

"McCade is already on his way to Cabrillo. He's taking the same train she is." He'd never thought McCade would act so swiftly.

But why not? The outlaw was free, back in his father's good graces—why not deal with that last complication while his luck was good?

Sebastian prayed his luck was better.

"You're not going after him, are you?" the judge demanded. "He's been found not guilty. There's nothing to detain him for."

Once, such a consideration would have stopped Sebastian. But he couldn't care about the rule of law at the moment—he only cared about her. "If McCade does any-thing illegal, then I'll detain him."

"I never said you could go," the other man challenged him.

Sebastian studied the judge's face.

"You want him to kill her." It was pure accusation, and farther than he should have dared, but not near as far as he'd like to go.

"No." The denial was quick, sharp. "But your role in this has ended."

It hadn't. He'd promised her—and he would see that promise through to the bitter end.

Sebastian spread his hands. "By all means, try to stop me."

The judge's throat bobbed. "Your father would dis-approve of this."

His father. As if his father's approval had ever meant anything to him. If Sebastian's actions would earn Judge Spencer's disapproval, then they must be correct.

Sebastian had to laugh. It scraped his throat as it went past, yet it still felt good to release it. Odd, but good.

Bannister didn't seem to agree, going whiter than Sebastian had thought possible.

Sebastian shook his head. "Her sister is married to your son, for God's sake."

Did the judge even think of such things? Señora Moreno had spent decades hiding from him, Isabel herself had been terrified when Bannister had faced her—did the man have the slightest notion of those who cowered under his long shadow? Of those who were affected by his political jousting?

Likely not. The judge was powerful and wealthy—and had convinced himself that he was an instrument of justice. No need for self-examination there.

Seabstian knew then that he could no longer obey this man's commands, bend himself to achieve the judge's ends. Even if it was in the service of justice.

There was no time to tell the judge that—Sebastian had a train to catch.

He set his hat upon his head and pulled open the door. "I'll return in a few days."

He only hoped he wasn't already too far behind the both of them.

CHAPTER TWENTY-TWO

ISABEL STARED OUT THE TRAIN window and wished she could press her forehead against the glass. It would be cool and firm against the fever of her headache, providing blessed relief from the pain set hard as a fist behind her eyes.

But she didn't dare do something so common, so coarse. Instead she stared at the crowd on the platform and wished the train would move.

A family stood there, parents and three small boys. The husband kept tossing his wife the most besotted smiles, as if it were nothing to smile affectionately at her in the midst of all these people, as if he had a neverending store of smiles to give to her.

Sebastian had given her exactly two smiles and one laugh.

She almost set her head against the glass, but stopped herself at the last moment. Her mother sat across from her, knitting in an abstracted fashion. Any lapse in Isabel's conduct would bring a reprimand.

She shifted on the hard wood beneath her and pulled herself straight. She could only look out the window, not touch it. No matter how the cool pane called to the flame burning under her skull.

The family left and the crowds thinned as the departure time neared. A slim man with serious intent passed under her window; a stout, elderly lady checked the watch pinned to her bodice; and there, near the waiting room, was—

Her heart stopped and she slapped a palm against the window. She blinked hard, her breath coming fast.

No. It couldn't be him.

She searched the entire platform, craning to see each end, ignoring her mother's worried frown. She'd seen him, she was sure of it.

Where was he?

Him—no. That man—no.

With each discarded subject, her pulse leapt higher.

He was there, she'd seen him, her eyes would not fool her so—

After what felt like endless minutes, she sat back when the platform was empty.

He wasn't there. It wasn't him.

Due to some mad trick of her eyes or her brain, she thought she'd seen McCade on the platform.

Foolishness. Why would he be here, on this train? No, he would certainly remain in Los Angeles, celebrating his victory next to the father who'd engineered it.

Her fear was producing sick mirages—and she was believing they were real. Perhaps she was going mad.

"Isabel?"

She summoned a smile for her mother. "It was nothing. I thought I saw something, but it was nothing."

But her heart kept bucking like some silly horse afraid of its own shadow.

With a jolt, the train moved out of the station. Finally, they were leaving this place.

She watched as Los Angeles began to slide away, taking with it all the foolish dreams of her youth. Along with her greatest enemy.

And the man who could have been her greatest love.

Her throat closed and salt pricked at her eyes. She breathed slow and steady to hold the tears at bay. She was done with him, him and this city. She had only to repeat it, over and over again, and soon enough it would be true. She would turn to stone once more.

She rummaged in the satchel at her feet for her schoolbooks. Lesson planning was a good way to lead her thoughts away from what she should not be thinking of. The book fell open with ease to the last topic she'd read of: Brazil.

She would *not* think of that evening in camp, when McCade had appeared out of the darkness like a demon summoned by a witch, would not think of Sebastian asking her if she were all right.

Would not remember the fall of his fist into the other man's jaw.

The hints had been there all along, the key to his true nature.

Or was it? A boy of seventeen was very different from a man of thirty, especially a man who had undertaken the mental rigors Sebastian had. In all those notebooks there had been no hint of violence until...

Until her.

He had struck McCade because of her. He had threatened the judge because of her. He had destroyed the furniture—because of her.

She snapped the book shut, unable to pretend to read any longer. She turned back to the window, watching the world slip by in a dizzying blur, the pain in her head pulling at her stomach and raising a wave of nausea.

For her, he made everything better. For him, she made everything worse.

That simple fact was why a future between them was impossible.

She pressed hard against her belly, hard against the pain tearing through the center of her. She dared not do more, dared not wail or weep or tear at her hair. Her mother was watching.

Dear God, what if there *were* a child?

He would do his duty, of that she was certain, but it would be nothing more. There would be no smiles or laughter—only that cold, inhuman indifference, as inexorable as stone grinding against stone. Such a fate would be worse than never seeing him again.

As soon as they were home, she would pray ceaselessly there was no baby in her belly. Even the love of a child would be poor recompense for a lifetime of Sebastian's iciness.

But for now she simply stared out the window. The emptiness within her was eerily familiar, a sibling to the silence that had taken her just after the attack.

No bruised neck or gawking gossips muted her in this moment—only the knowledge that her future had never looked darker.

She tried to find still points in the rush moving past the window. Small bits of fixedness to hang onto for half a second before they were lost. It made the nausea distinctly worse, but she kept to it regardless.

She had a sycamore in her sights and was turning to watch it disappear back into the blur when a shadow fell across her. A large, dark shadow.

Was that when one knew one was in love with a man—when one could identify him only by his shadow?

She looked up into Sebastian's gray eyes.

~~~

The expression on her face tore at Sebastian's heart.

Always before, always, she'd been lit from within by a fierce inner light, ready to do battle at a moment's notice. Now she simply looked vacant and drab, the light burned down to ash.

She didn't appear to be happy or sad or angry to see him. She appeared empty.

He missed her fierceness desperately. Missed all of her desperately.

"Marshal Espencer," Señora Moreno said in unwelcome greeting, her face flat and her neck stiff.

Isabel said nothing at all.

"Señora, Señorita. I apologize for bringing you distressing news again, but..." Lord, he hated this, hated having to hurt her over and over again. But it must be done. "I've received word McCade is returning to Cabrillo. I suspect he intends harm to the Señorita."

The Señora's mouth pinched tight, but she betrayed no other reaction. Isabel merely turned back to the window, as if she cared not that a man might be hunting her.

Or perhaps she could no longer stand the sight of Sebastian.

"I saw him. On the platform." It was spoken quietly to the window, but he heard Isabel's words clearly.

So McCade *was* here, somewhere. Thank the Lord Sebastian had found her before McCade had.

"Isabel!" her mother snapped. "Why didn't you say something?"

"I thought it was a trick of my mind," she answered dully.

"You're certain?" He pitched his words as if she were made of glass and his voice might shatter her.

"I saw him for only the barest moment, but yes, I'm certain it was him." Still she would not turn from the window.

"That's what you were searching for earlier," her mother said, "when you said it was nothing."

Her daughter gave no indication she'd heard.

Señora Moreno waved to the seat next to Isabel. "It seems we won't part company quite so soon, Marshal Espencer."

She sounded put out indeed by the prospect. He couldn't blame her for her fit of pique—hadn't he clearly proved he was a dangerous man?

The daughter in question didn't look his way as he sat, ready to keep watch over her. Only half an inch separated the folds of her skirt from his pant leg. Another half an inch, and there was her leg. A full inch between his flesh and hers. With her mother watching as they sat in a rail car, with everything that had happened between them, it might have been a full mile.

With her face turned to the window, she presented him with of a view of her profile eerily similar to the one she'd given at their first interview. The dark twist of her hair, the pale ridge of her cheekbone with the shadowed hollow beneath, and the wire of her spectacles as it disappeared behind the shell of her ear—it was all the same, and yet not.

He wondered if it pained her, the bite of the earpiece into the delicate skin behind her ear.

If they were alone—if things were not so terribly wrong between them—he could slide the frames from her face and massage the red mark he knew would be left behind, until she was soft and pliant against him. She might even breathe a kiss against his fingertips in thanks.

Well, that had been a pleasant fiction. He sighed silently as his fingers tingled with the imaginings of her lips. An ache tore through him, that it would only ever be imaginings.

So this was what pure misery felt like. It had been some time since he'd experienced it, but he recalled now. Distilled agony, heated and separated, then heated and separated again, until all that remained was the very essence of an ache, the same ache that made up the center of him.

This was going to be the longest train ride in the history of train rides.

He flinched every time the compartment door opened—but it was never McCade. Isabel faced the window the entire time—and never looked his way. Her mother knit ceaselessly—and never spoke a word.

When the train finally pulled into the station in the valley, he was half-convinced the ride would never end—the three of them stuck for eternity in this bizarre and tense tableau.

At least they could finally get off this train. Except there was still the ride up the mountain. He ground his teeth in memory of that bone-rattling journey.

The train halted with a jolt and a screech at the tidily painted depot.

Her mother rose and put away her knitting. Isabel finally turned away from the window, her gaze shunning his, and made to join her mother.

He held out a hand to halt her, stopping just before landing on her forearm. Not even an eighth of an inch, and he would grasp her.

"Wait." More plea than command. After all, she was the one who gave the commands.

Her mother went ahead, obviously assuming they were right behind her.

Isabel remained in the seat, staring at his hand. His skin began to heat with her gaze laid across it.

"What was he wearing?" he asked softly.

She looked up and the fire was back in her eyes.

His mouth softened in the barest beginnings of a smile.

"A dark brown suit, almost the color of wet clay." Her words were clipped and crisp again, not a hint of dullness in them. "And a Derby hat."

He searched the platform.

"Wearing a gun belt?" he asked.

"No. Not that I could see." She looked with him, the tilt of her body identical to his as they bent toward the window.

The crowd began to thin.

"Did you spot him?" he asked.

"No. I'm not even certain I saw him at the depot in Los Angeles. You know," she said, almost conversationally, "if he is coming, the men will hang him. You won't be able to stop them this time."

"It's the sheriff's job to prevent any violence." Although he knew Williams wouldn't.

"How many sheriffs do you know who stand tall when a mob comes, rather than stand aside?"

She was correct, but damn it, this was not a duty he wanted to assume. He only wanted to protect her. But the sense of justice he'd spent years honing, the one he hadn't entirely been able to leave behind in the judge's office, niggled—vigilantism was not justice.

He rose. "Hurry. We don't want to be on the train when it leaves."

She rose as well. "And if McCade is not in Cabrillo? How long do you plan to stand sentinel over me?"

How long? Forever, if need be. Perhaps standing sentinel would go some way to convincing her and himself he could be trusted. Perhaps if he stood guard over her forever, in that second before forever ended, she might allow him to touch her again.

Or perhaps not. Perhaps he was doomed to wander forever in the shade of her disfavor.

Her lips twitched. "Very well," she said with some disgust. "Search for him as long as you like. As long as necessary."

With that, she swept past him to rejoin her mother.

He followed behind, his jaw set against the knowledge that not only would he have to protect her from McCade, he would now also have to protect McCade from a lynching.

CHAPTER TWENTY-THREE

"JOAQUIN!" ISABEL HUNG IN THE DOORWAY of his room at the sanatorium, her lungs working like a set of bellows. Too fast. She'd run through the halls too fast.

Her gaze darted over his figure in the bed—sitting up. Eyes alert. Slightly hunched, but not crumpled. Thank the Lord.

"Isabel?" He leaned forward, gasping a little as he did. "What are you doing here?"

So much to tell him. So little time to do so. "I need your help," she began, trying to slow her breathing.

"My help?"

The disbelief in his voice made her pause. Perhaps this had been a poor idea. What was she thinking, to haul the man out of his bed like this?

She was thinking to stop a mob.

She needed his help. He *must* get out of bed.

But first, she must make her confession to him.

"The trial ended yesterday," she said baldly. "He was found not guilty." She wrapped her fingers around the doorframe to steady herself.

For half a moment, his expression went to pure accusation, and all of her flinched.

But then he sagged back against the bed, his gaze turning inward. "Well, we expected that."

That expression, those words—her entire family had the exact reaction when she'd told them. A resigned defeat, worn by all. They'd known she would fail—they didn't blame her.

They'd thrown off their defeat when she'd said the words she told Joaquin next: "He's—McCade—he's here. In Cabrillo."

"What?" Joaquin's horror at the news was deeper, sharper than her family's had been, his mouth opening into a wide gash as he spoke.

"He followed me here—the marshal thinks he means to harm me."

"Why aren't you at home then," Joaquin demanded, "under your father's and brother's guard? Isabel, if he comes here, I can't protect you!"

She pressed her fingertips into the doorframe, taking comfort from the unyielding wood beneath them. "Juan knows that McCade is here. You know what he'll try to do."

The look on her brother's face as he'd stalked from the room spoke to his grim determination. He would punish McCade, make no mistake.

She'd fled to her room right after Juan had left, pleading a headache. Then she'd gone in search of Franny.

Thank goodness her sister had been easy to convince—no blather about how mad Isabel's plan was, how Isabel ought to be keeping safe in the house—just steady determination as Franny had helped her prepare for their journey. They'd ridden hard for the sanatorium.

Joaquin's jaw worked in stiff jerks. "I'm not a sheriff any longer. I can't stop Juan."

This was what she must wrestle with if she wished to win him over, this terrible resignation to doing nothing, being nothing. "You cared about justice. Once. I believe you still do."

He raised a cold gaze. "Perhaps now I care about vengeance more."

Vengeance. She had to admit it sounded delicious. But would it still be delicious in the cold light of morning, knowing her brother had killed a man for her?

"I don't believe that," she said stoutly. "You can become the man you once were. You have only to take the first step."

She crossed the room to tug at his hand.

"I can hardly leave this bed." He pulled his hand away, set his face from hers. "I won't be taking any steps."

She was losing him. She wouldn't convince him to leave this bed, wouldn't stop them from killing McCade—she had nothing left.

"You don't have to walk far," she said. "We have the wagon."

She cringed at the pitifulness of that. *A wagon.*

He laughed humorlessly. "You think this is about the wagon? You think you'll just drive me up and I'll yell for everyone to go home?"

"I have a plan."

She watched his face carefully as she sketched it, waiting for the skepticism to ease.

It never did.

"That's leaving quite a bit to chance," he said. "If we arrive in time, if they even believe it, if McCade doesn't shoot someone first—none of it is near certain."

"We have to try, even if we're destined to fail. You used to believe that."

There, that flicker. Some part of her words was reaching him. She caught up his hand again.

"I know this man hurt us"—tears closed round her throat—"hurt us so much. But we can't let our family and neighbors take his blood upon their hands. His father won't hesitate to prosecute those involved. I can't see my brother go to prison."

Her voice splintered on the word *prison.*

"I don't know..."

He was considering it. She'd gotten him as far as consideration—only a little farther to go.

"Please." She put everything she'd once felt for Joaquin into that, praying he'd remember the man he'd been before.

His hand remained loose in hers. "I don't think I've ever seen you beg before," he mused. "It doesn't suit you." He sighed deeply. "Very well. I'll do it. For you."

Thank the Lord and all his saints. She pressed his hand and he squeezed back.

Oh, this might work after all—but they must hurry. How to get Joaquin out to the wagon, where Franny waited for them?

Isabel was looking wildly about the room when the little nurse appeared in the doorway.

"Why is someone shouting—oh. It's your fiancée." The flatness of the nurse's voice spoke to how unwelcome she found Isabel. "I'm sorry, miss, but you'll have to leave. It's time to settle the patients for the night."

"No," Isabel ordered. "You'll prepare him to come with us. You'll come along too, to attend to him."

"What? I can't do such a thing. Are you mad?"

There was no time for this nurse's objections. "Yes, I am," Isabel insisted. "Now hurry. A man's life depends on it."

Perhaps several men's.

The nurse crossed her arms. "No. If you don't leave, I'm calling an orderly. You can't upset the routine like this."

No. Isabel had not come all this way to be thwarted by this nurse. She prepared to lash the nurse with—

"Do it."

They both turned to stare at Joaquin.

"But, you..." The nurse dropped her arms, clearly flustered. "You can't leave."

"Yes, I can. Now help get me out of this bed." He held out an imperious hand to her. "And stop arguing."

Isabel allowed herself a moment to savor Joaquin's resolve, then gestured them to the door.

This was only the first of many battles tonight—the first and the easiest.

The worst was yet to come.

~~~

In the end, finding McCade had been easy.

Sebastian discovered his trail running along the creek, going up the mountain. McCade had avoided the road, using the creek to guide him, staying under cover. But clearly not expecting anyone to follow him.

Sebastian came across his hiding spot not half a mile from the Rancho Moreno. McCade's shock when Sebastian appeared was almost comical.

But McCade quickly dropped his surprise and put on a mocking smile. "Come to fetch me home again? You've nothing to charge me with this time."

That smile was a curve of razor wire against Sebastian's nerves. "Can we drop the pretense?" he demanded. "We both know you did it."

"Trying to force another confession from me?" McCade asked lazily. "I told you, it won't work. The jury found me innocent."

"It found you not guilty, which is another matter entirely." His voice dropped to a growl. "Whatever you had planned for her, you can forget."

McCade's smile went sly. "So it was true? You're sweet on that prune-faced hag? I never." He shook his head. "I want nothing to do with her. I'm only here for my horse."

Sebastian permitted himself half a moment to imagine breaking the man's jaw for the prune-faced hag comment, then put on his own air of disinterest. "*Your horse.* Which is why you're lurking outside her house."

"Lost my way."

He ought to leave this fool right where he was—but Isabel's entreaty and his own conscience wouldn't allow it.

"You'll lose your life if they catch you here," he warned. "They wanted to hang you before the trial—they'll be ravenous for your blood now." Perhaps an understanding of the threats assembling against him would turn McCade serious.

"They wouldn't dare," McCade sneered.

Or perhaps not.

"They know who my father is," the other man went on. "He'll see every man in this town hanged if anything happens to me."

"And if you're never found?" Sebastian pointed out. "If your body happens to end up somewhere in the desert on the far side of these mountains? They're not going to make a public spectacle of it. It'll be quiet—but probably not quick."

McCade's face sagged as the joviality left it—an unmarked grave in the desert clearly rattled him. "You won't stop them?"

She'd told him to stop them. She'd commanded him.

But Sebastian was tempted not to. With his control as frayed as it was, he was sorely tempted.

"Of course I'll stop them," he said. "I'm sworn to uphold the law." *And I swore to her.* "Now let's get out of here."

He gestured for McCade to go before him, out of the brush.

"If I don't go?"

Saints above. He'd just explained what would happen if the mob caught the man—and still he fought.

He crowded toe to toe with McCade, enjoying the shrinking of the other man's shoulders. "I'll handcuff you," Sebastian snarled in his face, "and haul you down the mountain. Threats of your father's power won't stop me."

Before, he'd never have done such a thing, let his anger run so clear and free—or use that anger to cow another.

"You want to ride down that mountain at night?" McCade asked, his swagger entirely gone.

"Would you rather wait here for the mob?"

"No, I wouldn't." McCade's expression flattened. "But we won't have to wait."

He jerked his chin toward a spot somewhere beyond Sebastian's shoulder.

Sebastian turned and saw the torches. There looked to be about a dozen, bobbing in the dark like malevolent, determined fireflies. The licking whoosh of the flames and their footsteps were the only sounds in the dark.

The mob had come.

CHAPTER TWENTY-FOUR

SEBASTIAN'S HAND WENT FOR HIS pistol as he crouched to snatch up his shotgun.

He'd put on a confident front for McCade, but he wasn't sure he could hold the mob off. He'd done it before, but they'd be even more determined now.

Truly, it was understandable. The man had injured two of their own and gotten away with it. The only justice McCade would see would be at the end of their rope.

But the law called that vigilantism, and he remained an officer of the law.

Which put him in the absurd position of protecting the attacker of the woman he loved. Of course, he might yet find himself in the even more absurd position of dying for the attacker of the woman he loved.

"McCade, come out! We see you there."

The man's voice caught at Sebastian's memory, but it was too muffled to snag upon its owner in his mind. He tightened his grip on the pistol and considered his options, of which there weren't many.

He released the pistol grip and raised the shotgun instead. He prayed that it and the badge on his chest would be enough to run them off.

If it wasn't, he might find himself hanging from an oak right next to McCade. His neck itched at the thought.

He stepped out of the brush into the clearing.

The full moon illuminated a dozen men wearing burlap hoods, all carrying torches and rifles—except for one, who was carrying a rope.

They'd come prepared.

They were about to find out he was prepared as well.

He pumped the shotgun, the slide and click catching every man's attention as he stepped from the shadows. He waited, his heart steady and his nerve strong, letting the shotgun and his badge to speak for him.

A man moved forward, tacitly designating himself the leader. "You'd best move aside, Marshal. We're here for McCade, but we won't hesitate to go through you to get to him."

That voice. He knew it. Dear God, let him be wrong about who it was.

"You know I can't allow you to do this."

The leader's head cocked, making him look like a curious scarecrow. "Allow? Who put you in charge?"

Sebastian tapped his badge with his free hand. "This. I'm sworn to uphold the law, and hanging a man is certainly against the law, no matter what you think he's done. Or what he might deserve. The court found him not guilty."

"So you think Obregon's a liar? That Isabel's a liar?"

Isabel. Why did you have to use her name, you idiot? I could have at least pretended not to know you before that.

"It doesn't matter what I think," he answered. "The law says he's a free man, and I've sworn to uphold that. You all need to disperse. McCade and I will be gone tonight."

The mob muttered and stirred, but their leader stood resolute. "We only have a few hours to get him strung up, then?"

The hint of amusement in the voice sent Sebastian's temper close to breaking. Did he think this some kind of joke?

Sebastian tightened his grip on the shotgun.

And paused.

Simple enough to step aside and let the mob have their way. No one would blame him for failing to fend off a dozen armed men. Most importantly, Isabel would be safe forever.

Easiest of all would be to pull out the pistol, turn, and put a bullet right between the man's eyes himself. He wanted to, wanted it more than his next breath. The pistol at his hip sang a siren's song to him, urging him to wreck upon those rocks.

And who would stop him? None of these men here. His father's name would be protection against any punishment.

As for Isabel, she would turn from him forever if she knew the truth—but given her silence on the train, she'd done that already.

If he killed McCade, he would know for certain she was safe.

He could live the rest of his life alone, unloved, unfeeling, if he knew she was safe.

He lowered the shotgun from the cradle of his chest.

And aimed it right at Isabel's brother.

"I don't believe that's what I said at all." As cold and hard as the shotgun in his hands. Sheer nerve on his part might yet win this encounter.

The mob leaned away as the barrel of the shotgun swung around. When the shotgun stayed steady on their leader, they stayed back.

Good. Go home.

But while the mob shrank back, the leader—*her brother*—stepped forward, until his chest was a few inches from the barrel. For the space of several breaths he and Sebastian waited for the other to break, each knowing the stakes should the other cry off first.

Then Sebastian felt it turn. The mob, in that queer way mobs had, came to a decision.

They were deciding against him. It was as simple as a slight tilt toward him, but all they had to do was lean a little harder, and then they'd be taking those first steps toward him, to shove him aside, or worse, seize him...

The thrum of a horse's hooves, coming toward them at speed, shattered the moment and turned every head.

The rider held a lantern aloft as the horse ran hell for leather, her skirt whipping behind her. She rode like an Amazon, her shouted words indistinct until she closed in on them.

"Stop! Stop!"

She pulled the horse to a halt and leapt off, transfixing every man there.

Sebastian wanted to close his eyes and pray that when he opened them again, she would prove to be nothing more than a mirage.

For if she were real, he would have to shoot her brother right in front of her.

"Stop!" Isabel shouted it one last time, her hair wild and her breathing quick.

The men merely stared.

"He deserves to die."

She gave a small start at the sound of the leader's voice, but otherwise betrayed no other signs of recognition.

That tiny flinch was all Sebastian needed to confirm the truth.

"I don't want this." Her voice vibrated with conviction.

The leader gestured to the outlaw. "You want him to go free?"

She hesitated. "No. But it's not for me to decide. I don't want any of you punished because of this. You are all too dear to me."

She glanced at Sebastian at that last, but her gaze slid away as soon as it touched his.

"The only person here that'll be punished is that animal," her brother said. "And this marshal if he doesn't get out of the way."

"You don't understand." A familiar irritation snuck into her voice. "It's a trap, set by the new sheriff to catch out what he called the 'vigilante element'."

"How do you know that?" the leader demanded.

"Because he told me about it."

Joaquin Obregon appeared from the shadows, leaning heavily on a cane.

The mob gasped as one.

"Sheriff Williams," Obregon spat out, "came to me asking if I would name the 'troublemakers' here in Cabrillo. I informed him the only troublemakers were the Carey boys and I'd taken care of them. He said I was lying and he would flush out any others like a dog with a quail." He gestured to the entirety of the scene before him. "McCade was the perfect bait. As soon as you lay

hands on him, the sheriff and his posse will come out"—
he pointed to the darkness surrounding them—"and arrest you all."

A prickling broke out on Sebastian's neck. He judged
the distance between himself and Isabel, knowing he
couldn't reach her in time if shooting broke out. But if
he moved closer, the mob could take that as their cue to
strike.

For a few moments, there was only the breathing of
the mob, the wind sighing in the trees, and the heavi-
ness that came to men when they knew they were within the sights of a gun.

"Please, don't do this to avenge me." The spell was
shattered by Isabel's plea. "The Lord said vengeance was
his." She turned to stare at McCade, something terrible
burning in her eyes. "God *will* punish this man. Perhaps
not in this life, but certainly the next. We must all trust
in that."

She stared at her brother, fierce enough to strain Sebastian's heart.

The hood concealed his expression, but the line of
her brother's shoulders eased. After a time, he sighed,
going as limp as the scarecrow he resembled. "Fine," he
allowed. "But if we see McCade here again, I swear by all
that's holy, nothing will stop us from hanging him."

Sebastian saw the concession for what it was and took it. "He'll never come back here again. I'll make certain of that—personally."

The leader gave a short nod. "We're only moving off because Isabel asked. I'd have shot you to get at McCade otherwise. And to hell with a sheriff's posse." He looked to the trees, limned in ink. "If they're even there."

With that, the mob followed him as he moved off, the torches licking at the night air.

"Go back to your camp," he ordered McCade, "and get your things. We're leaving."

McCade moved off without protest, thank God.

Sebastian turned to Isabel, only to find her in close conference with Obregon. She appeared to be thanking him, but he waved her off, the gesture more tired than dismissive.

There was no room for Sebastian by her side—she had Obregon. Who'd stopped all of this with a few words.

Sebastian had been ready to spill blood to stop them. Exactly what she'd said she didn't want.

A young woman appeared next to Obregon, her face twisted with disapproval. Sebastian wasn't quite sure what she disapproved of, but there was certainly plenty to choose from in this whole mess. The woman offered an arm to Obregon, which he took with obvious reluctance, and led him away.

Isabel watched them for several long moments.

Sebastian simply watched her watch them.

Finally, she turned to him and his heart clenched.

This was it. The last time he would see her.

She didn't come closer, only stared at him across the distance between them, her eyes unreadable behind her spectacles.

"That was my brother leading them." Her voice was aggressively neutral.

"I know."

Her throat worked, the moonlight flickering across the movement. "You held a gun on him to protect the man who attacked me."

"Isn't that what you wanted? For me to prevent bloodshed?" Christ, but she was maddening. He'd danced to her tune and still she wasn't satisfied. "I thought you meant to include McCade's blood in that." He paused, his mind working for a moment. "There was no posse, was there?"

She shook her head.

"You convinced Obregon to corroborate it since you knew they'd believe him more readily than you." He shook his head, impressed despite his anger that she'd put herself in danger—and that she hadn't confided in him. "No man ever won betting against you, did he?"

"Someone once called me terrifyingly brilliant." There was no humor in her words.

"He was correct." He took a step toward her and was gratified to see her hold her position.

"You held a gun on my brother." A tremor entered her voice. "Do you expect me to invite you to my family table after that? To tell them I love you?"

She was a sword once again, and the word *love* from her lips cleaved him in two.

"I never asked for that," he said. "I told you there is no happy ending for us."

"I never asked you for one."

"No, you didn't," he said softly. "I suppose that is why I love you so well."

The word *love* from his lips wasn't anything as savage as a sword swing—it was as slim and subtle as a stiletto blade between his ribs.

Something halfway between a whimper and sob escaped her before she smothered it.

"So what happens now?" she asked, her voice still shaky.

He didn't dare move any closer to comfort her. He had to be able to let her go.

"I take McCade back to Los Angeles. And I spend the rest of my life keeping him away from you."

"That pleases you, does it? To martyr yourself playing the eternal sentinel?"

His temper flared, but he reined it in. "I can't kill him for you," he retorted. "I wish to God I could, but I fought too hard and too long for this soul of mine. To shoot him in cold blood, even for the woman I love, would kill it dead. I'll do the next best thing—I'll ensure you never have to fear him again. But I can't kill him."

She blinked hard, as if something were in her eyes. "I never wanted you to." Her voice steadied. "You aren't a monster, Sebastian. You aren't your father. You've proven tonight you're a better man than he." She sighed. "And, of course, you're the man I love."

There it was again, just as painful as before, forcing him to cross the distance between them and gather her up for one last kiss. He put everything he had into it—his rage, his pain, his desire.

His love.

He took everything she gave in return, storing it up and hoping it was enough to last him the remainder of his days. However much it was, it would simply have to do for a long, lonely lifetime.

Finally, after too short a time, he broke off and simply held her against him. The moon turned her features to silver and onyx, light and shadow marrying to form the beloved features of her face. His heart ached at the thought that this would be the last time his arms encircled her, the last time his eyes beheld her.

"If he—" she whispered. "No. No, *when* he is gone... promise me you'll come to me. Fate will catch him soon enough, I'm certain of it."

Sadness washed over him. Fate was fickle, as they both well knew.

"As soon as he's gone," he lied, "I'll come straight to you."

~~~

Isabel watched his fine mouth form those words and knew he was false. His eyes never would obey his command to lie.

But what she asked was impossible, even more impossible than killing a man for her. He'd held a gun on her brother, prevented the lynching of an outlaw the entire town wanted to see hang, and he had a terrible past.

He'd stayed his need for vengeance not only for her, but for himself. When it had mattered the most, he'd not given in to the darkness within him.

These would be their last moments together. Unless...

"May I stay with you?" she asked. "Tonight? I can come to your room, after everyone's asleep..."

His face twisted as though her words had cut him. "Isabel, your parents, the townspeople... I've already damaged your reputation enough. Let me leave with him now, and let you go."

"If tonight is all we have," she argued, "let's take it."

Wrong of her, to ask more of him, when he'd already given so much—but she'd snatch all of him, if she could.

She felt him soften against her, as he subtly yielded in consideration. "What of McCade? I must keep watch over him."

"He's only just escaped a hanging. What would he dare tonight, with everyone's blood up?"

His lips parted and his breath washed over her, smelling of spice, and himself. "Isabel, I—"

A burst of sound pressed against her ears, then all was silent.

He looked down at her with a puzzled expression, the same one he'd worn when considering the dresser he'd pulled over. And then he slumped hard against her.

She only caught the barest impression of a man running past them, moonlight sliding along the barrel of a pistol as he made for the darkness of the woods.

Sebastian was falling, and she could hardly slow his descent, much less keep him upright. She clutched at him, her arms failing as something hot seeped under her hand, sticking in the webbing of her fingers.

"Sebastian?" The rush of her pulse filled her ears, loud in the silence enfolding them.

The puzzled expression remained on his face, although it was frighteningly taut and drawn now.

"Isabel?" The crease between his eyes deepened. "I do believe he shot me."

CHAPTER TWENTY-FIVE

ISABEL PULLED AND PULLED, BUT she could not move Sebastian. Not the barest inch. He was too large, she was too weak... oh God, she was going to fail him.

Blood coated the both of them. No matter how hard she pressed her hands against the wound in his shoulder, it just kept coming and coming—how much blood could a man have?

Enough to coat her arms to the elbow, her sleeves sticky with it.

"Sebastian."

No response. But his chest still moved—and the blood still flowed.

"Sebastian."

Nothing. She sent her fist into his torso. Still nothing.

"Sebastian, Sebastian, Sebastian..."

Her throat had never hurt like this, not even after the attack—the force with which she called to him seemed to strip the skin from it. But she kept on, because she would permanently destroy her voice rather than lose him—and she could think of no other way to call him back.

Finally, a faint threat of sound: "Don't cry. I cannot bear it."

She lowered her forehead to his chest in relief, her hair catching in the blood trailing along his arm. "I'm not crying," she sobbed. "Please, stay awake, don't—don't—"

The rest was lost in choking hiccups. She continued to push hard against his wound, trying to keep his life within his frame.

Suddenly she was roughly shoved aside. She battled the hands that were trying to take her from Sebastian as she fell to her back, striking wildly, connecting occasionally with flesh.

"Stop it," a voice hissed. "Step aside and let me do my job!"

Isabel didn't know that voice and didn't care to know that voice, she only wanted to get to Sebastian. She clawed her way up to do just that—only to be shoved back again.

"Get ahold of yourself! And stop screaming his name."

The little nurse. That voice was the little nurse.

The mad rush of her blood slowed to a quivering.

"Can you help him?" She caught at the nurse's sleeve. "You must help him."

"Stay back," the nurse warned, shaking off Isabel's hand. She pressed a length of fabric against Sebastian's shoulder. "You'll have to go fetch your sister."

Was the woman mad? Isabel caught her sleeve again. "I couldn't possibly leave him, he'll die if I leave him, you don't understand—"

"Enough!" The woman set her hand into Isabel's shoulder and shoved. The ground rose hard to slap her bottom. "Lord, what I wouldn't give for someone reasonable at the moment," the nurse muttered. "What's her name?" she asked more loudly.

"Who?" Isabel couldn't understand why this woman was trying to keep her from Sebastian, didn't she know—

"Your sister! So that I can call her here and have *her* help."

Her sister. Franny was here. Where was Franny?

"What the hell is going on?"

Both she and the nurse snapped around at that barked question.

Juan. He came striding out of the darkness, the mask off now.

"Who are *you*?" the nurse demanded. She shook her head and turned back to Sebastian's wound. "Never mind, help me get this man to the wagon. I have to get him back to the sanatorium."

Juan took in the situation with hanging jaw. "Is that the marshal? Did McCade *shoot* him? And where the hell is McCade?"

The nurse stood up, setting her fists on her hips. "I don't know and I don't care. Help me get him to the wagon."

Isabel wrung her hands together, dimly hearing the crack of her knuckles, as they lifted Sebastian. Juan took Sebastian's shoulders while the nurse took his feet.

"Where's the posse?" Juan grunted at Isabel.

"There was no posse," she answered dully, her fingers tingling with the force she was applying to her hands. "I made it all up. To save you."

She followed behind them. It would be all right now—Juan was here, the nurse was here, Franny was with the wagon—they would take him to the sanatorium and she would be there when he awoke and then—

"Jesus, Isabel, you could have been hurt," Juan seethed as he staggered under Sebastian's weight. "That son of a bitch deserved to be hanged."

"Perhaps," she allowed. "But you didn't deserve to take on such a sin on my account."

Juan made a scornful noise. "He hurt you."

They made their shambling way to the wagon, the nurse and Juan faltering under their burden, Isabel stumbling behind on numb legs.

"Jesus Christ Almighty," Juan roared when he saw who was in the driver's seat of the wagon. "You brought Franny with you, too! Isabel, what were you thinking?"

I thought to save you. And I did.

But I couldn't save Sebastian.

Her head began to throb.

"Oh hush," Franny chided him. "What happened to him?"

She jerked a thumb toward Sebastian, hanging between Juan and the nurse as they readied to lift him into the bed.

Sebastian didn't even moan as they slid him into the wagon bed, a two-foot-wide smear of blood marking his path.

"Shot," the nurse said succinctly, once her patient was settled. "You'll have to drive us back to the sanatorium, quick as you can." She peered in at Joaquin in the wagon bed. "And poor Mr. Obregon has fainted from the pain and exertion. I hope all of this was worth it," she finished scornfully.

Worth it? Sebastian injured, McCade loose somewhere—but the alternative had been to allow Juan to kill a man and possibly face murder charges.

"Franny's not driving you back," Juan said grimly. "I am. Franny's taking Isabel home."

"No, no, no." They must not take him from her, she would not let them. She grabbed the sides of the wagon bed and began to climb in.

Juan pulled her back easily, although she clung with all her might. He spun her around and caught her arms. "That outlaw is still loose. You have to get to shelter."

"But Sebastian could die. I have to be with him." She tried to pull free, went to elbow Juan aside, but her brother only shook her. Quite fiercely.

"He'll die for certain if we don't get him to a doctor," he urged. She stilled, studied him for a moment. His grip gentled when she did.

"Let him go," Juan urged.

She nodded and gently tugged her arms for him to release her.

Juan did so and stepped back.

She turned and dashed for the wagon, uncaring if McCade were still out there, because Sebastian needed her and she'd never leave him—

Only to be caught in Franny's inexorable grip.

"I've got her," Franny assured Juan as Isabel writhed in her clutches. "Get going."

Her sister dragged Isabel without mercy back to the house, Isabel screaming his name with every step she took away from him.

~~~

Sebastian woke to a clacking and a swaying.

Woke was perhaps the wrong word. The self he came to was not his own.

His thoughts were fuzzy with mold, his tongue thick and dry in his mouth, and his limbs deaf to his commands. He could only blink through the fog enfolding him.

"Ah, Marshal Spencer, good afternoon."

He turned to the voice, fighting through the haze in his mind to identify who was speaking.

A man...? Yes, a man sat next to him, something clenched in his mouth, rocking with the motion of the... *train.*

He was on a train. How had he gotten here?

The object in the other man's mouth coalesced into a pipe, the scent of tobacco hitting him in an overpowering wave.

"Do you remember me?" the man asked.

Sebastian could only shake his head.

"Well, you weren't conscious when we met, so that's understandable."

None of this was understandable, but his mouth wouldn't form the words to ask what had happened.

He became aware of an ache high in his chest. No, more than an ache—*pain*, but something was pushing the sharpness away, leaving only the press of the blunt edge. The same thing was pushing his thoughts from him.

"Dr. Arthur Goodwin, at your service. Lucky for you, Nurse McCallahan was close by. She kept you from bleeding too much. Lovely nurse, that girl. Wonderfully cool head in a crisis."

Something finally coalesced into solidity. "Where... where is she? Is she safe?"

"Nurse McCallahan? She's quite well, left her back at the sanatorium in Pine Ridge. She hauled you from Cabrillo to the sanatorium, I patched you up, and since I was already heading back to my teaching position in Los Angeles, thought I'd haul you back with me. Take you home and all that."

It made a kind of sense, and yet it didn't. He pondered the other man's words, waiting for the fog to thin further.

"Not the nurse," Sebastian said finally. "Isabel."

"*Isabel?*" The doctor raised an eyebrow. "Do you mean Miss Moreno? I understand her sister took her home. Nurse McCallahan said she was quite distraught. Near hysterical, actually. I suppose ladies' nerves can't handle the sight of blood." He gestured to the nurse in the corner. "Well, ladies that aren't nurses, isn't that right?"

The nurse—a broad-chested, hard-faced woman— shrugged in response.

Sebastian's mind finally wrapped clumsy fingers around what the doctor had been saying. *Hysterical.* She'd been hysterical.

Isabel was never hysterical.

She never screams.

Panic swelled in him and he tried to rise with it, but managed only to shift on the cot. The pain pressed harder against him.

"I have to…" He fumbled for the words. "I have to get off at the next stop. I have to see her."

The doctor exchanged a glance with the nurse, who rose to go fetch something. "I'm afraid that's not possible. Even if you could rise—which you can't—we're already to Pasadena. Cabrillo is hours behind us, and in a few hours we'll have you nicely settled in at the hospital."

"She can't… I have to reassure her." He closed his eyes, unsure whether the pain washing over him was from his wound or the thought of her in such distress.

"Of course, of course, send a telegram and all that. Once you're settled."

Despite his ruined state, Sebastian could tell the doctor was only humoring him.

The nurse returned with a cup in her hands. Before he could think to protest, she had it at his lips and tipped it down his throat.

The taste of alcohol and something even fouler had him gagging, but it all went down regardless, leaving his mouth and throat coated with horridness. His stomach rolled as the brew hit it.

"What...?" *Damn this haziness.* "What was that?"

The doctor waved his pipe at him. "Something to help with the pain."

That explained the fog—too late to spit the stuff out.

"The outlaw?" he asked. The man's name eluded him, but it was there in his mind. Somewhere.

"Oh, I heard he ran. I imagine the sheriff is chasing him now."

Not the most reassuring answer, but there wasn't anything to be done.

Once he was free of this doctor and his elixirs, hopefully by tomorrow, he would hunt down the fugitive.

First, he would send word to Isabel he was perfectly fine.

The mold fuzzing his brain bloomed, choking out any last bit of rational thought, and he was lost to sensation again.

~~~

It was the worst two weeks of Isabel's life.

The frantic need to know what had happened to Sebastian, the frustration at the lack of news—it was worse than the aftermath of her attack.

They'd locked her in her room after Franny had dragged her away, her screams and pounding at the door bringing no mercy.

When her mother unlocked the door the next morning, Isabel was dry-eyed. And threatened to claw the eyes out of anyone who kept her from riding to the sanatorium.

When she arrived, Joaquin's cold-eyed nurse informed her the doctor had taken Sebastian back to Los Angeles. She said he was expected to live—but *expected* was no reassurance.

Isabel had to see him for herself, touch him and know that life still quickened within him. Nothing less would soothe her heart.

She returned home to write letter after letter, to Señora Vasquez, to her cousins, to Don Enrique—to anyone who could tell her how he was. Her fingers ached, were stained with ink to her knuckles, and still she kept writing.

Her family tiptoed around her wishes, but they did not outright forbid any of it. Not that she would have listened.

No doubt her cousins were spreading the story far and wide, whispering it in every parlor in Los Angeles—how dear cousin Isabel was scandalously losing her head over the thrillingly frightening Marshal Spencer. The trial, the papers, the shooting; it would all be too much for them to resist.

Isabel found herself beyond caring. All she could do was wait.

Agony, that wait. A piercing misery. She begged the Los Angeles papers off anyone she could, but there was no mention of a dead marshal within them.

Finally, after a week, a letter arrived from Pilar. Isabel nearly tore it in half in her haste to open it—but it said only that Pilar had heard he was in the university hospital. More than that, no one knew.

From his mother she heard nothing, although she sent two letters a day: one to her and one to Sebastian.

When she could take no more of the waiting, she threatened to ride down to the valley and send a telegram to everyone she knew in Los Angeles and stay as long as necessary for a reply. Before her parents could forbid it, Mr. Merrill offered to go instead. He promised to wire his father, who ought to know everything. Or, at the very least, could find out.

She'd never imagined she could be so grateful to her brother-in-law.

While she waited for him to bring news, she thought on her future.

McCade was loose; where, no one knew. The sheriff claimed the fugitive was bound for Mexico, but whether that were true—or simply his excuse for calling off his search—was unclear.

If the outlaw intended to return and finish her off— she didn't care.

She felt no fear on her own account. The only fear she felt was for Sebastian. She prayed ceaselessly for him, bargaining with God, even though she knew it was wrong.

So she sat and waited, prayed and bargained, and watched for Mr. Merrill's return.

CHAPTER TWENTY-SIX

THREE DAYS AFTER MR. MERRILL had left for the valley to send the telegrams, Catarina came to sit with Isabel in the afternoon.

Her sister was looking less green and a little rounder these days. Isabel waited for some sensation to rise within her at her sister's appearance—gratitude, relief, irritation—but it never did.

There was nothing left in her but worry for Sebastian.

They sat for several minutes in companionable silence, Caterina's hands busy with her mending, while Isabel's own hands were still as she watched out the window. Autumn was creeping upon them, the air silver with chill instead of the golden light of summer.

She watched now not for McCade.

She watched for Sebastian.

"Oh, dear." Isabel caught sight of a familiar pony cart coming up the drive, heart racing as she rose from her chair.

Catarina was over in a flash.

"Oh, no." She shoved Isabel back down into the chair. "I'll take care of them; you stay here."

She waited in the chair, one ear cocked to decipher the voices coming from the hallway. Most of it was indistinct, but she did catch, "*not leaving*" and "*she has to explain herself*" in feminine tones she recognized all too well.

Caterina's strident responses carried clearly. "No! Teresa, Ines, she's not well!"

The skritch and thump of a scuffle came next, and then Joaquin's sisters were dashing into the parlor, huffing and red faced. Catarina followed close behind, her face screwed up in distress.

Isabel rose and held up a hand to her sister. "It's all right. They're entitled to this. And I deserve it." She gestured to the sofa. "Please, Teresa, Ines, sit."

"No," Teresa said, her body so rigid with tension, even her hair seemed to stand on end. "We won't remain long. Why did you do it? Why would you stop them? That man crippled our brother, and you let him go free!"

Isabel wasn't quite sure where to start in all that. "The trial was fixed from the very beginning—" she tried.

"So why didn't you let the mob deal with him?" That was tossed out by Ines.

They were beginning to suspect the truth of that night. Her cheeks and throat went clammy—her lies were being found out.

"How was I supposed to stop a posse?" she asked. Perhaps she could brazen her way through this.

Teresa shook her head. "No one knows anything about a posse. No one except for you and Joaquin."

Isabel's heart thumped as she waved a falsely careless hand. "Did you ask Joaquin about this? Likely not."

Both sisters began to blink hard, their eyes reddening. "Infection set in again," Ines said, "thanks to his leaving his bed that night. He's out of his mind with fever."

Isabel gasped, setting her hand against her breast. "Why wasn't I told?"

"Because you're not his fiancée any longer," Ines spat. "No, now you make up lies about sheriff's posses and flaunt yourself for that marshal."

The blood drained right to her toes. "I haven't—"

"Isabel has never flaunted herself for any man," Catarina broke in, her cheeks bright as coals. "I know a thing or two about flaunting—as do you, Teresa—and we all know Isabel's never done any such thing."

"Then why is she writing everyone in Los Angeles for news of him? Oh yes," Teresa sneered at Isabel's shocked expression, "you're not the only ones with cousins there."

"Because he took a bullet for her, you silly twit!"

Never had Isabel loved her sister more than in that moment.

"Joaquin took a bullet for you, as well," Ines hissed. "Where is your concern for him? You abandoned him just when he needed you the most!"

You abandoned me too, she wanted to cry.

Catarina looked ready to spit more harsh words, but Isabel held up a hand to stop her, even as her stomach rolled at the accusation.

"What happened between Joaquin and me is no one's business but our own," she stated with pretended calm. "If he hasn't seen fit to tell you the details, then I won't either. Believe me, he agreed it was best no blood was shed over this outlaw."

Teresa's expression wavered as if passing through rippling water. "This outlaw is loose once again. My brother couldn't have wanted that."

"I assure you, he didn't." Isabel felt her voice begin to slip from under her control. "McCade will be apprehended again."

"By who? Your precious marshal?" Ines's face twisted. "Will he hold a gun on our men again? And thwart the only justice Joaquin could have ever known? Besides, he's laid up in Los Angeles. Which is no more than he deserves."

A wave of hope and anxiety swelled in Isabel, forcing her toward the sisters. "You have news of him? What have you heard? Please, tell me anything you can."

They stepped back, their expressions going flat and white as new-fallen snow.

She'd betrayed herself most terribly—but if they had any word of him...

"Ines," Teresa said in clipped tones, "we're leaving. Now."

The two left without a backward glance, Isabel staring after them as they went, searching for something, anything to say to them.

Nothing came.

"Well," Catarina said, "now that you're not marrying Joaquin, I'm certainly glad I'll never be related to those two." She sank back into her chair and picked up her sewing. "Put them out of your mind. They always were spiteful harpies."

Easy for Catarina to say. She'd never liked the Obregon sisters. Isabel sighed, her heart slowing, though her limbs and her stomach held on to her jitters.

"They're correct," she admitted. "I did prevent that mob from meting out a kind of justice. And the marshal... I am..."

She could not name her feelings for Sebastian, so she ceased trying.

"Oh, I knew there wasn't any posse," Catarina said to her sewing. "You did the right thing. Juan doesn't need to be hanging a man, no matter what he's done. People around here will realize that. You simply have to give them some time."

Shame smoldered under her cheeks at her sister's kindly tone. "Catarina, after the attack... I was not as charitable toward you as I should have been."

Her sister set her mending in her lap. "I won't pretend that it didn't sting, but you were hurting. That was always your way when you were hurting."

"Even so..."

Catarina went back to her sewing. "There's no doubt you and I are different enough to rub wrongly sometimes. You don't have to apologize to me for your essential nature."

Isabel didn't answer. What words would suffice in the face of such generosity of spirit? None of hers, that was certain. So she simply turned back to the window, watching and waiting once more.

Somewhere out there was Sebastian, in a hospital bed, wounded, perhaps even dead. Joaquin, too, was trapped in a bed, perhaps even now burning with fever.

Here she was, trapped in a sitting room. Of the three of them, she was the only one who could move forward. But dared she?

She'd gone all the way to Los Angeles to testify against her attacker. She'd held off a mob who'd wanted to kill that same man.

She'd fallen in love with Sebastian.

None of those things had been in the grand life plan she'd assembled with Joaquin—but all of those were so much more daring than she'd ever dreamed she could be.

"I can't remain here," she announced suddenly.

"Of course not," her sister said, flipping the shirt in her hands to check the seams on the other side. "So where will you go?"

That was the question she'd been asking herself. Even if Sebastian had survived and was healing, she couldn't go to him in Los Angeles. McCade might be lurking in the city and even if he weren't, her reputation there was ruinous.

She couldn't remain in Cabrillo—the Obregon sisters wouldn't be the only ones angry that the mob had been stopped.

There was always the valley... But she wanted someplace bigger.

"Do you remember Aunt Esperanza?" Isabel asked. "In San Francisco?"

Her sister frowned. "Papa's sister? I remember she didn't like us children very much. Well," she amended, "except for you. She liked you because you were well behaved. I believe she wanted to drown the rest of us in the bay."

"Do you think she would allow me to stay with her? For a time?"

Catarina gave her a measured look. "She would be more than happy to have you. You always were her favorite."

The favorite child of a woman who had none herself and disliked them. What did that say of her?

"I suppose you're right," she said.

"Of course I am," her sister replied. "Everyone knows you weren't meant for Cabrillo. But San Francisco? That city was made for you. I'd wager it's even more exciting, more challenging than Los Angeles."

Isabel thought on it for a moment. It sounded exciting—enticing.

But so far away. From both Cabrillo *and* Los Angeles. *Perhaps. Just perhaps...*

"We would miss you," Catarina was saying, "but you would be much happier there, no?"

Isabel released a sigh. "Perhaps."

The clock ticked off many more seconds, how many she did not know, as she stared out the window and Catarina continued on with her mending.

How much longer to wait? If only she knew how he was...

Mr. Merrill came through the door without warning.

Her heart stopped at the sight, trying to read his expression for any news of Sebastian, but it was maddeningly unreadable. He clutched some papers in his fist.

A telegram. Or perhaps a letter.

His wife rose to greet him. He tossed her a smile so fond it hurt Isabel's heart. The smile dissolved as he looked to her.

"He's fine," Mr. Merrill finally said.

Isabel collapsed against the back of the chair. Undignified, but all she could do under the relief drowning her.

"The wound wasn't anywhere vital," Mr. Merrill said. "Wound fever did set in"—she gasped—"but he's past that now. He was released from the hospital two days ago."

"My goodness," Catarina breathed, "you must have sent a fortune in telegrams."

Mr. Merrill simply shrugged. He lifted the papers in his fist. "I brought the telegrams for you. And there was a letter."

A letter? She took the sheaf from him. There, written in the hand she'd come to know so well when she'd read those notebooks, was her name.

Isabel.

She rubbed a thumb across the ink, her face heating as she realized Mr. Merrill must have seen this, must know she and Sebastian used their Christian names. Which was silly, given her frantic need for reassurance that he'd survived. Mr. Merrill—all of them—must have suspected something long before this.

"We'll leave you to read it in private," her sister said as she drew her husband away.

As the parlor door clicked shut, Isabel tore open the letter and began to read.

~~~

After two weeks of being strapped to a hospital bed, the wind across Sebastian's face seemed odd, out of place.

He blinked against the autumn sunlight, cursing the weakness in his limbs. He'd need every bit of his strength for what he had to do.

His mother hovered at his elbow. This past fortnight had been agonizing for her, sitting by his bedside as he fought the fever. And he was about to hurt her yet again.

The last time. It would be the last time.

"Sebastian." He turned to her, puzzled by the hesitancy in her voice. "Now that you're well, I have something to give you." She lifted a stack of letters. "Señorita Moreno sent them. I kept them from you, which was perhaps wrong—but I didn't want them to distress you."

He took them, consternation tightening his jaw. "Did no one tell her I was all right? I distinctly remember requesting such when I was lucid." Which had not been often.

"Her cousins might have," she offered.

He closed his eyes against that. *She had been hysterical.*

No time. There was no time. He would deal with it later.

"Mother," he said gently. "You go home. I have to meet with Judge Bannister."

She frowned but went on without protest.

When he entered the courthouse, he took the stairs two at a time, ignoring the protests of his shoulder. He'd no time for weakness.

He barreled past the gaping clerk manning the desk outside Bannister's office, wrenching the door open without knocking.

To say Bannister was surprised to see him would have been an understatement.

"Where is he?" Sebastian demanded as soon as he opened the door.

The judge didn't pretend to misunderstand. "I have word he's in Mexico."

Mexico. Sebastian smiled at that. He doubted McCade had enough Spanish to get very far there.

"I'm going to bring him back, unharmed and un-touched." He pointed to the judge. "You are going to gather the evidence to try him for attempted murder. The victim being me, of course. You're going to see to it a competent prosecutor is put on the case."

"I can't interfere with that."

Sebastian leveled a look at him. "You're going to ensure he's convicted this time. I assume a US Marshal is a reliable enough witness for even a Los Angeles jury."

Bannister's answering smile was sardonic. "I would imagine so, yes."

"She is not to testify. Do you understand? She's been through enough."

The judge nodded. "Believe me, I have no intention of putting that girl on the witness stand again. But you can't be leaving now? You only just got out of the hospital."

Sebastian's shoulder ached at the reminder, but he ignored it. "I'm perfectly fine. I'll stop at home first and then I'm bound for Mexico."

He'd have to play the marshal for a while longer. And then...

And then...

Sometime later, he walked into his own home. He had only a few hours before the train left. Best to get right to it if he wanted to finish it all.

The first thing he saw was Junius, in the hallway. The dog thumped his tail once, regarding Sebastian consideringly.

"We are going to get someone to gentle you." Sebastian wagged a finger at him. "No more random attacks. If you're no longer a good guard dog, so be it."

Junius only wagged his tail.

Sebastian went to the library, taking a seat at his desk. He slit open the first letter from her. Ink-scrawled, tear-stained—her frantic sorrow bled through the paper. It pained him to look upon it. All the letters were like that, sobbing, begging missives asking for any news of him.

As if he were worthy of such an outpouring, deserving of her deepest feelings.

His breathing was harsh and his hand trembled as he reached for paper and a pen.

A letter to Isabel. He must write a letter to Isabel. He must answer that outpouring of hers with... with what?

Himself?

He lifted his gaze from the blank sheet, sought out the familiar sight of his notebooks. He could pour himself into those instead, as he'd always done. Lock her and the sensations she evoked—the *love* he had for her—away in them.

He could write her a perfectly correct, perfectly polite letter thanking her for her concern, telling her that he was well once more.

He wouldn't have to say that their association was at an end; she was clever, she'd understand what he hadn't written.

If he did that, they'd both be safe. Safe for the rest of their days from the emotions they inspired in one another.

He rose and picked up the first notebook, turned to that first page. He hardly recognized the writing there any longer—and not just because it was an illegible scrawl. He pulled down the next notebook and the next and the next, filling his arms with them.

He carried them out to the garden. Once they were piled there, he started a small fire in a bare patch.

He opened the first book.

There it was, in black and white and rust red, his terrible deed laid bare.

He tore the page out and fed it to the fire. The colors ran to black as the flames consumed it, then disappeared entirely into ash. He tore out every last page, giving them all to the fire.

When his sins of the past thirteen years were nothing more than a pile of ash, he crouched down beside the gray lump of it. Such a small bit of matter for so many sins. He dipped his fingers into the ashes before curling them into his palm and setting his fist against his forehead.

But only say the word, and I shall be healed.

He didn't believe he'd been healed, exactly, but he felt... light. Free. As if he'd been ridden with a heavy curb bit all this time and was only now experiencing the freedom of being without a halter. As if he might begin to move up the mountain once more. It would be a climb, no doubt, but he could manage. With Isabel as his companion.

He had to finish that letter to her first.

On his way back to the library, he ran into his mother.

"Sebastian, why are your cases out? Where are you going?"

The concern on her face tore at him, but hurting her further was unavoidable. "The man who shot me is in Mexico. I have to go bring him in."

She set her hand to her heart. "But you only just got out of the hospital! And *Mexico*?"

He took her hand in his—so familiar, the pressure of her fingers. She used to hold his hand, just like this, after one of his father's rages.

This would be the hardest part of leaving, this and the letter he had to write. "I must do this. For her."

Her rapid blinks were like paper cuts against him, each one tiny, yet agonizing. "Surely someone else can go to Mexico? Someone who hasn't just been grievously wounded."

He squeezed her hand. "I have to do this. For her and for myself."

Her expression dipped into melancholy. "How much more must you do to prove you're not like your father?"

How much? He wasn't certain. He'd thought a lifetime of burying his true nature and serving justice had done it... but it hadn't been enough. Not after Isabel had seen his true self and decided it was worthy of love.

"Just this last. I promise." This last to keep Isabel safe—and prove to himself he was deserving of her.

"I suppose you truly love her," his mother said thoughtfully.

His heart raced at the words, thrumming in his ears. "She's... Calling her my everything isn't enough." He reached for what she was to him, searching in both English and Spanish for something to encompass it. "She is my infinity, stretching far and wide and forever for me."

His mother's smile was the saddest she'd worn in years. "Then find this man and come back to her," she said. "I wish I could give you advice on a happy marriage, but I'm afraid I only know how to survive an unhappy one."

He shook his head gently. "Now who's clinging to the past?"

She embraced him then, squeezing him as tightly as if he were a child again and the clasp of her arms could soothe any hurt.

"Well," she said as she released him, "I suppose you'd better prepare for your journey."

"I'll be back, safe and sound. I promise."

He left her and made for the library, going straight to his writing desk. There was just enough time to finish this before he would need to pack and leave for the station.

He pulled out a clean sheet of paper, set the pen to readiness in his hand.

And sat there.

How to begin?

He wrote out *Dear Señorita Moreno.*

He pondered the greeting for a moment before tossing the sheet to the floor. Taking up another, he tried again.

Dear Isabel.

That went to join the other on the floor.

My dearest love.

Finally satisfied, he finished the letter.

CHAPTER TWENTY-SEVEN

ISABEL REACHED A HAND INTO her jacket pocket, felt the crinkling of the letter there, right over her heart. From beneath her hat, she took in the crowd clustered at the rail depot in the valley, everyone backing away from the track as the train eased into the station.

Time to say farewell.

She turned to her family waiting behind her, bracing herself for this final goodbye. For when the train left, her family would return to Cabrillo—and Isabel would be on her way to San Francisco.

Just as Sebastian had asked her.

She touched her pocket one last time, then went to Franny. She held her hands out to be squeezed, tilted her cheek to receive a kiss—but Franny, dear, dear Franny, crushed Isabel hard to her. A low noise came from her sister's throat, a sort of fond growl.

Isabel understood. She patted Franny's back, knowing her sister was too overcome to speak. "God bless you and keep you, sister."

Franny squeezed tighter, Isabel's ribs straining under the force of her affection. She released Isabel abruptly, averting her face as she stepped away.

Franny never liked for others to see her crying.

Isabel would miss Franny just as fiercely.

She moved on to Catarina, Juan following in her wake. He'd be accompanying her to San Francisco—she'd say her goodbyes to him some three hundred miles away.

Catarina gave her two swift kisses on either cheek and pressed something into Isabel's hand.

"Handkerchiefs," she explained. "A lady can never have too many handkerchiefs. Don't forget the box lunch I packed—you shouldn't eat that train food, it costs too much and is of poor quality."

Franny couldn't speak and Catarina couldn't stop speaking.

Isabel swallowed hard. Lord, but she would miss her sisters.

"Of course," she assured her, setting a kiss on Catarina's cheek. "Thank you for packing it."

She shared a solemn handshake with Mr. Merrill. "Thank you so much for your... assistance," she said.

His gaze was grave. "I only wish I could have done more. Wire if you need anything."

"I will."

Her father was next. She closed her eyes and bent her head when she came to him. He kissed her forehead and murmured, "God bless you and keep you, my daughter."

"And also you, Papa." *All of you.*

"Give our love to Esperanza," he said. "It will be good for her to have some company."

Isabel nodded.

Time for the last farewell.

Her mother squeezed her hands tightly, the kisses she set to Isabel's cheeks a heartbeat longer than the ones she usually bestowed.

"Be safe, my dear," she said. Her eyes were suspiciously bright, but her voice was unwavering. "I do wish you would remain close. But I understand."

Isabel wanted so badly to embrace her, to clutch tightly to that familiar form as she had when she was a child—but such a thing in front of all these onlookers would deeply embarrass her mother. So she simply gripped her mother's hands more firmly.

"Thank you, Mother." Her voice tried hard to break on *Mother.* "I know how hard this has been for you."

"Not as difficult as it has been for you." Her mother gave one last squeeze, then gestured toward the train. "Now go. And God bless you and keep you."

Isabel didn't look back as they climbed aboard, didn't glance out the window as they found their seats, stowed their bags, and settled in for the long hours ahead of them.

She adjusted her skirts instead, pulled a book from her pocket—and then, finally, she looked out the window.

Her family waited on the platform, her father's arm around her mother's shoulders—a rare show of affection from them—Catarina sniffling into a handkerchief as Mr. Merrill patted her back, and Franny staring resolvedly at the train, a fierce approval in her gaze.

The train started, jerking the portrait of her family within the frame of the window. As the train gained speed, pulling Isabel farther and farther from them, she turned to face forward.

It wouldn't do to be looking behind her the entire way.

~~~

Los Angeles, California
November 19, 1898

My dearest love,

All is well—I was laid low by my injury for a time but I am recovered now. They said you were in hysterics when I was shot. Please know that if it were in my power to have reassured you before this, I would have.

My every thought—when I could think—was of you.

Judge Bannister has informed me that McCade is rumored to be in Mexico. Of course you know I must go there to search for him. I won't stop hunting him until he is imprisoned or dead and unable to harm you again. But rest assured that his death will not be at my hands.

I know this because I burned all of my notebooks.

You might be surprised to read that, but I realized during my stay in the hospital that I no longer need them. You are now the star always pointing me true North.

I can't ask anything of you, not from Los Angeles and certainly not from Mexico. I cannot say when I will return with this outlaw or if I ever will—and what is between us must be resolved face to face, not through the dry medium of pen on paper.

However, if the other matter requires the immediate protection of my name, I will return at once to provide it. No matter what, please, please, allow me to write to you. I could not bear it if I didn't have even this slender link to you.

In closing, I do ask one thing of you, bold as it is. Don't remain in Cabrillo. Find a city with as many literary societies as you can and go there...

Sebastian

~~~

Cabrillo, California
November 25, 1898

My heart,

May I call you that? We began with the title Marshal Spencer between us, then moved on to Sebastian, and now we've arrived at the truth of the matter: you are my heart.

I was sick and sore with no news of you, but Mr. Merrill was kind enough to telegraph his father and he brought me your letter, for which I will be forever grateful.

Sebastian, you've no need of me to direct you—you've known your true North all along. When you had the choice to murder this outlaw—or allow the mob to do so—you chose the harder path. You and you alone. I would rather we be apart for the rest of our days than know I was responsible for blood on your hands, no matter how much this man might deserve it.

I am doing as you requested and moving to the city with the most literary societies I could think of—San Francisco.

As for the other matter you allude to, fear not—it has been resolved. I have only to wait until I see you again to speak what I cannot put to paper.

I beg you to write me as often as you can. If you need to put yourself into these letters to me, much as you did your notebooks, I am here waiting, greedy for you...

Isabel

~~~

Tijuana, Baja California, Mexico
December 3, 1898

...I've found his route here in Mexico—he can't help but leave destruction in his wake, which leaves an easily coursed trail. I travel south now, to Chihuahua, which he spoke of as a possible destination.

You may call me whatever you like as long as you continue to write. My every thought is for you, of you. If you are greedy for my words, I am ravenous for yours.

I know you think I react badly when I hear his name, but I am glad to know Señor Obregon is recovering. And that the two of you have made peace with one another. Without his help, I might have ended up dead that night—he has my gratitude for that.

Thank you for the poem you enclosed. I was unable to take any books with me, contenting myself only with that which my memory has retained. But if all I had in my mind was Martí's verse, the one about his lady's hair, it would be more than enough. I recite that each day and remember your hair surrounding the both of us, sheltering us from everything in this world but the other.

Tell me all of your new life in San Francisco—do any traces of Yerba Buena remain, or have the Americans made over the entire city...

Sebastian

~~~

San Francisco, California
January 10, 1899

...Aunt Esperanza and I rub along quite well together. We are two spinster ladies enjoying all that the city has to offer. She has yet to say anything of the prodigious number of letters I receive, none of which I share with her. I begin to think she might have a failed love affair in her past, which is why she overlooks my indiscretions in this case.

I must be true with you—for all that I'm enjoying it here, I yearn for you. Your letters are as precious as gems to me, each one I hoard close like a dragon with a treasure. But they are nothing compared to my memories of you and I together in the library...

Isabel

~~~

Chihuahua, Mexico
February 28, 1899

...I've arrived in Chihuahua, but his trail is cold. The Rurales claim he killed a prostitute, and just as in our own land, the lowness of the victim's station has prevented any real inquiry into the incident. (I do not blush to write that word to you, since I know you do not blush to read it.)

The Rurales are particularly uninterested in searching for McCade now that I've arrived, and I cannot fault them for it. Why shouldn't the American lawman solve the problem of their American outlaw?

Your description of your recent trip to the dressmaker made me smile. Yes, you should most certainly buy the most ridiculous hat they have. I hear tell that the sun never shines in San Francisco, so you must choose all your headwear for fashion's sake, rather than the sun's.

Speaking of myself, you would be shocked to see me these days. Dusty, unwashed, fraying elbows and cuffs—hunting an outlaw is terrible for a man's clothes. I've even begun to grow a beard to save myself the effort of shaving...

Sebastian

~~~

San Francisco, California
March 7, 1899

...I have some interesting news from Los Angeles—the city council has voted to keep the water supply in private hands— Mr. McCade's hands. I admit, I did smile at first to think of Judge Bannister so thwarted, but then I frowned to think of Mr. McCade so rewarded. I enclosed the newspaper clipping so that you might read for yourself.

I thought of your beard yesterday, quite unintentionally. My mind was wandering during a lesson, and suddenly, I felt your beard along my inner thigh, the hair rough and abrading, and right in the middle of all that prickliness, the soft, wet warmth of your mouth.

I entirely lost my place in the lesson...
Isabel

~~~

Chihuahua, Mexico
March 20, 1899

...Word has come that McCade was seen heading to the Barranca del Cobre, so of course that is where I must travel next. I will be unable to post letters every day, as I have been, but fear not—I will continue to write each day and post them when I can.

My heart is so full of you these days it is easily fooled by even the poorest facsimile. I see a lady with hair as dark as yours, or one as slender as you, or one as tall and straight, and my heart sings for half a moment "There she is! She has come!" And then my eyes see her for who she truly is and my heart is broken anew...

Sebastian

~~~

San Francisco, California
April 30, 1899

My only love,

There have been no letters from you for over three weeks now. Sometimes I feel as if I am writing to your ghost. If you were to die there, would I ever discover the truth? Or would I spend the rest of my life wondering what had happened?

I choose to believe you are alive.

A world where I cannot be by your side always is terrible enough—one where you are no longer present would be unbearable...

Isabel

~~~

Batopilas, Chihuahua, Mexico
May 20, 1899

I received five of your letters after arriving back in Batopilas just yesterday. I tracked McCade all the way into Sinoloa before the trail went cold again, forcing me to return here. I know you've sent more than five, but five letters from you are worth an infinite number from any other.

At times I wonder why I do this—why I track this man so ceaselessly, only to return him to uncertain justice in Los Angeles? If I come upon him, I still fear I will take the easy path and kill him in cold blood. After all, who would care here in the wilds of Barranca del Cobre?

But I have yet to find him, so I have yet to be put to that test. Again.

After so many months here, alone, searching for him, I am no longer certain of who I am. English no longer crosses my lips, my clothes are rags—and you... How can my arms continue to exist after not holding you for so long?

Sebastian

~~~

San Francisco, California
June 17, 1899

...I do not know if this letter will reach you before you apprehend McCade, but I send this anyway—you will not harm him. I say this not as a command to you, but as a reminder to your true nature. You return this man to uncertain justice because it is the moral choice. Anything else is vigilantism.

I trust you, Sebastian. And you must trust yourself...

Isabel

CHAPTER TWENTY-EIGHT

THIS WAS AN EASY PLACE for a man to die.

The Barranca del Cobre was a savage scar across the land, a deep green gouge made by the knife of a god. But still beautiful for all that.

For a man to survive such a place, he had to be more than half-wild himself. Sebastian felt no fear, facing that wilderness. Rather, it was anticipation building in him, the kind a wolf might feel when he spotted prey and prepared for the long chase ahead.

A chase crowned by the joy of the kill.

His prey waited in a shoddy camp in the canyon below. Sebastian was perched above him, well out of sight. McCade stumbled out of his tent, and Sebastian smiled to see his quarry flail like a dying cow.

He might be going a little mad, smiling like that. In his other life he would have recited all his familiar books, the lines that allowed him to retreat behind his reserve, to pretend that he didn't feel.

But in this life, the one where he embraced the wilderness, he simply smiled.

He raised the field glasses to his face, studied his reflection in the lenses for a moment.

After his return to Batopilas from his first trip into this landscape, Sebastian had almost shot himself when he'd caught a glimpse of his reflection.

That hadn't been *his* face. Not as dark as it was, streaked with grime, his too-long hair a salt-and-pepper cloud above it. And that beard—his mouth and neck were swallowed entirely by it.

How long had he been in the wilderness this trip? Sebastian counted the days.

Forty. He'd been here forty days.

How long since he'd spoken to another living being? Forty-three days. A man in Batopilas, when he'd purchased supplies.

How long since he'd seen another human? Thirty-nine days.

He thought he'd seen a shadow on the rock face at one point—the Indians here were known for their reclusiveness. But perhaps it hadn't been human—perhaps it had been an animal. He couldn't say for certain.

He ran a hand through his beard as he stared at his reflection in the lenses. Strange, that he hardly even felt the beard upon his chin any longer. Or the clothes across his skin. Such things would have irritated him to distraction before.

He lifted the field glasses to his eyes, watched his prey for several moments. McCade looked terrible. Gaunt, filthy, clearly out of his element.

In a week, or perhaps a few days, the problem would be solved. Barranca del Cobre would have killed McCade by then.

Sebastian pulled his pistol from its holster. He wanted to solve the problem now.

McCade didn't hear Sebastian approach. He stared at nothing as Sebastian came closer and closer, only the sound of the pistol's hammer cocking catching the man's attention.

He turned slowly, as if unsure if the noise were real or not.

Sebastian would prove soon enough that it was.

A ghastly smile pulled at McCade's lips. "Bannister sent you all this way to find me? My father was right—that man does hate him."

The man was this close to death, and he still couldn't set aside his jeering.

Let him have it for this last moment.

"Bannister didn't send me. I came for her." Was that his voice? He hadn't heard it in so long. He didn't remember it being so deep. So rough.

McCade squatted by the remains of his campfire. "So what happens now? You haul me back, there's another trial," he rattled off, "I serve a few years—and when I'm out, I find her." The mocking light fled his gaze, leaving it flat. Pitiless. Empty. "I'll make you watch as I carve her into ribbons, very, very slowly."

Sebastian raised the gun and put the barrel against McCade's temple. One flick of his finger, and he was done. He could return to her.

"Careful," the other man warned. "That's loaded."

"I know."

"Well, go ahead then," McCade urged. "You picked a good spot for it—no one will find me here. You win. You caught me."

There was no regret, no remorse, no pleading.

If the tables were turned, if McCade held the gun on him—there would be no hesitation. Sebastian would already be dead.

Sebastian tightened his grip on the pistol, the muscles of his arm flexing—causing the letter in his breast pocket to rustle.

Her letter. Her words.

She wouldn't want him to do this. If she were here, she'd lay her hand over his arm and stop him.

But she wasn't here. There was nothing to stop him from killing the man, from sending him to his final judgment.

One pull of Sebastian's finger and she would be safe forever.

She'd never know what truly happened here—he could tell her anything he liked.

But because she wasn't here, he must stop himself.

He slowly holstered the pistol, pulled the handcuffs from his belt.

McCade's eyes widened, the first time Sebastian had ever seen him baffled.

"You're under arrest," Sebastian said as he fastened the cuffs around the man's wrists. "I'm taking you back to Los Angeles to stand trial."

~~~

COMPANIA TELEGRAFIA MEXICANA 6 JULIO 1899

HAVE APPREHENDED MCCADE AM RETURN-ING TO LOS ANGELES

SPENCER

CHAPTER TWENTY-NINE

San Francisco
September 1899

ISABEL SWIPED THE RAG ACROSS the blackboard, coughing as chalk dust tickled her nose. The streetcar clattered faintly from a few blocks away. Her students chattered and laughed in the courtyard just outside the window, released for the day and on their way home to their mansions in Nob Hill.

The marine breeze blowing in from the open window stirred the hair at her nape, making gooseflesh rise there. After being in San Francisco for nearly a year, she still found the supposedly warm autumn weather chill-inducing.

She kept at the blackboard, swiping it with even strokes to ensure the last trace of chalk was gone. The neatness of her classroom at the California Ladies' Academy pleased her soul.

Setting the rag in the blackboard tray, next to the chalk lined up in readiness for tomorrow, she turned to her satchel. A single, solitary letter poked out from it.

She ran her fingers along the paper. Sebastian's latest letter. The other three hundred or so were in the bottom of the bag. One for every day they had been apart.

She hadn't received all that he'd sent—the mail service between here and Mexico was too inexact for that. But she knew they were out there, trapped somewhere in the ether, fluttering on translucent insect's wings.

The letters that *had* reached her were more than enough, a nearly ridiculous weight in her satchel. One she couldn't be without. He'd poured himself and his days into those letters, much as he'd once poured himself into those notebooks.

Now he poured himself into his letters to her.

His happiness, his anger, his smiles—not laughter, not quite yet—all presented for her. Along with his yearning.

Dear God, the yearning. The ache of it was a secret, delicious suffering residing in the center of her always, flaring each and every time she read over the words he poured for her.

Even when he was exhausted from his search, even when he wanted to do nothing more than sink into sleep, he sent a letter.

Te amo.

S.

Just those two words and his initial—but he still gave them.

She tucked the letter away. Already she had it memorized, but she'd spend this evening running her fingers along the same places his had touched, imagining it was his skin under them instead of thin, crinkling paper.

The only physical contact she had with him, and she snatched it up hungrily with each new letter.

As she hoisted her bag onto her shoulder, the tramp of booted feet came from behind her. Manuel, here to sweep the floors, no doubt.

"Buenas tardes, Señor," she greeted him. "¿Comó esta usted?"

"Bien, ¿y usted?"

She spun at those oh-so-familiar mellow tones, her heart instinctually leaping with joy, her breath hitching with anticipation.

And a fair amount of uncertainty.

Sebastian stared back at her, his broad length entirely in black, hat in hand, as immaculately turned out as ever.

The illusion held until she looked into those gray eyes. Eyes that looked tired, nearly exhausted, as if he hadn't slept for the past year. Had there always been that much gray in his hair? She wasn't quite certain; her memory wasn't infallible like his.

"I would have thought you'd still be at the trial," she said.

She'd obsessively followed the news of McCade's second trial for attempted murder, reading over and over again the accounts of his and Sebastian's testimony. The papers had indicated it would go on for a few more days.

"It ended yesterday." That impassive expression of his made her stomach lurch. If McCade had escaped yet again, she didn't know how she would survive it. Perhaps that was why Sebastian had come so quickly, to warn her.

"Guilty." His voice was harsh. "He'll serve twenty years at Folsom."

She exhaled deeply, trying to blow away her anxiety, trying to capture the elation she should be experiencing, seeing him after so long. "So in twenty years I'll need to worry about him coming after me?"

"You're overgenerous—he won't survive," he assured her. "Not twenty years there."

"It's finished then." There was triumph, yes, but it was tinged with a hollow sort of regret. "You did exactly what you promised. Delivered him to justice. And it was served, this time."

Perhaps if it had been done right the first time, if they'd been spared this year of bitter separation, she might have been entirely joyous.

"More than that, I delivered him unharmed. The only time I touched him was to put the handcuffs on him. I wanted to." He looked heavenward. "Lord, how I wanted to hurt him. He tried me severely, too." He looked back at her. "But I didn't."

She swallowed past the tightness in her throat. They remained nearly ten feet apart. Her heart strained to close the distance, but her reserve—and his—kept her where she was.

"I saw the account of it in the papers." Her steadiness matched his. "You're quite the hero in Los Angeles."

"Did you see the praise they heaped on my father?" His mouth twisted. "They painted me as following in his footsteps, heroically tracking that fugitive to the ends of the earth. For justice."

She knew how much that hurt him, felt an answering hurt within herself. The need to comfort him trembled within her, and yet...

He hadn't given the slightest indication he wanted her comfort.

"I know the true story," she said. "From your letters."

"When I came upon him, all alone in the wildness of the canyons—all I could think of was you and your words, your pale hand against my arm, restraining me. So I stayed my rage and put the handcuffs on him as gently as a mother dressing a child. To be honest, I don't think Mexico agreed with him."

She took a step toward him, her stomach clenching when he made no reciprocal move toward her.

"I was never so proud as when I received that letter from you." Her throat was near to closing completely.

"And now he's in jail. We never have to speak of him again."

"True." He ran his hand along a desk and looked about the classroom. "You're enjoying San Francisco?"

"Yes. My pupils are quite intelligent and willing, if a bit spoiled. The city itself is... well, quite beyond my imaginings."

Bustling with every kind of person, libraries, newspapers, temperance leagues, literary societies—it was a feast for the intellect.

"How many literary societies have you joined?" Amusement tinted that.

"All of them," she admitted.

He smiled, hitting her right at her knees, making them want to give way. *Steady.*

"How is your mother?" she got out. "She must be quite glad to have you back from Mexico safely."

"She's well. In fact, she's betrothed."

"Truly?"

"Yes. A very kind man who thinks the world of her. Even Junius likes him."

"Even Junius? The man must be a saint."

He cleared his throat. "Junius is a changed dog. I hired someone to gentle him while I was away. The effort required was prodigious, I understand, but the results have been... extraordinary."

Tears clotted in her throat and chest. "I see," she said, the words wavering as they left her throat.

Oh, this was painful, this slow stumbling past these inane pleasantries. But all of this politeness must be exhausted before they could come to the heart of the matter.

He tapped his hat against his leg, looking everywhere except at her. "All that time hunting McCade, it gave me quite a bit of time to reflect." He paused. "There is no doubt that a strain of violence runs within me. As I... unbent with you, I did not take the proper mental precautions to control it." He looked straight at her now, his eyes as cool and clear and deep as a lake in autumn. "I can control it now. But I have... *unbent* as far as I can. I will always be reserved."

Nothing of marriage, of affection, of love. Only *control* and *reserve*.

The tears came then, damp and shuddering. She could no longer hold them back.

He closed his eyes, averted his face. "I cannot... I cannot look at you when you do that."

His pained words twisted through the center of her.

"As I said, I will always be reserved," he said to the floor, "but even so, never doubt that I love you to the profoundest depths of my soul."

A sob escaped her. Here, here was the declaration she'd been aching for.

His jaw clenched and his fists flexed as he went on speaking to the floor. "Knowing all of that—all of me—I must ask you..." He looked up and his eyes were ablaze. "I must ask you, will you have me?"

She closed the distance between them, nearly throwing herself at him.

"Of course, of course," she breathed between kisses, shivering with the release of finally touching him after so long apart. "I love you with everything I have."

His arms went round her and the sensation of it, the heavy clasp of them against her after only imagining for so long, smashed the ache she'd been living with right to pieces.

Here. Here is right where I belong.

But he wasn't kissing her in return.

He frowned down at her. "Are you certain? I can't... I will never be ardent. I can't give full rein to every emotion within me. But it is there, I swear it."

She ran a hand along his jaw. So warm, so smooth. She would never tire of the feel of his skin under hers.

"I know all that. Didn't I read your letters?" Her fingertips traveled to his lips and he breathed a kiss into her palm. Finally.

"Ah, my Isabel. These things seem easy when we're so far apart, with only letters to speak for us. You must be certain. For once I take you to wife, you're never leaving my side."

He kissed the tips of her fingers and a thrill ran through her. After imagining the touch of his lips for so long, the reality was almost more than she could bear. "What things are difficult now there's nothing between us but flesh and speech?"

"I will never be an easy man to live with." His breath caressed her hand. "My reserve, my taciturn ways—those won't change."

"I wouldn't want them to. I myself am *magnificently difficult.*"

A smile flashed across his face. Two smiles in less than a quarter of an hour. He *had* changed.

"And—" His expression twisted in hesitation. "I don't know that I want to be a father. I would never want to be like my—"

She held a fingertip to his lips. "You would never be like him. And I don't know that I want to be a mother."

His frown eased, but didn't erase. "If we marry, it would be in the papers."

"I have found that San Franciscans cultivate an active disinterest in the affairs of Los Angeles." Her heart slowed. "Unless you mean for us to return to Los Angeles. I suppose you would have to." Breathing was becoming difficult. "Since you are a marshal there—"

He shook his head. "I turned in my badge."

"What about your duties?" She frowned at him now. "What about justice?"

He shrugged. "As you said, I've done my duty. Justice isn't quite so alluring when it can't protect the ones you love."

"So we can remain here in San Francisco?" she asked eagerly.

"Wherever you like. As long as it's far away from your brother. I imagine he's still put out I held a gun on him."

She smiled. "I believe San Francisco is far enough away."

He rested his forehead against hers. "If I were to travel the whole world, I would never find another to fit me as well as you do."

"I'm here right at hand," she whispered.

Lord, to be so close to him, to be touching him after all this time... if they weren't in the middle of her classroom, she'd be tempted to strip him naked.

He breathed kisses along her jaw, nibbled along her lips. "What shall we do next, my Isabel?"

"First," she said, "you are going to kiss me. Then you are going to marry me."

He proceeded to do just as she commanded.

EPILOGUE

A MAN WHO'D NEVER INTENDED to take a wife was allowed to feel a bit unsettled upon waking the morning after his wedding.

It was a good kind of unsettled though.

Sebastian looked around the ridiculously ornate suite they had taken at the Palace Hotel, pulling his wife—*his wife*—closer to him as he did. She shifted, settling more of herself against him.

After a year apart, and a month's wait to marry her, having all of her nakedness pressed against him was the purest pleasure.

He gathered the ends of her hair with his free hand, studying the dark lines of it against the fainter lines of his palm. He would wake like this every morning for the rest of his life. He would sleep as serenely as he had last night every night for the rest of his life. Contentment rippled within him.

Releasing her hair, he simply enjoyed the rhythm of their entwined breaths, the slip of her skin against his, the slow beat of his heart in his ears. He could almost be lulled back to sleep like this...

She raised her head slowly, those dark eyes solemn without the protection of their spectacles.

"Good morning," he said gravely.

Was that the correct way to greet a wife? He wasn't certain.

"Good morning," she said just as gravely.

"Did you sleep well?"

A smile curved her mouth, her lips still rosy from their exertions of last night. "As well as you did."

He smiled in return. "Then very well indeed."

Yes, this was the way to greet a wife, with gentle teasing and a reminder of the night before.

"What shall we do today, wife of mine?"

"Hmm." She trailed a hand down his torso, scattering his thoughts. "Breakfast, of course, and after, we should continue our search for a house."

"Certainly." A little strained, but her hand was in a very sensitive spot indeed.

"But first"—she rolled to her back, tugging him along to raise him over her—"you have some duties to attend to."

A command. Now *this* was the way to greet a husband in the morning.

"Of course." He began to kiss his way down the slender length of her, lapping up the taste of her skin. "What kind of house shall we have?"

She lifted to meet his lips. "Close to the streetcar, so you can travel to work easily. How lucky for you they needed an experienced marshal so badly they were willing to overlook your resignation in Los Angeles."

"Being a celebrated hero has its uses. Besides, how was I to know I would miss being a marshal until I wasn't one?"

"Better to serve an imperfect justice than none at all?"

"Exactly."

He'd come to that realization after some weeks of pondering what he might do next. After all, he *was* the marshal.

But he was also *Sebastian*.

"Mmm," she replied. "The house should be large enough that we'll need at least two maids."

He smiled into her stomach. "As many maids as you like, all to wait on you, wife of mine."

He'd give her all of that and more—she would never want as his wife. And books... He'd give her books the way other men gave their wives flowers.

She squirmed as his breath dusted her skin, and tapped his head. "No tickling. It will need to have a large library."

"Of course." He moved lower, spreading her knees apart as he did. "We will take all the papers, even those in languages we don't speak." He nipped at the softness of her inner thigh, running his tongue to the hot, wet center of her.

She made a noise beyond language, the kind of noise Eve must have made when Adam first did this, before the words for it existed.

"And roses," she gasped. "As many roses as we can plant."

"As many as you like," he whispered as she writhed beneath him. "Anything and everything for you, my heart, my love. My Isabel."

ACKNOWLEDGEMENTS

Major thanks go to my critique partner, Emma Barry, who had to guide me through not one, but two massive breakdowns about this book—a year apart, no less. Every time I wanted to be a coward and delete this book, Emma forced me to be brave.

Thank you to my editor, Mallory Braus, who after reading the first draft said, "I think we can go darker with this." And we did.

Simone St. James did a wonderful job copy editing the book—and over the holidays! I am forever grateful for that.

Thanks also to Melody and Cindy, world's greatest lab mates; they know what they did. And again, I would never have taken this step without the excellent advice from the community at Romance Divas.

And, as always, thanks to my family. You guys put up with a lot so I can tell my stories.

ABOUT THE AUTHOR

Genevieve Turner writes historical romance fresh from the Golden State. In a previous life, she was a scientist studying the genetics of behavior, but now she's a stay at home mom studying the intersection of nature and nurture in her own kids. (So far, nature is winning!) She lives in beautiful Southern California, where she manages her family and homestead in an indolent manner.

You can find her on the web at www.genturner.com.